ABOUT THE AUTHOR

Claire Merchant is an Australian author and storyteller. She is best known for her collection of fantasy, contemporary, and romance novels set in fictional South Coast. In 2018, Claire was voted one of the '50 Great Writers You Should Be Reading' by The Authors Show.

CHRISTIAN AND LAYLA

Post Encounter and Prior Engagement

ALSO BY CLAIRE MERCHANT

Mistry by Moonlight

South Coast Son

Foresight

Forever Ruby

Knowing Nora

Midnight Mistry

Mistry at Dawn

A Lady Born, A Pirate Bred

Finding Hope

Dreaming of Reality

Linger

Heart Strings

Daughter Departed

Ebony Rose

Light and Shadow: The Story of Luna Lake

For those who have loved, lost, and never stopped looking

Acknowledgements

To my family and friends. Thank you for coming back every time you leave.

To those I have loved, to those I have lost, and to those that I have never stopped looking for. Your presence in my life has and will be forever imprinted on my soul. You will never be forgotten.

To Ed Sheeran. Thank you for creating such beautiful music that inspires me, especially when I hit a writing brick wall.

To my readers, my lovelies. Thank you for your desire and passion to experience a world outside of your own. I've said this before, and I'll say it again – you are always welcome in South Coast. If I'm not there, don't fret; just wait for me to come home.

Be yourself. Be thoughtful. Be kind.

Claire x

Part One: Christian

"Post Encounter"

You could call it a love story, but I just call it our story. There was love, there was loss, there were family interferences, and there was an ending. There was more than one ending.

Regardless of what happened, it appeared that our lives were intertwined, our hearts somehow fused, our futures seemingly tethered.

It all started with an ending.

**

The year that I turned fourteen, my father, Mitchell Turner, moved my mother, Nancy, and me to Almanbury for his work. It was the beginning of spring and nearing the end of term three at school. I'd loved living in South Coast. I loved the atmosphere and the slightly laidback yet still businesslike city. I used to believe that South Coast was more of a country-town compared to some capital cities, and then realised that this was far from accurate when I actually moved to the country.

Almanbury was the last place that I wanted to be. It was every bit a sleepy little country-town and, after living in the city, was a much different pace to what I was used to. *"Salt of the earth, Christian,"* my mother would say. *"The people of Almanbury are salt of the earth."* Sure, but maybe I was more of a pepper guy.

The drive from South Coast to Almanbury was unreasonably long for the nothing that was in between. Despite its name, South Coast wasn't the southmost point of the continent. No, that spot was reserved for Almanbury. Tucked far beneath civilisation where no one would pass by unless they were looking for it. Almanbury.

I started at Almanbury Senior High four days after arriving in the town. It felt appropriate to me that the locals abbreviated the school to ASH since it certainly felt like my life had gone up in smoke.

I walked through the short and narrow halls to the principal's office one fateful Monday morning knowing absolutely no one. My mum had tried to encourage me to wander around town after we'd arrived, but I didn't see the point. The whole town centre was almost as small as a suburb back home so, to me, circling it in less than an hour would only depress me more. If I didn't see how small it was, maybe I could trick myself into believing I was somewhere else. It was worth a shot, even if that shot missed the target.

The principal, Mr Coleman, walked me to my form class. All I could think of was *three years*. Three years. That's all it took before I was out of here and city-bound again. I had practically calculated and begun counting down the hours as I walked into the class of a mere sixteen people. It was sixteen less than the smallest class that I had at my old school, South Iris High. My spirits dropped to a new low. Three years felt like an eternity away.

But then I saw her.

I remember the moment so clearly, that moment when I first saw her face. She was the epitome of beauty. I remember how the dim sunlight reflected in her shoulder-length auburn hair like a halo and the way that she stumbled through the door laughing at herself after tripping over her own feet.

I knew right then that, whatever it took, I would know her. I would stay in Almanbury forever if it meant being close to her.

"Whoopsy daisy." She giggled. "Morning, Mr Coleman."

"Layla Thomas, good morning." The man nodded.

Layla Thomas.

"Who's your friend there?" she asked, her gold eyes settling on me. I adjusted my stance and then reached my hand towards her. I couldn't help it. I needed to know if her hands felt as soft as they looked.

"Christian Turner," I said. "It's nice to meet you."

"But we haven't met yet, Christian Turner." She smiled and shot out her hand, clasping mine with a snap. "Layla Louise Thomas. *Now* it is nice to meet you."

I laughed. *Layla Louise Thomas.* I was already in love with this girl.

"Well then, now that you've *officially* met," Mr Coleman sighed. "Layla, can you look after Christian and show him around today?"

"Sure, it won't take that long." She laughed again. "This school is teeny."

Mr Coleman cleared his throat. "Thank you, Miss Thomas."

Another adult entered the room, and she looked as if she had just rolled out of bed, and that bed was in a barn.

"Ms Tottle, this is Christian Turner. He has just moved here with his family. His father is the new police sergeant in town."

And bam. Instant repellent.

Layla's eyebrow rose at me. It was distracting but intriguing. Usually people didn't care who my dad was until they found out. Then they proceeded with caution.

"Come on, Deputy Turner," she said, pushing me sideways in the direction of a desk. I stumbled into it, and she sat beside me. "So, what's your story?"

"My story?"

"We've all got a story," she replied. "Tell me about Christian."

I smirked. "Well, I was born in March—"

"Pisces or Aries?"

I blinked. "Um, Pisces."

"Well, that's a relief," she sighed.

"Why is that a relief?"

"I'm a Scorpio. We're compatible." She shrugged. "So where did you move from?"

"South Coast."

"What's your favourite colour?"

"Gold."

She blinked. "Are you for real? Who picks gold as their favourite colour?"

I laughed. "No idea, it just popped into my head."

"Favourite song?"

"*Here Comes the Sun* by The Beatles," I said. "Or *Layla* by Eric Clapton."

"You're lying." She smiled and her nose wrinkled.

I shook my head. "I'm not."

"Live acoustic version or album version?"

"Album."

"Who picks the album version? The live acoustic version of *Layla* is so much better. Everyone knows that, Christian Turner."

I lifted a shoulder. "You're right. What was I thinking?"

She giggled. "Okay then, now for a serious question."

I shuffled in my plastic chair. "Shoot."

"If a tree falls in a forest, and no one is around to hear it, does it make a noise?"

"Let me answer your question with another question, Layla Thomas," I said. "Is there ever really no one or nothing with ears around to not hear something?"

Her pretty eyes narrowed. "I like you, Christian Turner."

I just smiled because no words could escape me. She looked up and waved at three more people who were dribbling through the door. At South Iris High, if you were late to form, you got a late slip. Here, people seemed to rock up to class when they felt like it. Maybe ASH wouldn't be so bad after all.

"Hey, guys, I want you to meet an old friend of mine," Layla said as she looked at me and winked.

Yup, I was definitely in love with this girl.

The two guys and girl walked over, pouring into the surrounding seats.

"Wayne, Abbie, Stuart, this is Christian Turner," she announced. "He just moved here from South Coast. He is a Pisces and don't bother messing with him because—"

I looked down expecting the inevitable *because his dad is a cop.*

"—because otherwise, I'll shoot you," she said, and then added, "with my camera."

Her hand lifted, and something flashed in front of my eyes. I blinked and saw that it was a disposable camera in her grip. Her thumb wound the roll of film on. It surprised me. I didn't think people used film any more.

The guy with light brown hair huffed, and I looked over at him.

"Hey, Christian," he said. "I'm Stuart. I see that Layla has already gotten her hooks into you."

You have no idea.

I smiled at her, and she beamed back at me.

"Apparently." I nodded.

I was in so much trouble.

"Wait, Layla, did we break up?" the other guy who had orange hair asked. Wayne, I guessed.

Layla pushed him, and he theatrically half-fell out of his chair.

"We were never together, Wayne," she sighed. "Unless you count *in your dreams*."

He laughed, and I sort of felt sorry for the guy. He genuinely looked as if he did dream about her. I guess he was only human.

"I'm Wayne," he said, nodding towards me. "Good to meet you, bro. Welcome."

"Cheers, man."

The girl, Abbie, I assumed by deductive reasoning, tipped her head.

"Is your dad the new cop?" she asked.

I pressed my lips together.

"How do you know that, Abbie?" Layla asked. "Did Christian's dad already bust yours for handing out bogus scripts again?"

Wayne burst into hysterics. Stuart rolled his eyes. Abbie's eyebrows lifted.

"Wow, back away from the new guy, or Layla will *shoot* you down," she grumbled. "Even if you happen to have been her best friend since we were four."

Layla seemed to blush. "I'm sorry, Abigail, but who really cares about who his dad is? He is probably just as scary as anyone else's dad."

Wayne laughed again. "Except yours. Henry is the greatest."

Layla glowed. She seemed proud of the fact.

"So, Christian, if you're free after school, a few of us like to hang out at the forum," Stuart said.

"You guys have a forum here?" I smirked. "Go figure."

18

"Well, it might not be as big as the city complexes, but it's something to do." Abbie shrugged. "It's hard to miss though. Haven't you been there?"

I lifted a shoulder. "No. I haven't really been anywhere. I've been, uh, unpacking." I glanced at Layla. "Do *you* normally hang at the forum after school?"

She nodded. "But if you haven't seen the rest of the town then I can show you around. After all, Mr Coleman assigned me to give you the grand tour."

"I don't think he meant beyond school grounds, Layla," Wayne sighed.

"That sounds good to me," I answered.

"What does? Hanging at the forum or Layla playing tour-guide?" Stuart asked. He looked amused.

"The tour guide thing mostly." I smiled at Layla, and she straightened and smiled back. "But the forum thing sounds pretty cool too."

Stuart smacked me in the shoulder. "You're going to fit in just fine here, Turner."

The school was a bit bigger than I initially thought, and Layla was thorough in showing me all the little nooks and crannies that ASH had to offer. I tried to make a mental note to remember some of them because they looked as if they might come in handy. But, I was too distracted by her voice and her eyes, the smile that glowed from her cheeks, and the way she would randomly click that camera in her hand to take a photo of me. Everything about her captivated me. I had never considered myself a romantic—I couldn't tell you any fourteen-year-old guy that would—but the things I would do for Layla Thomas, the lengths I would go to if only she asked me, it scared me a little.

"Any questions?" she asked.

It was the end of lunchtime, and I was only faintly aware that people still stared at me as if I was a blue M&M that had fallen into a bowl of red ones.

"Just one," I replied.

"Then that's all you get, so make it count."

I smiled. I couldn't help it. I'd smiled so much today that my cheeks began to ache. I pressed my fingers into my dimples.

"Do you want to hang out sometime? Just you and me, I mean." I was a bit impressed that my voice held so steady. In the past, girls scared the hell out of me with all their eyelash flapping and hair tucking that they do to try and throw you off. Layla didn't scare me. Maybe the way I felt about her did, but everything about her felt... right.

"Christian, we are hanging out right now, just you and me." She smiled.

"Well then do you—"

"You said one question."

I frowned. "Can I buy another one?"

Her arms folded. "With what?"

"I don't really have much, to be honest. What did you have in mind?"

She held up her fingers to make a rectangular frame around my face. "Christian Turner, you may have another question if you let me photograph you sometime."

"You've been doing that all day anyway, Layla Thomas." I smirked. "Anything else?"

"Was that your second question?"

"What? No."

Her lips curved. "What about that?"

I chuckled nervously and ran my hands through my scruffy hair. "You are making this impossible."

"Okay, second purchase," she said. "You have to get a haircut. I think it would look nicer a little bit shorter."

"Done," I sighed. "Do you want to be my girlfriend?"

Her smile was blinding. "Why, Christian Turner, I thought you'd never ask."

After school, Layla showed me around the town centre, which I guess was a more downscaled version of a city centre. Basically, it was just a cluster of shops which included a post office, where her mum apparently worked, plus a tavern, and a cemetery just on the outskirts. Nothing seemed that far from anything and, although there wasn't much, the way that Layla regarded the small town, I began to see the awe in it. Almanbury was home to her. That was good enough for me.

One thing that I couldn't quite seem to get used to in the four and a half days of being here though was the weather. The cold felt colder, even in the warming spring. The locals didn't seem to notice and seemed to treat it like a South Coast summer. I guess it wasn't all bad though. I mean, I couldn't deny that I enjoyed seeing Layla in her little yellow dress.

Apparently, most people brought a change of clothes to school even if the uniform wasn't that bad. I mean, a black polo school shirt with any kind of bottoms was much better than the checks and purples of my old school. Layla trumped everyone else though, underneath her black polo shirt and denim skirt was the yellow dress. She had already torn her uniform off as we walked through the front gates. We started walking around the small town. Well, I was walking while Layla danced around in a circle. Her dress twirled as she stepped.

"Aren't you cold?" I asked after an hour had passed.

"Are you?" she countered.

"No. Well, a little."

"City slicker." She smiled.

"So where to now? Is the tour over?"

I looked up as we headed between the brick walls of the malls. I tried to ignore the disappointment that I felt that we'd soon be surrounded by people.

"The forum. If you want," she answered. "You said that it sounded cool to hang out, so I thought I'd introduce you to everyone."

I caught her hand as she spun again. She landed up against me, and my back fell against the wall behind. The closeness was a little thrilling.

"Or we could just make another lap of the town?" I offered.

Her gaze dropped to my mouth, and I moistened my lips. She lifted her eyes back to meet mine.

"Whatever you want," she whispered.

I could feel her heart beating, and it was quick. Her hands were resting on my arms. They didn't make any attempt to move, and it pleased me to know that she liked being this close to me too. I bit my lip, and her eyes followed the motion again then returned to mine.

"Layla?" I said.

"Christian."

"Is it okay if I kiss you up against this wall?"

Her breath caught in her throat. "As long as that's all you plan to do."

"And what if it's not?"

She responded by lifting her lips to meet mine, her hands clutching my arms to better reach. I spun her around, pressing her gently but firmly against the wall, and cradled her mouth to mine.

I had kissed a girl before, sure, if you call a peck a kiss. But kissing her was like poetry in motion. It wasn't perfect in the Hollywood sense, but it was perfect because it was real. It was messy, and it was laced with a passion and a hunger that was beyond our years.

I didn't stop kissing her until my lips felt bruised. I didn't regret a thing.

**

Time is a funny thing. Sometimes it feels like it's going at double speed, but sometimes it feels like it has stopped altogether. My life began to straddle both at different times of the day and in different company. One thing that didn't change was that Layla and I became inseparable both in school and out. It was as if we were drawn to each other like magnets, like I had suddenly stumbled across a part of myself that I didn't know that I'd lost. I was fourteen, but I knew what love was from the moment that I met Layla Thomas. From that day, we were Christian and Layla, Layla and Christian.

The first few days were intense. We tried to keep our budding relationship to ourselves because we felt like if we shared our moment, somehow it would take away the magic that seemed to make us work.

Days turned into weeks, and during that time, I learnt a lot about Layla. I learnt a lot about her lips and her curves. I learnt that she loved taking photos. Her camera, or one of her many cameras, was an extension of her arm. She saw beauty in everything. She saw colours, quirks, and characteristics that most people glazed over. Her favourite colour was yellow. She loved daisies. She told me that she liked to collect memories. She took pictures with her camera so her mind wouldn't forget. She was scared of forgetting, of being forgotten. But I would never forget her. I don't know how anyone could. We created our own world. It was a world that fit in with reality but immersed us in the fantasy that people called love.

But then the inevitable happened. Friends started asking questions, parents started butting in, and the next thing we knew, we were facing a firing squad of opinions on what they all considered was best for us.

It started at school.

"Dude, do you think that you spend a little too much time with Layla?" Stuart asked one Tuesday. I'd been in Almanbury for just over two weeks, almost three in fact, but it already felt like home to me. I gave Layla the credit for that.

"No." I shrugged. "I like spending time with her."

"But what about your other friends? What about Wayne and me?" he said. "You've been together since you first arrived, and you've spent most of your time with her. No one really knows you without her. What happens when you guys break up?"

"We're not going to break up, Stu."

"But what if you do?"

I exhaled. "Look, I know what you're saying, and I probably should make an effort to spend more time with you guys. But Layla and I are never going to break up."

Stuart smiled. "She's got her hooks in deep, huh?"

I shrugged again. "Yeah. I'm happy for her to keep them there though."

"You know, I've known her since pre-school. I always thought that eventually she and Wayne would get together. But, dude, I've never seen her light up around anyone the way she does when she's with you."

I nodded and couldn't hide the dumb smile. "Good."

"But just don't forget about us guys, okay?"

"Sure, I hear you, man." I tapped my pen against the back of my head. My fingers felt for hair that was no longer there.

I'd cut it the week before. "Hey, since it's warmer today, how about instead of the forum after school we head to the beach? Just the guys."

Stuart's eyebrows lifted. "You want a bunch of guys to just hang out at the beach? Better the girls join us for that, bro."

I laughed. "Your call."

"I'll check with Lindsay."

Lindsay. Stuart was dating her, or they were just regularly making out behind the sports shed. She'd tried to put the moves on me on my second day here, a day after Layla and I had kissed against the brick wall on the way to the forum. I hadn't even noticed that she was flirting until she asked me to go to a movie with her. It's funny what meeting the right girl can do. I see the other girls, but they don't register. I don't consider that they might want something more with me because Layla was the only girl that I saw. She was the only girl that I wanted to see.

I nodded slowly. "So, should I, uh...?"

He rolled his eyes. "Yeah, check with Layla."

Layla bounced towards me at lunchtime. I threw down my books and caught her before she landed.

"Hi." She beamed, and then kissed me quickly.

"Hi." I kissed her again, slower.

"I forgot to tell you something this morning," she said. "Or ask you, rather."

"What is it?"

She made a face. "My dad wants to meet you. My mum too, but more my dad."

"Oh, sure, okay." I nodded. "When?"

Her eyebrows lifted. "Really?"

"Yeah, I might as well meet them. I'm bound to eventually."

"Really?" She smiled. Her arms lifted around my neck. "Well, what about dinner tonight then?"

"Tonight? I'll have to check with my folks. Or, I mean, you... you could come with me, and we could ask them to-uh-gether."

She giggled. "Are you asking me to meet your parents too?"

"If you want."

Her gold eyes looked to the side. "Well, I might as well meet them. I'm bound to eventually."

I laughed.

"Do you think we're crazy?" she asked.

"Probably, but does it matter?"

"Not to me." She kissed me again. "Oh, wasn't there something that you wanted to ask me too?"

I blinked. "Oh, yeah. Um, beach today?"

"Beach? Okay."

After school, we walked to Layla's house to get her little yellow two-piece swimsuit, and then headed back to mine. Layla stuck to me as I led her through my house. She was clutching my arm as if something was about to jump out at her.

"Relax. No one's home yet." I chuckled, but she didn't loosen her grip.

"Everything is really neat here, Christian," she whispered.

"That's because we've literally just unpacked it all."

I walked through to my room, and she stopped at the door as if she was barred from the threshold.

"You can come in," I said as I walked straight to my set of drawers.

She looked around the doorframe and then hesitantly stepped in.

"You're probably like the cleanest boy on the planet." She smiled, and her head bobbed around from my made single bed to my ordered desk. There was nothing on the floor, but that was because I didn't have much stuff. I'd always been more of a bookworm than a baller, though I did skateboard a little back in South Coast. I'd snapped my deck on a grind before I left, so I was between boards right now.

"So, you've been in every guy's room on the planet?" I glanced at her and raised an eyebrow. "Layla Louise Thomas, what would your parents say?"

She groaned and fell back onto my bed. "I've only been in one other boy's room, and his was *super* messy."

I turned and backed up against the draws. My arms folded. "Who was that?"

"Wayne-o."

"Wayne?"

She nodded. "You literally can't see the carpet."

I looked down at the shorts in my hand. I knew that there was nothing to be jealous about since Layla and Wayne were nothing but friends, but it still irked me that she'd been in his room.

"Hey," she said. "What's that look?"

"Nothing, no look."

"There was a look." She stood up and walked towards me. "I told you that Wayne and I are friends. He's your friend too."

"I know."

Her arms moved around my neck.

"Okay, so no more looks."

I kissed her, and every ounce of jealousy melted away. Then she gave a small sigh and something else burned through me. I pulled her closer, and she did the same. A second later, she stepped away.

"What's with all the books?" she asked.

My head was spinning so fast that she might as well have been speaking French. She took another step back, and the confusion of that made me focus.

"What?"

"Books." She smiled. "What's with them?"

"Oh," I sighed. "Um, I like reading."

"What's your favourite?"

"I don't know."

She pressed her lips together. "I'll let you think about it, but I want an answer soon."

"Why?"

"Because, Christian Turner, I want to know everything about you," she said. "So, when people say that we're crazy and that we can't be whatever because we don't hardly know each other, I want to be able to tell them that I know all of your favourite things."

"Who cares what anyone else thinks?"

"I just don't want them to try to change your mind about us. I know we're young, but we're good, aren't we? You and I."

I smiled. "We're definitely good."

I took a step forward, and she blushed.

"What?" I breathed. "You okay?"

"We should go, or the sun will go down," she said. "Plus, we still have to make it back to my place for dinner."

I nodded. "I'll just change then we can go."

"Great, I'll wait in the kitchen."

I bit my lip. The kitchen was halfway out of the house. If she waited further away, she would be out the front.

"Layla?"

She looked over her shoulder at me. "Christian."

"If you're uncomfortable with anything, like, we don't have to do anything if you're not comfortable with it."

She smiled. "I like you, Christian Turner."

By the time I had changed, which was in record time, Layla was talking to my mum in the kitchen. I hadn't even heard her get home, but maybe it was because my heartbeat was so loud that it drowned out any other sound.

"Christian, why have you not introduced Layla to us sooner?" Mum crooned. "She is absolutely delightful."

"Us?" I frowned. "Is Dad home?"

"He's just changing. He picked me up from the pharmacy after his shift."

I exhaled. Mitchell Turner was a decent dad, but he tended to treat most people as if they were suspects. I wanted Layla to meet them both, but I wanted to pace myself with the two of them. At least with my mum here, Dad might be more likely to behave himself.

Layla smiled, and my mood instantly lifted.

"Mitch, sweetie, come here," Mum called. "There's someone that Christian wants you to meet."

I walked over to Layla and dropped my mouth to her ear.

"We should go soon. The sun will go down," I whispered.

She nodded. "After I meet your dad, we'll go."

Footsteps echoed, and I took half a step back from Layla. She straightened and was already smiling before my dad had rounded the corner.

"Who is... a girl?" Dad mumbled.

"Dad, this is Layla," I said. "Layla, this is my dad."

"It's lovely to meet you, Mr Turner." She smiled. Her hand outstretched towards him, which he took and shook.

"Layla, a pleasure." He nodded. "Are you working on a school assignment with Christian?"

"No, Dad," I sighed.

"Mitch, sweetie, Layla is Christian's girlfriend, remember?" Mum added. "He told us about her."

Layla's eyes flashed up at me. She looked a little victorious.

My dad frowned. "Girlfriend, hm, well. I didn't think you were old enough to date, Christian. You've only just learnt to walk."

"Mitchell," Mum sighed. "I think it's lovely. Layla, feel free to come around anytime. There is too much testosterone around this house."

"I'm okay with that too." I smiled.

Layla was practically glowing. "Thank you, Nancy. I'd really love that. You have a beautiful home. I was just telling Christian that it's so neat and tidy."

Mum laughed. "You're sweet, but that's probably because we just finished unpacking."

"That's what Christian said."

Mum grinned at me. "Would you like me to fix you something to eat?"

"Actually, we were heading out to the beach," I answered. "And Layla has asked me over for dinner tonight, if that's all right with you?"

"Of cou—" Mum started.

"On a school night?" Dad interrupted.

"I promise, Mr Turner, I'll have him home at a reasonable time," Layla said. "My parents don't like me staying up late on weekdays either."

"Hm, okay." Dad nodded. "What do your parents do, Layla?"

Layla's shoulders rolled back. She was proud of her parents – it was evident in the way she spoke of them in such high regard. However, given the way she reacted to Abbie speaking

30

about what my dad did, I know that she hated people judging her parents for the same thing.

"My mum works at the post office, and my dad is a plumber," she said. "I'm sure that they'd love to meet you."

"I'm sure they will soon," Dad answered. Layla's smile faltered. My dad sounded so ominous that I wanted to roll my eyes at him, but I knew better than that. Instead, I looked to Mum pleadingly.

"Mitch, for goodness sake," she exhaled. "Layla, sweet, that would be lovely. Why don't we arrange an afternoon tea this weekend or something like that? Let Christian know which day will suit them best, and we'll set it up."

Layla nodded. "I will, Nancy, thank you. I'll ask them."

I kissed her head. "Come on, the others will be waiting."

"Would you like me to drop you both at the beach?" Mum asked.

"Oh, we don't want to disrupt your afternoon. We can catch the bus," Layla replied.

Mum shook her head. "Nonsense. It's no trouble."

My mum and Layla had their own personal jokes by the time we reached the surf club car park. Then, for the rest of the afternoon, Layla didn't stop talking about how much she loved my mum. I only liked her more for it. I liked that my family life and Layla were now overlapping. I just wished that my dad wasn't so intense towards her. He had a heart of gold, but he often let his head rule it.

"Your dad is a bit scary. I don't think he likes me," she said as we walked towards the bus.

It was nearly six thirty, and the sun was dipping towards the horizon. I hoped that her folks didn't blame me for being out so late after school.

"Sorry about him," I replied. "He means well. It's not you, trust me."

"I do." She smiled. "And don't worry. He'll love me eventually."

I chuckled. "I have no doubt that he will."

She skipped up to her door and unlocked it.

"Hi ho!" she called, pushing it open. "I'm home."

"Hi, honey," a female voice called. "How was your day?"

"Super-duper."

I laughed, and Layla led me down the hallway. A head popped out at the end of it.

"Is this the Christian that we've heard so much about?" Layla's mum asked.

"The one and only." She smiled. "Christian, this is my mother, Patricia."

Patricia rolled her eyes. "Come now, who calls me that? Honestly, Layla. Christian, call me Pattie."

I stepped forward and offered her my hand. "It's a pleasure to meet you, Pattie."

Layla's mum glanced at her daughter then stepped around my hand to hug me.

"Christian, honey, forget the formalities," Pattie said. "Welcome. Can you stay for dinner?"

"Yes, ma'am." I nodded.

Pattie's eyebrows rose.

"I mean, yes, Pattie," I amended.

She smiled. "Henry, your daughter has brought a boy home."

"Grief, kiddo," her dad's voice echoed from somewhere. "It's not Wayne, is it? I mean, the kid is nice enough, but he's not the brightest crayon."

Layla rolled her eyes. "No, Dad. It's Christian. Remember? I told you all about him."

Her father appeared from the hallway. He looked friendly. A real salt-of-the-earth type.

"Of course, the Beatles and Eric Clapton fan." He smiled. "How are you, Christian? I'm Henry, Layla's very protective and very strict father."

Layla rolled her eyes again. "As if, Dad."

I was still caught on the fact that he seemed to know my music preferences. She really had told them all about me. I hoped that she didn't go into too much detail about how we passed the time.

"Henry, it's good to meet you," I answered and shook his hand. "And, noted."

He slapped my shoulder. "Good lad. So, you're staying for dinner then?"

"Yes, sir, if it's okay with you."

Henry pulled a face. "What's this 'sir' business? I'm not old enough for that, am I?"

"No, sir, I—"

Layla laughed. "Christian was just raised right, that's all."

"Is that it?" Henry asked. "Well, it sounds like you picked a good one, kiddo."

"The best." She beamed.

I smiled. I really, really liked this girl.

By the end of the evening, the Thomas family had accepted me as one of their own. Henry drove me home at eight forty-five, and my dad met him out the front as we pulled up. Out of respect, I didn't get close enough to hear but, given the fact my dad didn't mention anything about Henry to me, or even Layla, I assumed that everything had gone okay with the meeting.

"What did my dad say to yours last night?" I asked the next morning. Layla was colouring in my nails with a black marker, and it didn't occur to me to stop her.

She didn't look up, but her shoulder lifted. "He asked about how business was and then said something about the two of us spending time together and how it shouldn't affect our school work."

"Are you for real?" I frowned. "Did he really say that? School work?"

Her gold eyes lifted. "Yes, I would never lie to you, Christian."

I nodded. "I believe you. I just don't believe him."

"Don't sweat it. He's just concerned about you. Any parent would say the same."

"Yours didn't."

She smiled. "My parents tend to be the exception to the rule. They're bigger kids than me."

"I like them though. They're great."

"They like you too."

I kissed her, curling my fingers around her hair. I felt her body rise as she moved her hand to the nape of my neck. Her fingers tugged on the short bits of hair around my hairline.

"Hey, three feet apart you two," Ms Tottle bellowed from the front.

I opened my eyes and found Layla looking back at me. We both smiled then parted.

"Seriously." Wayne huffed from behind us. "You two are nauseating."

Layla poked her tongue out at him, but he just smiled back.

Wayne was a cool guy, but even then, after seeing Layla with me, I could see the stars in his eyes when he looked at her. A part of me hated the way that he looked at her. I felt territorial when I had no real right to. But, another part of me felt a sense of triumph in the fact that she didn't notice it. All she saw was me. I could see the glow in her eyes when she looked at me, and that wasn't there when she looked at anyone else.

So, I looked past the stars in Wayne's eyes and saw the dude who was behind them who was the class clown and skateboarded everywhere. He was the guy who couldn't manage to wear his trousers anywhere other than halfway down his butt, and who would probably need to get his cap surgically removed if anyone ever requested that he take it off. ASH was pretty good with the dress code – they weren't too strict, so individuality was able to flourish.

Come the weekend, Pattie, Henry, and Layla Thomas were all set to come to our newly established home for afternoon tea. My dad was being a bit difficult, saying that as the sergeant it wasn't easy for him to drop everything and have scones with jam and cream. But, somehow my mum tipped him over, and he agreed to make a little effort. I knew what he was thinking – that this was all just a waste of time because Layla and I had only known each other for three weeks; we were fourteen years old, and no one found their soulmate at fourteen years old. Maybe my mum thought that too, but at least she humoured me.

Pattie and Henry were incredible though, and Layla sat beside them just as proud as ever. I sat beside her with a similar sense of pride that these two people would probably end up being like parents to me too. As far as I was concerned, Layla was my soulmate and, if time was the only thing that would prove to anyone else of the fact, then I would happily take it.

Time.

It felt like it was flying and hardly moving. One thing that was constant was the fact that every day I seemed to fall more in love with Layla Thomas. I wanted to tell her so many times from that first day that she stumbled into my life and twirled around me in her yellow dress. But, there was never the perfect moment. When was the perfect moment to tell someone that you were in love with them? Did it exist?

It took me a while, but then I realised that there wasn't such a thing as the perfect moment. I realised that when you loved someone, you should tell them as often as you could so they never doubted it or had the chance to forget.

**

It was mid-autumn, and Layla and I had been together for about seven months. We'd spent her fourteenth birthday, Christmas, and my fifteenth birthday together. Everyone around us appeared to be waiting for our flame to snuff, but it kept burning warmly between us. I knew then for sure, and for a reason that I couldn't comprehend, that I loved her in a way that would never disappear no matter what we were faced with. So, I decided to tell her.

I thought about ways to say it, to express it. I wanted it to be more than words because what was between Layla and me was unexplainable. But, I still believed that words were powerful and had the power to change lives, so I wanted to do it right.

On a Saturday, which started like any Saturday, I got up early and had a shower, then inhaled a coffee and two slices of toast before heading over to Layla's house.

"Hi." She smiled. She was wearing a denim skirt and a blue T-shirt, and her arm hung off the wooden door.

"Hi," I replied.

She stepped back, and I stepped forward. She grabbed a handful of the shirt on my chest and pulled. Her head tipped back as my lips sank forward onto hers, and her arms wrapped around my neck.

"Hi," she whispered.

I moved my hands up her arms. "What do you want to do today?"

"I have a couple of ideas."

"Really? Like what?"

"Well," she sighed, and stepped back again. "There is something that I've wanted to do with you for a long time."

My heart squeezed. "What's that?"

"Build a fort."

"A what? A fort?"

"Like a little cubby house out of sheets."

I laughed. "Okay. Where?"

"My room."

"But I'm not allowed in your room, remember?"

Henry had instilled the rule when we'd hit the three-month mark. It was the strangest third monthiversary present ever.

"Well, my dad isn't home," she said. "He got called out to an emergency plumbing job."

"And Pattie?"

"Grocery shopping," Layla answered as her nose wrinkled. She hated grocery shopping.

"You mean, we have the place to ourselves?" I asked. "And you want to build a fort?"

She grabbed my hand and tugged me down the hallway. I pushed the front door to close behind me and then allowed myself to be dragged.

"Layla, I don't know if this is a good idea," I said. "When Henry gets home, he'll throw me out."

She laughed. "Not if he doesn't know that you're there. That's the whole point of a fort, Christian."

"Layla."

She stopped and pivoted. "Are you being a chicken?"

"No."

"You're being a chicken."

I exhaled. "I just don't want to abuse his trust in me. As it is, it sucks that my dad is so strict on you coming around my place."

My father had decided that Layla was only allowed over when either he or my mother was home. It seemed ridiculous to me, but I knew better than to question him. We were just lucky that Pattie and Henry didn't mind having me around so much. The only condition, Henry's *only* condition, was that I didn't go into Layla's room. It was a condition that I was going to break because I would do anything for this girl, including breaking only conditions.

Layla's fingers drew zig-zags on my chest, and I caught her hand.

"Fine," I said. "But, for the record, if your dad asks, I took a lot of convincing."

She giggled. "I'm sure he'll believe that. Come on."

We'd managed to get Layla's blue doona cover suspended between the foot of her bed, the chair from her dressing table, and her windowsill when Pattie arrived home.

Layla crawled out from the fort and slid towards the door.

"I'll throw her off the scent. Wait here," she whispered.

I had to laugh, but I made it quiet. Five minutes later, Layla returned with a bag of pretzels and a giant glass of orange juice. She kicked her door closed and shuffled back under.

"All good?" I asked.

"I told her that I was studying." She giggled quietly. "She gave me brain food."

"Pretzels?"

Layla shrugged. "I guess so."

She crawled up the length of me and sat on my lap. Her nose grazed mine a second before her lips did. I moved my arms around her.

"Christian?" she said.

"Layla."

"I don't want to do *that* yet," she murmured. "Is that okay?"

"You mean sex?"

Her brow pinched. "You knew what I meant."

I smiled. "I just wanted to make sure that we were talking about the same thing."

"Right," she sighed, and her gold eyes rolled. "Well, it's just that I know that Wayne and Abbie did *it* recently, and we've been together for longer, but I just want to wait a bit. The whole thing still sort of scares me."

"Scares you? Why?"

"It just does. The whole… everything. It's so adult, you know?" She shrugged. "I just want to make sure that I'm ready for it and what happens after it. Abbie keeps going on about it changing everything. I don't want to change anything just yet. I like how things are between us."

I stayed quiet. I didn't want to pressure her, but I didn't exactly know how being intimate would change things for the worse. Stu and Wayne had both said that it made them closer to their girlfriends. Nevertheless, that wasn't why I wanted to be with Layla. I wanted to be with her because I loved her and wanted to be with *her*. I was in this with her for as long as forever allowed. So, as far as I was concerned, things would happen when they happened.

"Are you disappointed?" Layla asked, as her perfect lips were downturned.

"Not unless you're saying never," I replied. "But I told you months ago that we don't have to do anything that you're not comfortable with."

She nodded. "I do want to do it with you. Just not yet."

"Okay."

She kissed me again, and her fingers scrunched the collar of my T-shirt. I tipped my head back.

"Layla, I will support your request to wait, but you've got to work with me a little," I sighed.

Her eyebrows lifted innocently. "What do you mean?"

"Studying on a Saturday?" Henry's voice said.

A fraction of a second later, Layla's bedroom door flew open. Layla scrambled off me and peered out of the fort.

"Hey, Daddy," she squeaked. "You're home."

"Layla Louise Thomas," he exhaled.

"Yes?"

"If I look in there and see that you are not alone, I am going to be very, *very* disappointed in you *and* Mr Turner."

Layla sat back on her heels. "Dad, Mitch isn't in here with me."

I tried not to laugh and failed. Layla looked back at me and rolled her eyes.

"Christian, come out please," Henry said.

I slid towards the entrance of the cubby.

"For the record, Henry, I took a lot of convincing to break—"

"Sure you did, kid," Henry groaned.

"Truly." Layla nodded. "Daddy, don't be mad. We weren't doing anything. We were just eating pretzels and telling stories."

"Kiddo, I don't care if you were playing bridge under there."

Layla pulled a face. "What's that?"

"It's a card game, Layla."

"Isn't that with four players?" I asked. My mum used to play.

Henry huffed. "Christian, out. Come on. I thought that I made myself clear."

I crawled past Layla, and she grabbed my shoulder.

"No, Daddy, please," Layla sulked. "Honestly, we're not doing anything different here as we would in the lounge room. We'll even keep the door open if you're going to get all authoritative on us."

Henry rubbed his brow. "I'm your father, kid. It's my job to be authoritative."

"Oh, sure," she sighed.

Henry glanced at me as I kneeled just outside the opening. He stared me down with a similar shade of golden brown eyes that Layla had.

"Door stays open," he said. "And I will be coming in every five minutes to check that there is no funny business going on, so don't even think about getting any ideas. Do I make myself clear?"

"Crystal clear." Layla beamed. "Thanks, Daddy."

"Opposite sides of that little tent."

I nodded. "Got it, sir."

Henry lowered his head in reply. I knew we were stretching his tolerance because for once he didn't correct me for calling him 'sir'.

Layla backed under the cubby. I held Henry's gaze for a moment longer and then shuffled back under myself.

41

"No lengthy silences or I'll be back in here huffing and puffing so quickly that your little house will blow down," Henry finished.

"Noted, Henry," I called.

"Layla?"

"Yes, Dad?"

"Am I clear?"

"As a daisy." She grinned.

I heard Henry sigh. "Door stays open."

Layla smiled at me as his footsteps sounded.

"See, no sweat." She shrugged.

"You are going to give him a heart attack one of these days," I replied.

"Nuh, my dad is as strong as an ox."

She crawled to the opening and reached for something. A moment later, she sat back, and a flash went off.

I rubbed my eyes.

"Layla, love, don't you ever get sick of taking photos of me?" I sighed.

There was another flash from Layla's camera, and I blinked.

"No, Christian blue-eyes, I could never get sick of you." She smiled. "Besides, I need to fill up my Christian album."

"Christian *album*?" I frowned, and there was another flash.

"The one you bought me for my birthday. I'm making it a Christian album."

I wrinkled my nose. "I didn't realise that the present would be encouragement for more paparazzi shots."

Flash.

My eyes rolled. "Can't it be a Christian *and* Layla album instead?"

"No, baby, we'll have another one for us. Lots of them."

I smiled, and there was another flash. My hands rested on my jeans, and I felt the pocketknife in my pocket that my dad had bought *me* for *my* birthday. *"Every man should have a decent pocketknife,"* he'd said. *"Just don't go using it for the wrong thing or I'll arrest you myself."*

Ah, Dad.

I pulled it out and held it in my palm. Layla took another photo, and I looked up at her then glanced down at the wooden skirting that ran around her room. Maybe this was the perfect way to mark the occasion. Maybe this could be my grand gesture. I opened the blade.

"You're not going to stab me, are you?" She smirked.

"No. But, I may stab your wall. Is that okay?"

She shrugged and then shuffled around to rest her head in my lap.

I was momentarily immobilised and then slowly relaxed. My fingers ran through her hair, and then I twisted towards the skirting. I sank the tip of the knife in and began carving.

While I worked, Layla kept the conversation going by telling me stories about when she was growing up and all the different friends that she'd had as she moved from year to year. Apparently, since she'd started high school, she had just stuck with Abbie, even if sometimes she was mean. I tried to concentrate on my task, but there were times when I just found myself staring at her as she spoke. She was the kindest soul, and had the most innocent heart. Even something small like calling her best friend 'mean' instead of using a few other choice words that I would have used to describe her. I didn't like hearing that Abbie ignored Layla sometimes, or that she dominated the conversation just so Layla couldn't tell her about how happy she was with her life.

When Layla was done telling me about Abbie, she moved on to talk about all the places that she wanted to travel to and photograph. Eventually though, she ran out of steam and looked up at me with her wistful eyes.

"Do you think we can stay in here forever?" she asked.

I looked down at her and laughed.

"I think your dad will drag me out before forever comes," I said. "I don't think he likes me very much right now."

"Sure he does." She grinned. "He thinks you're great. But your dad still doesn't like me."

"Well, at least he doesn't come into my room every five minutes to make sure we're not doing anything inappropriate."

She rolled her eyes, shuffling around to sit on her knees.

"I'm his only child, and you're the first boy I've ever brought home. Of course he's going to be a little protective of me."

"A little." I nodded.

"A lot."

I smiled and put my blade down. I was nearly finished carving, but I couldn't wait. Looking into her eyes, having her look back at me the way she was – as if I was the most amazing thing she'd ever seen. It made no sense to me, but I took it gratefully.

I leant down to brush the tip of my nose against hers and then dipped further to reach her lips in the lightest of kisses.

"I love you," I whispered. I couldn't help it; it needed to be said. I had waited long enough.

Layla was silent, so I sat back to make sure that she wasn't flipping out over my little revelation.

She blinked. "You do?"

"Yes, is that okay?"

I must have looked dumb. I know I felt a little dazed. It had only just occurred to me that if Layla was worried about sex changing things, my telling her that I loved her would probably have about the same effect.

She giggled, and I relaxed a little. Giggling was good. That meant she was happy, right?

"Yes, it's okay. God, Christian, I love you too," she answered.

I let out a laugh of relief. "Do you think we're crazy?"

"Probably." She shrugged. "But does it matter?"

"Not to me."

I shuffled around to kiss her again, scooping her into my arms, so our bodies were mashed together in twisted limbs. I felt the breath hitch in Layla's throat, but she didn't stop like she usually would when things got too heavy between us.

I was only vaguely aware of her boundaries as I lowered her onto the blanket that we'd laid on her wooden floor. I kissed her firmly, hotly, and when it felt like the oxygen had been sucked from the room, I rested my forehead against hers to catch my breath. She was panting as hard as I was.

But then the clock stopped ticking, the trees stopped swaying, and everything around us faded away. There was only Layla, and she was the centre of my world. I have never been particularly religious but, at that moment, I would have knelt before any higher power that led me to Almanbury to meet Layla Thomas.

Layla watched me intently, staring into my eyes as if under a trance. I had to admit that I felt a certain amount of triumph that I seemed to have that effect on her.

My fingers moved to tuck her hair behind her ear, and then, testing her limits, I let my hand drift down her neck, over her sternum to her waist. I felt for the bottom of her T-shirt and ran my hand over her skin. She pulled in her lower lip to bite down on, and my chest clenched. God, she was beautiful.

Then there was a sound of someone clearing their throat, and my life seemed to flash before my eyes. Every image I saw was of Layla.

There were two knocks on wood. I guessed it was on the opened door.

"Layla, Christian," Henry's warning tone said. "It's a little too quiet in there. What's going on?"

Layla's head turned towards the voice.

My gaze followed, and I was eternally grateful for the sheets of material that concealed us. I was sure that the alternative was my dad showing up to charge Henry with murder.

"We're, um, miming, Dad," Layla answered. She was still a little breathless.

My eyebrows lifted, and I considered moving from our compromising position but with Henry so close, it would sound even more suspect.

"Well, I think maybe you should stick to verbal conversation. Right, Christian?"

I cleared my throat. "Yes, sir."

Layla giggled against her hand.

"Layla, enough please," Henry said. "Behave, or I'll ban any boys from being in your room."

"Sure, Dad, I promise I'll behave," Layla replied.

Henry sounded like he was leaving again.

My eyebrow lifted. "Any boys? Are there more?"

Layla's eyes rolled. "Does he count himself as a boy, do you think?"

I huffed a laugh and slowly sat up, peeling my arms and legs from around her.

She shuffled around to sit as I turned back towards the skirting and picked up my pocketknife.

"What exactly are you doing to my wall?" she asked.

I moved my hand in front of my etching. "I'm carving something into it so you'll never forget it."

"Do I get to see it? I mean, it is my wall."

"Yes, but I want to finish it first."

"Well, how long until you finish?"

I looked over my shoulder at her and saw that she was pouting. I was at the mercy of that pout.

"Close your eyes and count to ten, and then you can see it," I answered.

She perked back up and closed her eyes. I began chiselling faster, and she giggled again.

"One, two, three, four," she counted.

Wow, too fast. I gave a breathless laugh and put my elbow into it. I moved in front to get a better angle, and to shield it, should Layla try to sneak a peek.

"Five, six, seven, eight, nine—"

I squirmed to finish. "Wait, wait, wait."

"Nine and a half, nine and three quarters—"

I moved one of my hands to cover her eyes. "Okay."

"Ten!" she squealed, and then moved to peel my fingers from her face.

I swallowed as her eyes found the engraving, and her excitable smile faded as she read it. My eyebrows lifted as I glanced down at the inscription. It was an impressive job considering what I was working with. I just hoped that she didn't think it was completely lame.

Christian Turner loves Layla Thomas.

Layla exhaled slowly. Her eyes twinkled as a smile crept back onto her lips.

"My dad's going to have a fit." She grinned.

"Totally worth it," I said.

My head tipped, and my shoulder lifted, and then I leant forward to kiss her again. She moved her hands to settle on my face and pulled her body against mine. I threw the knife in the general direction of the corner and wrapped my arms back around her.

I didn't even hear the footsteps.

"Right. Out," Henry said. "Come on, before I throw some cold water on the two of you."

Layla groaned and unwrapped herself from around me.

"Dad," she groaned. "You really ought to trust us more."

"Telling stories, my foot," he mumbled. "Christian, why don't you come and help me mow the lawn?"

I stumbled to my feet. "The lawn, sir?"

Layla's shoulders dropped. "Dad, you can't make him—"

"Well, he's around here enough; he might as well pull his weight with the chores," Henry huffed.

I scratched my neck. "I've never worked a lawnmower before, Henry."

He patted me on the back, and it nearly made me spit out my stomach. "Well, kid, I'll teach you. Every man needs to know how to work a mower."

Layla pouted. "What am I going to do then?"

Henry lifted his hands. "Well, you could study, kiddo. Isn't that what you told your mother you were doing today?"

Layla folded her arms, and Henry moved his hand to the base of my neck and guided me out of Layla's room. I wouldn't see the inside of that room again for another year or so.

I regretted nothing.

Even if the day had taken an unexpected turn, I really enjoyed hanging out with Layla's dad. Henry had become like a second father to me even in the less-than-a-year that I'd known the Thomas family. He took me under his wing as an honorary son and taught me things that my dad didn't have time to. I was glad that he thought so much of me. He and Layla were pretty close – closer than Layla was with Pattie. Layla and her dad seemed to connect on a different level, as if they had a mutual understanding and a kind of honesty with each other that I'd never seen between a parent and a kid before. I kind of envied it, but I liked that I could at least witness it from the outside.

**

About a month after I had etched my affection into Layla's skirting, I managed to score myself a job. My mum told people that it was in distribution, but I just told people that it was delivering newspapers. It took me two hours before school to cover the small town, but it meant that I could still spend my afternoons with Layla on most days of the week – most days because my dad decided that I was spending too much time with her and not enough on my school work. So, Mondays and Tuesdays were devoted to that. It didn't matter too much, since Layla and I still found ways to hang out.

At first, we weren't that clever, so we kept each other on speaker phone for hours. But then my phone bill came in, and Sergeant Turner hit the roof. He wanted to confiscate my phone, but my mum convinced him that I needed one for emergencies, so he compromised with a pre-paid. Then we texted instead, but I used up all my credit in the first two days. Then we got a little smarter, and I used some of my savings and birthday money to invest in a cheap laptop with a webcam. I hooked that up to our internet, and we did our homework together until one day my father walked in my room unannounced and decided to cut off our Wi-Fi. Then it sucked for a few weeks until term ended.

The fourth of September marked our first anniversary, and the anniversary of when my family and I had arrived in Almanbury. With the cash that I'd saved from the paper delivery, plus a small contribution from my mum, I bought Layla the best thing that I could afford at the only jewellery store in Almanbury – a goldstone pendant that was encased in a woven gold cage. I had picked it out especially because it perfectly matched her eyes. I thought I'd done a great job in picking something that she'd like but, when I gave it to her at the picnic that she'd planned for us, she started to cry.

"No, no, no, no, no, don't cry." I frowned. "If you don't like it, I can take it back."

Her head shook in quick jerks, and she hugged it to her chest.

I blinked in confusion. "Layla, darling, I'm going to need words to understand why you're crying if you don't want me to take it back."

"I… I… I… I just," she sobbed.

I rested my hands on her shoulders. "Breathe, Layla."

She sniffled. "I got you a new skateboard. My present is crap compared to yours."

I laughed in relief. "You got me a skateboard? That's not crap. That's awesome."

"Don't lie, Christian. It's not awesome; it's pathetic."

"I wouldn't lie to you, Layla. Come here," I murmured. I pulled on her hand and tugged her onto my lap. She wrapped her arm around my shoulders and buried her face into my neck. It sent tingles down my spine.

"I'm sorry that I'm a dud girlfriend," she mumbled.

I frowned at her. "Says who? Why? Because of a gift? There's more to being a girlfriend than that. I actually think you do everything perfectly."

She pouted. "Almost everything. We've been together for a year, and we still haven't done… it."

"Layla, please," I groaned. "Give me some credit. I love you, and I told you that I'm prepared to wait."

"You love me more than I deserve."

I rolled my eyes. "Damn it, you are so frustrating sometimes."

"But you still love me?"

"Yeah." I huffed. "A lot. More than a lot."

"More than I deserve."

I pressed my fingers into my eyes.

"Christian?" she squeaked. Her fingers wrapped around my wrist to pull my hand away.

I dropped it then moved it around her. "What?"

"I love you more than all the photos I've ever taken, and all the words you've ever read," she said. "I wish that there was a way to show you how much I love you, but I can't capture anything that fits it."

She looked down at the necklace that was still curled in her dainty little hand. She was wearing gold nail polish that had started to chip off.

"Will you please help me put this on?" she asked. "I'm never going to take it off."

I had barely registered her question because I was too busy staring at her, wondering what ridiculously good thing that I had done to deserve the golden karma that meant this girl was in my life, declaring to an unquantifiable amount just how much she loved me.

It had been a year, but it had been a whirlwind. I felt like it had been longer, but only because I couldn't remember my life before I'd met her. I didn't want to remember it because it wasn't worth remembering.

I clipped the clasp of the gold necklace around her neck, and her hand moved to the pendant.

"Now, Christian Turner, even when we're apart, a piece of you will always be near my heart," she said.

I reached to tuck her hair behind her ear. "That's very poetic. I couldn't have said it better myself."

"Nonsense," she sighed. "You're better at words than I am."

"Maybe, but that was pretty perfect."

"You are."

Her lips brushed mine, and I tipped my face up at the same time she gasped.

"You still need to open your skateboard," she said.

My head shook as my hand rose to catch her cheek so I could guide her lips back to mine. "In a minute."

Her gold eyes glistened. "Don't you want it?"

"I actually kind of want to kiss you first." I shrugged. "If that's okay."

She smiled and clapped her hands to my cheeks then gave me a quick peck. "Open it."

"You've changed your tune." I laughed. "Okay, let me have it."

Layla bounced off my knee and scrambled for the picnic basket.

"I hid it in here because I didn't want you to find it and guess," she said as she dragged out a long gift wrapped in brown paper. "I think I may have squished all the sandwiches though."

"Well, squashed sandwiches happen to be my favourite. It makes the toppings really sink into the bread."

Layla laughed, and her head tipped back. "Oh, how I love you, Christian Turner. You're my favourite."

I accepted the parcel and peeled back the sticky tape at the fold on the side that had less of it. I glanced up at Layla, and she was gnawing on her lower lip.

"My mum wrapped half of it because she thought I was wasting sticky tape," she said.

"I take it this was her side then?"

She shrugged. "The paper looked flimsy. I thought the wheels might break it open."

"I wonder what it is," I replied with a laugh as I started to tear the wrapping.

As I pulled it clear, I froze to stare at it. The deck was custom printed with a photo that Layla had taken of me at the beach. I was a silhouette against the sunset, but I recognised the photo right away. More than that, the wheels were a light blue that matched the blues of the ocean in the picture. The reverse-side grip tape was bright yellow like the sand in it – and Layla's favourite colour.

"Are you kidding me?" I sighed. "Layla, this is *incredible*."

"It's not as good as your present."

I turned it over in my hands. "This is so amazing. How did you…? This would have cost a fortune."

"Not as much as my necklace."

I groaned. "Will you please just accept the fact that this is the most thoughtful and insanely remarkable gift that anyone has ever given me?"

Her eyebrows lifted. "Really?"

"Truly." I nodded. "I love it. Almost as much as I love you, but that's not possible."

53

She giggled, took the board from my hands, and threw it aside before lunging on me. I fell back with impact, and it winded me a little, but I didn't care.

"Do you like the yellow grip stuff?" she asked before she kissed me.

I laughed. "I love it."

"I got blue wheels though." She smiled, and then kissed me again.

"They're perfect. It's—"

She kissed me again, and then ran her fingertips under my eyes. "I got blue wheels because your eyes are blue. Blue is my second favourite colour."

I looked up at her. "It's perfect."

"You're perfect. Your soul is perfect. I am so lucky to have you in my life. The last year has been the most favourite year of my life. Christian Turner, I want every year to be as amazing as the last year."

"It will be. They will be," I murmured. "Each as incredible as the last."

"I believe you." She nodded. "Because we will spend them together."

"Deal."

It was something that was so easy to promise because neither one of us could imagine that anything would or could come between us to make it so we were apart.

We spent our second Christmas together, along with the summer holidays, and my father was thawing a little over Layla and me spending time together. However, I wasn't sure whether it was because we had lasted over a year, or whether it was because it was the holidays. I didn't bother stopping to question it because, for whatever the reason, it only meant that there were fewer obstacles in our way to ensure that our promise to each other remained intact.

**

We thought that this meant that, as we went into our sixteenth year of life and our second year together, the hardest part was behind us. We thought that we had done enough to prove that we were Christian and Layla, and that wasn't going to change no matter what. But, then school started back and, after a full term of good grades, my dad decided that two Layla-free afternoons were not enough for my year eleven workload.

"I think that Mondays to Thursdays should be spent without Layla hanging around so you can just focus on your school work," Dad said the evening before the first day of term two.

"I appreciate your opinion, Dad, but I think that's unnecessary," I replied.

"Beg yours?" He asked. "It wasn't an opinion, Christian, it was a command."

"Honestly, Mitch," Mum sighed. "Do you really think that Layla is such a bad influence on Christian? He has never done so well in school before coming here and meeting her."

Dad shook his head. "Well, that's because he went without her for two days last year, and he doesn't have the city influences that he did before."

"Dad, with all due respect, I don't know what you think we get up to when we hang out after school. Layla has schoolwork to do too, so we normally just do homework together. Nothing sinister, just two people—"

"Two hormone-charged teenagers," he interrupted. "I know what kids your age get up to, son, and I'm not going to sit by and watch while you and her stuff up your futures by putting all your eggs in each other's baskets – or worse, by doing something completely irresponsible like a teenage pregnancy or—"

"For goodness sake, Mitchell Turner," Mum reprimanded. "Give Christian some credit."

I glowered into my peas. Anything that I said to defy my father would make things worse, so I really was banking on my mum saying what I couldn't.

"Christian, sweetie, do we need to have a talk with you about—"

"No," I replied. My voice dripped with discomfort. "Mum, no. We're... no."

So much for having someone in my corner. My mum clearly thought that we were as *hormone-charged* just as my dad did. To be fair, the fact that we hadn't had sex yet wasn't my decision, but at that moment, I was glad that Layla had taken the stand.

Mum gave me a small smile that looked a little apologetic. "See, Mitch. Let Christian and Layla see each other or we'll just have to face the fact that they'll only defy us and sneak around."

I had never loved my mother more. I glanced at Dad for his reaction, but he was a statue. Her hand moved on top of his.

"Mitch, sweetie, do you remember when we first started courting? You can't sit there and tell me that if our parents had told us not to see each other that we wouldn't have taken matters into our own hands."

"Nancy, we were older than Christian and Layla," Dad said. "They're still kids, and they're talking about love and forever; it's just not realistic. I don't want Christian to look back when this is all over and regret that he let that girl decide his future."

I pushed out my chair. "Layla *is* my future, Dad. You can learn to accept that, or you can live in denial, but the fact is that I'll never regret anything when it comes to her. I love her and, one day, I'm going to marry her. When that day comes, you'll remember this conversation and, on that day, I'll be waiting with a big, fat 'I told you so'."

"You are fifteen years old, son. You don't know what you want," Dad muttered. "Now sit down and finish your dinner."

"I'm sixteen," I said. "And what the hell has age got to do with anything? Pattie and Henry have been together since they were fifteen and were married straight out of high school. Just because you don't understand how I could find my soulmate at fourteen, it doesn't mean that it's not possible."

Dad's hand slammed on the table making all the cutlery and crockery jump, as well as Mum and me.

"Now you listen to me, Christian David Turner, you will not speak to me with that tone again, *do you understand?*"

"Yeah," I breathed.

"Pardon me?"

"Yes, Dad."

He frowned. "And I don't care about what Pattie and Henry did or did not do. You are my son, and while you are living under my roof it is my job to have *your* best interests in mind. They can let Layla run off and do whatever she wants to but, so help me God, I *will not* allow her to take you along for the ride."

"Mitch," Mum growled. "Stop that."

"No, Nancy, don't challenge me on this."

"Fine," I sighed. I stepped around my chair. "If that's how it's going to be *living under your roof* then I'll find somewhere else to live."

"Christian, no." Mum frowned.

"Sorry, Mum," I murmured. I leant to squeeze her shoulder and then headed to my room. I figured that, as soon as my father stopped blowing steam out his ears and caught his breath, it was where he'd send me anyway.

"Christian, get back here," he bellowed. Okay, so maybe not. "Don't behave like such a child."

"But I'm not a child, Dad, can't you see?" I yelled. "I'm sixteen. People leave school and get jobs, start lives, have children or whatever at this age. I'm not saying that I *want* to move out but, for the love of God, I just want to go to school and spend time with my girlfriend who is not a felon, by the way. Layla is the best thing that has ever happened to me and comes from the greatest family that I've ever met. If you are so unhappy with the fact that, for the first time I am actually happy with my life and doing well at school, then it's not me who has a warped idea of my future; it's you."

I watched as Mitch Turner's face went from purple to red then started to fade back to normal. There was a long silence that made me question my existence on this planet, since I knew that speaking to him the way that I had would generally result in my death. But, instead, he just looked back to his dinner and continued eating.

Mum took a breath. "Christian, sweetie, come and finish your dinner."

"I'm not hungry, Mum," I replied.

She kept staring at me, so I walked back over and sat back down. I began moving the remaining peas around my plate.

"No one is moving out," she sighed. "I don't want this family to be broken just because we can't come to some sort of compromise."

"We have compromised. I already don't see Layla two afternoons a week," I said. "I'd prefer that it was zero, to be honest."

Dad exhaled. "I think two days away from the girl is perfectly—"

"Layla, her name is Layla," I replied.

"Two afternoons apart is perfectly reasonable."

My mum gave a slow nod that told me that she didn't entirely agree but didn't necessarily disagree.

"Christian, are you willing to agree to keep up Monday and Tuesday afternoons?"

"Well, I don't *want* to not see her but—"

"Okay, so two days as they stand," Mum sighed. "Do we agree?"

Dad looked down at his plate. "Three."

"No," I grumbled. "I won't agree to that."

My mum exhaled. "We will start with two, but if Christian shows any signs that he's struggling, then we will have this discussion again. Can we agree on that?"

"Fine." I shrugged.

My dad cleared his throat.

"Mitch," Mum warned.

"Yes, Nancy, fine," he sighed. "Christian, the duty rests on you then."

As always.

The conversation cast a dark cloud over my first day of school. I had never really felt pressure when it came to getting good grades since I'd never found school that difficult. I enjoyed reading, so I found it easy to teach myself any theories that I missed in class. I liked writing too, so that covered most subjects. The only ones I had to spend more time on were maths and science. You couldn't write your way out of those. You were either right or wrong.

"What's wrong?" Layla asked. Her finger traced my lips at lunchtime. They tasted like the orange she had just been peeling.

"My dad was trying to extend our two afternoons apart to four last night," I said. I never lied to Layla; it wasn't worth it.

"Why?"

"He thinks that I'll need to focus more on school this year."

She pouted. "But you're like the smartest person in the year. This isn't about you, this is about me. He hates me, Christian."

"He doesn't hate you," I sighed. I didn't know why I was defending my dad because he clearly didn't seem to especially *like* Layla. "I think he's just concerned about the future."

"Your future, you mean." She frowned. "Not mine or ours, just yours. He doesn't think I'll be in your future."

"Well, he's wrong," I said. "One hundred per cent. I told him that."

"You told your dad that he's wrong?"

I smiled and nodded. "He didn't take it well."

She laughed and wrapped her arms around me. Her forehead rested on mine.

Wayne groaned, "Another year, another episode of the Christian and Layla show."

"Block your eyes, Wayne-o," Layla murmured.

"How do I block my eyes?"

I laughed. "Hey, you should come over for dinner on the weekend, Layla."

"Is that smart?" Stuart asked. It amazed me how everyone around us decided that they were entitled to an opinion in our relationship.

"Why?" I frowned.

"Because Sergeant Turner just said he wants you and Layla to spend less time together, you really think that asking her over for dinner is going to make things better?" Stuart replied. "Dude, you're delusional."

I pulled a face and glanced at Layla. She bit her lip.

"I don't care. He's just got to deal with the fact that we're together, and that's never going to change." I shrugged. "Besides, it's on one of the days that we *can* see each other."

Layla smiled. "I'm going to buy new jeans for the occasion. Count me in."

My dad wasn't pleased, but my mum was planning things to cook for the rest of the week. Layla was set to come over Saturday afternoon, so I helped mum cook most of Saturday. My dad made himself scarce, but there were the odd mutterings about the fact that I was in the kitchen when I should be doing homework or anything else that normal teenage boys would do.

At ten minutes to four o'clock, I waited out the front for Layla to arrive. Almanbury was small, so it didn't take long for her to walk from her house to mine. We timed it once and discovered that if we ran, it was eight minutes from door to door. Layla didn't run today, but she was still earlier than we'd planned.

I stood up as she appeared down my street. She waved and started to jog and then stopped. I ran towards her.

"I don't want to dirty my new jeans," she called, and then did a little spin.

"Very nice." I laughed and opened my arms to take her into them.

It was crazy to think that it had only been a day since I'd seen her. I missed her every minute that we were apart, and I kept waiting for that feeling to run out, but it didn't. After almost a year and a half, I was convinced that it probably wouldn't. It would only intensify.

"I've been so excited all day." She giggled. "I started getting ready after mum and I got back from the shops at one o'clock."

I took her hand, and we started walking towards my house.

"You could have come earlier," I said.

"I didn't want to push my luck." She shrugged. "Your dad already—ouch!"

I stopped and looked at her as she leant over and pressed her hand to her right leg just above her knee.

"What's up?" I frowned. I glanced at my dad's ute beside her. The bumper had been cracked and half broke off a couple of weeks ago when someone had clipped it. They'd gone to lock up for it, but Dad still hadn't had the chance to get it fixed.

"Your dad's car just attacked my new jeans," she squealed. "Apparently, *that* hates me too."

I gave a small laugh.

"It's not funny." She pouted. She removed her hand, and the tear had gone through the denim and cut her leg.

"Holy crap," I sighed. I leant over and scooped her up to carry her back to my front porch. I sat her on the stairs. "Layla, we need to clean this. It'll get infected otherwise."

She whimpered.

"Is it painful?" I frowned.

"No, but these jeans weren't cheap, and they're only new today," she cried. "I'm so angry that they're *already* ruined."

I tried to hide a smile as I wiped her cheek dry.

"Christian, sweetie, are you going to show Layla inside?" Mum asked. "Oh dear, what happened?"

"Dad's ute attacked Layla's new jeans," I answered. "Can you please get the first aid kit?"

Layla sniffled. "I'll just wash it. It'll be fine."

"Nonsense, come inside, Layla. I'll get the medical kit and find you something to wear," Mum said.

I smiled at my mother and helped Layla stand. She limped a little, so I picked her up again and carried her inside. Mum and I fussed over her, cleaning the wound and making sure that she was okay. It wasn't too deep, but it was deep enough to bleed, so her jeans needed soaking too. Mum let her borrow a pair of shorts. By the time she was all fixed up, and Mum returned to the kitchen, our lasagne was topped with charcoal.

"Oh, bother." Mum frowned as black smoke poured from the oven when she opened it. "I forgot that I turned up the oven before coming to check on you two. I've burnt dinner."

My shoulder's dropped. "Is it edible? Maybe if we take the top layer off?"

"I don't know, sweetie, it's probably all dry."

Layla stood up. "I can help."

"Layla, sweetie, you sit. You're our guest," Mum said.

"But it's my fault that it got ruined," Layla sighed. "Please, all I need is pasta, cheese, milk, an onion, plain flour, and a bit of salt. Oh, and bacon or chicken if you want some meat protein in it."

Mum and I exchanged a look.

"We have that, don't we?" I asked.

"Yes, of course." Mum nodded. "What are you thinking, Layla?"

Layla shrugged. "I learnt how to make macaroni cheese by heart when I was twelve. It might not be as lovely as your lasagne, but it's pretty yummy if I do say so myself."

"She's not lying; people write songs about how amazing her mac and cheese is," I added.

"It sounds perfect." Mum laughed. "Set us to work."

Layla breezed around the kitchen like a professional, albeit she only knew how to cook one meal. At least it was an incredible one.

We finished throwing it together in less than fifteen minutes, and then it baked for another thirty. When the top breadcrumbs turned golden, we all set ourselves at the table for mac and cheese with chicken, and a garden salad to share.

"I thought we were having lasagne?" Dad said as my mum began serving up.

"We were, but I burnt it by accident." Mum smiled. "Luckily, Layla saved the day."

Layla blushed. "It was the least I could do after being the cause of it burning."

Dad frowned, and I reached out to take Layla's hand.

"It wasn't your fault," I said. "Besides, this looks better. Sorry, Mum."

My mother laughed. "No apologies necessary. It looks wonderful."

"I was looking forward to lasagne," Dad said.

"Well, I'll make it tomorrow night then, Mitchell. Tonight we are having macaroni and cheese."

Dad huffed.

"Speaking of which," Mum continued. "Layla cut her leg on your broken bumper, so why don't you look into getting that fixed on Monday. You can use my car until we get it back."

"Well, what was she doing so close to my ute?" Dad asked.

"Mitch, you are missing the point," Mum scolded.

I groaned. "We were just walking by it. For goodness sake, Dad, give her a break."

Dad's eyebrows lifted. "Now—"

"Mitchell," Mum snapped. "Don't start."

"Fine," he sighed. "So, kids, selections for classes next year will come out soon. Do you know what you're choosing?"

I frowned. "Dad, it's only April. We have until, like, October to decide."

"Yes, well, surely you both have some idea on what you want to do when you leave school," Dad replied. "That should narrow down the options on what you need to study as prerequisites."

I exhaled. Of course, he was doing it again. Why was I surprised?

"Well, Mr Turner, I would like to pursue photography when I finish school," Layla said. "But the university course for it isn't offered anywhere outside of the city, so I think I'll just study it through TAFE."

"Why not just relocate to a place where they offer the course?" he asked.

"Because Almanbury is my home."

"So, you would jeopardise your career for that?" he pressed. "What about work? Is photography something that is likely to offer a steady income?"

"Mitch," Mum warned.

"Dad," I groaned at the same time.

Layla shrugged. "It's what I want to do, Mr Turner. Besides, I believe that some things are more important than money."

"Well, you still need to consider it. It's all well and good to want to pursue a hobby, but some people aren't talented enough to build a career off of it."

"Mitchell, enough," Mum gasped.

I pushed out my chair. "I'm done. Come on, Layla."

Layla's face was red, and her mouth fell open as I offered her my hand.

"Where are you going, boy? Sit down," Dad said.

"No, I'm not putting up with you talking to her like that. She is my guest. She is my girlfriend," I answered. "Show her some respect."

"Respect?" Dad huffed. "I was merely trying to help the girl realise—"

"She has a name!" I shouted. "Stop talking about Layla like she is a criminal that you need to lock up."

"Christian, sweetie—" Mum started.

"Christian, please just sit down. It's fine," Layla whispered as she clutched my hand. "I know that he didn't mean anything by it."

I glanced down at her, and the pleading in her eyes was enough to weaken my knees. I folded into my chair.

"For goodness sake, what a carry-on," Dad mumbled. "You're too sensitive, son."

I stared at my dinner. "Right."

Layla squeezed my hand. I laced my fingers through hers and squeezed back.

"Nancy, I almost forgot," Layla sighed. Her voice was as pleasant as it always was – as if none of the shouting had occurred a minute ago. "My mum asked me to invite you to a candle party that she's holding next Tuesday."

My mother smiled. "Oh, lovely, tell her—"

"We don't need any candles, Nancy," Dad said.

I gritted my teeth.

"Regardless, Mitchell. Layla, please tell Pattie that I would love to come," Mum replied. "And I will bring a plate of food."

Layla smiled, but her eyes didn't smile with her cheeks as they usually would. Dad was chipping away at her. I resented so much that he was being so difficult.

We continued eating, and the silence was a gift.

"How is work at the post office going, Layla?" Mum asked. "Are you enjoying it?"

Layla had started helping her mother sort mail on Mondays and Tuesdays since we were forced to spend them apart. She didn't love it, but at least it was a job. They were hard to come by in a country town where every kid and their friend wanted a casual means to earn money.

"Well, let's just say that Mondays and Tuesdays are my least favourite days of the week for two reasons now." She laughed. "No, it's fine really. It's a job, and I'm really lucky to have one."

I stared at my dad, daring him to comment. He didn't.

Layla squeezed my hand, and I looked over at her. She smiled, and I tried to return it.

"Christian, have you thought about getting a decent job and giving up that paper round?" Dad asked. So close to silence. No cigar.

"Actually, Dad, I was considering getting a trade or something like Henry," I replied. "Maybe start earning a proper income as soon as I can."

Dad glowered. "Since when?"

"Sweetie, I thought that you wanted to study English?" Mum asked.

Layla was watching me carefully, not reacting, just curious.

"Well, sure, I enjoy English." I shrugged. "But it's just a hobby. I'm not sure if I'm good enough to get paid for it."

"Oh, for goodness sake," Dad groaned. "Surely you can see that English has more job prospects than… than other things."

"Please, the two of you, please don't start again," Mum sighed. "I'm so sorry, Layla, they are both behaving terribly this evening."

Layla lowered her head. "It's okay, Nancy. But, for what it's worth, I think that Christian *is* good enough to make a career in

Literature. He's the best in our class by a long shot. He makes me want to be more. He makes me want to be better."

I squeezed her hand and leant over to kiss her cheek. She giggled.

"You're great. You make me better," I breathed.

"Aren't they sweet?" Mum crooned.

Dad stayed quiet. It was the smartest thing he'd done all evening.

**

I started to spend more time at Layla's house after that night. We rarely went to mine. It was too hard, and I wasn't going to tolerate my dad treating her the way that he had at dinner. Life with the Thomas family was great though. Henry showed me more handy things around the house, like how to clean the gutters and build shelves, just general tinkering, and then car maintenance. I loved my dad, but Henry felt like the dad that I'd always needed. I suppose I was just lucky to have them both in my life. Pattie was terrific too, and she taught me how to read a recipe properly and bake things. She also shared with me her collection of little ceramic models that she had painted. The ceramics were amazing, and she even let me paint my own dragon ceramic figure. She explained how the paints she used were ones that could be glazed, then after she was finished, she baked them in an oven to make the paint stick. It was cool.

Layla was never far from me through any of it. Naturally, she was there to capture all of it on film, including when I'd hammered my thumb with Henry, to the moment that I knocked over one of Pattie's good oil paints. Things had never been better between the two of us and, even if my father was still sceptical, we at least had three supportive parents between us. Henry even began to let me into Layla's room as long as the door stayed open.

Her hands ran up my side, dragging my T-shirt with it.

"So, how many kids do you want?" she murmured.

I groaned. "You really want to talk about this when we're making out? Isn't that jinxing it?"

"Why?" she panted. "You're not getting a home run, not just yet anyway."

I sighed. "I don't know. Four?"

She frowned. "Five?"

I kissed her neck. "Four is even."

"But five is more," she sighed. It was the only thing we ever really disagreed on, but I had to admit that she had a point. She pushed my shoulders and pinned me down. Her hair cascaded down her neck and shoulders, rising and falling with the quick breaths of her chest.

"Six?" I breathed.

She grinned and turned to look towards the door, and then climbed off me.

"Hey… what?" I asked.

Layla giggled and carefully closed the door.

"Henry is going to murder me," I hissed.

Layla pulled a face. "Better that he gets mad at us for it being closed than for him to see what we're about to do."

My mouth went dry. "Which is?"

"I could tell you." She shrugged, pulling off her top. "Or I could just show you."

I sat up on my elbows and watched as she shimmied out of her ripped jeans. Layla had refused to fix them. She said that it was a reminder of us being stronger than people like my dad, who didn't believe that we would last.

She crawled back onto the bed and sat on my thighs. Her fingers began unbuttoning my jeans.

I didn't say anything because, for once, words wouldn't help. That, and I couldn't seem to find them. The wasps that were thoughts in my mind seemed to fly out my ears. My heartbeat shook me, and my short breaths didn't issue enough oxygen.

Layla laughed. "You're falling apart."

"I... I'm..."

Her lips silenced me, which I was glad for because I wasn't making any sense anyway.

My hands ran up her side, and I felt her breath catch. Mine did the same as her hands ran down my chest. I thought my heart was going to break my ribcage and burst through.

I probably should have been thinking about what *could* happen if we were interrupted, but every part of me was enthralled with Layla and her fingers.

"Layla Louise Thomas," a voice bellowed. "Christian David Turner, what did I tell you about this door?"

Layla gasped and sat back on my legs as she scrambled for her clothes – or any clothes. I was too concerned with my jeans.

The door flew open and bashed the wall, and both of us were still in an extremely compromised state.

Layla stumbled onto her feet and threw me my shirt. I turned towards the wall.

Henry let loose, screaming so loudly that his words were unintelligible. The only words that I could make sense of belonged to Layla.

"Daddy, I am nearly sixteen years old. There is no need... stop shouting... this wasn't his fault!"

Henry stomped over to me as I turned towards the edge of Layla's bed, thankfully now fully clothed, and well and truly calmed down from before. He grabbed the scruff of my shirt and dragged me out. Layla trotted alongside us as he walked me to his shed and grabbed his toolkit, and then dragged me back to her room.

Henry let me have the honours of removing Layla's door from its hinges. If he wasn't kicking me out, and this was the worst we got for being sprung, then we would both take the punishment without dispute.

I had a dumb smile on my face the whole time I worked, which only made Henry's frown deepen. Layla found it rather amusing too until she realised that she wouldn't actually have a door any more. She got a stern talking to about being responsible and, well, celibate. I managed to dodge that talk, but I was back to being banned from her room and from basically the entirety of the lower end of the house. Essentially, only the public areas were open to me.

Regardless, we both took the punishment without question since neither of us wanted to give Henry a heart attack. Plus, even with the bans, he was still more supportive of me than my father was of Layla.

Layla's door wasn't returned to its hinges until mid-August, which was just in time for a figurative door to slam on us – at least for a while. It was a Sunday, the week after Layla had her door back, and at 9.44 a.m., there was a knock on my front door. My parents had gone to the markets in town for our weekly fresh fruit and vegetable supply, so I was alone in the house.

As soon as I opened the door, Layla flung herself into my arms.

"They're taking me away," she sobbed.

"Where? Who?" I asked. "For how long?"

Layla pulled back and was shaking from her hysterical crying. "M-Mum and D-Dad are taking me to W-Wales next weekend for the whole of September."

"Next week? What?" I frowned. "Was this just planned?"

She rolled her eyes causing more tears to leak from them. "No, they've been planning it for months. They only just told me though. It was a surprise."

"But... for the whole of September? We're going to miss our second anniversary."

She nodded and wiped her cheek from the tap of tears that seemed to be falling from her reddened gold eyes.

"I don't want to go," she cried. Her arms wrapped around my waist. "Don't make me go, Christian. Run away with me. We can go somewhere. Somewhere they can't find me, and stay there."

I wrapped my arms around her, and she grabbed a handful of my shirt, sobbing harder. I had always had the utmost respect for Henry and Pattie but, right now, I would willingly defy them just to see Layla smile again.

"Say that you'll run away with me," she bawled. She sounded as if the crying was hurting her throat. I would have done anything that she asked in that moment.

Anything.

So, I did.

I packed my backpack and grabbed my skateboard along with any kind of food that we could carry between us. We didn't know where we were heading, so we just started walking in one direction and hoped for the best. We kept to alleyways and backstreets because they were the roads where fewer people were likely to see us and report on our whereabouts. We walked north towards South Coast because at least I knew what to expect from that place. Plus, we both agreed that it was easier to hide out in a city than another country town.

We didn't get very far because it started to rain. It was still winter and being more south than South Coast, weather wasn't as perfect in Almanbury. We headed towards the beach because we knew that there were some decent caves to hide in until it stopped.

It turned out that the reason Henry and Pattie were taking Layla to Wales was to visit family. Henry was born there and moved over to South Coast when he was four. His family moved down to Almanbury, and he hadn't been back to his home country since. It sounded reasonable in theory, but the way that Layla told it made it seem like there was something more sinister going on. If it were my dad, maybe I would have believed it, but I found it hard to believe that Henry would act with any kind of motive. Regardless, anything that meant we would spend a month apart was not okay with me. It wasn't just our anniversary that we'd miss; it was the whole of the September school holidays too. What was I supposed to do without her?

"All we need to do is stay here for a week." Layla shivered. "Then they'll go without me, and I'll have the house to myself."

We both had wet clothes and were rubbish at making fires. I hadn't thought to bring matches. Our runaway clearly wasn't very well planned. I peeled off my hooded jumper and laid it out to dry. The air was damp, so I wasn't sure if that was going to happen anytime soon.

"Do you think that we'll survive that long?" I asked. I tried to warm my arms, but my hands were cold too.

Layla frowned. "I can't go back, Christian. I won't go back. I don't want to spend a whole month without you."

"Well, maybe there's a different way," I sighed, and knelt down in front of her. "What if I came with you?"

Her pout lifted with her eyebrows. "You mean, come with us to Wales?"

"Sure." I shrugged. "I still have a little money from the paper round. Maybe... maybe my parents could let me borrow some too."

"Do you think that they would?" She blinked. "Do you think they would let you?"

My parents didn't let me. They never would have let me but, by the nightfall of the same Sunday, I had convinced Layla that they might long enough to allow me to take her home. Layla's skin was a shade of blue, and I couldn't let her suffer, even if it only put off the suffering for a little while.

Henry, Pattie, and my mother were worried sick about us being missing for the day, but my dad was merely furious. To him, it was another reason why Layla was a wrong fit for me. She was impulsive and emotional, and those were two traits that he held at the lowest regard. As a sergeant, he had too often seen the effects of people who possessed them.

Layla was forced to have a couple of days off school to recover from our escape attempt, which meant more time that we were apart. I tried to imagine it being extended over a month and couldn't – or wouldn't.

The following Saturday morning, I climbed out my bedroom window and walked to Layla's house before sunrise. The Thomas family were due to fly out from South Coast the next morning, so were starting their five-hour drive at ridiculous o'clock. I waited on the corner of her street under the lamppost and counted the passing time with the heat that blew out with my warm breaths. At a few minutes past six, Layla bounded out from the front door and jumped into my

74

waiting arms. She breathed me in, and we created our own fire between us with our embrace. I savoured every second, every touch, and every sigh. It felt like *goodbye* even if it was only *see you soon*.

Then, too soon, Henry called her, and Layla's lips left mine.

"I love you," I said.

Her forehead rested on mine.

"I love you, always," she whispered. "Wait for me to come home."

Those were the last words that she said to me, and I clung onto them as if they were the last breath of oxygen that I would breathe until October.

I missed her like the sun missed the stars. I felt like a daisy in the dark. I felt the absence of the whole Thomas family but, moreover, it showed me just how much of my life now belonged to Layla. I was proud of what we had, but I was wildly aware that due to the amount of time that we spent together, I had neglected my friendship with Stuart and Wayne. I started to spend more time with them, but I wasn't much company. So, more often than not, I just resorted to reading whenever I wasn't at school or work.

My dad was in cheery spirits, which bothered me considering I felt as if the darkness of winter was extending into spring. It became painfully apparent by the time the school holidays came that I needed to do more than read. So, instead of hiding out in the public library to gloss over books, I got a job there too. It paid rather well and meant that my days were filled after my early paper round.

Wayne and Stuart came to visit sometimes, and they were the greatest at taking my mind off the fact that I was alone. It was fine when it was just the three of us but, the second the girls showed up, I was reminded that Layla was across the world, and the dark cloud returned.

My mum was worried about me. So, in the evenings when I was home and running out of things to do, she began to teach me some of her recipes. Pattie had shown me how to bake, but cooking was something different. I didn't care what I was doing; I just wanted to be doing something. I just needed to keep occupied.

"Christian, sweetie, how are you doing?" Mum asked. It was the middle of the holidays, and I still had another week until Layla was back. I didn't like to think of the days ahead of me. I just focused on the ones that I had lived through.

"I... I'm surviving."

She glanced up from chopping carrots. "She'll be back soon, you know."

"Not soon enough."

"I know that it feels like the end of the world, sweetie, but you're still young. Maybe this is a good—"

"No," I sighed. "It's not good. Mum, I know what you're going to say. You're going to say that I'm young, and I don't know what love is, and maybe she'll get back and realise that there's a world outside of me, but you're wrong. You are all wrong. Layla and I are in love and, one day, I'm going to marry her. When she gets back, we're never going to be apart again. You'll see."

Mum smiled weakly and lifted her hand to my cheek. She looked a little sympathetic, but I think it was because I sounded like someone who was trying to prove to people that their imaginary friend really existed.

"She didn't leave me, Mum," I murmured. "She went away against her will. We would be together now if it weren't for that."

She nodded. "I know, sweetie."

"She's coming back, you know. When she comes back, things are going to be the same as they were before she left," I answered. "I don't want your pity. I don't need it. Everything is going to go back to the way it was."

It wasn't.

But that wasn't a bad thing. Time doesn't stop, no matter how much you will it to. People don't stay the same when they experience different things. Travel is one of those things that changes a person. Absence is something that will either make two people grow apart or grow closer.

We were the latter.

Layla and I had planned to meet in our hideout cave on the Monday that she got back. It was a public holiday before school went back for term four.

I decided to camp in the cave, so I wasn't late. So, on the Sunday night, I packed my backpack again, threw on a backwards cap and headed down there. I brought lanterns this time, blankets, and wet-weather gear even if rain wasn't forecasted. I settled in for the night and waited for the sun to return. It felt like it had been the longest winter in history – or maybe that was just for me.

I woke up to warm lips and fingers that were peeling off my clothes in the flickering light. My eyes shot open, and I sat up and then began helping Layla tear the layers off that remained between us.

No words were spoken because it was a waste of breath to talk. Instead, we kept our lips occupied on more important things.

Neither of us really knew what we were doing, but it didn't really matter. We knew the basics, and we improvised the rest. It might have been a bit sloppy and awkward at first, but there was a mutual need that surmounted any cause for self-consciousness. It was Layla, and it was me, and we were finally together again in every way. Any doubt that had been planted in my mind in her absence had been extinguished. There was no doubt in my mind now that, as a couple, we would stand the test of time.

Layla had said once that she wanted to wait to have sex because it would change something between us. I didn't understand it at the time or at any time leading up to it, but it did change things between us. Maybe it was because being with her was like a tsunami after a drought but, that night, we tapped into something to make whatever was between us bigger. The bond between us seemed to expand, to grow like we had in the two years we'd been together. There was maturity to our relationship. There was also a vulnerability that was strangely empowering. It made us stronger.

"I've been planning that since the moment I left your arms," she whispered into my neck. "I missed you so much that I thought I wouldn't survive."

I smiled because I knew exactly how she felt. "I can relate."

"When I saw your lantern, I nearly cried with relief. A part of me was worried that you wouldn't be here."

I glanced down at her. "Where else would I be?"

She shrugged. "Anywhere, somewhere."

"Nowhere," I breathed. "I would have waited here all month if you'd asked me to."

She moved up to kiss my mouth, and the feel of her skin on mine felt like the most natural thing in the world.

"Did you have fun in Wales?" I asked. I wasn't sure whether I wanted her to answer yes or no. I wanted to believe that us being apart was for a good reason, but I also wanted her to have felt my absence too.

"I wouldn't call it *fun*, but it was amazing," she replied. "I took lots of photos. The countryside is so pretty, it's like driving through a painting."

I nodded. I didn't know exactly what to make of that.

"I wished you could have been there," she whispered. Her hand ran over my cheek. "Did you have fun here?"

"No," I said. My response was instant. Almanbury didn't feel like home without Layla.

She pouted. "I'm sorry."

"Why?"

Her head shook. "It was horrible being away from here. I got really homesick, and I missed you. God, I missed you, Christian. I'm so sorry that I had to leave you—"

"Hey," I murmured. I guided her lips to mine. "Hey, you didn't leave me, not really."

"I didn't want to go, and then, every time I let myself get distracted, I felt so guilty for it," she cried. "I thought of you all the time even when I was trying not to be sad."

I was nodding. "I know."

"I'm never leaving again, not without you," she breathed. "From now until forever, we go everywhere together. Wherever life takes us, we'll be there side-by-side."

"Deal." I smiled.

She kissed me again, and it was a side of Layla that I hadn't seen before. She had changed since she was away, and she was surer of herself now. She wasn't the girl who had kissed me under the lamppost when she left, but she was the girl that I had always loved. The girl that I would always love.

She moved her head to rest on my heart, and I noticed that the sky was beginning to lighten. I had no immediate plans to move.

"You're quiet," I said.

"I'm just thinking."

I sighed. "That can't be good."

She turned to look up at me. Her chin rested on my sternum.

"No, it's not bad. I was just thinking that I like being close to you," she whispered. "I trust you with everything, and I want you to know every part of me, but I'm just scared that I won't be everything that you deserve."

I frowned. "All I want is you. You're more than I deserve."

Her eyes rolled. "Christian."

"I mean it. Being with you, growing older, having a family, that's all I could ever want. Everything else is just a means to get there."

"That's what I want too," she whispered. Her eyes smiled from her cheeks. "But I want you to have everything else. I want you to study English and do everything you want. I want you to have it all."

"I will. We will." I nodded.

"But we'll also have that big family too with our eight kids," she laughed.

I huffed. "It's eight now, is it? I'd better get myself a good job before they all come along, or we'll be living in a shoe."

Layla laughed. "Naturally, we'll wait a couple of years before kids. I want you all to myself for a while."

"That sounds good to me," I sighed.

"Christian?"

"Mm?"

She drew circles on my abdomen. "We're going to need loads more practice if we're going to have ten kids."

I laughed. "Ten? Lord Almighty."

Layla's enthusiasm for the whole 'practising' thing expired after a couple of weeks when she needed to make an appointment to see her doctor for another birth control injection. Apparently, she'd gotten the first one a couple of months before going to Wales because she had been thinking about doing it for a while. I knew that she'd been thinking about it since we'd talked about sex more than any normal couple should who weren't actually doing it, but I didn't know about the injections.

I walked with her to the appointment because she was nervous about it. Layla had this weird aversion to doctors as if all they did was hand out death sentences. I guess that was because her strongest memory of them growing up was when her grandfather had died.

We weren't far from the GP when she squeezed my hand.

"Oh no," she gasped.

"What?"

"I… I need to have those things now, those… those pap-smear things," she cried. "I'll need testing and stuff. People are going to find out that I'm not a virgin any more."

I pressed my lips together. "Well, it was bound to happen eventually, love."

She smacked my chest, and it made a sharp noise. Her eyebrows lifted at the shock of it then she started sobbing harder.

"I'm sorry. I didn't mean to hurt you," she whimpered.

"God, Layla, don't cry, you didn't," I sighed. "All of this – everything you're feeling, it's okay. You know, it's part of growing up."

She sniffled. "Yeah, I… I—"

"Besides, I'm sure when your dad walked in on us all those months ago, he suspected something."

Layla cringed and wiped her nose on her hand. I smiled and wiped my sleeve under her eyes. It smeared all her running gold eyeliner on the fabric.

"He pretty much alluded to a chastity belt when he caught us," she mumbled. "He'd kill me if he found out."

"You mean he'd kill *me*," I replied.

Her head shook. "I was the one he warned. Besides, he'd never kill you, he likes you too much. You're the son he never had."

"And you're the daughter he does have. His only daughter," I countered. "He loves you more, as he should."

"Thank heavens for doctor-patient confidentiality."

I nodded. "Let's just keep Henry in the dark, so he'll spare both of our lives, okay?"

She wiped her nose with her hand again. "Okay, he can just assume that we waited until we were married."

"When we start having our ten kids?"

"Twelve," she murmured. "We'll need a really big shoe."

I laughed. "Okay, but we should at least graduate first because I only want the best shoe for my family."

"Deal," she sighed. "Besides, I've still got a ton more years of wearing sundresses until I have to wear frumpy *Mum*-clothes."

My eyebrows lifted. "I like the sound of that."

"Okay, well, Christian Turner, you wait here. I'll go and baby-proof myself so we can still keep up the practice."

I frowned. "You managed to make that sound very unsexy, Layla, thank you."

She jumped up to kiss the corner of my lips. "You're welcome. I love you."

"Good luck."

82

Layla took two steps towards the clinic door then turned and frowned at me. "On second thoughts, can you come and hold my hand while I wait? I really, really hate doctors."

I smiled and stepped forward, locking my hand to hers, and we both went inside.

It was the first of many visits that I walked her to and, each time, she had the same request – that I was there to hold her hand. I always had the same answer for her – that I always would be.

**

Time marched on, and Layla's yellow dress got a little shorter as she grew a little taller. It wasn't much taller, but it was a signifier that we were both getting older, and adulthood was closer than we anticipated. We always knew that it would come, the day that we started our final year of organised schooling, and the day that would end it. I began to realise that those days in between were the precious ones since they were the ones that dictated what would happen after. I realised that there was something in what my dad had been reminding me about – the future, my future, our future, and our plan for the future.

I kept up working in the library on Sundays and after schools on Monday to Wednesday. On Mondays and Tuesdays, Layla still worked at the post office but, on Wednesdays, she would bring her schoolwork to sit with me and work there. It was a public space, so my father couldn't have a problem with it. I wished that I had thought of it months ago because it meant that we could still see each other on the days that we were told not to.

Thursdays were ours, and that sometimes meant hanging out at the forum with our friends, but sometimes it was just us. Layla eventually switched her Tuesdays at the post office for helping Pattie on Fridays, so that meant my afternoons and evenings were free for a guys' night. It was a necessary time where I could just hang with my friends, which was something I realised I hadn't done enough of before Layla went away. Even though I loved her beyond reason, I needed more than just her in my life. I needed my friends, and they were great because they understood and supported Layla and me. They also accepted me for who I was and made a point to remind me that I wasn't just Layla Thomas' boyfriend. I was also just Christian Turner, and they allowed me to be both.

The guys and I usually didn't do a lot. Sometimes we'd hang at someone's house playing the newest Xbox game, or if the weather wasn't too cold and rainy, then we'd go down to the skate park, or the ship near the beach.

The ship.

It was completely random to have a wooden sailboat perched on the coastline when there was no port in Almanbury. Regardless, it was a cool place to hang and chill out. Sometimes Wayne would bring a six-pack of beer that his older brother bought for him, and he'd pretend that he was a pirate. Stuart occasionally joined in the drinking and threw bottle caps at Wayne, but I never took the risk with a police sergeant at home. I was pretty sure that my father kept his own alcohol breathalyser in a drawer somewhere.

Despite the underage drinking that my dad wasn't aware of, he approved of a weekly guys' night. He always liked the idea of time I spent away from Layla. I knew that he was just worried because I seemed to have skipped the whole casual dating thing and jumped right to the serious relationship-settling-down kind of thing, but I didn't want anything more than what I had with Layla. I would never want anything more than what we had, and I was sure of that beyond the shadow of a doubt. I never told my father just how much I loved her because he didn't deserve to know. He didn't want to know, so I wouldn't let him take the happiness I had with her away from me. It was blissful, and it was ours.

**

The year that I turned seventeen, I learnt to drive and got my license. I'd managed to use all the money that I'd saved through the paper rounds and the library to buy my first car. It was a beat up old Holden sedan circa 1985, but I loved it along with everything that it represented. Freedom.

The only thing was that, because Almanbury was so small, it wasn't worth the petrol to drive around the town, so Layla and I planned to take a road trip when final exams were over at the end of the year. Until then, we pretty much spent our time studying and preparing.

I wasn't really looking forward to this year because it meant that I needed to make a decision about my future – or at least the part that didn't revolve exclusively around Layla. I didn't want to go to university if that meant leaving Almanbury. I'd always wanted to study English Literature, but there weren't a lot of universities outside of the city that offered it. My car had wiped out my funds, so I'd planned to work for at least a year before actually making any kind of move to study anyway. Even so, it wasn't a decision that I wanted to make without Layla because she was as much a part of my future as any sort of pending university degree was. If I moved, we both would move, but neither of us was fond of the idea of leaving the place that had come to feel like home to both of us.

"This is unreal," Layla said with a giggle.

We were sitting in our cave as the forks of electricity struck over the ocean, lighting up the sky with silver every few seconds. Naturally, Layla's camera was attached to her like an extension of her hand. It was the winter school holidays in our final year of high school, and we'd just finished our first lot of exams. Camping out in the thunderstorm seemed like a good idea at the time. I'm not quite sure when but, regardless, it was a beautiful sight in more ways than one.

"I just love this place," Layla sighed. "I love Almanbury."

"I love you."

She looked over and smiled, pressing her lips to my shoulder. "Can you imagine if you hadn't moved here, and you were stuck in silly South Coast?"

"No," I sighed. "I can't imagine never knowing you. But South Coast isn't all bad. It's not as cool as here, but it still has its pockets of perfection."

"Well, from what I saw of it on the way to the airport, I wouldn't want to live there." She shrugged.

"Not even if I was there?"

She took another photo then lowered the camera. Her brow was pinched. "Are you planning on going there?"

"Not exactly, but I've been thinking about next year and the year after. We'll need to have the discussion about what we're going to do since both of the courses we want to study are only offered at universities based in South Coast."

She nodded. "It's not as easy as we thought it would be, is it?"

"Not everything will be, but we'll sort it out," I replied. "Do you still want to study photography and multimedia stuff?"

We hadn't talked about it between us in a while since it was something we heard a lot between school and home. But it was something we needed to start thinking about considering we only had about ten weeks left of classes before our final exams began.

Layla glanced down at her camera. "You should see some of the shots I got. I'm going to send them to the local newspaper."

"Layla."

She sighed. "My grades aren't so good, Christian. There's no way I'll get a high enough score to get into any of the university courses that I would pick. Maybe TAFE could work, but I don't like any of the courses that are offered locally. Maybe... maybe your dad is right, and I should just think about pursuing something other than photography."

I frowned. "No, he's not right."

"But I can't—"

"You can do anything you want to, Layla," I answered. "If that means we have to move, so we'll move."

"Do you want to move?" she asked. "Because I don't. Think about it, Christian, we don't have a lot of money, and we don't even have much of a plan. All we know is that we want to be together."

"So?" I shrugged. "That's enough, isn't it?"

She sighed. "I don't have a future, Christian. You're the only thing I'm certain of, and I don't want to hold you back. You'd never forgive me for it."

"You're not holding me back."

"I feel like I am. You're really smart and talented, and if you just settled for me, then your dad would hate me even more than he does now. You deserve better than to be stuck here working a trade. You can do so much more."

"I don't want any of it if it means being without you," I murmured. "Besides, I don't have much money either, so it's not like I can afford to go anywhere anytime soon. We don't need to make a decision about studies now, we can just get jobs and save a bit, and even go to study as mature age students in a couple of years."

Layla stared at me for a moment and then lifted her camera, and a flash went off in my face. I blinked, and she leant across to kiss me. I could hear her jeans – her formally new jeans scraping on the rocks below, but she didn't care about ripping them any more.

It was the last that was said about studies for a while, but I was sure that our plan still held. We would stay in Almanbury next year and work, saving whatever money we could to invest in whatever future that waited for us beyond that.

**

The year marched on, and we put in our preferences for higher education as was expected of us. Layla's photos got published in the local paper, and she managed to get credit and bragging rights for them. It gave her the boost that she needed to believe that she could make something from photography, but her grades still weren't as strong as her eye for talent. Layla tried really hard, but she still struggled with the subjects she was taking. She began doing more freelance photography for the newspaper, but it wasn't enough to make a career out of, so, when school was over, she was looking to increase her hours at the post office. I wished I could do more to support her since I knew how much she disliked working there but, even with my good grades and promising prospects, I was in the same boat when it came to getting a full-time job when school finished up.

We sat our final exams and kept planning for our little road trip for after they concluded. Stuart, Wayne, and Abbie were planning to take a trip too as a kind of schoolies celebration. Lindsay was still around a little, but she and Stuart hadn't been making out as often these days. Layla and I were going to meet up with them all after a few days of being on our own.

Layla decided that she wanted to drive first having just gained her driver's license before school broke up. She cursed it as one of the drawbacks of having a birthday so late in the year. We set out along the southern coast in my car since the old yellow Volkswagen Beetle she'd bought needed a bit of tinkering before any kind of extended journey anywhere. I'd made a mixed tape for the trip, so, as we began driving just after sunrise, the tunes of Eric Clapton, the Beatles, and a few more of our favourites filled the car. We had been driving for around two hours when another of my favourites, *Don't Dream It's Over* by Crowded House, started playing. It was the last song we heard for a while.

The car started to grumble and protest, and Layla flapped her arms around as I reached across to take the wheel and guide it out of traffic.

"What's happening?" she squeaked. "What did I do?"

I frowned at the dashboard. "Why didn't you say that the petrol was so low?"

"Why didn't you check it before now?"

"You're the one driving, Layla, you're supposed to keep an eye on it," I sighed.

"It's your car. I'm watching the road!"

I exhaled as the car cut out.

Layla pouted. "What do we do now?"

"Call for someone to bring us petrol, or start walking," I groaned. "So much for our road trip."

"I'm sorry."

My head shook. "It's not your fault."

"My dad normally checks the little sticky thing to make sure it has enough petrol."

"You mean the petrol gauge?"

She shrugged. "Whatever it's called."

I couldn't help but laugh as I glanced down at my phone. "Do you have any phone reception? Mine is out of range."

"Darn it, mine too," she whimpered. "What now?"

"Now we walk until we find help or reception."

Her eyebrows lifted. "Walk in this heat?"

"It's not so bad." I shrugged. I got out of the car, remembering how the summers in South Coast used to be so much worse.

Layla climbed out and locked the doors, then walked around to hold my hand. We started walking straight ahead rather than go back the way we'd come considering we hadn't passed civilisation in a while. I hoped that a petrol station wouldn't be far, but I didn't know this area at all. It was more east around the coast rather than looping back northwest towards South Coast.

Layla hummed *Don't Dream It's Over* for the hour that it took for us to reach phone reception. When we had bars, we called Henry since he was the one most likely to come to help us out without demanding that we abandon our trip. I also rationalised it by the fact that it was a weekday, so my dad was probably working the office hours that being a sergeant enabled him to. While we waited for Henry to arrive with a barrel of petrol, Layla and I started walking back towards my car. He reached us shortly after we got there. It was lucky that we had been so thorough with our planning because neither of us had a clue as to where we'd broken down. We didn't think to look at roads, but the map we'd left Henry, Pattie, and my mum was enough for him to find us.

I took over driving as we got back on the road, and we listened to *Don't Dream It's Over* on repeat for the rest of our little getaway. We decided after our few days away from Almanbury that we'd just head home rather than meeting up with the others. For some reason, Layla and I didn't like being away from the place that had become as much a part of who we were as a couple as it was home to both of us. It was evident then that the two of us probably wouldn't end up leaving Almanbury for any reason. I loved Layla and was willing to favour the prospect of our future over any concept of study. As far as I was concerned, as long as I was earning money, and I could still read, that was enough for me. Layla was enough for me. The rest didn't matter much.

I started working more hours in the library and gave up my paper rounds. Some days, I'd go out to help Henry with plumbing jobs as his pseudo apprentice, and I enjoyed spending time with him as much as the change in scenery.

My father was at peak disappointment with me and the decisions I'd made for my future, considering I'd been offered places in every university that I'd applied for. He couldn't understand why I'd pass them up, but held Layla accountable as the influence. We stopped spending any time at my house at all, which meant I was hardly ever there unless I was rolling into or out of bed. I felt bad for leaving my mother alone so much since she hadn't done anything to push me away, but I knew that she somehow understood. It was my decision not to be home so I could spend time with Layla as much as it would have been my decision to leave and go to university.

Layla worked four days a week in the post office and had every Wednesday off to drive around and take photos that she would offer to the local paper to buy. They bought a few of them, which kept her beaming, but I couldn't help but feel that she was destined for more. It just sucked that something like school grades could prevent her from being recognised for the thing that she loved, and happened to be remarkable at. It made me want to work harder to provide for her so she could focus more on it.

**

Although we weren't meeting our own expectations in the careers that we wanted, as a couple, Layla and I were stronger than ever. It both surprised and thrilled me that, after four years of being together, I was even more in love with her than the day I first saw her and kissed her against that wall.

However, there comes the point in every relationship when there's a shift. Something changes and, all of a sudden, it's not just about the here and now, it's about what lies ahead. I knew that Layla would be in my future from the moment I saw her, or I'd at least hoped. Then when we started dating, and we fell in love, I knew that the possibility was more like a probability. But we were still kids, and we thought about the future in terms of next week or next year, of what we were doing in the summer holidays, or, at a stretch, what career ladder we'd try to climb. But, then the shift happened, and I was thinking seriously about the very real prospect of marriage and kids, where we would live, and the adult issues that went beyond the superficial. It went from what people conceived as puppy love to the idea of eternal love. We weren't just a boyfriend and a girlfriend; we were becoming partners in life. I loved Layla with everything that I was and, for me, there was no better fit, no one more perfect in this world. I had known early on in our relationship that one day I would marry her, and one day I woke up and I wanted that to be today.

The idea of marrying Layla became my reality, my immediate future. I wanted to make it official, to sing it out to the world. I wanted to be with her forever, and I wanted forever to start now. I knew that it wouldn't always be easy, but I wanted her to be beside me through it all. I knew that she felt the same way, so I wasn't scared. Loving Layla never scared me, only losing her did.

On a Monday in late August, I took the day off work to look for a ring. I tried the jewellery store in Almanbury, but none were right, so I decided to go for a drive outside of Almanbury to a jeweller that I'd looked up on the internet. It sold pieces that didn't look as stock standard as the ones in the retail stores. When I saw the ring, I knew that it was the perfect one for Layla. It was yellow gold with a diamond setting. The diamond wasn't huge, but it was all I could afford. It wiped out a lot of my savings, but I didn't care. I loved her, and I wanted it for her.

I thought about proposing on our anniversary, but it seemed too cliché. So, we celebrated our fourth anniversary on the fourth of September and then, the following week, I went to speak to Henry and Pattie to ask for their permission. Henry wasn't as enthusiastic as I hoped about his daughter getting engaged so young. He was dubious as to why I wanted to since we had barely graduated from high school. Naturally, he initially jumped to all the usual conclusions. That said, it didn't take long to convince him and Pattie that I loved their daughter more than anything. Layla and I had been unwavering from the start, we complemented each other as a couple in every way, and I was confident that if I didn't ask for her hand now, nothing would change in time. I would still want to marry her every day until I did, and I would never regret it for all the days after.

It was inevitable. We were endgame.

Once I had the support of Layla's parents, I told my mother about it. I didn't want to break the news to my dad because I knew that he would try to talk me out of it, but Mum had been my pillar of strength from the beginning. She was shocked but not surprised since I had already mentioned to her my intention when Layla had gone away. To my amazement though, she told me to hold off telling my dad until it was official. It amused me a little that she was as sure of his reaction as I was.

The only other person that I told before I started planning the proposal was Stuart because he was my best friend beside Layla. Stuart thought that I was crazy but was happy for me. Maybe I was crazy, but if this is how crazy felt then I'd willingly stay that way for the rest of my life.

On the fourth of October, I'd planned a picnic for the two of us just like the one we'd had on our first anniversary. I chose the fourth because that seemed to be a lucky number for the two of us. We were both born on the fourth of a month, and our anniversary was on the fourth, too. I liked the symmetry in it all, and I liked that the number would be ours. The fourth of something was the date that had changed my life more than once, so it was only fitting that it should be responsible for doing it again.

I remember the day perfectly. I took photos in my mind as if I was a camera with its shutter open, watching and recording.

Layla wore the yellow dress, my favourite yellow dress. She had just had a haircut, so her hair was short, reaching just beneath her chin. I brought her daisies, and her face lit up like the sun when I gave them to her.

My stomach was in knots, but it wasn't because I was scared, it was because I was excited. I wanted to ask her from the second I saw her, but I also wanted it to be perfect. Layla didn't seem to notice because she was too busy taking photos of everything.

I rubbed my face and groaned internally at the stubble across my jaw. I should have shaved. Why hadn't I shaved? I'd meant to. Layla, who was sitting across from me, tipped her head.

"Are you okay? You look weird," she said. There was a pucker between her eyebrows as she squinted to take aim and snapped another photo.

"Yeah, I just forgot to shave," I replied. "Sorry."

Layla laughed. "I like that sexy five o'clock shadow thing you've got going on."

I smiled and reached towards the camera. "Give me that."

"But—"

"Come here."

"Christian, I—"

"You should be in it too," I said.

Her shoulders dropped in defeat, and she smiled, crawling over to sit against me. I moved my arms around her and turned the camera around, my lips dropping to her ear. I felt her squirm but clicked the button. I didn't feel a flash, but the sun was shining on us. Layla giggled and took the camera back.

"Enough of me." She smiled. She shuffled around and pushed me back against the red tartan picnic blanket then climbed on top of me. My eyebrows lifted.

"More of you," she sighed.

I moved my hands behind my head and watched as she took another photo. It was bizarre that it was such a norm to me now. I never thought that it was something that I'd come to expect.

"That's it, work the camera," she said with a laugh. Her free hand dropped to my abdomen and began to push up my black buttoned shirt. I struggled against it.

"Layla, cut it—"

"No need to be shy." She giggled. "You've got it."

I huffed. "Layla, stop, just—"

She dropped the camera and smiled, leaning forward to kiss me. I sat up, feeling a tingle all the way down to my toes. The words that I'd been waiting to say rose to my throat as Layla's fingers began to unbutton my shirt. I didn't stop her. I was too busy thinking about what I would say next. I'd rehearsed it over and over in my head but, for some reason, I couldn't remember any of it now.

Layla pulled back to look me in the eyes. I sat back and sighed, running my hands down her arms. I could feel the crease in my brow as I tried to find a place to start with this proposal. Of all the times to clam up, this was probably the worst.

"What's the matter?" Layla pouted. "Did I do something wrong?"

"No, Layla," I breathed. "It's not you."

She leant back against my knees and straightened her dress that had begun to ride up her thighs. I bit my lower lip.

"Then what is it?" she asked.

My hands caught hers as they played with the hem of the fabric.

"Um, there's another reason why I wanted to come here today," I started. It wasn't the best way to phrase it, but it would suffice. At least words were coming out now. I reached up to tuck back a piece of hair that had fallen out from behind her ear then slid a daisy up with it.

Layla smiled and glanced over at a group of giggling school kids. "So, it wasn't just to have a picnic and make out in front of a bunch of tenth-graders?"

I twisted to look at them and laughed. "Yes, well, apart from that."

I lay back as she leant forward to rest a hand on either side of my head. The daisy fell out from behind her ear and landed on my bare chest.

"Then why did you bring me here, Christian?" she asked.

I looked into her eyes. "Layla."

She sat back suddenly and blinked. Her forehead creased. "What? What is it?"

I drew in a breath and opened my mouth, but nothing came out. I wished that I could remember how to speak because I could feel Layla's heartbeat shaking her and hated that it was probably because I wasn't being clear. I tried to sit up and, after a second, Layla climbed off me so I could. She moved onto her knees and pouted.

"You're breaking up with me, aren't you?" she said. "This was a mercy picnic. You're buttering me up before letting me down gently."

"No," I sighed. "Of course not."

She exhaled. "Then what's going on?"

I reached towards the picnic basket and fished around for the film canister that I'd shoved the ring in. It was an idea I'd had that I thought she'd like, though, now that I thought about it, it was probably a dumb one. I frowned at it, then handed it to her. It was too late to go back now.

"Um, Christian, you know that I don't use film any more. I have my digital camera," she answered.

My eyes rolled. "Just open it smarty-pants. You're ruining the moment."

Her lips pressed together, and she pushed off the top of the small cylinder. It popped off, and the ring tumbled out onto her lap and then bounced onto the blanket. Yeah, this wasn't really the best idea. It was pretty clumsy, actually.

Layla blinked at it then picked it up. "What is this?"

I tried to smile. "I would have thought you'd know what a ring is."

She laughed lightly. "Yes, but what is it for?"

"It's for you." I shrugged.

She nodded slowly. "I get that, but why? It's not my birthday, it's not our anniversary, it's not Christmas…"

I could see that she knew what it was for, but I could also hear in her voice that she didn't want to jump to conclusions, even if there was excitement in her tone.

I smirked. "You're not honestly going to make me say it, are you?"

Her head tipped. "If you're really doing what I think you are, Christian Turner, then you are going to do it right."

I chuckled to myself and shook my head, moving my foot in front of me, so I was kneeling. I rested my chin on it, and Layla handed me the ring.

I exhaled. "Layla Louise Thomas—"

She pulled a face. "Come on, you can do better than that."

"I'm asking you to marry me."

"Yes, I got that much." She shrugged. "So go on then."

I bit my lip and looked around. "So, will you marry me?"

She folded her arms. "Why?"

"Uh, because I love you."

She pressed her lips together, and I realised that I was messing all of this up. The words that I'd been planning to say came back to me like a tsunami wave.

"Layla," I sighed. "My life means nothing if I don't have you to share it with. I don't want to spend a single day without you. Every day, from now until forever, I want to wake up next to you and remind you just how much I love you."

Her gold eyes turned glassy. "Well, that was better."

"So, are you going to give me an answer, or do you need me to go on?"

She smiled and threw herself into me, making me fly back with a groan. Her lips were on mine with so much enthusiasm that they felt like they might bruise.

"Yes," she breathed against my mouth.

I laughed in relief and fumbled for her hand to slide the ring onto her finger, and then spun her onto her back. My hand made its way down to her waist, and I pulled her against me. I could hear the school kids giggling, but I didn't care because, other than that first time I'd seen Layla, this was the most profound moment of my life.

I pulled back to look at her, to take another mental picture so that I could remember it correctly to tell our grandchildren about it one day.

"Nothing can tear us apart now," I murmured.

She smiled and lifted her hand to run through my hair.

"They never could," she whispered.

She guided my lips back to hers as her hand moved down my neck to the skin of my chest. My heart was soaring, but I was pleasantly surprised to find that hers was beating just as fast. In fact, they were in perfect unison, as they had always been.

Naturally, once we'd come up for air, Layla proceeded to take a million photos of her hand, me, and every little detail that surrounded us. I managed to wrestle the camera from her and took a few more of the two of us, and then even convinced her to take a timed photo of the both of us so there was a proper one that could mark the occasion. It was arty, as most of Layla's photos were now, and it was one of my favourites. She sat back against me, turning her face up towards me as her hand lingered around my neck. We were a breath apart, and the closeness still sent my heart into a sprint. Layla said that she'd print it for me to keep in my wallet. I planned on keeping it there forever.

We stayed out at the picnic all afternoon, and I wasn't sure whether it was a conscious thing or not. We didn't say it out loud, but we both knew that when we started to tell people about our engagement then they'd have an opinion about it, as they always seemed to have had an opinion about our relationship. Layla was excited to learn though that I'd already spoken to her parents, so at least we already had people on our side. The only person that I was really dreading to tell was my dad. Everyone else might have had an opinion, but he was under the impression that his opinion was law. As far as I was concerned, his opinion became mere advice from the moment that I turned eighteen.

"I don't want to go back." Layla pouted as her eyes lifted towards the sky.

I looked up from packing everything away. "Back home?"

"Back to reality."

"But this is our reality now."

Layla smiled. "We're engaged, Christian. We're going to be together forever."

I laughed. "Yes."

"Can forever start now?"

"It started four years and one month ago if you ask me."

She giggled and lifted her hand again to admire her ring.

"Why don't you come and stay at my place tonight?" I asked.

Her eyes lifted to me. "Your house? With your dad? With your scary police sergeant dad?"

"Sure." I shrugged. "We're engaged now. He'll need to learn to deal with that fact sooner or later."

"And you picked sooner?"

I smiled. "Henry still probably won't let me in your room since we're technically not married yet."

"So, let's elope."

"Or you could just come to my place."

She thought for a moment then frowned. "Don't you want to marry me now?"

"Well, I kind of thought that we'd do a bit of planning first. You know, white dress, guests, the whole shebang. But, hey, I'll marry you now if that's what you want."

She grinned. "Or we could just go to your place."

I nodded and picked up the packed basket. "The white dress was the hook, huh?"

"I've always wanted to wear a white dress."

"I like yellow dresses."

She laughed. "I know *you* do. Oh, well, maybe I can wear a gold one and be different."

"You can wear whatever you want," I replied.

"Whatever I want?" she asked. "What if I just wore your underwear?"

"My underwear? Well, that would be awkward... and strangely hot."

She giggled and took my hand. We began walking in the direction of my house. It was empty when we got there, so we headed straight to my room.

Layla backed against my door and stepped forward, pulling her yellow dress above her head. She threw it at me, and it fell against my chest and then onto the floor beside my bed. I didn't have a lock on my door, so she dragged and dropped my old school bag against it. It wouldn't stop anyone who wanted to come in, but it would slow them down at least. I unbuttoned my shirt and shrugged out of it. She smiled and walked over, running her hands up my body to my shoulders and around my neck.

My hands moved around her waist, and I heard her breath catch in her throat. It amazed me how we still had the same effect on each other as we always had – always would.

I didn't hear my parents get home that night, but I heard them in the morning. I woke up with Layla in my arms and marvelled in the thought that I would get to do that for the rest of our lives. There was a lot that we would need to figure out beyond planning the ceremony, but we'd have time for all that. The important thing was that we would do it together.

"Hi," Layla whispered.

I smiled down at her. "Hi."

"We got engaged yesterday."

I brushed my hands through the front of her hair. "Yes, we did."

"I probably need to find some clothes before your parents come looking for you," she breathed. Her cheeks seemed to flush, but it only made me love her more. Her hands moved to my arm that was around her, and I tightened it.

"Christian, let me find clothes and then you can have me back," she said.

"No," I mumbled. I nestled into her neck, and she giggled.

"Shh," she gasped. "I don't want your parents to find me naked in your room, even if we are engaged."

I smiled at the reminder. Her eyes seemed to glitter each time she said it.

My arm loosened, and she slid out from my grip. She looked around my floor and pressed her lips together as she reached into my dresser. I watched her curiously as she pulled on a pair of my underwear and then hooked on her bra. She found a navy singlet of mine that she dragged on over the top and then lifted her arms.

"Ta-dah," she said quietly. She looked so perfect.

I smirked. "You want to wear that when we tell my folks that we're engaged?"

"Too casual?"

I laughed. "At least borrow a pair of my shorts too."

She spun around and found some denim ones, and then began throwing clothes at me.

"Get dressed. We need to be ninjas and sneak—"

"Christian?" My mum's voice said, followed by two quick knocks on my door. "Are you awake?"

I quickly pulled on the white singlet and pants.

"Uh, yeah, Mum," I said. "Give me a sec."

"It's fine, sweetie, I was just making sure that you were home," she replied.

I wondered if she really was, or whether she was checking if I was alone. I was sure that I'd left the picnic basket on the table. I would have thought that would have given away my whereabouts.

"I am."

"Okay," Mum answered. "Morning, Layla."

"H-hi, good morning, Nancy," Layla called back. She bit her lower lip, and I froze before kicking the bag out the way and then opening the door.

Mum smiled. "Well? I take it you both have some good news then?"

Layla lifted her bejewelled hand. "Yes."

My mother smiled and walked in to capture us both in a hug. "Congratulations."

"Thank you, Nancy. Christian and I are both very excited to start the planning."

"But it's going to be a long engagement, isn't it?" Mum said. "I mean, you two will need to sort yourselves out before getting married."

Layla and I exchanged a look.

"Actually, Mum, we don't really want to draw it out too much," I said.

"Right." Layla nodded. "We were thinking of maybe getting married this time next year. Or maybe even on the fourth of September. We haven't discussed specifics yet."

"Next year?" Mum repeated. "But where will you live? Who is going to pay for it all? What will—?"

"We don't know yet, Mum," I replied. "We'll figure it all out. We don't need a huge wedding."

Mum nodded slowly, and I didn't miss how her eyes appraised our attire. "Is there a reason you're in a rush?"

"N-no, Mum, of course not," I groaned. "No, Layla and I are... no. We're waiting for the whole starting a family thing. We have loads to do before then, right?"

I looked to Layla who was nodding enthusiastically.

"Definitely," she said. "We just, well, Nancy, we love each other so much. We just don't see the point in waiting."

I could see in my mother's face that she wished that we would still wait, but she didn't say as much. I was sure that she was saving it because she knew that my dad wouldn't hold back.

He went ballistic.

In fact, I wished that I had forewarned him because at least then Layla wouldn't have had to witness Mitch Turner at his worst. Most people were happy for us, most of our parents were happy for us, but my dad just wouldn't budge. He stopped speaking to me and eventually demanded that if this was really something that I wanted to do – if I was adult enough to make adult decisions, then I was mature enough to support myself.

I packed my backpack and planned on sleeping in my car until Henry found me and insisted that I stay with them, considering I was practically already part of the family. I nearly refused since I knew that Henry's invitation meant that he was getting involved in the feud between my dad and me, but he wouldn't take no for an answer. It shouldn't have even come to it, but at least I knew that, once Layla and I were married, we'd have a place to live together until we found one of our own.

I stayed with the Thomas family for three nights until, on the fourth, my mother came around begging for me to come home. I didn't want to upset her, but even she knew that it hadn't been my choice to leave. I loved my dad but, apparently, we couldn't live in the same home together. She came back later that day with him, and we all sat down, my parents, Layla and me, and her parents, to discuss what was going to happen. They urged us to give the engagement a little more time – not call it off, but just wait a couple more years. Even my father begrudgingly agreed that he could support us if only we were a bit older and more stable in our plans for the future.

Layla didn't see any of it as an obstacle, she saw it as encouragement since they had all come around to agree that us getting married was inevitable. We both spent the better part of the summer defending our choice to get married within the year. Eventually, we stopped having to convince them all and just started cementing the plans for the wedding that would take place on the upcoming fourth of October.

We held an engagement party on the fourth of January, and the support we received from our friends and people of the town was overwhelming. Everyone was excited and unsurprised by the news since Layla and I had been inseparable since the day we met. The anticipation seemed to catch like the flu and, from then, everyone wanted to be involved in helping with the wedding arrangements.

My mum and Pattie were instrumental in the preparations and, even though Layla and I didn't want or need anything big, they managed to organise everything with the help of people around Almanbury at a reduced cost. Our only request was that it had lots of yellow, and the floral arrangements were made of daisies. Everything else we didn't really concern ourselves with – or at least, I didn't concern myself with since, as a nineteen-year-old boy, I didn't know the first thing about planning a wedding. Layla still had some input, and between her, Mum, and Pattie they seemed to know what they were doing and did well with pulling it all together.

Probably the hardest thing that Layla and I had to decide on was what song to pick as our wedding song. I was pushing for *Layla* by Eric Clapton, but Layla didn't want a song with her name in it, and one that was relatively melancholy for such an exciting occasion. Nevertheless, I put it on our shortlist along with *Here Comes the Sun* and *Don't Dream It's Over*. Eventually, after months of toying with them, we decided that the latter fit the two of us best as a couple. The second decision that I had to make was who was going to be my best man and groomsman. It wasn't even a choice that Stuart and Wayne would be up there with me, but I chose Stuart to be my best man. Layla chose Abbie as her maid of honour and Lindsay to stand beside her as her bridesmaid. Layla didn't seem to stay in touch with too many people from school any more, but both Abbie and Lindsay were usually there if we did anything with Stuart and Wayne.

**

Time seemed to fly that year and, the next thing I knew, Layla and I were sitting in my kitchen the night before the rehearsal dinner. Layla and my mother had cooked Dad and me a banquet, and it was nice to at least pretend that we were a functional family. My dad had slowly begun to give up on interfering with my relationship and even started being civil to Layla. I suppose he had finally accepted that the wedding was going to happen whether he liked it or not. The only variable factor was just how much of an input he was going to have in mine and Layla's life as a result of his attitude towards it.

Layla didn't eat much that night because, in the worst timing ever, she had caught a bout of the flu in the week or so leading up to the date. She'd eventually given up and gone to see the doctor to get something that might take the edge off the nausea, and he'd run a pile of tests. Since then she had a little more colour in her face, but she still seemed to have a sensitive stomach. I just hoped that she'd be okay in two days when we finally made *us* official.

Then, the next morning, a whole series of events began to fall into place. That evening would be our rehearsal dinner, and then tomorrow would be the main event. I spent the morning helping Henry finish off an emergency plumbing job that he was called to, and then, in the early afternoon, I went back to see Layla before the party. She was practically glowing with excitement when she saw me.

"Not long now." She beamed. "I can't wait to be Mrs Christian Turner."

"Me neither." I smiled. "Are you all set?"

"Almost." She nodded. "I need to start on my hair soon though."

I frowned at it. "It already looks great."

"Don't be silly. I need to spend a couple of hours making myself beautiful for you."

"Hours? You are already beautiful."

She laughed and shook her head.

"Well, I should go and let you get organised then," I said. "But I'll be counting the minutes before tonight."

"I'll be counting the seconds," she replied. She walked me to the front door. "I can't wait."

"It's going to be perfect," I whispered.

Layla smiled and stepped towards me. She breathed me in, her body rising as her mouth moved harmoniously against mine. She pulled away, running the tip of her finger around the perimeter of my lips, her golden eyes holding me at their mercy.

"Christian," she sighed, moving her fingers over my cheek. "I think you need a haircut."

I laughed, and she giggled. It was the most amazing chime in the world, Layla's laugh. I longed to hear it, to be the reason for it. The fact that she'd agreed to let me try to make her smile for the rest of our lives made me happier than I'd ever been.

She opened the door, giving me a cute wink, and blew me another kiss before closing it behind me.

I slowly turned, heading towards my car and went straight to the hairdresser's to get a trim before our rehearsal dinner.

Rehearsal dinner.

I could hardly believe that the wedding was so close. After all the planning, the wedding was only a day away. Everything had gone so effortlessly for us in recent months, and I could only hope that our future was just as smooth sailing.

But that wasn't to be because little did I know that storms were forecast on our horizon, and the little boat of bliss that I was sailing on was about to capsize. I thought nothing of it. I thought it was normal for things to run a little fashionably late. Even if it was unusual for Layla to ever keep me waiting.

She was supposed to drive herself to the party since I was off being groomed, and Henry had to meet with the minister to finalise some details for the service tomorrow. Pattie had been at the hall for hours with my mother making sure that everything was organised, and the amount of effort that they had gone to was astounding. They'd covered almost every surface in fairy lights, and it glowed like a dream. I couldn't wait for Layla to arrive so I could see the way they would reflect in her gold eyes.

"Pattie, do you know when Layla was going to get here?" I asked.

People had already started to arrive, but she was supposed to come before that – or so I thought. Maybe there had been a last minute change in plans.

"She's not here?" Pattie blinked. "She was nearly ready when I left her. Well, she was working on her hair, but I wouldn't imagine it would've take too long. Have you tried calling her?"

I frowned at my phone. "It just goes to voicemail."

"I wouldn't worry, honey, just give her a little more time," Pattie said. "She's probably just fussing overlooking perfect."

"She always looks perfect," I answered and then gave a laugh. I hadn't meant to say it out loud.

More people trickled in, and Layla was still nowhere to be seen. When she was nearing forty minutes late, I went to find Henry.

"Henry, Layla still hasn't arrived," I said. "Have you heard from her?"

"No, son." He frowned. "Are you sure she's not around here somewhere?"

My head shook. "No one has seen her."

He nodded. "I'll go and check at the house. It's unlike her to be late, especially when you're the one left waiting."

"That's what I thought."

He patted me on the back. "Sit tight, Christian, I'll be back in ten."

"Thanks, Henry."

I did another round of our guests, talking and filling up their glasses of champagne. I checked in with Mum and Pattie as they did rounds with the food that they and a couple of other ladies had been cooking all day. I really underestimated the greatness of living in a small town – everyone bonded together in times of need.

Amidst my socialising, I kept watching the door for Henry to return with Layla. I got a bit worried when ten minutes became fifteen, and then twenty. When twenty-five minutes had ticked over, he walked through the door looking sombre. I was over to him in a heartbeat.

"What's wrong?" I asked. "Where is she?"

His eyes looked vacant as they found mine then traced around the room for Pattie. I looked around and then clutched at his arm.

"Henry, where is Layla?" I asked again.

Pattie was suddenly beside me. "Is something the matter?"

Henry swallowed and lifted his fist. His hand slowly opened palm-side up. In his hand was the gold diamond ring that I'd given Layla almost a year ago.

I stared at it. "What's that?"

I knew what it was, of course, but I didn't know what it meant. Surely it didn't mean that she didn't want to get married any more. Less than four hours ago, she'd been just excited as I was for this.

"Layla has left," Henry said.

I frowned. "Left where?"

"Almanbury."

"Why?" Pattie breathed. "For how long?"

His shoulder lifted. "I don't know. It didn't say."

"What didn't say?" I asked.

Henry's head shook. It looked like he was experiencing some kind of shock. He pulled a note out of his pocket, which Pattie took from him. I was still trying to add up what Henry was telling me and how it compared to the Layla I knew.

"I don't understand," Pattie muttered. "What does this mean?"

I looked at her and wondered how she was reading my mind – then I realised that she was reading the paper in her fingertips. The ink was smudged, but the words were still legible. I took it from her.

"I'm sorry. I can't stay. I love you, please don't hate me."

It was definitely her handwriting but not her words. It wasn't addressed to anyone, and it didn't say goodbye. So what did it mean?

"Her car is gone," Henry said. "I... I think she's left. She's gone."

"But why?" I asked. My voice was louder now, but it wasn't Henry I was mad at, it was the fact that nothing was making any sense at all.

He didn't reply, so I walked past him out the door and over to my car. I had started it before my mum was at my window.

"Christian, sweetie, what's going on?" she asked.

"I need to go, Mum, something's happened to Layla," I said. I shifted into reverse, but she didn't move.

"What do you mean?" she replied. "Is she okay?"

My head shook. "I don't know. Henry found her ring and a note."

"What does that mean?"

"I don't know. I need to find out."

She stepped back. "What about the party?"

"I can't, Mum, I need to find Layla."

I didn't wait. I just tapped the accelerator and headed straight to Layla's house. As Henry said, her car wasn't there, but nothing else made sense to me. I couldn't understand how she could leave and not tell me. She wouldn't. She wouldn't leave Almanbury or me. We were home to her. She would never leave her home.

I unlocked the front door to her house using the key that she had cut for me when my dad kicked me out. Henry and Pattie let me keep it for emergencies, and this felt like one. I called out Layla's name, even if I didn't expect her to reply. If her car was gone, unless someone had stolen it, it was unlikely that she would be here. I kept moving around the house, noticing that the fruit bowl looked emptier than it had been earlier in the day. The pantry was also open, and there was an empty muesli bar box lying on the floor of the small area. The breadbox was also bare. But what did that mean?

I continued through the house to her room and stopped in the doorway. The gold dress that she had been planning to wear to the rehearsal dinner was still laid out on her bed. The shoes that she was going to wear were buckled in the corner. Her curling wand was still on the floorboards where she had left it, and there were pieces of scrap paper and pens scattered across her desk. Her cupboard door was cracked open with her dressing gown caught in the gap. The third drawer down on her dressing table was also not properly closed, but appeared to be empty. It was the one where she'd kept her underwear.

The thing that caught my eye and worried me the most though was what was *on* her dressing table. It was her goldstone necklace, the one I'd given her on our first anniversary. Layla never took it off. She wouldn't leave it behind unless she was in a rush. She loved that necklace and, if she were planning to go for any length of time, she would have at least taken it with her. I knew that with certainty. I picked it up and sat on the floor with my back to her bed. I didn't care how long I had to wait here, but I would wait until she returned. If I knew her as well as I thought, then it would be sooner rather than later.

Henry showed up not long after. I don't know how long because time seemed to stand still from the moment he had shown up at the hall with the note and Layla's ring.

"Son, you need to get back to the party," he said. "People are asking questions."

"Well, they should get in line because I have a few questions of my own," I murmured. "Some of her things are gone, Henry. She's taken food, her wallet, and her camera, but she's left other things – things that she wouldn't leave behind if she'd really left." I gripped the necklace in my hand. "I spoke to her earlier, and she was excited about the party. Why would she just leave?"

"I don't know, son," he whispered. "But I'm… there has to be a logical explanation."

I nodded. "She'll be here. She always comes back. She can't be away from me for long. She's never been able to."

"I know, son, you're right," he answered. "But, for now, we need to get back and tell people."

I frowned. "Tell them what?"

Henry stared at me but didn't say what I was afraid to hear. I didn't want to hear out loud what I feared – that she wouldn't be back in the next twenty-four hours, and it wasn't just the rehearsal dinner that would be called off, the wedding would be too.

"I should tell our guests that Layla won't make the rehearsal dinner," I said. I lifted myself to my feet and shoved the necklace in the pocket of my trousers.

Henry shuffled. "What about the wedding?"

"The wedding is tomorrow." I shrugged. "She'll be back by then."

Henry frowned. "Okay."

I nodded and walked past him, back through the house and out to my car. The hall wasn't far, and I hadn't been gone for too long, I don't think, but people were starting to get restless in the absence of both the guests of honour.

I found Pattie and my parents and told them that Layla wouldn't be coming, and that people were welcome to stay until the food ran out. Other than that, the rehearsal wouldn't be going ahead. I did a circuit to tell the guests something of the like and added that Layla wasn't feeling well and needed to rest until tomorrow. I didn't bother telling them about the note because it wasn't real. She'd be back for the wedding. There is no way she'd miss it. We'd been waiting for this day since the day we met. This moment was five years in the making. She wouldn't just walk away from that. Maybe it was just a simple case of cold feet, even if that didn't sound a thing like Layla, but then neither did leaving. In fact, of the two stories, getting cold feet was probably a more believable one.

I stayed at Henry and Pattie's place on the couch in their living room that night. I knew that it was bad luck for the groom to see the bride before the wedding, but I wanted to make sure that she'd be back in time. The ceremony was planned for two o'clock, so at least she had a few hours in the morning to get back before she'd be pressed for time to get ready. I didn't know exactly what appointments she had planned, but I knew that she had to get her hair and makeup done before getting dressed in the white gown that she'd chosen to marry me in.

I woke to voices. Though, if I was honest, I hadn't been sleeping. I'd been waiting and listening. I just hoped that Layla wouldn't get mad at me for the dark circles under my eyes. But then again, I probably had more reason to be annoyed at her for not making it to the party last night.

"Someone needs to start telling people, Henry," Pattie's hushed voice said. "She's left—"

"She could still come back—"

"She has gone, Henry," Pattie replied more slowly. "The note said everything."

My eyes opened, but I still felt vacant. It was that feeling of recording my surroundings but not reacting to them.

Henry huffed. "But it's not like Layla to—"

"Face it, Henry," Pattie sighed. She sounded calm. "Our little girl has run away."

I sat up but still couldn't find the words to react to what was being said. None of it made sense, none of it. It was just so unlike the Layla that I knew to do something like *run away from home*, from me. This was Layla Louise Thomas, the girl who wanted to run away *with* me when we were sixteen because she was going on a four-week holiday away from me. This was the girl who used to call, text, and skype me on the days that my father wouldn't let us see each other. It was the girl who defied rules to *be with me*. If she left, then she must have left for a reason, and when that was fulfilled, she would come back. I knew that she would. Without each other, we didn't function on our own. We needed each other to exist, and that wasn't a weakness on either of us, it was a strength.

I just couldn't get those words out of my head. The words that she'd once whispered to me under the lamppost, and then down the phone when she was in Wales. When we were apart, when the world seemed at fault, when the balance was off... *Wait for me to come home.*

Layla hadn't left *me* a note. The words had not been spoken, they had been written. There was no evidence to the world that she didn't *want* to be here, only that she wasn't here. She wasn't running from me, or it would have been my name on the paper. She was running from something else. Or towards something else.

She hadn't left me. She'd left Almanbury and, if I believed anything in the world, it was that she would eventually come home. So I would wait for her. We would be together again. She just needed to realise that I wasn't going anywhere. I would wait for her to come home, and when she did, we'd pick up where we left off, only this time we'd be stronger because the

116

absence would boost both of our hearts into a new capacity to love like it had before.

"Christian, honey," Pattie said. "Would you like a cup of tea?"

Tea? No, I didn't want tea. I wanted Layla.

"No, thank you, Pattie," I murmured. My voice was thick and tired. It sounded as hopeless as I was beginning to feel. "Any news?"

"No, honey," she sighed. "I… I don't think we're likely to hear anything new."

I looked up at her. "Why? What makes you say that?"

"Nothing new. I just know my daughter. She wouldn't leave unless—"

"No, unless, Pattie," I said as I stood up. "Layla wouldn't leave. I know her too. I know her better than anyone. Layla wouldn't just leave. She wouldn't. She… she's going to come back. She'll be back."

Pattie frowned and looked at Henry. Henry looked as pale as he did yesterday, but I could see that he agreed with me. None of this sounded like something she would do.

"Well," Pattie sighed after a moment. "Maybe you're right. Maybe she'll be back. But I don't think that it will be in the next few hours, so maybe we should—"

"She's going to come back," I answered. "She'll be back for the wedding. I'm not calling it off. She'll be back. We've been planning it for… Pattie, she'll be here."

This time Henry stepped forward. "Son, I don't think she will be."

"Henry, not you too." I frowned. "Of course she will be. Why wouldn't she be?"

His head shook. "I just don't think… maybe it's not a coincidence that she left when she did."

117

I felt my heart hit the floor at my heels. "You think this was her way of leaving me? But the letter wasn't even left for me."

Pattie and Henry exchanged another look, and I heard the front door open and close, followed by footsteps. I lunged forward and skidded to a stop as my mother appeared.

"Any news?" she asked.

I exhaled. "Nothing *yet*."

"Christian, sweetie, do you think maybe it's time that we—"

"No!" I shouted. "I'm not cancelling the wedding. She'll be here."

The room was filled with another charged silence, and the door opened again. I turned my head as my father stepped in behind my mum. Perfect, that was just what I needed. An *I-told-you-so* while my world was crumbling around me.

"Mitch, how did you go?" Henry asked.

I frowned at my would-be father-in-law.

"No word, I'm sorry, Henry. No one saw anything," Dad said.

I stared at him. "Who did you ask? Did you check the security footage from around here?"

"Christian," Dad sighed. "This is not a missing person's case. Layla is an adult who left on her own accord—"

"But—"

"She left a note, son. She doesn't want to be found," he added. "Maybe it's time you move on and let people know that there won't be a wedding today."

My head was shaking, but I couldn't speak to rebuke him. Everything he said was true, but it was the wrong truth. My mother walked over to me and rested her hands on my arms.

"Sweetie, would you like me to start calling people?" she asked.

My head was still shaking.

"I can help, Nancy," Pattie said. "It's better that we start sooner rather than later."

"No," I snapped. "Everybody stop. No one is calling anyone because Layla will be here."

Now the four of them were exchanging a look as if I'd gone crazy.

I exhaled. "Shouldn't you all be doing something else like getting ready? What time is it?"

"Eleven," Henry said.

I frowned at him then at the clock behind him. How could it be so late? I wasn't sleeping that long. I wasn't sleeping at all. Why wasn't Layla here? She was cutting it really fine.

"We're running late," I mumbled. "Maybe someone should call the minister and tell him that we might be a bit late."

Pattie's hand lifted to cover her mouth, and Henry glanced at her then put his arm around her. My dad folded his arms and Mum reached out to rest her hand on my cheek.

"Christian, Layla has gone," she said quietly. "I think we need to start telling people."

I blinked at her. "She didn't die, Mum. She… she might have left, but she'll be back."

It was the first time that I had said the words aloud. That she *had* left. I still didn't believe it, but I couldn't deny the facts. She had left because she wasn't here. That was fact.

There was another sound at the door and, this time, everyone looked up. A moment later, Abbie appeared with Lindsay on her heels.

"My dad said that he saw Layla's car outside the bank last night as he was closing up the surgery," Abbie said. "She was wearing jeans and looked like she was making a withdrawal."

More looks were exchanged between them before their eyes crept to me. I couldn't deal with it any more, any of it, so I

119

walked out of the house without another word. A few called after me, I couldn't be sure of whom, but they didn't follow.

I felt as if I'd been thrown into another world, another life of someone who wasn't me. Everything that I had been sure of was suddenly cracked. My heart was cracked, and none of this made any sense at all. I rolled up the sleeves to my pale blue shirt from last night as I walked. The sun was out now, and it was balmy outside even though it was a dark day for me. I kept walking without purpose until I remembered that the last time Layla and I had tried to leave we had ended up in our cave by the beach, so I walked there. Maybe she'd gone there again.

She hadn't.

The dunes and the caves were empty, but a few people were enjoying the October sunshine. I wondered if we weren't supposed to be married today, whether Layla and I would be too. Layla loves the beach… loved. No, loves. She wasn't dead. She was just away for a while.

I kept walking past our cave when I saw that it was empty because I didn't want to be there without her. It was a place that didn't seem fitting without us there together. So, I walked to the wooden pirate ship and sat there. For a while, a few kids came to play on it but, eventually, they left me alone again too. I didn't know whether I preferred hearing their laughter and chatter to the silence that surrounded me. It felt less lonely with them here.

"Christian," Stuart called. "Dude, you all right?"

I didn't look up.

"People are looking for you, mate," he continued.

"People are looking for a lot of people today," I mumbled. I shrugged out of my shirt because the heat was getting too much. The sun felt nice on my skin.

"I heard," he answered, and then handed me a bottle of vodka. "Sorry to hear, man, that's rough."

"I'm not drinking, Stu," I sighed.

He took it back from me. "It might help."

"Not on an empty stomach… or in this heat." I frowned up at the sun. Why was it still shining?

"Do you know why she left?" he asked. "Did she say anything to you?"

I looked down. "No, and I don't want to talk about it."

Stuart unscrewed the cap of the bottle and took a swig. He put it down beside me.

"Hey, Turner, you up there?" Wayne yelled.

"Wayne, he's here," Stuart called back. "We're here."

Wayne's orange hair popped up into view. He'd stopped wearing his hat when school finished, and it was still strange to see the tuft of hair in full light.

"Oh, hey," Wayne said. "You okay, bro?"

I glanced at him and ignored the question.

Wayne looked at Stuart and then pulled himself up. He had a backpack on.

"I bought you something," he continued as he pulled out a bottle of whiskey. "But I see that Stu beat me to it."

Stuart took another sip of his vodka. "He doesn't want to drink."

"Well, I do, and I wasn't even the one she was supposed to marry today," Wayne answered. "Right now actually."

I looked up and snatched the whiskey from his hands. I'd never been a big drinker, and it burnt all the way down my throat. I hated the taste in fact, but if it came with temporary memory loss, then I'd take it.

"Just shut up and sit down, Wayne-o," Stuart said. "What else do you have in that bag?"

"Don't worry, I'm not planning on going anywhere," he huffed.

Stuart leant behind me and smacked the back of Wayne's head. I didn't see it, but I heard a thump and then Wayne's protests. A beat later, he unzipped the bag further and pulled something else out. He stuffed a packet of crisps in my lap.

"So you don't drink on an empty stomach," Wayne said. "Thought you might have forgotten to eat breakfast with all... with all that's been happening."

I opened the yellow packet and frowned at it. I didn't feel much like eating, but I didn't feel like doing anything so that probably didn't mean I wasn't hungry. Wayne stuffed his hand in to grab a pile of the cheesy potato crisps and dropped them in his lap. He then leant over, took the whiskey from me, and gulped a mouthful.

"I just can't believe she left," Wayne sighed. "It's really unlike her to leave though. Like, you and Layla are so functional and, like, close. It doesn't make a whole lot of sense."

I exhaled and stuffed the packet of crisps against Wayne's chest. Stuart leant over and smacked him in the head again as I stood up.

"Mate, where are you going?" Stuart asked.

I pulled my shirt back on but didn't bother buttoning it. "I'm going to tell people that the wedding is off."

Stuart and Wayne exchanged a look. It was the same look that everyone else seemed to be exchanging in my presence today.

"Bro, you don't have to do that," Wayne replied. "Abs and Linds were helping Pattie and Nancy spread the word when I left them."

I shook my head. "It's not their responsibility, it's mine."

"What are you going to tell everyone?" Stuart asked. "You don't really know anything, do you?"

I shrugged. "I know that she's not here, and there is no wedding without her. She left for reasons that are her own. When she comes back, she can tell her side of the story."

"You think she's coming back?"

"Of course she'll be back."

Wayne shoved another crisp into his mouth. "I want to believe it too, bro, believe me. But Abbie said that she withdrew all her savings. It sure sounds like she was planning on staying away."

I ran my hands through my hair. "None of this was planned, Wayne. None of it. Whatever made her leave won't keep her away forever. Besides, she doesn't have a lot of savings. She's going to come back."

Stuart put the cap back on the vodka. "Okay, I've got your back. Let's do this."

"Listen, you really don't have to—"

"Bugger off, we're coming," Wayne answered. He smashed another few crisps in his mouth and dusted off his hands before standing. Stuart put the vodka in Wayne's bag, and Wayne piled his stuff in with it.

"Right, we're all set." He nodded.

My eyes rolled. "Wonderful."

It wasn't easy, but I never expected it to be. In fact, this was the last thing that I ever expected today to turn into. I hated every minute of it. I hated the looks that people gave me, the sympathetic exchanging of glances that questioned my sanity. I hated the glint of "*I told you so*" that some people had in their eyes, or the slow nodding of "*well, they were very young; what did they expect?*"

I hated every second of the day that should have been the happiest of my life.

So, in the afternoon, I went back to the ship with Stuart and Wayne and drank the whole bottle of vodka and half of the whiskey. I wanted to be drunk and stay drunk so I didn't have to feel any of it. It worked for a while but, for some reason, every time I closed my eyes, I saw Layla, and it all came back. After a while, I started to miss her more, and the pain was tenfold. So I drank a little more and eventually passed out.

Stuart was the least hungover in the morning, so he set out to get greasy food for Wayne and me. I didn't feel like eating though. I was pretty sure that I was still drunk, and the sun didn't help. At least it was only the Almanbury sun and not the South Coast sun.

When I could walk again, I stumbled back to Layla's house. Henry and Pattie were out, but I didn't know whether they were working, or if they were just trying to return all the gifts that people had started to leave before they were told about Layla's disappearance. I was mildly aware that there was a line of other people that were let down by the event being cancelled. Those who had catered for us, the cake maker, the people arranging the flowers, those organising the canopies by the beach, the DJ, everyone who had loaned us tables and chairs. There was a multitude of people that I harboured guilt for, but I couldn't get over my self-pity to take on remorse for theirs. Again, I still couldn't understand why Layla would leave never mind at a time that meant so many others would be let down. She wasn't a selfish person, but the decision had been a selfish one. It only made me angrier because I didn't want people to think of her that way, and yet, I was thinking of her that way.

I collapsed on the floor of her room, careful not to disturb anything from the way she had left it. It was stupid, and even in my drunken stupor I knew it, but I liked the thought that her hands had been the last ones to touch things. I liked that the room that I was seeing now was the same room that she had seen, and being in it made me feel closer to her. But even so, I still felt paralysed from the pain, from the loss of a girl that I never thought I'd lose. Moreover, the girl that I never thought would leave on her own accord. I just couldn't stop thinking that I needed to wait for her and that she needed to come home. That hope started to fade into the belief that maybe we would never be how we used to. Maybe I wouldn't get to hold her again.

Henry and Pattie let me stay in the house because I think they felt sorry for me as much as I felt sorry for myself. I knew that my mum called periodically to check on me, but I couldn't take on the guilt of upsetting her too. I just needed to be close to Layla, and being in the place that we had last been together felt like the best way to do that.

After a week had passed, the denial that she'd left and shock of it all turned into anger and a new, lower stage of misery than I'd ever felt before. I didn't know whether I wanted to cry or punch something.

On the eighth day after she had left, I discovered that my pocketknife was still in the corner of Layla's room from when I'd carved my affection into her skirting. I was caught between the impulse to scratch it out or just alter it, and I spent the better part of a day pondering over it and eventually decided to keep it there and just add to it. So, by nightfall, the inscription read: *Christian Turner loves Layla Thomas, but not enough.* It was one of the only things that I had achieved since she'd gone. Everything else, living, existing, felt like an effort that wasn't worth it. Nothing seemed to matter without her. What was the point? My future had been wiped clean. The promise of a life with the love of my life had gone with Layla, and I was left with nothing but memories and sympathetic looks.

The hardest thing was that I didn't actually *want* to think about the future because any kind of future without Layla wasn't one that I wanted at all. I didn't want to think about moving on and building anything without her. I didn't even want to consider the fact that maybe she would be moving on without me. It physically hurt me to think that there was a real possibility that she wouldn't come back, but I didn't allow myself to dwell on it. I needed to believe that I would see her again and, once she'd done what she needed to do on her own, she would return to me. Anything contrary to that I couldn't think about it because I fell apart. I couldn't function if I had to revise my entire belief system. I couldn't.

"Christian, son, if you're going to stay in here and sleep then at least use the bed," Henry said one day. I didn't know what day it was since I stopped counting them. It felt like a lot had passed, but I didn't care. It wasn't as if I had anywhere else to be. I wondered if the library had even noticed that I was gone. But, then again, this was supposed to be my honeymoon period, so I didn't really bother much about work.

I looked up from the floor. Pattie had given me spare pillows and blankets from the linen closet.

"No, I'm not moving anything," I sighed. "No one can move anything. When Layla gets back, she won't like that people touched her things."

"Son, I—"

"Henry, I'm fine where I am," I answered. "Thanks, but I'm fine."

I rested my head back down but didn't hear him leave.

"You know, son, Pattie and I were talking, and we were thinking about making some improvements to things around here. You know, like maybe painting the place and renovating. I'm going to take some time off work, and if you're free, then maybe you'd like to help me out."

I sat up. "You're changing things?"

"We're making some improvements."

I frowned. "Why do they need to change? Everything works, right? Why do you want to change it?"

"Well, son, change is inevitable, and we've been thinking about it for a while. We thought that since… since Layla isn't around then maybe we can update her… her bathroom for when… when she gets back."

I stared at him and saw the sheen of glass pool in his eyes. He held as much hope for her return as I did. I was just more outspoken about it. It seemed like he needed to keep busy as much as I probably needed to.

"Okay, I can help," I replied. "Layla never liked the idea of going without things, and she hates the smell of paint. Maybe it's better that we do that stuff now."

Henry's expression softened. "I agree."

We both nodded at each other.

"So, um, when do you want to start?" I asked.

He drew in a breath. "What about tomorrow? It's a bit late in the day today."

I looked towards the window and noticed that the sun was slanted. "Okay."

"Good then."

I pressed my lips together.

"Pattie is making meatloaf if you're hungry," he added.

"Sounds good." I nodded. "Sorry if I'm an imposition. I don't mean to be. I—"

Henry took a step forward then took then step back, so he wasn't inside Layla's room. I noticed that he didn't like to come in here. Unlike me, he preferred to stay outside of Layla's space.

"Son, as far as I'm concerned, you're family no matter what. You are as welcome here as you always have been for as long as you want to be. Know that, okay?"

"Thanks, Henry," I whispered. "I just… it's always felt more like home to me here than it did at my house."

Henry nodded. I didn't need to expand on that since he'd witnessed the uphill battle that Layla and I had fought with my dad. I couldn't even consider being there now and facing him when I didn't have the complete faith in what I was fighting for as I did before. The faith that I was surviving on was blind, and Mitch Turner didn't believe in things that he couldn't see.

**

Henry and I started renovating the bathroom first because we figured there was the possibility that we'd bash the paint off the walls anyway. Between the two of us, it took us a few weeks to do, from the destruction to the designing and measuring, and then the fitting and tiling. It was lucky that Henry was a plumber because that saved time in waiting for everything to be connected properly. Wayne helped us with the tiling since he was in his second-year apprenticeship as a tiler, and given that Stuart was a trainee electrician, he came over to look at the wiring for new power points. Renovating the bathroom was the best project I could have had because there was so much to it that it kept my mind off anything else in my life. That was mostly because there wasn't anything *left* in my life to fulfil me the way that it used to when I was with Layla.

When the bathroom was done, we painted the entire house except for Layla's room. That took us more time, but it was still only a couple of weeks before we were finished, and then I was back to where I started, having no direction other than to Layla's floor.

And then, one day, I realised that I needed to leave the Thomas house for a while. The walls started to feel empty to me, and I wasn't sure whether it was because they were no longer the walls that Layla grew up in since that had changed in her absence, but I needed a change of scenery. I hadn't spent a lot of time outdoors since Layla left, so, even walking around the town, I noticed subtle differences. It was hard to accept that people's lives had continued on when mine felt like it had stopped. I didn't like to think that one day Layla would only be a memory to the people of Almanbury when she had been so vital to what made Almanbury significant to me. Without her, it didn't feel like the same town, but they didn't seem to notice.

My mum was glad to have me back home but, again, it was hard being in my room when there were traces of Layla everywhere I turned. Photos, letters, even her yellow sundress that was still tucked under my bed from the day I'd proposed. I put it in my drawer because it was difficult to look at without her body being in it. It didn't represent happiness without her. Everything just felt empty.

**

I turned twenty, and it was my first birthday without her. I wished for her on my candles, and I still held onto the thought that she hadn't actually said goodbye to me. I couldn't accept that we were completely over because she would have told me. She would have set me free. So, even when Lindsay threw herself at me, it felt wrong. I couldn't see her. No other girls existed to me because my eyes and heart were still focused on Layla, my love, my life.

I went back to work at the library and even started back on my paper rounds just to pass the time. I got by as best I could with what I had and even made a pathetic mix of sad songs that reminded me of Layla for my car. I needed to hold onto the memory of her even if it hurt. Pain was good because it made me remember that I was still alive. It was relevant. It hurt. It allowed me to live in the memory that what we had was real and not just some school grade crush that fizzled out after graduation.

More time passed and, after a suggestion from my mum, I started to write. I wrote down everything that I could remember because then, even if my memory faded, our story would be immortalised in words. I started with the day we'd met – with my first encounter with Layla Thomas, and worked through from there. My diary became an ode to Layla, and it was liberating to free my mind from thoughts of her that I was scared I would otherwise forget. I became addicted to it, to documenting everything and phrasing every detail. When I wasn't at work, or with Stuart and Wayne, I was writing in the journal. And then my ideas bled into stories, into fiction, and my desk that had once been kept neat became a canvas for post-it notes with ideas that I could write about. My brightest idea was writing a story about Layla and me – about how we'd met and fallen in love. I stuck it on my desk lamp and stared at it every day until I eventually decided to put pen to paper and write it out. I found it harder than I thought to revisit, so I kept it short. I turned the story of Christian and Layla into a short story that I put aside to focus on other fantastical ideas that ended happily. But everything I wrote seemed to end in loss. I suppose it's hard to write about things that I didn't know.

"Christian, sweetie, it's lovely to see you doing so much writing lately," Mum said one Tuesday. It was the first time in weeks that I'd been home for dinner, and we were eating reheated lasagne. It was nice, but not as nice as Layla's mac and cheese was. "Have you thought about maybe reapplying to study English?"

"No." I shrugged.

"It's just that you have so much potential and… and it's such a waste for you to… to…" She stopped and appeared to be struggling for breath. It had happened before, but never this bad. She also hadn't touched any of her food. But, to be fair, there was hardly anything on her plate.

"Are you all right, Mum?" I frowned.

"Yes, I—"

"Nancy, you need to tell him," Dad interrupted. Despite his words, his tone was soft and sounded defeated. It sounded wrong coming from his mouth. "You can't keep putting it off."

I looked between them. "Tell me what?"

"I didn't want to say anything until I knew for sure," she answered.

"What's going on, Mum?" I pressed. Now that I was looking at her, she didn't look well at all. How long had she looked that way? I felt horrible for not noticing. "Are you sick or something?"

She drew in a breath and replied on the exhale. "Yes."

"How sick?"

"Very sick, sweetie," she breathed, and then coughed.

I shifted in my chair. "Well, maybe we should get you to a doctor or something."

She tried to smile. "There's nothing they can do."

"What do you mean?"

My mum glanced sideways at my dad. It looked like she didn't want to tell me, and I didn't want to make any assumptions that would cause premature hyperventilation. Dad's hand moved over hers, and I frowned at it. My parents were as affectionate as any, so that wasn't what alarmed me. It was the way he looked at her, and the delicacy in which his hand caressed hers as if it was a soap bubble about to burst.

"Mum," I said. "Tell me."

"I have cancer, sweetie," she whispered. "Stage four."

My head shook. "I don't know what that means."

"I'm dying, Christian," she replied. "The doctors think I probably only have another two or three months."

I blinked in shock. "What? How long have you known about this?"

"I... we've known for a few months—"

"Months!" I shouted. "Why didn't you say anything?"

She smiled weakly. "You've had a lot on your plate, sweetie, you didn't need this too."

My eyes were wide as my hand moved over my mouth then dropped to rest on my mother's.

"You still should have told me, Mum, I... I would have..."

"Would have what, Christian?" She smiled. She sounded tired. How could I have missed this?

I shrugged. "I would have been here more."

"There's nothing you could have done here that would have changed my prognosis."

"So, what? You're just going to give up?" I frowned. "No, you can't. You have to get a second opinion or something. You need to live."

Her hand turned over to grip mine, but it was really weak. I squeezed hers softly to make up for it.

"It won't make a difference, sweetie, it's grown too big," she exhaled. "It's spread to my bones and my liver, my lungs… brain, my brain."

My head was shaking. "But I can't lose you too."

"I'm sorry," she breathed. "I'm so sorry, sweetie."

"Why are you apologising, Nance?" Dad replied. "Unlike Layla, you didn't choose this."

I flinched.

"Please, Mitch, don't say that. We don't know the circumstances of…" Mum sighed and panted for breath. "But when I'm gone, you need to look after each other, so please be kind to each other."

Mum's eyes closed.

"Nancy, why don't you go and lie down?" Dad said. It was phrased as a question, but it sounded rhetorical.

Mum nodded but didn't try to move. I stood up and walked around to help her, only just noticing that she was in her nightdress. A fresh surge of remorse flooded through me. For the last year and a half, I'd been mourning the fact that Layla had left. I'd been keeping busy, but it meant that I'd been so caught up that I'd missed the fact that my mother was terminally ill. I felt as if the kicks just kept coming.

**

In the weeks that followed, I changed my routine. I stopped the paper rounds again, and sold my car to help pay for the care that my mum needed at home. I also dialled back on my hours at the library so I could be there for her when Dad was at work. We put aside any quarrels that we might have had over everything else and just focused on her.

A couple of months passed, and then a couple more, and it was the summer before my twenty-first birthday when she took a turn for the worst. She had lasted longer than the doctors had predicted, but I had hoped that she would at least live until March so we could spend one last birthday of mine together.

In early January, I got mail. I never usually got mail, so it surprised me a little. Though, what shocked me more was that it was postmarked from South Coast University.

"Mum," I called. I walked into her room and stopped in the doorway. She opened her eyes.

"Mm, sweetie," she exhaled.

I went to sit beside her. "I got a package from South Coast University."

Her eyes were closed again, but she smirked. "Oh. What... does... it...?"

"I haven't opened it yet," I answered. "Mostly because I'm confused as to why they'd be sending me mail considering I haven't done anything to warrant it."

"Open it." She smiled. Her blue eyes opened and twinkled. They were the only part of her that hadn't changed. They were still so full of life.

I nodded and looked down at the A4 envelope, sliding my finger underneath the folded seal. I slid out the contents and frowned at it.

"This is an acceptance letter," I said. "It's a scholarship acceptance letter which is weird because I never applied for a place there never mind a Literature scholarship."

"Congratulations, sweetie," she breathed.

I looked up. "The dean of the School of Arts and Sciences thanked me for my short story. Did you send them something of mine?"

She pouted. "Don't be mad at me."

"I'm not." I smiled, although my heart felt as if someone had it in their fist. "Which did you send? When did you send it?"

"About a month ago," she answered. "It was the Layla one."

My lips pressed together. "Did you read it?"

"Don't be mad, sweetie," she murmured. "I didn't mean to breach your privacy. It was amazing though, I... you two really were perfect together. You fit together like... like two parts of the one whole."

I was a little embarrassed that she'd read my words, the ode to my broken heart and lost love, but I couldn't be mad or stay mad at my mother. She was the only one who ever understood and humoured my continual struggle without Layla, and with my dad.

"I'm not mad, Mum," I replied. "I'm just a little surprised that you went to the trouble of applying for me. I just..."

"I know you don't want to leave," she exhaled, and her hand lifted to my cheek. "But, sweetie, you need to start living your life and not keep waiting for the life that you and Layla planned out to begin. She's not keeping up her side of the dream, so go out and chase your own."

I rested my hand on hers. "I can't, Mum. I can't leave Almanbury. Not now, and not in case..."

"Just think about it," she said.

Her hand moved to my overgrown hair, and mine fell back to my lap.

"You need a haircut, Christian," Mum whispered tiredly. "It's dreadfully long."

"I know." I nodded. "But I can't bring myself to cut it. The last time I had it cut was—"

I looked down and frowned at the memory of the day that Layla had left. My mum seemed to understand. She ran her hands through it and brushed it over my ear.

"When did you get that piercing?" She blinked.

I lifted my hand to the single captive ring in my left upper ear. "When school finished. I got it with—" I stopped and edited myself, so I didn't say her name. "I got it one weekend, remember? When Dad saw it, he went ballistic, saying that pierced ears are for girls."

She gave a weak chuckle. "Oh, yes."

"I forgot it was there."

"Because your hair's all grown out... but I suppose it makes you look more rugged this way," she sighed. "In an unkempt... raised by wolves... kind of way."

I smiled. "I suppose Dad can get a little gnarly at dinner time."

She laughed and then gave a small cough. "My boy, be nice to your father, he... he just wants you to reach your potential."

"Isn't happiness more important though?"

"Are you happy, Christian?" she asked.

I looked down. "I was... for a while. Ironically, that was when he was pushing me in another direction."

"That's because you have always been far too bright to shine in such a small town."

"This, again, is ironic considering he was the one who moved us here." I smirked.

Her head moved in a shake. "He moved *for* you. You were losing your way in South Coast. You weren't happy there. We could see that, but you were too proud to ever say."

"I... it was high school, Mum, no one is ever happy in high school." I shrugged.

"You were happy at ASH. You were happy here," she answered. "*Were*, but now that has changed, so you need to seek happiness elsewhere."

Her eyes drooped closed, and I knew that I had probably occupied her long enough in her weak state.

"Mum, you need to rest," I whispered. "I'll let you rest."

Her hand caught mine as her eyes peeked open. "I love you, Christian. All we ever wanted was the best for you. It's time that you start making decisions for yourself and shine in your own light."

"Okay, Mum." I nodded. "I love you too. Now get some rest."

**

Time ticked slowly, as slow as laboured breathing and, although she didn't improve, my mum still clung to life. Some days I wished that she would just keep holding on, others I felt terrible for willing it considering the pain she seemed to be in. She was bedridden and couldn't do anything but sleep and try to breathe. Her appetite was all but gone, but she still kept fighting. I took more time off work to watch over her, and it became my full-time job to make sure that she had everything she needed. Pattie and Henry were a fantastic support too, and Pattie would come and visit every day with a new casserole for Dad and me so we could focus on Mum. Wayne and Stuart were here also, though, they didn't visit as often. I don't think they quite knew how to be there for me, but the fact that they were there was enough.

On the third of March, a day before my birthday, I woke up to find that my mother had a little more colour in her cheeks than usual. She was still weak and struggling to breathe—louder and more congested than it usually was—but she appeared to be a little less tired than the day before. I made her some dry toast, and she nibbled on it a little. I was so relieved that she seemed to be a bit better, especially because that meant she would be around to see me turn twenty-one. It was more than I could ever have asked for.

"The weather has been real nice lately. It's not as hot as it has been," I said to her that morning. I was eating my cereal with her, and she was taking slow blinks as she watched me. "Dad and I were thinking that maybe tomorrow we could try and do something special like have a picnic. I mean, we'd have to stay in here, but maybe we could move you around so you can see out the window or something."

"Mm, sounds nice."

I nodded. "I mean, we don't even have to do anything. I could just read to you for a while. I've been writing more lately. In fact, I've decided to turn that short story that you sent into SCU into a novel, well, a short novel, a novella."

Mum smiled weakly. "That's lovely, sweetie."

She started to cough, and I frowned. I put my cereal bowl down.

"Are you okay? Do you want me to get you some more pillows? Maybe sitting up will be better?"

She exhaled. "No, I... I'm..."

Her hand weakly searched the side of the bed, and I reached for it. She gave my hand a squeeze, and the firmness of it surprised me. She took another breath and then started to choke again. I stood up.

"Mum, I'm going to get you another pillow," I said. "And maybe a glass of water."

"Sweetie, no, stay," she sighed.

"I won't be long, I promise. I'll be right back."

I gave her hand a light squeeze then slipped out of the room that we'd transformed into a home hospital for her. It didn't take me long to find the pillow, but it took me a couple of minutes to find a clean pillowcase for it. I tucked it under my arm then looped back to the kitchen for the water.

I should have known before I stepped foot into the room that something was wrong. It was far too quiet in there.

"Sorry, Mum, I—" I blinked. "Mum?"

I waited and frowned. Her eyes weren't fully closed, and her mouth was a little droopy. There was no sound coming from her, and I couldn't allow myself to comprehend why. I was just here. I was just talking to her. She had even felt like eating today. Today was a better day than yesterday, so why wasn't she alert now? I couldn't even fathom the reason. I couldn't deal with it. I couldn't forgive myself for leaving her on her own as her breath was taken from her. I couldn't handle the fact that I wasn't there, that I never got to say goodbye to her. I shouldn't have moved when she asked me to stay.

I had never wanted to say goodbye to her, so I didn't, but that didn't mean that she wouldn't go. That she wouldn't die. I knew she would, but I tried to avoid it because I couldn't deal with it. I couldn't deal with losing someone else in my life, even if I knew that I couldn't control any of it.

My heart had cracked when Layla left. It had been the hardest thing that I had lived through. But, then I found out that my mum was sick and, watching her health deteriorate, I felt as if another piece of my heart had detached and disintegrated. And then, on that day when one minute I was talking to her and the next she was gone, that was another wave – another tsunami of agony that drowned me. I couldn't even acknowledge my birthday the next day because I didn't feel as if it was a day to celebrate. If four was my happy number, then three was beginning to be a date associated with sorrow and loss.

My dad didn't talk to me for a while after Mum died. I was sure that it was because he blamed me for not being there with her too, but maybe it was also because, without her, we didn't have any common ground. Mum had been our Switzerland. She had linked our warring sides and brought peace to the household. Without her, we didn't know how to communicate. So, for that reason, I spend the weeks after her death with Pattie and Henry again. They were great, as they had always been. In fact, the whole town was great in offering their support to Dad and me. We were a real community in Almanbury, and I was sure that without everyone's kindness, particularly the Thomas family's, as well as Stuart's and Wayne's, I wouldn't have coped at all with what had happened in the past two years of my life.

**

I moved back in with my father in May and slowly, surely, we began building up our relationship again. We clashed a little, as we always had but, unlike before, we worked through it this time. My mother had been right when she'd said that we both needed each other. Neither of us wanted to let my mum down. She had always wanted us to be together as a family, so that's what we were committed to – we were committed to finally being there for each other, no matter how difficult it was sometimes.

Regardless, he wasn't happy when I deferred my place at university for a year, and then two. The university almost wasn't going to let me, but I didn't feel like I could leave Almanbury or my father in the state that we were in. I was still mourning, and I felt like I needed to be here for that. I felt closer to Mum and to Layla when I was here, and I needed to come to terms with that loss before I relocated to follow any new path for myself.

"You can't keep working at the library forever, Christian," Dad mumbled into his soup one night. "That and paper rounds, they're not careers, they're fillers."

"People work in libraries as their career. That's what librarians are."

He frowned at me. "Librarians have qualifications, not high school diplomas."

"Yeah," I sighed. "Well, I'll get there eventually."

He dropped his spoon. "When?"

I shrugged. "When I'm ready."

"Christian, you should have been ready when you were eighteen," he muttered. "You're now twenty-two."

"I'm aware of my age, Dad."

"Well, son, these last few years you have just wasted, and for what?" he asked. "You could be something more by now. You could be qualified as something."

"I needed to be here," I said. "I made the decisions that I needed to at the time."

"And how did they turn out? If only you had listened to me when I—"

"Then what?" I exhaled. "Then I would have been in the city when Mum died. I would have missed the last three years of her life."

"Yes, well, you did anyway because of that Thomas girl."

I flinched. "Don't."

"Well, it's true."

"It's not. I was still here," I replied. "Don't hang any more guilt on me than I already feel. I have been doing the best I can to cope, and it's not easy, Dad. I wouldn't wish the last couple of years of my life on my worst enemy. So, just back off and let me try to survive through the rest. I'm doing the best I can, okay? I'm trying."

Dad's lips pulled down as his hand lifted to rest on my wrist.

"I know, son." He nodded. "I… I know that you've been through a lot, and maybe I don't say this enough, but I'm proud of the man that you've become. Selling your car and putting your life on hold to… to look after your mother was a real honourable thing to do."

"I would have done more if I could have." I shrugged.

He squeezed my wrist. "I know, son. But you can't do anything more now."

I looked up at him. He'd gotten better at talking to me in the thirteen months that we'd been alone under the same roof. He'd definitely calmed down from the tough police sergeant that I'd grown up with. I didn't know whether it was time that softened him or loss, like in the opposing way that it had hardened me. He withdrew his hand and I folded mine into my lap.

"Christian, don't take this the wrong way, but it's been nearly three years since Layla left. I think it's time that you accept that she isn't coming back. You need to move on with your life. It's not healthy to dwell."

"I'm not… dwelling," I replied, twisting my would-be wedding band around my right ring finger. It seemed a waste not to wear it, and I couldn't bring myself to sell it. I also couldn't bring myself to say that I wasn't still holding onto that last ounce of hope that Layla might still come back. I actually didn't think about it often, but the hope was still there, buried deep in my heart so I could live each day normally.

"It's time that you stop hiding behind fear, or whatever it is, and start living the life you should be living," he said. "Don't defer university any more. Go and make something of yourself. It's what your mother wanted. She went through all that application stuff because she believed in you, son. Even... even Layla wanted that for you. I remember her saying once that you were good enough to make a career out of that reading stuff."

"Literature."

"Right, that." He nodded.

I tried to smile. "I'll think about it."

"Don't just think about it, Christian." He frowned. "As much as I'd miss you, you need to go. Call the university and get your place back. You can have my old car, and surely you've got a bit saved too. I can send you money for rent if you need it. You can work or what not. You've got skills."

I breathed a flat laugh. "You're really keen for me to leave, Dad."

"I just don't want you to waste away here," he answered. "I never... we never wanted that for you, son. That's why I pushed you so hard when you were in school."

"But I did my own thing anyway."

Dad frowned but didn't take the bait. I was proud of him since it was a perfect opening that he let pass.

"Okay, I'll call SCU tomorrow and see if they'll let me in." I nodded. "It's what Mum would have wanted anyway... and me, I guess."

He smiled. "That's real good, son. I'm glad to hear it."

**

It was lucky that I called when I did because South Coast University hadn't yet filled all the places for scholarships for the beginning of next semester, which was the first semester of next year. They were willing to let me in, which meant that I had the summer to save money before making the move back to South Coast. I helped out where I could, doing whatever jobs that people needed doing. I worked as many shifts as I could at the library, helped out in my mum's old pharmacy, and even assisted Pattie in the post office after hours sorting the mail.

In late January, I did a tour around the town telling people that I was moving. Probably the hardest people to say goodbye to were Henry and Pattie because I had come to be like a surrogate son to the both of them. I knew that my dad would be okay because he knew that I needed to do this, and he wanted me to do it, but Henry and Pattie had never wanted Layla to leave. I felt terrible for leaving them too, but they were as proud of me as if they were my own parents, so that alone gave me the strength to go. Besides, unlike others, I would make an effort to keep in touch and come home to visit as often as I could.

On the fourth of February, a month before my twenty-third birthday, I loaded up what little possessions that I needed and, with Layla's gold necklace still in my pocket, I made the move back to South Coast. It was harder than I thought it would be to find a rental property but, after spending the first week or two in a backpacker's motel, I finally found one that was close enough to transport to get around.

The public transport was just as bad in the city as I remembered, but it was a cheaper alternative to all day parking, so I made do. I even managed to find a job in the city that I could work around my uni hours. It wasn't the kind of work that I expected. In fact, it was the furthest thing that I would have thought to find myself in.

The place was called *Montage*, and it was a huge warehouse-looking clothes store that was situated down one of the corners of the biggest forum in South Coast. It was concrete everything, with industrial lighting and a red sign that hadn't yet had the store's name painted on it. Regardless, they needed workers and paid well, so I jumped at the chance for a job. I got into a good routine for myself and managed to make it so I could even do a couple of hours of work in the shop before heading in for afternoon classes. Things were finally starting to look up.

The literature course was intense in terms of the number of books that I had to read a week, but I loved it. I found it a bit hard to get back into the swing of study but, once I had, I felt like I was smashing through it. I made the drive down to Almanbury every second Saturday afternoon and stayed overnight to drive back for classes and work on Monday. Luckily for me, most places didn't open for business on Sundays, so it meant that I could still make it down and back without giving up a shift. On the weekends that I wasn't back at home, I was reading and writing so I could keep up with my units. I was committed to making a good go of it all and, as I completed my first semester at SCU, I was sitting on high distinctions.

I went back home to Almanbury for the first two weeks of the winter break at uni, and it was amazing just how much everything had changed in my absence, or maybe it just felt like it had. I spent a lot of time with Henry since he seemed to need the help a little more now. His knees weren't too great, so he appreciated the assistance on jobs. Stuart and Wayne were the same as always, and Abbie still hung around them too. She and Wayne were back together again and, by the sounds of things, they weren't too far off from settling down. He didn't say much about it since engagements were still a pretty delicate subject amongst us, but anyone could see that they were going to make things official soon.

I spent the second and final two weeks of my winter-term break working at *Montage* and starting on the reading list for my next semester's units. By the time August came around, I was shaping up for another successful semester, which was lucky considering I needed to maintain my grades to keep the scholarship. The weeks ticked by and, although I was in a good rhythm with everything, it was becoming more difficult to find the time to drive the five hours back home to Almanbury. So, every second weekend became every third but, even if I couldn't get down there as often as I wanted, I made up for it with phone calls. I spent a lot of time on the phone, and it was the least I could do.

**

Everything was going smoothly until, one Friday morning, I slept through my alarm and was late to work. It threw me off because I had never been late to anything before. When I finally made it in and saw the date, I concluded that it must have been the universe poking fun at me. The fourth of October. Time passed so quickly. Had it really been five years since I had proposed to Layla on this day? Had it really been four since she'd disappeared from my life?

It was the first time I'd spent the anniversary away from Almanbury, and I couldn't shake the feeling of weirdness. It didn't make a whole lot of sense to me though because I'd spent our *actual* anniversary in September away too, but there was something about today specifically that made me feel as if I should be back there. That maybe this might be the day that she would finally come home and…

I turned a corner in *Montage* without looking and bumped into someone. The piles of black designer T-shirts that I had been carrying fell to the ground at our feet. I didn't know what made a T-shirt designer, but I supposed I didn't work here because I was any kind of expert on fashion.

I heard the girl that I'd walked into mumble an apology, and we both lowered to gather them.

"It was my fault," she said.

"No, I wasn't watching," I answered. I thought I must have been going crazy. It must have been because today was the day that it was, or because I'd just been thinking about her, but I could have sworn that she sounded just like…

I looked up. "Layla?"

She was looking down, but I had memorised every freckle and follicle on that girl in the five years that we were together. Her eyes lifted, and my heart felt as though it had literally stopped as the familiar gold irises pierced into my cracked soul.

"Christian," she breathed. She paled and looked as if she'd just seen a ghost. "What are you…? I mean, hi."

I didn't know what I was expecting to feel when I finally saw her again. I'd thought so many times about what I would say to her, what I would ask her when I did see her. I thought that maybe I'd want to hug her and kiss her, scoop her into my arms and make sure that she didn't leave again. I'd imagined our reunion as a happy one, as a re*union* because she was coming home to me, and we would be together again. I didn't expect it to be a chance encounter in a clothing shop in a city that she didn't even like. In fact, when I looked at her now, I didn't see my Layla. I saw a girl who had deserted me and who had no intention of coming home.

I tucked my shoulder-length hair behind my ear and took the clothes from her before offering her my hand to help her stand. She took it and straightened, and I noticed for the first time just what she was wearing. It twisted something inside of me that I hadn't felt since finding her room empty and her goldstone necklace on her vanity. I was reminded of the way that Henry looked when he came to the party with the note and her ring.

She glanced down at the white gown and looked back at me with something that resembled regret. It was the first sign of it on her expression since I'd seen her again.

I worked to smooth my features, but I couldn't stop staring at her. I still couldn't believe that this was Layla Louise Thomas standing in front of me.

"You grew your hair," I said. It was a stupid thing to say, but it was all that I could think to say.

Her hand lifted to run through it. "You too."

I took a breath and tried to say something with more substance.

"So, South Coast? That's where you ended up."

Layla blinked, and I could see so many words in her eyes that she wanted to say, but I wasn't sure whether I wanted to hear them.

"Christian, I—" she started.

"Layla, I think I found one," someone interrupted.

Layla glanced over her shoulder as a girl with short light blonde hair appeared.

The girl smiled when she saw me. "Apparently, you did too. Hey, I'm Madeline. I mean, Maddie, call me Maddie."

"Christian." I nodded. "It's nice to meet you."

Maddie looked at Layla as if expecting her to speak, but Layla still looked as if she didn't know how to. I knew how she

148

felt. A part of me felt sorry for her, but another part was relieved that she couldn't confuse me with an explanation.

I cleared my throat. "Well, I need to put these away."

Layla's eyebrows lifted. "You work here?"

I gestured towards the employee badge I wore on the green polo shirt that was part of my uniform. It wasn't particularly fashionable if you asked me, but what did I know?

"It's not ideal," I said. "But I needed a job. It pays the bills."

Her head shook in confusion. "You mean, you live in South Coast now?"

"Why wouldn't he?" Maddie laughed. "He works here."

Layla looked a little irritated with her friend, but she also seemed a bit comforted that the girl didn't realise this was somewhat of a reunion for us.

I sighed. "I used to live down south in Almanbury. Layla and I—"

"Went to school together," she interrupted. "But, gosh, it's been years, hasn't it?"

I flinched at the blow. We went to school together? Is that all we did?

Maddie looked over at me, and I tried to compose myself before her eyes could settle. When they did, they were practically glowing with lust.

"No kidding?" She smiled. "Layla never said that she was from down south. Or that she went to school with such a hottie."

"I guess she didn't think it was important," I mumbled, looking towards my feet. I looked back up in time to see Layla's mouth close, and then pressed my lips together.

"Well, it was nice to meet you, Maddie." I nodded. "Layla."

"Lovely to meet you, Christian." The blonde girl waved.

I turned and walked off without a second look. I wished that I could have left work, but I couldn't rationalise bailing on responsibility just because I was in an uncomfortable position. It wasn't my style, it was Layla's.

I dropped the black T-shirts where they needed to be folded, and began putting them away.

After about five minutes had passed, I saw movement at the corner of my eye. I didn't want to admit to myself that I wished it was Layla, but I couldn't help but feel deflated when I glanced up to see her friend coming towards me. She was carrying a dark pink dress in her arms that she must've just tried on.

"Hi again." She smiled.

I nodded. "Hello."

"I thought I'd come and have a chat to you while I wait for Layla." She shrugged. "I love shopping and trying on things, but she hates it. Getting her to wear a dress is like trying to get her to go to the dentist. I don't know what her problem is."

I felt myself frown as I folded. Layla didn't like wearing dresses? The Layla I knew wouldn't wear anything else. It seemed that her hair growing out and her apparent indifference weren't the only things that had changed in this new version of her. Did Maddie even know Layla, or was I the one who didn't?

"Right," I sighed. "So, how do you know Layla?"

"We work together at *Flash Magazine*. I'm the fashion guru, and she's the chief photographer."

I found myself smiling with some sort of pride that she had actually achieved what she'd always wanted for a career. With that pride came sadness because I hadn't been a part of her life when she'd finally made at least some of her dreams come true.

"So, do you just work here or are you studying?" Maddie pressed.

I blinked back into reality. "I'm studying on scholarship at SCU."

"Cool, what are you studying?"

"Um, Literature."

Her eyebrows lifted. "Wow, that's amazing."

I laughed. I didn't know what she found so amazing about reading. I mean, I found it amazing, but she didn't strike me as the kind who had read a novel since high school. A fashion magazine, maybe. But then, maybe I was being too presumptuous.

"What's your favourite book?" I asked. I couldn't help myself.

She smiled and opened her mouth, then laughed. "I liked Harry Potter."

"Which one?"

"The one with Robert Pattinson in it," she said. "Busted. Yeah, I really don't read anything other than magazines."

I chuckled.

"Hey, do you want to maybe hang out sometime?" she asked.

Her question caught me by surprise, and I blinked. I was about to decline when another, terrible, terrible thought struck me. This girl was the new Layla's friend. Maybe if we just hung out, I would get to see Layla more too. Could I do that to Maddie? I mean, it wasn't as if we had to *date*. Hadn't her exact words been just to *hang out*? Had she asked Layla if it was okay to ask me? Had Layla said yes? Did it matter what Layla thought?

"Um, sure." I shrugged. "Sounds like fun."

She beamed and was suddenly offering me her phone. "Chuck your number in, and I'll be in touch."

My eyebrows lifted. I'd forgotten how forward the girls in South Coast were – or maybe it was just the ones that I remembered.

I took the handset and punched in my number, then gave it back to her. She wiggled her shoulders in excitement as she put the device away. I frowned as I caught sight of Layla's auburn hair and looked back to my folding task. After a few seconds, I glanced back up as she stopped by Maddie and poked her.

"How'd you go with that one?" she murmured. Her eyes looked a little glassy as if she'd been crying. I didn't like to think of Layla being upset, but I couldn't understand why she would be. It sounded as if her life had undergone a considerable upgrade since moving here.

"It's great." Maddie beamed. She didn't notice a change in Layla. "I'm going to get it, but I might just try on some more just for the fun of it."

Layla tried to smile. "Okay then, shall we?"

I mashed my lips together since she looked about as uncomfortable being here as I did. The only difference was she could leave, and I was paid to stay.

"Well, you've changed your tune." Maddie laughed. "Christian and I were just getting to know each other better."

"I can see that," Layla mumbled.

I folded my arms. "Maddie was just telling me that you guys work at *Flash Magazine*. That's a big achievement."

"Yes," Layla breathed. "It is."

Maddie looked between us. "And Christian is studying literature on scholarship at South Coast Uni."

"Scholarship?" Layla repeated, but she didn't look surprised. "Wow, congratulations."

I nodded. I didn't know what else to say, so I didn't say anything.

Maddie was rocking on her feet like a little kid.

"Well, we should stop distracting Christian while he's trying to work," Layla sighed. "Besides, I still need to find a dress."

Maddie blinked. "Right."

"What's the occasion?" I asked. I was impressed that my voice sounded indifferent even if I was budding with curiosity. It was Maddie who answered.

"Work ball," she said. "It's the magazine's fifth anniversary."

I glanced at Layla but didn't allow my eyes to settle. "Fifth?"

Maddie nodded. "Fifth."

Did Layla remember that it was our anniversary today? Five years since I'd proposed — it also should have been our fourth wedding anniversary. I shook my head to stop the thoughts.

"Well, if you look in the back right-hand corner, you might find something there that you like," I said.

"Thank, um, thank you," Layla stuttered.

I nodded down at the T-shirts and saw that they were all folded, so turned to head towards one of the four payment counters that were positioned around the store. I wished that I could have stayed and spoken to Layla more, but I still wasn't sure what I wanted from her. I didn't want to hear the reason for her leaving, even if it still existed because that would mean that there was no chance for us at all.

But then I didn't know if I wanted there to be a chance if she wasn't my Layla. I didn't know if this Layla was one that wanted me back. This Layla had left Almanbury and let four years pass. This Layla I would have never seen again if it wasn't by accident, I was sure of that. So, maybe it was better for me not to talk any more to this Layla because I was scared that it would shatter my memory of the real one. Maybe I should have said no to Maddie. Maybe I could still say no next time she asked.

I knew that I wouldn't though because, even after all this time, I still couldn't bring myself to stay away from her. I still wanted to know more about what she'd been up to and what had kept her away. Maybe not why she'd left because that was obviously something that she had chosen over me, and I didn't really want to know that something existed that she wanted more. Maybe it was egotistical, but it was there.

I kept Layla at the corner of my eye as she looked through the gowns where I suggested and saw her pick up a few to try on. One was black, one was dark blue, and the last was gold. Without seeing her in them, I would have picked the gold for her. I'd always loved the way the colour brought out her eyes. Plus, it was something that the Layla I knew would have picked. It was something that the Layla I knew would have considered getting married in.

She went to the change rooms and tried them all on, and I made myself busy nearby to see her in them. Physically, other than having longer hair and more of a pucker between her eyebrows from frowning, she didn't look different at all. She was still petite – maybe a little slimmer than when she'd left. There was no question that she would still fit into the clothes she had left behind.

She smoothed her hand over the dark blue gown as Maddie groaned.

"I don't know, Layla, they all look good," she said. "You look good in everything."

I smiled to myself because I couldn't disagree with that.

"Come on, Maddie, you're a fashion editor, give me useful criticism," Layla sighed. "What about colours? Which one do you think goes better?"

"Everything goes with your incredible golden skin tone," Maddie huffed. "I really don't know!"

There was a silence, and I peeked out from behind a rack to see Layla frowning.

Maddie shook her head. "I'm getting kind of bored though, so please make a decision."

Layla sighed and turned towards the full-length mirror. Like a stickler for torture, I stepped out.

"Pick the gold lace one," I murmured. "It brings out your eyes."

She blinked, and I thought I saw water glisten in her eyes again. Maddie sighed from behind me, but was smiling in relief. I gave Layla a small nod, and pushed off the wall that I'd been leaning on. *Enough, Christian, walk away.*

"Well?" Maddie asked as I paced slowly back through the racks.

"I… agree. I think the lace one is the one."

I exhaled and shook my head. I hated that even a small agreement made me believe that she was still in there. Layla Louise Thomas, the Layla Thomas that loved Christian Turner. The little seed of hope budded in my heart. *Enough, Christian.*

I watched as Layla and Maddie paid for their purchases and then left the store. I don't know if I was relieved or distraught, for the fact. I was scared that when she left, it would be another stretch of years until I saw her again. I never thought that would ever be a worry when it came to Layla. It used to be hours that I mourned without her, not years. Definitely not years.

As she disappeared into the crowd, I couldn't handle it any more. That tsunami wave of emotions hit me again.

"Hey, Troy," I called.

The bozo that I worked with, that looked as though the only definition he knew of love involved his reflection, looked up.

"Yo, Christo." He nodded.

I frowned. "I'm taking a short break."

He lifted his hand up in a peace sign. "Mint."

"Okay."

I headed straight back to the crew room and made myself a coffee. I was more of a tea drinker myself but had acquired a taste for it in the last five years. Layla had started drinking the stuff about ten years ago, but I never understood why. As far as I could establish, the only perk to it was the caffeine. The taste wasn't brilliant.

I hardly drank any of it. I just stared into it, into the warm gold liquid that was almost the colour of Layla's skin. I wished that I could call someone to tell them that I'd seen her, but I didn't know what to say. I still didn't know why she'd left. I just knew that she was alive, and in South Coast of all places. I shouldn't have been surprised. Deep down, I had assumed that she'd come here since we'd plotted it once when we were going to run away. A city was the best place to hide because there were more people, more pockets, and more possibilities to be anonymous. Layla had done that – she'd done that and more. In fact, she'd become the person that she'd always wanted to be, only without me. A huge part of me resented that she had achieved it on her own because I always liked to think that we needed each other. Maybe it was just me who needed her, but then here I was paving my own future without her. A future that seemed to collide with her regardless.

I frowned down at my ring and spun it around my finger. Maybe we needed to be apart for a while to become the people that we wanted to be. Maybe us meeting again could be our second chance? Is that what I wanted? Is that what she would want?

Of course it wasn't. I was getting way ahead of myself. She didn't come home. I waited for her, but she didn't come home. As far as I knew, she never intended to see me again. This was all just coincidence, and it was messing with my head after I'd just started to move on with my life.

I knew that today was going to be tough. I just never considered that it would be *this* tough.

I exhaled and glanced at the time. I'd been on break for about half an hour. That was longer than we usually had for a cup of tea or coffee. I rose to my feet, stuck my finger into the cold liquid, and then poured it out before returning to the floor.

I headed straight over to a shelf of blue T-shirts that were in a pile and began straightening them as if I'd been there for the last fifteen minutes. I'd almost gotten through them when I saw someone walking straight for me from the corner of my eye.

"Is this some sort of game to you?" Layla shouted.

I sighed and ignored the people that looked up to stare. "What are you talking about, Layla?"

"Are you trying to hurt me or something?" she continued. "Is this some sort of sick payback?"

I frowned. "Hurt *you*? What have *I* ever done to hurt *you*?"

"You mean, apart from dating my best friend?"

I huffed. "Oh, I'm sorry. Are we still engaged? Because *I* was under the impression that when you abandoned me at our rehearsal dinner and left your ring, family, and life behind that meant we'd broken up."

Layla's brow pinched. "Christian, I—"

"I don't want to hear it, Layla," I sighed. "Really, you have no idea what I went through when you left—"

157

I stopped and shook my head. I wasn't going to do this here, not in public, and in the middle of my workplace. Besides, she didn't deserve to know when she never bothered to ask. I continued my folding with more enthusiasm.

"Christian," she sighed, my name rolling off her tongue as it always had.

I clenched my teeth. "Please just leave, Layla. It's what you do best."

She frowned and took a moment before turning.

I shook my head. "And just so you know, not that whoever I date is your concern any more, but it was your friend who asked *me* out. If you've got a problem with it, then I suggest you take it up with her."

Layla had stopped in her tracks but didn't turn. When I finished speaking, she just continued walking towards the door.

I swallowed back the pain as I watched her leave for the second time today. It was a tough day.

She was almost at the door when Troy stepped out in front of her, and she collided with him before toppling back on her heels. He flicked his hair from his eyes and started talking to her with the creepy smirk that he used to chat up the other girls who came into the store.

Layla tried to step around him, but he seemed to mirror her movements. I frowned because I didn't like the fact that he was harassing her. He reached over to pick up a lacy bra and held it towards her. That seemed to be the final straw. She gave him a shove and continued towards the exit. I exhaled in relief.

"You don't like red?" he called after her. "We have it in black."

I groaned. The loser just couldn't leave it alone and, Apparently, neither could Layla. She stopped and spun around, pacing back towards him with a look of determination. I dropped the shirt that I was folding and darted towards her. The last thing she needed was an assault charge against her – and something told me that if she discoloured Troy's face, he would cry about it. I think I remembered hearing him tell someone that he was a part-time model. Typical.

I grabbed Layla from behind to pin her arms to her side as her hand lifted towards him. She struggled against me, whipping and thrashing as if she was being kidnapped.

"Layla, stop fighting me," I mumbled.

She seemed to relax. "Then let me go."

I didn't let her go until I had reached the door. Then I put her down and dropped my arms back to my side.

"What were you thinking?" I muttered. "You're picking fights now?"

She shook her head. "That guy was being a creep. He needed to have some sense knocked into him."

My eyebrows lifted. "By you?"

"What is that supposed to mean?" she snapped. It was a little refreshing to see her annoyed rather than upset.

"You're a bit of a flake, Layla." I smirked. "You always have been."

"A flake? What does that even mean?"

"Just get a hold of that temper of yours. Man, the city has corrupted you."

"I'm not corrupted." She pouted and then folded her arms. "I've just grown up. It's not easy living on your own."

I ran my hands through my hair. "Right, well, no one forced that upon you. Speaking of, you should call your folks. I'm sure they'd like to know that you're still alive."

She flinched, and I looked down.

A beat passed, and I turned to go back inside. No doubt Troy would be complaining to someone that I was slacking off.

"Wait, Christian," she called. "How are you? I mean, really?"

I shook my head. "Layla, I haven't heard from you for four years, and now you care?"

"I… I always cared, I—"

"You don't just abandon someone that you care about."

She blinked back moisture. "At the time, I thought it was best—"

"I don't want to know, Layla," I mumbled, turning towards the store.

"Christian," she sighed. "Please."

I exhaled. "No, Layla. This time it's my turn to walk away."

With each step that I took, I wanted to turn back. It felt wrong to walk away from Layla, even if it was a Layla that I didn't completely recognise. I wanted to believe that the Layla that I once knew and fell in love with was in there, and that she was broken, remorseful, and maybe even a bit homesick. Maybe in time I'd see her emerge again, but maybe not. Maybe I wouldn't ever see her again at all.

I glanced back down at the band on my right ring finger and sighed.

"Hey, Christo," Troy called.

I rolled my eyes. "It's Christian."

"Yeah." He nodded. "Don't you have to be somewhere, like, reading something? I think you're actually, like, working overtime."

I lifted my other wrist to check my watch. He was right. I had a late tutorial that started in half an hour. My shift had actually finished an hour ago, but I was too thrown by Layla's sudden reappearance that I'd forgotten all reason. Sounds about right. It figures that I hadn't been late anywhere in all my life, but then pushed it twice in one day. Of course, it had to be today.

I hastened back into the crew room, grabbed my uni bag, and then powerwalked back towards the exit.

"Later then, Troy," I called. "Can you let the floor manager know that I left?"

"I think she thought you already had."

I huffed. Typical city folk.

I headed out of the store and ran down to the bus shelter. My bus was just pulling up as I arrived. It was totally unlike South Coast public transport to be on time, but I was running a bit late so it was a stroke of luck that it was so unreliable. I had to admit, I really missed the ease of being able to walk everywhere the way you could in Almanbury. I never thought I'd miss something like that, but it's funny what becomes normal to you when you gave it enough time.

I barely listened all through the hour-long tutorial, and my tutor was eyeing me curiously the whole time. I was usually pretty forthcoming in my readings of the texts. It was all part of the university experience after all.

I dragged my feet back to the bus stop after class to catch it back to my rental, which was just outside of the city. It was late, but I expected it to be. In fact, I didn't expect anything else from the day.

As I got off at my stop, I felt my phone vibrate in my pocket. I didn't know who would be texting me on a Friday night since Henry and Dad usually just called me. Stuart and Wayne were pretty silent on Friday nights since they had their own version of after work drinks, which only sometimes involved drunk-dialling me at obscene hours. But, it was far too early for a call from them.

I didn't recognise who the text was from, but it turned out that it was from Maddie. I'd forgotten that I'd given her my number.

"*Hey, Christian! Just wondering if you were free to maybe have dinner tomorrow night? Maddie x*"

I frowned at my phone. Crap. "*Hi, Maddie. I think I may have plans tomorrow. Can I let you know? Christian.*"

Okay, so it was a stretch of the truth, but tomorrow was supposed to be my weekend when I drove home to Almanbury. I'd already considered deferring the trip when I was given two more essays during the week, and in light of today's events, deferring was probably my best option. I still wasn't sure what I was going to tell people, especially Henry and Pattie. I still didn't really know anything myself.

I rounded the corner to my block of apartments, and my phone lit up again. I walked across the front pavement and into the spiral stairs as I read her reply.

"*Sure, no worries. If tomorrow doesn't suit, then it looks like I'm free all weekend. Layla is abandoning me to go down to Almanbury. Let me know if/when you're free to catch up. Mads x*"

I nearly tripped up the stairs. Layla was going to Almanbury? About time. Only four years late.

It definitely would not be a good idea for me to be down there at the same time. She needed to sort out her own mess without me getting in the way. Besides, at this rate, it sounded like I'd get my time with her in due course.

I backed up against the wall to allow people to pass me as they headed down the stairwell. I stared at the screen and deliberated on how best to proceed. Maddie was a nice girl, and it was evident that she was interested in me. I was no way near together enough to even contemplate dating her, even if she wasn't Layla's friend. But, I couldn't deny that I was curious about how Layla was doing. I could just agree to hang out with her and be upfront about things. Maybe even tell her that I'd just come out of a relationship and I wasn't ready to rush into anything. It was the truth, even if that relationship had dissolved four years ago. But, to be fair, Layla had never really properly ended things.

I exhaled and began typing.

"What about Sunday? Crescent has a Sunday session that I've been meaning to check out. C."

Clubs were good. They were crowded, and they were more impersonal when it came to hanging out with someone that you weren't really interested in dating.

"Sounds amazing! Let me know what time and I'll be there with bells on. Mads x"

I dropped my phone back into my pocket and took the remaining stairs two at a time, trying not to dwell on the fact that I'd just made a sort-of date with a friend of the girl that I had a prior engagement with. Considering it meant that I was one step closer to finding out why said girl had suddenly up and left town on the eve of our wedding, and without any explanation, I couldn't muster any regrets.

Our story might have started with an ending, but I was determined, now more than ever, for to end it with a beginning.

Part Two: Layla

"Prior Engagement"

Preface
Not So Forever

Christian sat back and sighed, running his hands down my arms. His expression was conflicted, as though he wanted to say something that was wedged in his throat.

"What's the matter?" I frowned. "Did I do something wrong?"

"No, Layla," he breathed. "It's not you."

I shuffled nervously. "Then what is it?"

He moistened his lips then bit down on his lower one. I sat back against his bent knees, straightening my yellow summer dress to cover my exposed thighs.

Christian put his hands over mine.

"There's another reason why I wanted to come here today," he began, lifting a hand to tuck a piece of my short light auburn hair behind my ear with one of the daisies he'd brought me.

"So, it wasn't just to have a picnic and make out in front of a bunch of tenth-graders?" I asked, nodding over to where a small crowd of mixed gender teens broke into giggles.

Christian twisted to look at them and smiled. Small dimples dented his cheeks.

"Yes, well, apart from that," he replied.

I leant forward to rest my hands on either side of his head, forcing him onto his back. The daisy behind my ear tumbled onto his chest.

"Then why did you bring me here, Christian?" I whispered.

"Layla," he murmured.

His serious tone made me nervous so I sat back again. I could feel my forehead creasing with stress.

"What? What is it?" I sighed.

He took a steadying breath, and the silence only made me feel worse. I could feel my thumping heart shake my body and wondered if he could feel it too.

Christian moved to sit and, as I realised what he was trying to do, I tipped myself off him and sat back on my heels.

"You're breaking up with me, aren't you?" I mumbled. "This was a mercy picnic. You're buttering me up before letting me down gently."

He blinked. "No, of course not."

I relaxed only slightly. "Then what's going on?"

He leant towards the picnic basket on the corner of the red tartan blanket, and pulled out a film canister. He stared at it intently before handing it to me.

"Um, Christian, you know that I don't use film any more. I have my digital camera," I sighed.

He rolled his eyes. "Just open it smarty-pants. You're ruining the moment."

I frowned and cracked open the cylinder. A flicker of gold tumbled out onto my lap then rolled onto the blanket in front of me. I stared at the gold ring encrusted with an elegant diamond setting. It took me a moment to move, but then I picked it up.

"What is this?" I asked.

"I would have thought you'd know what a ring is," he answered with a small smile.

I breathed a weak laugh. "Yes, but what is it for?"

"It's for you."

"I get that, but why? It's not my birthday, it's not our anniversary, it's not Christmas…"

He cleared his throat. "You're not honestly going to make me say it, are you?"

My eyebrows lifted. "If you're really doing what I think you are, Christian Turner, then you are going to do it right."

He shook his head but propped himself up on his knee. His chin rested on it, and I passed him the gold ring.

"Layla Louise Thomas," he mumbled.

"Come on, you can do better than that."

"I'm asking you to marry me."

"Yes, I got that much," I answered. "So go on then."

He looked to the side uncertainly. "So, will you marry me?"

I folded my arms. "Why?"

"Uh, because I love you." He shrugged.

I mashed my lips together, and he exhaled.

"Layla, my life means nothing if I don't have you to share it with. I don't want to spend a single day without you," he sighed. "Every day, from now until forever, I want to wake up next to you and remind you just how much I love you."

"Well, that was better," I laughed, and the pool of salty tears spilt over my eyelids.

"So, are you going to give me an answer, or do you need me to go on?"

I lunged forward to kiss him, and he fell back onto the rug. He groaned then raised his hand to my cheek, guiding my lips to his before resting his forehead against mine. I caught my breath.

"Yes," I whispered.

He let out a throaty chuckle and picked up my left hand to slide the glorious piece of jewellery onto my finger. Before I had the chance to admire it, he rolled me onto my back, dropped his hand from my cheek to my hip, and pulled my body towards his. His lips enclosed on mine again, and I heard the giggling teenagers' wolf-whistle.

Christian pulled back to look at me, and his sky-blue eyes were sparkling with adoration.

"Nothing can tear us apart now," he murmured.

"They never could." I smiled, running my fingers through his short light brown hair.

I pulled his lips back down to mine, and then my hands moved down to his open black shirt and onto his smooth skin. His body flinched at my touch, and I left them to rest over the rhythmic thud of his heart and as it sped up.

I felt as though I might explode from happiness. If there was a law for being so blissfully ecstatic, then we were surely breaking it. That day we had pledged forever to each other, but little did I know that forever would soon end. Nothing lasted forever. Forever was a dream that didn't coincide with reality.

Chapter One
Ghost of Lover's Past

I woke up from the dreamlike memory reeling in sweat. My breathing was short and quick, but it was still barely able to keep up with my pounding heart. It had been five years today since the day that Christian had proposed to me. It felt like another lifetime ago now.

"Bad dream?" Madeline called from across the room.

I looked up from the desk and sat upright. The transparent sheet that was stuck to my cheek fell back down in front of me.

"How long was I asleep for?" I asked, trying to regulate my heart again.

"Not long." She shrugged. "Twenty minutes or so."

I nodded. So why did it feel like years? "You shouldn't have let me sleep. We've got a deadline."

"You needed it, Layla. You've been working around the clock for almost a week now."

I began ordering the papers in front of me. "Because I'm behind, Maddie. I'll sleep when all of this is over."

She glanced at her watch. "Only a couple of hours now."

"Are you serious? I need to have ordered all the shots that we're going to use for the entire magazine in a couple of hours? That's impossible."

"Calm down, Layla," she sighed. "You're forgetting that you've already done the feature articles, and the advertisements were done by marketing. The only thing you need to select is the cover image."

"Oh," I exhaled. "But the editor in chief does that. That's Ebony's job."

Maddie shrugged. "Ebony said for you to choose the best shot."

"Do you remember who Ebony said she wanted it to be?"

"Gabby Black, the actress that you photographed a couple of days ago," she replied. "You know, the year's new breakout star from South Coast."

"Right, Gabriella Black," I mumbled. "The twenty-five-year-old orphan who made it in the big time."

"She was in my brother's class at school." Maddie smiled. "Doesn't it make you sick that she's only two years older than us, and she's a millionaire?"

"You can talk, Maddie. Your father is, like, a billionaire."

She shrugged a little smugly. James Butler was a hotel tycoon. He made his first million at twenty-one. By the time Madeline was born, he could have probably built a hotel out of wads of cash. The only catch was that he was away more than he was here. Maddie was raised mostly by her two older brothers, Jake and Dean.

"Do you know where the sheet with my shots is?" I asked, doing a three-sixty spin.

Madeline grinned. "It was the one that was stuck to your face before."

I looked down at my pile and searched for the right page. When I found it, I rested it on the light table and put my magnifier over the first of the shrunken images.

Choosing a photo was hard, especially for the photographer. There was enough pressure on choosing the right frame without the image being for the cover of the magazine. It was one that had to grab people, but that didn't always mean it was the most stylistic.

When I looked at the photos, all I could see was how they could have been better. How the light screen should have been a little more left to stop the shadow forming under the model's eye, or how she should have tilted her head back slightly to open up her smile, or maybe I should have used a blue filter instead of a green one.

There were a rare few photos that photographers found flawless. They were the ones that truly captured the intended feeling without any technical faults. That wasn't too important for the cover image I chose now. Whichever shot I chose would be airbrushed in some way. It was different working for an acclaimed fashion and lifestyle magazine like *Flash* than it was just taking photos for fun. My audience expected more obvious beauty than understated beauty. It was my job to give the people what they wanted.

"I think this one," I said, pointing to the thirteenth one along. "All we'll have to do is lighten that shadow below her neck and make her skin look a little silkier. The teasers will fit around it perfectly."

"Done." She nodded. "I'll let the art department know and get them to send it off to Ebony for final approval."

"Thanks, Maddie."

"No hassle." She smiled. "Now go and make yourself a coffee. You still look dead tired."

I yawned at the reminder, covering my mouth with the back of my hand before heading down to the pokey little kitchen across from where the writers sat. I always wondered why we never got so much as a kettle for our department, whereas they got entire kitchenette. It wasn't as if photographers didn't drink as much coffee as the writers did. We did, after all, spend more time in the dark developing room.

Maddie rounded the corner into the kitchen a few minutes later. She was efficient.

"So, I was thinking about going to the city tonight to find a dress for the ball next week," she said.

I wrinkled my nose. "Do we really have to go to that thing?"

"Are you kidding? I'm the associate fashion editor. I'm practically the guest of honour. Why would we not go?"

"Oh, I don't know," I sighed. "Because it sounds like a form of cruel and unusual punishment. Who even has a ball on a Friday night?"

She rolled her crystal-blue eyes. "Okay, Miss Negative, Miss I-never-want-to-be-seen-wearing-a-puffy-dress."

"They're uncomfortable."

"Uh-ha, so it has nothing to do with the fact that you've probably never even *worn* a dress in your entire life."

I shrugged. I didn't dare tell her that I used to wear them all the time. "So what if I feel more comfortable in a pair of jeans than a stupid dress? This isn't the seventeenth century."

She chuckled. "So, do you want to come to the city with me to shop tonight or what? They might even have a nice pair of flares you can wear."

"Funny," I mumbled. "And sure, I'll come."

"Great. Do you want to go straight from work? We can get dinner or something?"

"Sounds good."

We both looked up as footsteps sounded, and Ebony appeared in the doorway. Ebony Marrone was the stunning raven-haired beauty who looked hardly old enough to be the owner of her own magazine, never mind an acclaimed novelist too. She was brilliant though, and was filled with great ideas and wisdom way beyond her years.

"How'd you go, Layla?" she asked, and her jewel-like blue eyes were bright with excitement.

"Good." I nodded. "I selected a photo, and the artists have it to tweak before sending it to you."

"Great. I hope they don't tweak it too much. Gabby is stunning as it is," she murmured, mostly to herself. "I'll tell them just to forward it to the subs to place the teasers and then we'll be in business."

"You don't want to see it before it goes to the publishers?" I frowned. "What if you don't like it?"

"I trust you, Layla. You have a great eye."

I smiled and suppressed another yawn. Her eyes narrowed at me.

"Have you slept at all this past week?" she asked.

"Sort of."

Maddie giggled. "Yeah, for twenty minutes about half an hour ago. Layla has barely made it home before midnight lately."

Ebony folded her arms, and I was half expecting a lecture about sleeping on the job.

"Layla Thomas," she said sternly. "I am hereby giving you the rest of the day off. Go, now."

"What?" I sighed. "But the edition goes to press—"

"Let me worry about that, I am the editor. You, my brilliant shutterbug, have only been the chief photographer for two weeks, and I'd like you to stay that way."

"But don't you want me to double check—?"

"No, I don't." She smiled. "I know this is your first issue in the role, and you want to make sure it's perfect but, seriously, everything that I've seen is wonderful. Just relax and take the rest of the day, okay? Come Monday, it's only going to start all over again."

I exhaled. "Good point. Thanks, Ebony."

Madeline took a deep breath. "Well, I guess I'll see you later then."

Ebony turned to her.

"Miss Butler, you can go too," she continued. "I know that you and Layla make a great team. You've both been putting in extra hours lately. Go and enjoy."

"Really?" Maddie smiled. "Oh, that's great. Layla, we can spend the *whole* day shopping for ball dresses."

"Great." I grimaced.

Ebony laughed as she picked up her mug and headed towards the door.

"Well, you girls have fun," she replied. "And I'll see you at nine o'clock Monday for the ideas workshop."

"Okay." Maddie beamed. "Thanks again, Ebony."

Ebony waved behind her as she walked.

Maddie turned on her heel towards me.

"South Coast City, here we come!"

**

It took Madeline and me less than ten minutes to get to the shopping complex from the office, and that was only because traffic was terrible. Maddie made a beeline straight to a small coffee shop for a late breakfast before we began our gruelling shopping expedition.

In South Coast City, there was one main forum, and it took up an entire block.

I didn't really go there often. In fact, I'd probably only been there a handful of times with Maddie since I moved to South Coast from Almanbury, which was a small country town south of the coastal city.

The novelty of being at the forum outshone my lack of enthusiasm for shopping for ball gowns. I didn't always dislike the idea of dressing up like a Disney princess. I suppose it just reminded me of the last gown I went shopping for – a gown that I never got to use.

"What colour dress are you going to get?" Maddie asked. She sounded far away. "I think I might get a pink one. Or maybe a gold one, what do you think?"

I blinked back into reality. "Sorry, what did you say?"

She giggled. "Lucky you didn't stay at work, Layla. I don't know how much help you would've been."

"I know. Were you saying something about pink or gold?"

"For dresses, which colour?" she asked, running her hands through her short platinum-blonde hair.

I stepped back to appraise her, and she slowed to a halt.

"Pink," I said. "It will go nicely with your olive complexion and bright blue eyes."

She clapped and continued in the direction we were headed.

We slowed at a dead end, at a bag shop, but then Maddie grabbed my hand and towed me towards a red shopfront with the word *Montage* not yet painted on. It looked as if it had just popped up, all concrete flooring and industrial lighting. It seemed a little out of place next to all the glass and gloss of the other shops.

The exterior was deceiving because, inside it unfolded into an extraordinarily large warehouse, which was filled with every brand and designer I could think of.

Maddie's eyes glowed as she assessed the couture. I felt my girlish tendencies creeping back to me as I followed her gaze.

"Lucky we've got all day, right?" she sighed.

"This place is absolutely huge," I mumbled.

She grinned mischievously and tugged on my arm, leading me down the long aisle.

We only got halfway down the length of the shop when she turned sharply.

"Oh my gosh! Ambrosia White, I *love* her," she gushed, running over to the wall dedicated to the designer. "Did I tell you that my cousin Anna works for her?"

"Once or twice." I smiled. "I might go and look over there."

Maddie was in her own world, gazing up at the couture-like it was some kind of religious monument. I had only walked a few meters when I bumped into a rack of clothing. They seemed to be everywhere. Surely it was a fire hazard.

"Layla," Maddie gasped. "I found a dress for you."

She tugged me back into the aisle and stopped me in front of an incredibly intricate looking gown. I felt my forehead crease.

"Maddie, I'm not wearing a white dress," I said. "It's just not going to happen."

"Oh, come on, Layla," she groaned. "At least try it on, *please*."

"If you like it so much then why don't you try it on?"

She frowned. "They don't have my size."

I looked at her, and she pouted like a puppy, then picked up the hanger and began waving it around.

I rolled my eyes. "Fine, give it to me. But I'm only trying it on."

She clapped. "Thank you."

The change rooms were adjacent to the Ambrosia White collection, so, in next to no time, I had yanked off my pinstriped slacks and navy blue shirt, and replaced it with the silky white gown. It made me nervous to be in a dress again, especially a white one. The last time I wore a white dress…

I pushed open the change room door and stepped out, and then lifted up my below-shoulder light-auburn hair to show the intricately beaded neckline.

"Oh my gosh, Layla! That looks *incredible* on you," Madeline gasped.

I took a deep breath and turned to face the mirror. I could barely hold my gaze because the déjà vu was overwhelming. I looked back in search of Maddie, but she'd disappeared.

"Madeline?" I called. "Maddie, where'd you go?"

I couldn't see her anywhere, not even gazing at the Ambrosia White collection. I took hesitant steps to search the aisles, and then decided just to change back into my regular clothes. I'd only taken one step back towards the change rooms when I bumped into someone, and the black fabric they'd been carrying tumbled to the floor between us.

"Sorry," we both murmured at once.

I lowered to help pick it up.

"It was my fault," I said.

"No, I wasn't watching… Layla?"

My heart stopped at the voice, and my eyes lifted to find his face.

It couldn't be. How could it be?

Christian Turner.

"Christian," I breathed. I felt numb. "What are you…? I mean, hi."

He looked almost the same as he always had except his usually short brown hair was now shoulder-length and tucked neatly behind his pierced upper ear. He took the clothes out of my arms and straightened, offering me a hand to help me stand. I took it without thinking. His expression was a mixture of confusion and pain as he assessed me in the white gown. I glanced down at it and mentally cursed Maddie's selection, and when I looked back at him, I saw that he'd composed his features. His usually clear blue eyes were guarded as he stared at me, as if re-familiarising himself with the plains of my face.

"You grew your hair," he said.

My fingers reached up to feel for it. "You too."

He lifted his head slightly. "So, South Coast? That's where you ended up."

I sighed. How could I begin to explain to my ex-fiancé why I'd suddenly left without an explanation? I had to try at least. "Christian, I—"

"Layla, I think I found one," Maddie said, and I looked over my shoulder as she appeared.

"Apparently, you did too." She grinned. "Hey, I'm Madeline. I mean, Maddie, call me Maddie."

"Christian," he answered. "It's nice to meet you."

Maddie was glancing at me from the corner of her eye. I had no idea what my face looked like, but I felt wide-eyed and pale, as if I'd just seen a ghost. In a way, I had. Christian Turner was *the last* person I had ever expected to find in a clothing store, in a shopping centre, in South Coast City.

What was he even doing here? Why wasn't he in Almanbury?

Christian cleared his throat.

"Well, I need to put these away," he said, answering one of my questions as he gestured towards the clothes he held.

I blinked. "You work here?"

He nodded, pointing to the badge pinned to the sea-green polo he wore. "It's not ideal, but I needed a job. It pays the bills."

"You mean, you live in South Coast now?"

Maddie laughed. "Why wouldn't he? He works here."

I forced a smile and was glad that she hadn't seemed to cotton on that we'd known each other for more than a few minutes.

"I use to live down south in Almanbury," Christian replied. "Layla and I—"

"Went to school together," I sighed. "But, gosh, it's been years, hasn't it?"

Christian frowned at me but managed to compose it before Maddie turned back to him. Her eyelashes batted.

"No kidding?" She smiled. "Layla never said that she was from down south. Or that she went to school with such a hottie."

Christian looked down. "I guess she didn't think it was important."

I opened my mouth to deny it but then thought better of it. My mouth snapped closed, and Christian mashed his lips together.

"Well, it was nice to meet you, Maddie," he said politely. He paused and then nodded at me. "Layla."

"Lovely to meet you, Christian," Madeline answered, waving enthusiastically as he left without another glance.

My body felt frozen in place. I fought back the tears that threatened to give me away, but Maddie didn't notice. She was too busy ranting on about how attractive Christian was as she led me over to the dress she had found to wear to the ball. She held up the French-rose coloured gown, and I blinked back into the now.

"It's perfect isn't it?" she sighed.

I willed myself to react and managed a nod.

"I'm going to try this on," she said. "Are you going to get that one?"

I looked down at the white dress. "No, I… I'm, I need to get changed."

"But it looks great on you."

I shook my head and paced quickly towards the change rooms. I could hear Maddie following me but didn't slow. I managed to keep my composure until the door was closed, and then felt my façade crumble. My back leant against the door for support, and then I sank to the floor in the white gown.

I started sobbing and pressed my hands to my face to suppress the sound. I knew that I'd need to see Christian again eventually. But, after four years apart, I didn't think I'd see him for the first time again wearing a wedding-type dress that closely resembled the one that I'd left behind – the one that he'd never had the chance seen me in.

The irony was not lost with me.

Chapter Two
Worlds Collide

When I'd finally pulled myself together and changed back into my regular clothes, I left my cubicle to find that Maddie was no longer in the change rooms. After I'd hooked the white gown onto the return rack, I began searching for her again.

I was dreading to find her buried under a mountain of dresses for me to try on, but I would have gladly taken that when I saw her talking to Christian instead. My past was apparently coming back to haunt me, and my present self couldn't do a thing about it. I forced my legs to carry me forward even if I would have willingly gone running in the other direction.

Christian looked up as I advanced but took no notice of me. He was clearly expecting to see me again so managed not to react. When I was close enough to Maddie, I poked her in the arm.

"How'd you go with that one?" I asked her quietly. I made a conscious effort to keep my voice low to hide the quiver in it. I was still a little emotional. Maybe it was due to the lack of sleep, but maybe it wasn't.

Madeline smiled. "It's great. I'm going to get it, but I might just try on some more just for the fun of it."

I attempted to smile. "Okay then, shall we?"

Christian pressed his lips into a line, and Maddie giggled.

"Well, you've changed your tune," she said. "Christian and I were just getting to know each other better."

I cleared my throat. "I can see that."

"Maddie was just telling me that you guys work at *Flash Magazine*," Christian answered. "That's a big achievement."

I nodded slowly. "Yes, it is."

"And Christian is studying literature on scholarship at South Coast Uni," Maddie said.

"Scholarship?" I wasn't that surprised. Christian had always loved reading and was a very talented writer. "Wow, congratulations."

He nodded, and there was a short, uncomfortable pause in the conversation. Maddie looked between us silently.

"Well, we should stop distracting Christian while he's trying to work," I sighed. "Besides, I still need to find a dress."

"Right," she said slowly, curiously.

"What's the occasion?" Christian asked. He didn't sound interested, in fact, his tone was rather detached.

"Work ball," Maddie replied. "It's the magazine's fifth anniversary."

"Fifth?" Christian repeated. His gaze flickered to me for such a brief second that I wondered if I'd imagined it.

"Fifth." Maddie nodded.

There was another awkward silence, and I wondered if Christian was trying as hard as I was to avoid thinking back to where we were five years ago – newly engaged and tangled up in each other.

Christian cleared his throat. "Well, if you look in the back right-hand corner, you might find something there that you like."

I wasn't sure if he was talking just to me or to both of us. I could only assume that since Maddie held the dark-pink gown in her arms that he meant the tip for me.

"Thank, um, thank you," I stuttered.

He nodded and turned to head towards one of the payment counters situated around the large stockroom.

"Gosh, I think I'm in love," Maddie sighed.

I tensed. "What?"

"With this shop." She laughed, studying my features. "Layla, are you okay? You look kind of pale."

"I guess I'm just tired."

She looked as though she didn't quite believe me but nodded weakly.

I exhaled. "Let's just find a stupid dress so we can leave here, okay?"

"Now there's the Layla we all know and love."

**

The back right-hand corner of the store where Christian suggested that we look was incredible. Maddie and I ended up spending almost an hour looking through the different dresses that were the last of their kind. There were lots that I liked, but I couldn't commit to a decision. In the end, I had cut it down to three: a tight-fitting strapless black gown, a long gold lacy halter-neck gown, and a midnight blue one-shoulder dress with a split to the thigh.

I tried them on one after the other, but I still liked them all evenly. If my bank account could handle buying all of them, I might have. But, even then, I rarely had the occasion to wear them. I flattened the midnight blue dress that I had on.

"I don't know, Layla, they all look good," Madeline groaned. "You look good in everything."

"Come on, Maddie, you're a fashion editor, give me useful criticism," I sighed. "What about colours? Which one do you think goes better?"

Her blue eyes rolled. "Everything goes with your incredible golden skin tone. I really don't know!"

I pouted.

"I'm getting kind of bored though," she added. "So please make a decision."

I turned back to the mirror and saw Christian appear in it behind me.

"Pick the gold lace one," he said. "It brings out your eyes."

I nearly burst into tears again but managed to compose myself. Madeline, on the other hand, beamed a smile.

Christian pulled his lips into a half smile, an adorable dimple forming in his cheek. He nodded once and pushed off the wall before pacing away. I cleared my throat and looked to Maddie whose eyebrows had almost climbed to her hairline.

"Well?" she prompted.

A tiny and stubborn part of me wanted to reject his help because I knew that I didn't deserve it. The more substantial part of me still remembered how my heart always stopped when he looked at me the way he just had.

"I… agree," I said slowly. "I think the lace one is the one."

Madeline smiled and waited as I changed back into my work clothes. We both headed to pay for our dresses before finally getting some lunch in the food court. I didn't realise how hungry I was, or maybe the guilt of seeing Christian again was still eating me up.

We didn't see him on the way out of *Montage*, but I was glad for it. I knew that I'd already seen too much of him today, and I'd pay for it later. Even before today, his face haunted my thoughts whenever I closed my eyes.

Madeline threw a piece of tomato at me that had fallen out of her focaccia.

"Layla!" she sang.

I blinked. "Madeline."

"Layla."

"What did you say?"

"So, you and Christian." She smiled. "Were you two ever a couple?"

I kept my face even, but my insides were on fire. I'd never spoken about my past because I'd never had the inclination to. It wasn't something that I was proud of, so I didn't want to talk about it.

I swallowed. "Why do you ask?"

"You just seemed a little tense around each other, that's all." She shrugged. "I wasn't sure whether it was because something happened between you two."

"It's been a few years since we saw each other," I sighed. I wasn't sure if it was any kind of reason for our weirdness, but she didn't question it.

"So, if I was to say, have dinner with him, would you be okay with that?"

My eyebrows lifted. "Did he ask you out?"

"I can tell him no if it will be too weird for you."

"No, don't be silly."

The words only just came out, and I took a bite of my roll to mask the sound of strangulation that threatened to surface. It was a bad idea. I could barely swallow the bite due to the emotion bubbling in my throat.

"Are you sure, Layla?" she asked. It didn't sound much like a question. She sounded excited.

I just nodded.

Madeline bounced in her seat as we finished lunch in silence, or at least I was silent while she mused between mouthfuls about what jewellery and shoes would go with her dress.

After lunch, we decided to leave since we'd been out for most of the day. It was a great effort for me. I hadn't spent this much time at a shopping complex since I was fourteen in Almanbury, surrounded by a group of friends.

When we reached the door, I stopped.

"Maddie, can I meet you at home?" I said. "I just, I forgot something."

"It's okay. I can wait." She shrugged. "After all, we did come in the same car."

Since Madeline and I worked together, we saved on petrol and pollution by carpooling. It worked fine so long as we both went to and from work at the same time. The fact that we were able to leave early was a first for us.

"That's okay," I replied. "I'll just take the bus home."

Maddie pulled a face. Public transport was a dirty couple of words for her having been raised in one of the wealthier suburbs.

"I can wait, Layla. It's no trouble," she answered. "I don't *need* to be home."

"Maddie, seriously," I sighed. "I'll be fine."

"Okay. Well, at least let me take your dress home for you. I'll put it in your room."

I smiled, handing her the bag. "I'll see you soon."

Maddie waved, and I waited to make sure she left, and then turned and found my way back to Christian. I suppose it took me long enough.

The sadness that I felt for our time apart seemed to melt as I stepped, and the anger of the prospect of him dating Maddie took over, seeping through my pores. I stormed into *Montage* and found him arranging a shelf of T-shirts to the left of the store.

"Is this some sort of game to you?" I exclaimed.

A few nearby shoppers turned to glare at me, but Christian didn't flinch. He turned slowly as if he'd expected my return.

"What are you talking about, Layla?" he sighed.

"Are you trying to hurt me or something? Is this some sort of sick payback?"

"Hurt *you*? What have *I* ever done to hurt *you*?"

"You mean, apart from dating my best friend?" I snapped.

"Oh, I'm sorry. Are we still engaged?" he said a little too casually. "Because *I* was under the impression that when you abandoned me at our rehearsal dinner and left your ring, family, and life behind that meant we'd broken up."

I exhaled. "Christian, I—"

"I don't want to hear it, Layla," he mumbled. "Really, you have no idea what I went through when you left—"

He stopped and composed himself, and then shook his head and went back to his folding.

I blinked back moisture. "Christian."

"Please just leave, Layla. It's what you do best."

I flinched again. Maybe I deserved his hostility. I knew that I did. But that didn't make it any easier to swallow. It didn't make my intentions any worse. It just further proved that my actions were not well thought-out. Again.

I turned to leave.

"And, just so you know," Christian said. I stopped but didn't look back. I couldn't look at him when his blue eyes were so flat. "Not that whoever I date is your concern any more, but it was your friend who asked *me* out. If you've got a problem with it, then I suggest you take it up with her."

I exhaled and continued towards the exit.

I was only halfway there when another sales assistant stepped out in front of me. My hands lifted to keep from slamming into him, and I rolled back on my heels. He had short brown hair that was slicked messily to the side. His lips twisted into a smile, and I sighed impatiently.

"Hello there." He smirked. I saw on his badge that his name was Troy. "Can I be of any service to you?"

My eyes rolled. "Not a chance."

"What?"

"No."

I went to step around him, but he stepped too. My shoulders dropped.

"Can you move please?" I groaned.

"I could pick out something that you'd look great in," he continued. He reached to his right to grab a red lacy bra. "Now, this would be perfect on you."

I scoffed and pushed past him towards the exit.

"You don't like red?" he called after me. "We have it in black."

I gritted my teeth and turned on my heel, ready to knock the stupid grin off Troy's dumbly attractive face. I lifted my hand and then felt someone grab me from behind, pinning my arms to my side in an unbreakable hold. I struggled against them.

"Layla, stop fighting me," Christian whispered.

I frowned. "Then let me go."

He didn't release me until he'd walked me all the way to the front door, then his muscular arms returned back to his sides.

"What were you thinking?" he growled. "You're picking fights now?"

"That guy was being a creep," I replied irritably. "He needed to have some sense knocked into him."

His brows lifted. "By you?"

"What is that supposed to mean?"

He shrugged. "You're a bit of a flake, Layla, you always have been."

"A flake? What does that even mean?"

"Just get a hold of that temper of yours," he sighed. "Man, the city has corrupted you."

I folded my arms. "I'm not corrupted. I've just grown up. It's not easy living on your own."

"Right, well, no one forced that upon you," he mumbled. "Speaking of, you should call your folks. I'm sure they'd like to know that you're still alive."

I deserved that too.

He turned to go back inside.

"Wait, Christian," I sighed. "How are you? I mean, really?"

He shook his head. "Layla, I haven't heard from you for four years, and now you care?"

"I… I always cared, I—"

"You don't just abandon someone that you care about."

"At the time, I thought it was best—"

"I don't want to know, Layla," he sighed, turning towards the store.

"Christian," I murmured. "Please."

He took a deep breath. "No, Layla. This time it's my turn to walk away."

I watched as he walked and then disappeared behind a rack of clothes. I knew that I deserved everything that he dished out. I had given him enough cause for it. I just thought that maybe he might want to listen to me so I could explain my reasoning for leaving so suddenly.

I blinked back tears, but it was futile. They spilled over, and I brushed them off my cheek before they rolled off my chin. I started heading back down the mall, only stopping when I'd reached the end. I took pause against a glass storefront to dry my eyes properly, and then looked up to see where I was.

The store that I stood against was a jewellery store named *Reflective Jewellers*. Everything in the window glistened gold and silver with splashes of gemstones to colour.

I reached the end of the window then looked up into the small shop. I didn't really want to go home yet. I didn't want to face Maddie's questions until I had collected myself.

"Can I help you, miss?" someone said.

I looked up to see a guy who didn't look much older than me standing behind the glass counter. He didn't seem to be wearing a uniform or any other form of identification tying him to the store.

"Do you work here?" I asked. My tone sounded breezy.

He tipped his head. "Yes, why else would I be back here?"

"Sorry, I guess I'm just not used to seeing a young male in a jewellery store, never mind working in one."

He smiled, running his hands through his grown out dark brown hair.

"Well, it's a family business," he said. "I just help out when people call in sick."

"That's why you don't have a badge or a uniform?"

"Is that your way of asking me my name?" He grinned. His pearly teeth were perfectly straight and seemed to glow against his tanned complexion.

I smiled and looked down. "That was my way of asking why you're not identifiable as an employee."

"Well, I'm the real deal, I promise." He chuckled, and held his hand out towards me. "I'm Jeffrey, for the record."

I nodded but didn't take his hand. "Layla."

He curled his fingers before dropping his hand back to the counter. "Is there something I can help you with, Layla? Or are you just looking?"

"Just looking. I can't really afford anything here, but it's fun to browse."

He smiled. "Just let me know if you see anything you like."

I rolled my eyes. "Will do, Jeffrey."

He chuckled, and I could feel his eyes trace my movement with every step.

I would have felt self-conscious if I wasn't lathering in so much self-pity. No matter how hard I tried, or how much sparkly jewellery caught my attention, Christian's face still haunted my thoughts. I kept comparing the man that I'd just seen to the man I'd left behind. He was mostly the same, but there was a definite difference in him. The way he carried himself was as if he had the weight of the world on his shoulders.

I didn't realise that I had wandered towards the door until Jeffrey called out to me again.

"Layla?" he said. I looked up, and he smiled. "Will I see you again sometime?"

"Maybe." I shrugged.

"Layla?"

"Yes?"

"I'd really like to see you again sometime."

I smiled weakly. "Goodbye, Jeffrey."

I left the store and headed down the passage towards the direction of the food court. Or so I thought. The shopping centre was huge and, although I considered myself to have quite a good sense of direction, I completely lost my bearings. Every shop front seemed to look the same as the next. Ten minutes had passed when I found myself back at the jewellery store. Jeffrey glanced up and chuckled, and then began speaking in a language that sounded like Italian to someone I couldn't see.

I kept walking.

"Layla," he called from behind.

He caught up to me quickly, and I turned to face him.

"So, when I said I'd like to see you again, I didn't think it would be so soon." He smirked.

I mashed my lips together. "I got a little lost."

"Bummer, I thought you just wanted to see me again too."

I scratched my head. "So, what, are you on a break or something?"

He grinned. "Why?"

"Because you're out here and not behind the counter like you probably should be."

"Right," he replied. "Then I suppose I am. What about you?"

"I'm about to head home. Well, once I find the exit in this stupid shopping centre."

He chuckled. "I'll do you a deal. You have a coffee with me, and I'll personally escort you to the exit."

"Or I could just take my chances?" I countered.

Jeffrey rested his hand on his heart. "Ouch. Come on, it's just a coffee, not a marriage proposal."

"What?"

"It's just a coffee, not a commitment."

I exhaled. "Fine, one coffee."

"Don't sound too enthusiastic."

"Sorry," I sighed. "So, which way is it?"

Jeffrey quickly led the way back to the food court. In fact, I was a little embarrassed that I'd missed it. When we got there, he veered off down another corridor towards a coffee shop with an Italian name. We found a table, and he went up to order. I checked my watch and hoped that Maddie didn't think

194

I'd been kidnapped given my reluctance to come here in the first place.

"So, what do you do, Layla?" he asked as the barista put our coffees down in front of us. He picked his up and took a sip. "I mean, apart from hanging out in jewellery stores accusing staff members of not being real employees."

I huffed. "Actually, I'm the chief photographer for *Flash Magazine*."

"No kidding?"

"Why? Don't you believe me?"

"No, I do." He laughed. "That's quite impressive though, how'd you score that gig?"

"Hard work and determination, I suppose."

He smiled. "You suppose? Did you have to study for that, or do you have a natural eye for it?"

"I did TAFE for a year to complete a certificate four in multimedia. It was all I could afford as far as tertiary study went, but I've always had an interest in photography. Most people, professionals, prefer credentials over raw ability."

"And *Flash*?"

"Right place, right time, I guess." I shrugged. "I met the editor in chief, Ebony Marrone, at an art show. She had only just started the magazine and was looking to hire a freelance photographer. At the time, I was only doing portraits for a local business, but she took a chance on me and, over the years, I worked my way up."

"That's pretty amazing, Layla. Well done."

"Thanks." I nodded. "So, what do you do, Jeffrey? I mean, apart from hanging out in jewellery stores pretending to be a real employee?"

He laughed. "Well, when I'm not helping out my folks at *Reflective*, I work part-time at the South Coast Museum of History."

"Oh, cool. Doing what?"

"I sell tickets and wander around teaching people about the past."

The past. Something that I didn't like to dwell on, even if it seemed to be catching up to me now.

"So, did you have to study history to do that?" I asked.

"Probably not, but I studied history at university."

"South Coast Uni?"

"No." He smiled. "We're not all from the rich upper class. I studied at North Iris Uni."

I nodded. "I thought I was the only one without a trust fund in this place."

"Yeah, there are only two classes in South Coast, the rich and the not rich. Or as the locals refer to it: South Coast and Iris Cove."

I breathed a laugh. "Well, if you ask me, the locals have it all wrong. Iris Cove is much prettier than the city. There are some spots by the Waning River that I swear you can see all the way to Heaven."

"Spoken like a photographer." He smiled. "You're not from around here then?"

"No. I... I'm from Almanbury. I moved here four years ago."

He beamed. "A country girl?"

I sighed into my empty coffee mug as Jeffrey finished his espresso.

"So, do you live in Iris Cove?" he asked.

"East Iris with my friend Maddie," I answered. "She is one of the rich South Coast folk, but she's rebelling against her father so moved north of the river."

He laughed. "Where did you park? I'll walk you to your car."

"Maddie drove me. I'm just going to catch the bus home."

"The bus?" He blinked. "Wow, you really aren't from around here. Everyone in South Coast knows that the public transport here is crummy. Can I give you a lift?"

I pressed my lips together. "Thanks for the coffee, but I'll just catch the bus."

"Are you sure? I really don't mind, and I promise I'm not an axe murderer."

"Well, I didn't think that until just now but, honestly, I'm fine. Besides, I don't, I'm not... I mean, you seem like a nice guy, but I'm not really looking for anything—"

"Relax, Layla, it was just a coffee. I enjoy your company, so let me know if you want to do it again."

I nodded. "It was fun, actually. I'll let you know."

Jeffrey smiled as he led me out of the Italian coffee shop and pointed down a wide corridor of shops.

"See that passage? If you follow that to the end, you'll find an exit which leads right out to the bus terminal."

"Thanks," I sighed. "And thanks again for the coffee."

"Anytime." He nodded. "You know where to find me."

I waved weakly and headed down the wall to the exit and, thankfully, found my bus home easily. When I got there, Madeline threw the flyscreen door of our rental open, and it slammed against the brick wall.

"Layla! I thought you were dead!" she exclaimed.

I couldn't help but laugh. "Charming, Madeline."

"Where were you? What on earth were you doing there?"

"Sorry, I got lost and then gave up and had another coffee. I'm not that late, am I?"

"Still." She pouted. "I've been home for, like, two hours. I was worried."

"Sorry," I repeated sullenly.

She took a deep breath. "So, I was going to go shopping tomorrow—"

"Maddie, we just went," I groaned.

Her eyebrows lifted, and I mashed my lips together. Madeline hated being interrupted; it was no doubt a result of being the youngest in her family. As an only child, I never understood the sibling thing. It was only my parents and me when I was growing up, but we were a team, and Christian had become a part of that team. I thought about what he'd said about calling them and realised that he was right. I had put it off long enough. It had already been too long. They deserved better from their only child.

"For shoes," she finished. "Do you want to come, or do you have some stilettos that you've been hiding in your cupboard for the last four years?"

I bit my lip and made a decision. "Actually, I was going to take a little road trip tomorrow."

I walked past her into the house, and Maddie followed me in.

"Awesome, anywhere with decent shops?" she asked.

"No," I sighed. "To Almanbury to see my parents."

Maddie frowned. "Is that wise? You haven't seen them or even spoken to them for as long as I've known you."

"I know but, after seeing Christian, I realised that I owe some people an explanation. I can't keep running. My past will catch up with me. It has already started to."

She laughed. "You make it sound so sinister."

198

"It's been four years, Maddie. I'm their only child, and I've neglected them for four years. I don't think they're going to welcome me back with open arms after that, and I don't blame them."

"You'd be surprised what parents would do for their kids though. They love them regardless of what they do."

I sighed. "But is it fair to test that love?"

She shrugged. "You were only doing what was best."

"For me," I breathed.

And for Christian. Or so I thought.

Chapter Three
The Land That Time Did Not Forget

On Saturday morning, I pulled up by the curb of my old house in Almanbury almost five hours after leaving. It looked smaller than I remembered, but I guess childhood homes generally do. My fingers strummed restlessly on my steering wheel, and I looked towards the wooden front door. I had spent the entire drive running over everything in my head that I would say to my mum and dad but, now that I was here, I could barely remember my own name. My forehead rested on the wheel, and I took a few deep breaths.

"Layla?" a voice said. I would have recognised the voice anywhere.

I looked up to see my mother as she peered in the far window. I swallowed and pushed the door of my Volkswagen Beetle open, and then stumbled to my feet.

"Hi, Mum," I sighed. "How are you?"

She blinked before quickly moving around the car to pull me into a back-breaking hug.

"Honey," she whispered. "Oh, Layla, you came home. I knew that you would find your way back eventually."

"I'm so sorry, Mum," I breathed. "I'm so sorry that I didn't come back sooner."

She pulled back to look at me and ran her thumbs over my cheeks.

"You're here now," she said. "Your father will be so happy to see you."

"Where is he? Is he inside?"

"He's just gone to get milk. He should be back anytime now."

I nodded, and she took my arm, leading me across the small front yard.

When we got to the front door, she ushered me inside. It looked like an entirely new house despite the unchanged outside. The once-white walls were now coloured in earthy tones.

"You guys painted," I said. "It looks great."

"We thought it could do with some colour," she replied. "It took ages, mind you. You know how your father gets with putting things off. It was lucky that we had Christian to—"

She stopped and turned at the mouth of the kitchen as I slid up to sit at the breakfast bar. Hearing his name was hard enough without hearing my mother saying with such reverence. It shouldn't have surprised me that he'd stayed close with my parents after I'd left. It was comforting, but still made me sad. It shouldn't have come to that, him supporting them without me. It shouldn't have, but it did.

"It's okay, Mum, you can say his name. I won't burst into flames," I said.

She bit her lip. "He moved away you know. He got a scholarship and moved to that city where you went."

"I know." I nodded. "I saw him yesterday."

I had called my mother from South Coast the morning after I'd left. We had always been quite close, so I felt like I at least owed it to her to let her know that I was alive. I'd told her where I went and sworn her to secrecy. It was because of that, I think, that no one came looking for me. She'd kept the promise.

I hadn't kept in contact with her since that call though. I knew that it would make things harder for her if she had to keep more secrets.

"You saw him?" she asked, her voice jumping a few octaves. I glanced up to see that her eyebrows had done the same.

"Yes, I… he wouldn't even let me explain—"

I heard the front door close and looked towards the hallway.

"Pattie," my dad's voice called. "There's a Volkswagen outside that looks exactly like the one that belonged to—" He stopped when he saw me. "—Layla."

"Hi, Daddy," I breathed.

My dad, Henry Thomas, lifted his eyebrows and then frowned. A shadow darkened his honey brown eyes that were the same shade as mine.

"So, it is you," he mumbled.

I shrugged. "I thought I'd come and say hi."

"And the phone didn't work?"

He walked past me into the small kitchen to put the milk on the counter.

I sighed. "I'm sorry I haven't called—"

"Called?" he scoffed. "Layla, the last I saw or heard from you was when you were preparing to get married. And then you disappear, and we don't hear from you for years. Now you just waltz in, expecting, what? A welcome home parade?"

I frowned. "I wouldn't really call it waltzing."

"Where have you been? Why did you go? And do you even know what that little Houdini act did to that fellow of yours?"

I looked down, a pucker pinching between my eyebrows as they pulled together. "I'm sorry, Dad."

"You should be, kid. I thought we raised you better than that. After everything… the preparations, the planning, the money spent—"

202

"I'll pay you back the money." I frowned, brushing the tear that had spilled onto my cheek.

"It's not about the money, Layla," he snapped. "You didn't only leave him and us, you know, you left everyone… a whole life behind without so much as an explanation."

"Henry," my mum sighed.

"No, Patricia, she needs to hear this," he said. "Have you taken responsibility for what you did? Where you were? Why you left? Well, have you? Your note didn't exactly explain much. *I'm sorry. I can't stay. I love you, please don't hate me.*"

I cringed at the memory of the words in tear-stained ink.

"You don't understand," I sniffled.

"Damn right I don't, so help me to," he answered.

I rubbed my forehead. "I had to leave. It was the right thing for everyone. If I stayed, I think I might have stuffed up everyone's life, especially Christian's."

"What does that mean?"

"I loved Christian, and I honestly wanted to marry him. But if I stayed, this is where we would have ended up."

My dad's frown-lines deepened. "That makes absolutely no sense at all."

"It's the only way I can explain it."

Dad folded his arms. "You could've just called off the wedding and faced the music before you left him to face it alone. That would have been the less cowardly, too."

"Henry!" Mum shrieked.

Dad shrugged lightly. "True, isn't it?"

"Maybe, but it wouldn't have changed anything," I whispered.

"So, where did you go?" he asked.

"North, to South Coast. I went to TAFE and got myself a job. I work for a magazine now as the chief photographer. It's great."

"South Coast?" my dad repeated, seeming to miss the other gold nuggets of information I'd shared. "That's where Christian went."

"I know. I bumped into him yesterday."

Dad huffed. "So, that's why you came back."

"What?"

"You were waiting for him to leave, so the coast was clear."

"No, Dad," I sighed. "That's not it at all. If anything, seeing him made me realise how gutless I've been. I came back to make things right and apologise for everything that I put everyone through."

"Did you do the same to him?"

"I tried to, but he doesn't want to hear what I had to say," I whispered. I blinked back tears, but they fell anyway. I looked back to my father and watched the anger and disappointment melt from his expression as he looked over my face.

"I've missed you, kiddo," he mumbled. "I wish you'd have just stayed."

I cried. "I'm sorry, Daddy. I missed you so much."

I stepped over and threw my arms around him. He hugged me back, squeezing me even tighter than what my mother had. Neither of us made any attempt to move, and a couple of minutes must have passed before we parted.

"So, how long are you back for?" he asked, and he managed to look hopeful.

"The night if you'll have me." I sniffled. "I don't really want to drive back today."

"That sounds reasonable. I think we can find somewhere for you."

I rubbed my eyes. "Do you mind if I go and freshen up? It's been a long drive."

"Go ahead." Mum smiled. "I'll put the kettle on."

"I'll be right back."

"You'd better be," Dad taunted.

I breathed a humourless laugh and continued toward the bathroom.

The bathroom had been renovated too. The beige tiles were now white and reached the ceiling. I didn't know what I expected when I'd left, maybe for time to stop because it had in my memory but, instead, everything had changed.

I splashed water on my face and ran my wet hands through my tangled auburn hair. I wished I'd taken more care in making myself presentable this morning before I left South Coast. My appearance right now didn't exactly scream independent. I looked a little haggard and stale, and my eyes were puffy and lacking the normal honey-warmth that they once had. If I was honest, they hadn't been that way since the last time I was here.

I mashed a charcoal coloured hand-towel into my face to dry it as the kettle clicked off from boiling. I took a deep breath and hung the towel back up before heading back into the hallway.

My footsteps faltered as I looked down towards the white door where I used to spend most of my time. My old bedroom – I wondered if it had changed as much as the rest of the house. Maybe it was a study now, or perhaps a weight room? Or maybe my mother had turned it into a sewing room, or a room for her ceramics, or a guest room? My parents had always joked about what they'd do with it when Christian and I were making plans to get our own place. I was almost too afraid to look and see if they'd really moved on. I stepped slowly towards it and rested my hand on the gold handle. My eyes closed as I pushed the door open and the hinges squeaked. I took a breath and let it out, then opened my eyes and stood frozen as I appraised the room.

I felt like I had transported back in time.

It hadn't changed at all. Nothing, not one single detail had changed from how I'd left it. The gold dress that I was planning to wear to the rehearsal dinner was still laid out on my bed. The shoes that I was going to wear were buckled in the corner. My curling wand was still on the floorboards where I'd left it, and the pieces of scrap paper and pens were still scattered across my desk. My cupboard door was cracked open from when I hastened to pack. The third drawer of my vanity was not properly closed.

It was as if my last moments had been photographed, and I was walking around in the picture. I wondered why they'd kept it this way, like a crime scene that needed to be appraised for answers. Maybe that's what they wanted – reasons, explanations, evidence, anything they might have missed to explain why I'd left.

They wouldn't find it here.

"He wouldn't let us change it," Dad said quietly from behind me.

I turned to look at him as he leant against my doorframe. After a moment, he stepped in and looked around.

"Christian wouldn't let us move anything," he continued. "He always thought that you'd be back and you'd want everything as you left it. He knew how you valued your space."

"It sounds like he spent a lot of time with you after I left," I murmured. I had intended to speak at a normal volume, but the emotion in my throat wouldn't permit it.

Dad nodded and rubbed his hand through his short light brown hair. "That kid spent almost every day in this house, in this room, just sitting beside your bed waiting for you to come home. It was heartbreaking, Layla."

I frowned deeper, feeling a pinch of emotion at the back of my eyes. My dad continued regardless, rubbing reality in.

"He was here so darned much that we had to put him to work just to keep him from moping around," he said. "It helped him for a while but, as soon as we were done, the moping started all over again. The worst part was that we couldn't comfort him because we couldn't understand ourselves just what would drive you to leave."

"I'm sorry, Dad. I really am," I sighed. "I don't know what else to say. I can't change what I did, but I really do regret hurting so many people. I honestly thought that I was doing the right thing at the time."

I frowned again becuase I couldn't think now why I thought it would be better to run. Maybe I thought that Christian would be able to move on. I mean, I had never moved on but...

"Anyway." Dad shrugged. "Christian began writing and ended up finishing a short story or novella thing, whatever it's called. He wouldn't let anyone read it, but Nancy found it and sent it to the dean of that university in South Coast. They offered him a scholarship there, I guess, but he kept deferring it, well, until the beginning of this year that is."

I tipped my head. "What made him change his mind?"

"Not sure, love, he didn't say much about it. Just did the rounds one day telling everyone he was heading to the big smoke. We all thought it was real good. It seemed like he was finally moving on."

I brushed my nose with the back of my hand. "I really hurt him, didn't I?"

"You sure did, kiddo."

"I thought it was right, but I never wanted to hurt him. I didn't think it would stop him from living his life, but hurting him and stopping him from moving on sounds like all I did."

"He was in love with you, Layla, did you really expect any less?"

For some reason, that sentiment warmed me and chilled me at the same time. I'd known that we had a love that was bigger than both of us, but I didn't think of what that would mean when we were apart.

"No," I replied belatedly. "I guess not."

"Did you move on?" he asked.

I frowned. "No, how could I? Christian was my entire life. I never wanted anyone else. I never would."

"So, why did you leave then? That's what makes no sense. You spent months trying to convince your mother and me, Nancy and Mitch, that you and he were getting married no matter what, and then you left the night before the wedding. If you fell out of love with Christian, then that's something we'd all understand, but you're as in love with him now as the day you left."

I nodded.

"Then, kiddo, how was that not enough to make you stay?" he sighed. "Explain it to me."

"At the time, I thought it would benefit him more if I left."

"I don't know what that means, Layla, but I think you're wrong," he answered and then sighed again. "Well, anyway, your mother mentioned something about going out for dinner as a family tonight. Are you interested?"

"That sounds great, but I don't think it would be very wise, Dad."

He seemed genuinely confused. "Why not?"

"Because the whole town must hate me," I replied. "And what if we bumped into Mitch and Nancy Turner? No doubt they have a voodoo doll of me after what I did to their son."

"You mean just Mitch," he said, and his eyebrows pulled together solemnly. "Nancy died about a year and a half ago."

"No," I breathed. The tears came almost instantaneously, and I felt as if I'd been kneed in the gut. Christian's mother had been like a second mum to me. She'd never had a daughter, and I was more than happy to be her surrogate. "How did she die?"

"Cancer." Dad frowned. "It shocked us all."

I sank onto the floor. My legs didn't feel strong enough to hold me up any more.

"Why didn't anyone try to find me?" I asked. "Didn't you think I'd want to know?"

"We didn't know where to start, Layla."

I exhaled as a new sheet of tears cascaded from my eyelids. His mother had died through the fault of no one, while I had just up and left on my own accord. One loss was a cruel twist of fate, but one was a choice. I was selfish.

"I wish I could have been here," I sobbed. "God, poor Christian."

"These past few years haven't been kind to him, that's for sure."

I buried my head in my hands, and I felt my dad's hand rest on my head.

"I should have been here." I sniffled. "I should have known. How could I think that everything would stay the same when I left? God, I'm so selfish."

Dad sighed but didn't reply. I knew him well enough to know that it was his way of agreeing with me without using words. My dad had always been honest with me, even if it hurt my feelings. It was a trait that I appreciated, even if sometimes I didn't want to hear it.

My mother was different, honest, but more tactful, and a lot more optimistic. She wouldn't lie necessarily, but she would always offer the bright side of a situation.

"Come on, your mother's made tea," Dad murmured. "I know you're upset, Layla, but you made your decisions, and now you have to make do with the consequences."

I looked up through glassy eyes. "Are you trying to make me feel better? Because it's not working."

"I'm just telling you what you already know, kiddo."

"I know. I just wish—"

"What's done is done, Layla. No use torturing yourself with things you can't change."

My dad offered me his hand, and I took it and stood beside him.

"Hey, Dad?" I asked.

"Layla?"

"Thanks for being so… you."

He looked to the side. "Anytime."

I nodded, and he turned to lead the way back.

"Oh, and, Dad?" I said. "Can you tell Mum that I'm just going to pop out for a bit? I think I'm going to go to the cemetery."

He mashed his lips together. "Layla, I—"

"Better late than never." I shrugged.

He frowned but nodded. "Don't be too long."

"Promise," I breathed. "Thanks, Dad."

**

I walked to the cemetery since it wasn't far. Nothing in Almanbury was. Plus, I thought if I left my keys with my parents, then they'd know for sure that I'd be back. The day had taken a cold turn in the southern town. After spending so much time in sunny South Coast, it seemed bizarre for early spring day to be so cold. I felt like I was getting all the seasons in one day today.

When I arrived at the cemetery, an involuntary shiver wiggled its way down my spine. I'd never been particularly squeamish around graves, but I never had voluntarily wanted to go to one. Knowing that I was going to visit someone that shouldn't be there seemed to make it worse. My dad had tried to explain where Nancy Turner's gravestone was and, after I'd located the maple tree, it was quite easy to find. The headstone was understated, but beautiful, and chiselled into the pale marble was elegant script of how she was a beloved wife and mother. I'd brought some yellow carnations from a deli on the way and rested them beside the several bunches of pink roses. The site was otherwise pretty grey.

"I'm so sorry, Nancy," I whispered. "You were like a mother to me. I... I'm so sorry."

I glanced around self-consciously, feeling a little silly about talking to a pile of sand and stone. Then I realised that I didn't care because my apology was long overdue. I moved my hands over the cold marble and let the tears fall.

"I can't imagine how it must've been for you after I left, with Christian spending so much time with my parents, and then you finding out about your illness. It must've been so hard for you and Mr Turner." I sniffled and wiped my eyes, but it was a little futile. "God, you two must hate me so much for what I put Christian through. But, you need to know that I never wanted to hurt him. I just wanted him to be able to share

211

his greatness with the world before he settled. He got into uni on scholarship, but I guess you already knew that. I saw him recently, and it broke my heart to see him looking so sad. I am so sorry that I played a part in that. I still love him so much. I don't like to think about it too often because it hurts, but I just hope that I haven't damaged him to the extent that he can't find happiness with someone who deserves him. He has so much to offer. You did such a great job with him. You and Mr Turner should be so proud of the man that he's become."

"We are," a voice rang from behind me.

I jumped and then lost my balance from my crouch and toppled into the dirt. I scrambled to my feet and found Mitch Turner towering over me.

"Oh," I sighed. "I'm sorry. I didn't see you there."

"I know." He nodded. I noticed that he held another bunch of pink roses in his hand.

"So, exactly how long have you been standing there?"

"Since you started talking about Christian's greatness."

He stepped forward to lay the flowers beside mine. "You were right about that, and about Nancy... she was a great mother to him," he said.

I mashed my lips together to stop myself from crying but was unsuccessful. "Am I right about anything else?"

Mitch straightened, and his eyebrows pulled together. "Are you asking if we hated you?"

I shrugged weakly. "I wouldn't blame you if you did."

He took a steadying breath that unnerved me. "Nancy never hated you, Layla. She didn't understand you, but she could never hate you. She already thought of you as a daughter."

"I thought of her as a mother too."

He nodded, and I wrapped my arms around my chest.

"And what about you, Mr Turner?" I pressed. "Do you hate me?"

He raised his head and brushed his greying blonde hair from his eyes. "I feel a lot of things, Layla, but hate isn't one. I guess I'm just disappointed. I thought your parents raised you better than that."

My brows pulled together defensively. "Better than what?"

"Better than to run away when things got tough. I always thought that you were one to face things head on."

"It was a little more complicated than that, Mr Turner."

Mitch shrugged. "If you say so."

I took a deep breath and looked back to the grey headstone that was brightened by the roses. "I am really sorry for your loss. I wish I'd known sooner. I would have come—"

"It's probably better that you didn't," he interrupted, kneeling to pull one wilted rose out from an underneath bunch. "It was a hard time for Christian, and seeing you would have only made it worse."

His words pricked a nerve, and I realised that he was right. It would have been selfish for me to come back even to pay my respects to my almost mother-in-law. I owed Christian a lot, but it wouldn't have been the time when he was dealing with the loss of his mum. I shook my head slowly, and another tear dripped from my swollen eyes.

"I'm sorry for that, too," I whispered. "I never meant to hurt—"

"I know. I heard you before."

I pressed my lips together. "Well, I should go. I told my parents that I'd be home for dinner."

"Well, you'd better not be late or they might think you've skipped town again."

I drew in a deep breath and released it slowly.

"Right, well, goodbye, Mr Turner. It was…" I paused and wondered if 'nice' was the right word for our brief reunion.

Mitch lifted his eyes expectantly, but I didn't bother finishing my sentence. Instead, I just turned to leave.

"Layla," he called.

I looked back at him, and I didn't want to admit to myself that I was hopeful, but I was.

"You said that you saw Christian recently," he said, shuffling his weight from foot to foot.

"Yes, I did," I replied.

"He saw you too, I take it."

"Yes, why?"

He looked at the wilted rose in his hand. "I know that I have no right to ask—"

"What is it, Mr Turner?"

"Stay away from him, Layla. It took him almost four years to get on with his life after you left. It would be a shame if your reappearance stopped him from reaching that potential you spoke about."

I exhaled slowly, wondering whether it was a promise that I'd be able to keep. It wasn't me that I was worried about, and I was pretty sure that my being away from him would suit him too. I was more concerned because Maddie seemed to be besotted with him.

"I'll do my best." I nodded. It was the most I could give him with the unforeseeable circumstance.

Mitch nodded once, and his expression reminded me of Christian's the other day. "Thank you, Layla."

I lowered my eyes and headed across the field of the fallen, back in the direction of home.

**

214

My parents were waiting for me at the table when I got home, and when I saw them, I felt like crying again. Seeing Mitch was harder than I thought it would be. Not that I ever expected it to be easy.

My mum stood up. "What happened?"

"I bumped into Mitch at the cemetery," I sighed. "He's not happy with me."

"Oh, honey."

Dad pressed his lips into a line. "What did you really expect, Layla? I mean, in all honesty, if the situation was flipped, I don't imagine I'd be too thrilled with Christian either."

"I know." I shrugged. "But still."

"Mitch has been through a lot, kiddo, don't be too hard on him."

I nodded and pulled out a chair to sit beside him. Mum, who was still standing, wandered over to the kettle and flicked it on to boil.

"Would you like a cup of tea, Layla?" she asked. "I had to drink yours before since you left so quickly."

"Um, sure, thanks." I nodded. "But can you make it a coffee? I don't really drink tea."

Mum's thinly plucked eyebrows lifted. "Honestly, Layla? But you don't like coffee."

I looked towards my father who raised an eyebrow.

"Pattie," he sighed.

"Yes, I do, Mum."

"When did this happen?" she huffed. The way she was reacting was as if I had just confessed to committing a crime.

I shrugged. "Oh, ten years ago."

"Really? Huh."

215

"Coffee is more effective at keeping me alert. I acquired a taste for it."

"Acquired a taste," she muttered, taking the jar from the cupboard and reaching for a spoon. "Well, how do you take it then?"

"With one sugar, and cream if you have it. It takes the bitter edge off."

Mum turned around, and her expression was blank. "You know, for someone who has *acquired a taste* for coffee, you certainly add a lot of things to suppress the flavour."

"If it's going to be a problem, Mum, then I'll just have the tea," I sighed.

"No problem. I'm just saying," she sighed. I rolled my eyes and saw Mum smile to herself. "So, what do you think about dinner, Layla? Would you like to go out as a family?"

The kettle clicked off, and she poured the boiling water into my old mug. The aroma filled the room instantaneously. I glanced over at my dad and saw him looking between my mum and me.

"Sure." I nodded. "I mean, I've seen Mitch now so the rest of the town can't be worse than him."

Mum gave a half shrug. "We can always just get take-away from that little Chinese restaurant you like?"

"I honestly don't mind. Whatever you want," I replied.

She walked over and set my coffee in front of me. "Coffee, cream, with one sugar. Enjoy."

"Thanks, Mum."

She nodded. "And I vote for Chinese takeaway and a good movie."

"Sounds great." I nodded. "Dad?"

"Fine with me," he agreed. "I'll get the menus."

Chapter Four
Forgetting to Remember to Forget

I was about ninety-eight per cent sure that I was dreaming. Of course, watching an exact scene I had already lived through in the third person was a bit of a giveaway, but that didn't deter from the fact that it seemed so real. I felt as though I'd been gagged and bound, watching as an unwilling witness to the exact time when everything changed, when everything went wrong...

"Now, there's your dress, Layla. I'll hang it on your door," Mum said.

She held up the glorious golden silk cocktail dress, and I turned around from my glossy white dressing table, still in my dressing gown.

"Thanks, Mum." I smiled. My natural-looking makeup with subtle golden tones made my bright honey brown eyes sparkle in the afternoon sun that was streaming through my window.

"Okay, honey. I'm going to the hall to help Nancy set up, so I'll see you in a couple of hours."

"Sounds perfect."

She lowered her eyes before turning towards the door and then stopped. *"Is your father picking you up, or are you coming with Christian?"*

"Dad's went to see the minister about something, and Christian had to take care of a few last minute things," I answered. *"I'm just meeting everyone there."*

"Okay, well drive safe, and I'll see you soon."

"I will do. I'll see you soon."

My mother nodded and then stepped out, leaving me with my thoughts to get ready. I saw myself reaching for the curling wand and began twisting my shoulder length hair around the metal shaft.

Then the picture faded into another.

It was as if time had passed, like a montage in a film.

My hair was now completely curled in little light-auburn curls. I wore a golden headband and stood to dress in the gold dress that was hanging on my door. I took it off the hanger and laid it out on my bed.

My stomach turned as I watched because I knew what came next – the shrill ringing of the polyphonic mobile phone chime.

I watched myself reach towards the vanity to answer it.

No. My head screamed, but I was bound in place. I knew that not even avoiding the call would have changed my fate. It would have caught up to me eventually. Maybe when I did find out, I would have done the same thing, but no doubt it would have been harder to leave as Mrs Christian Turner.

The ringing stopped, and I held the phone up to my ear.

The crease on my forehead deepened, and I backed to sit on the bed for support.

The picture changed again.

It faded to me in a mad dash as I gathered my belongings to leave. I jammed my dressing gown in the cupboard that was left ajar. I scooped underwear from the drawer that didn't properly close. I dressed in my nearest clothes and left the gold dress on my bed. I removed the sim card from my phone and snapped it in half. I took my wallet and grabbed my car keys. I clutched at what little food I could carry – fruit, muesli bars, bread. Nothing that would sustain, but it would have to do. I ran out to my car and piled my things inside.

The only stop that I made out of town was at the Almanbury bank to withdraw as much cash as I could before heading north to South Coast. I didn't know I would stay there until I drove through the borders of the bright city a little after sunset.

The party would have been in full swing, or maybe it would be over. They would have noticed I was gone by then.

I stopped in at a gas station since it was apparently the only thing open on a Saturday night. I bought a new pre-paid sim-card and some food before finding a cheap motel in one of the more modest suburbs in South Coast called Delwyn. It was a place that I still couldn't go back to even today.

I cried myself to sleep that night, haunted by the thoughts of what I was missing in Almanbury, taunted by the darkness in my mind as I tried to sleep.

I passed out around sunrise, but it was only from exhaustion. My eyes had finally run out of tears, and my body felt dehydrated.

My restlessness made the picture change again.

Enough. I can't take much more.

This time it was an earlier memory of Christian and me. It was during our first year together. We were fifteen and huddled under a fort that we'd made with my comforter that was suspended between my bedpost, the chair from my vanity, and the windowsill. My head rested in Christian's lap as he twisted towards my skirting. In his hand was a pocketknife that his father had given him.

"*Do you think we can stay in here forever?*" I asked dreamily as I looked up at him.

Christian glanced down at me, and his incredible crystal-blue eyes glimmered in the light from my lamp, which we'd pulled under with us.

"*I think your dad will drag me out before forever comes,*" he chuckled. "*I don't think he likes me very much right now.*"

"*Sure he does. He thinks you're great. But your dad still doesn't like me.*"

"*Well, at least he doesn't come into my room every five minutes to make sure we're not doing anything inappropriate.*"

"*I'm his only child, and you're the first boy I've ever brought home,*" I whispered, shuffling around to prop myself on my knees. "*Of course he's going to be a little protective of me.*"

"*A little.*"

"*A lot.*"

Christian put the knife down and leant forward, so our noses were touching. He closed his eyes and moved his head slowly from side to side, so the tip of his nose brushed mine. Then, so softly that I hardly felt it, he pressed his lips to mine.

"*I love you,*" he breathed.

My eyes lifted, and he sat back to read my expression. It looked blank. I tried to remember how it felt.

"*You do?*" I asked.

"*Yes, is that okay?*"

I gave a burst of hysterical laughter. "*Yes, it's okay. God, Christian, I love you too.*"

He chuckled. "*Do you think we're crazy?*"

"*Probably, but does it matter?*"

"*Not to me.*"

He took me in his arms and kissed me again. His mouth was hot as it moulded against mine, like two perfect entities moving in unison. I felt my breath leave my body as laid me down on the wooden floor that was covered ineffectively by a woollen blanket.

He pulled back an inch, his breathing as heavy as mine as we both gasped for air that we couldn't seem to catch.

The palm of his hands ran from the side of my face, down my neck and abdomen to my waist. His fingertips ran lightly under the bottom of my T-shirt, and I could feel my skin tingling in the trail they left.

I bit my lower lip as his eyes caressed the plains of my face.

Someone cleared their throat, and my heart stopped.

There were two knocks on my door.

"*Layla, Christian,*" my dad's voice said. "*It's a little too quiet in there. What's going on?*"

I looked back in the general direction of his voice and was thankful that our makeshift tent covered the compromising position that our bodies were twisted into.

"*We're miming, Dad,*" I sighed. My voice was too breezy to be convincing.

"*Well, I think maybe you should stick to verbal conversation. Right, Christian?*"

"*Yes, sir,*" Christian answered. His arms were still tight around me, and he didn't make any attempt to move.

I muffled a laugh with my hand.

"*Layla, enough please,*" my dad warned. "*Behave, or I'll ban any boys from being in your room.*"

"*Sure, Dad, I promise I'll behave.*"

Christian lifted an eyebrow, and we both heard footsteps as my dad left.

"*Any boys?*" he asked. "*Are there more?*"

"*Does he count himself as a boy, do you think?*"

Christian laughed and twisted his body back towards the skirting. He picked back up the pocketknife, and I frowned.

"*What exactly are you doing to my wall?*" I said.

I noticed that there were wooden filings piled on the floor below the skirting as Christian quickly covered his artwork with his spare hand.

"*I'm carving something into it so you'll never forget it,*" he replied.

"*Do I get to see it? I mean, it is my wall.*"

"*Yes, but I want to finish it first.*"

I pouted. "*Well, how long until you finish?*"

"*Close your eyes and count to ten,*" he whispered. "*And then you can see it.*"

I smiled and squeezed my eyes shut. "*One…*"

I heard the sound of wood protesting under the sharp metal blade and laughed.

"*Two… three… four…*"

Christian breathed a laugh as he exerted force against the lower border that framed my room.

"*Five… six… seven…*"

I tried to peak through my eyelashes, but Christian must've guessed my thinking and moved his body in front to block my view.

"*Eight… nine…*"

"*Wait, wait, wait,*" he squeaked.

"*Nine and a half… nine and three quarters…*"

"*Okay,*" he sighed.

I felt one of his hands rest over my eyes.

"*Ten!*" I exclaimed, peeling his warm hand from my face.

My smile faded as I read the intricate inscription. Although it had been carved with a pocketknife, the words were in perfect script. *Christian Turner loves Layla Thomas.*

I let my breath out slowly as a smile stretched across my face.

"*My dad's going to have a fit,*" I breathed.

He shrugged. "*Totally worth it.*"

He leant forward to gently press my lips again to his.

Dreamy memories swirled into darkness, and the picture faded to black.

I sat up with a start from my bed, and I wiped the perspiration from my forehead.

It took me maybe half a second to remember why I had woken, and what I had awoken from, and then I was throwing off my covers and scrambling out of bed. I clicked on my lamp and dropped to the floor, crawling over to where Christian had once engraved his declaration of love to me.

My heart sank as I stared at the only visibly changed detail in my room: *Christian Turner loves Layla Thomas* it read, *but not enough* he had scratched carelessly into the wood after it.

I choked as I tried to swallow the lumps that had formed in my throat. I fleetingly wondered if anyone had ever died from lack of air from their own emotional state.

So, Christian had thought that it was his love that had driven me away, or rather that he hadn't loved me enough.

Preposterous.

If anything, it was because of the enormity of his love that I had to leave to save him from throwing his life away; it was because of his blind devotion to me.

The tears came, and I couldn't stop them. My weak whimpering turned into uncontrollable sobbing, and I curled myself into a ball at the foot of my bed to try to silence myself. I really didn't want to wake up my parents, and I thought that I was doing well, but a few minutes later, there was a light tapping at my door.

"Layla?" Mum whispered.

The door creaked open, and I peered up through my folded arms.

"Oh, honey," she sighed. She hurried to my side and tipped my head onto her shoulder. "What's wrong?"

I sobbed hysterically. "I… I was… I was so… so cruel to him, Mum. He… he loved… loved me so… m-much… and I just… just threw it back in his f-face."

"Shh, it wasn't your fault."

"But it was," I cried. "It w-was, Mum, I didn't want to l-leave, but I did… I did it for him."

She pulled back to scrutinise my face. "What do you mean? You left *for* him?"

Nothing got past my mother.

"I… I just wanted more for him. Being m-married to me, I couldn't see how that would be p-possible."

Her brows pulled together. "Honestly, Layla. I know you don't really believe that. Being married doesn't mean things need to change in a relationship. You and Christian seemed to have everything planned out to suit yourselves. The wedding was merely a formality."

"I know."

My hysteria had calmed down, so I was able to focus on not giving too much away with my words.

"If you loved him so much, then why did you leave?" she asked. "What on earth could have changed to make you think that you needed to be apart for him to have a fulfilling life?"

I sniffled and sat up, wiping the dampness from my cheeks. It all seemed redundant now, but I knew that telling my mother about the phone call that made me leave would only upset her more. Even if it cleared my conscience, I didn't feel right about it.

"I'm tired, Mum," I breathed. "I'm going to try to go back to sleep."

She stared at me for a moment and then nodded. "Okay, Layla, I'll see you in the morning then."

"I'm sorry for waking you."

She shook her head and pushed off the floor to stand. I did the same as she made her way back over to the door.

"Layla, I know you seem to want to punish yourself for what happened, but trying to deal with it alone is the wrong way to go about it," she said quietly. "There are a lot of people who love you who just want to understand, and you may not want to tell me about it but, if you need someone to talk to, I'm here. You're my daughter, and I love you. I'm not here to make judgements."

"I just don't really—"

"I know." She nodded. "You don't want to talk about it. But maybe you should – if not with me, then try to get Christian to listen. I'm sure that, despite what he says, he'd like to know what went wrong."

I thought about the promise I'd made to Mitch about staying away from him. It was going to be harder than I thought. But, anyway, Christian was seeing Madeline now, so it wasn't as if what I said would make a difference. Even if a small part of me wanted it to, the more significant and more logical part knew that it was just wishful thinking. As perfect as Christian was, even I knew that his forgiveness only extended so far. Knowing might make him hate me less, but even I could now see how skewed my logic had been at the time.

**

I didn't sleep for the rest of the night. My mind wouldn't switch off, so I gave up and began searching through my drawers and wardrobe to distract me. It didn't work. I kept thinking about what would have happened. What if I had stayed and married Christian? What if I'd faced my concerns head-on rather than running and hiding? What if I'd handled everything differently? The rhetorical questions turned over and over in my head like restless waves on a beach. I needed to believe for my own sanity and ego that it wouldn't have helped anything, and that I made the right decision for everyone at the time. I needed to believe it, but I couldn't seem to convince myself that it was the right choice any more.

My father was right. It was cowardly and selfish, even if that was exactly what I had been trying to avoid. I had done what I'd always hated. I had made a decision for someone because I thought that I knew what was best for them. But then, would telling Christian now, when he didn't want to know, be a repeat of that? Wouldn't easing my guilt and lifting the burden be as selfish as not telling him four years ago?

When first light came, I got up and changed into the only other set of clothes that I'd brought with me from South Coast, and went out to make breakfast for everyone. I found some bacon, eggs, sausages, and tomatoes, and began frying everything up. When I was finished, I put some bread down to toast and boiled the kettle. It was then that my dad came out to see what was going on.

"Layla, what in God's name are you doing?" he asked. "It's twenty past six."

I frowned at the time. "I'm making breakfast for you. Sorry, I didn't realise it was so early."

Dad rubbed his eyes and then sighed, pulling out a stool at the breakfast bar behind the plates I'd set out.

"So what's for breakfast then?" he sighed.

"Everything."

"Marvellous."

I smiled. "Would you like it with tea or coffee?"

I dished my dad up some breakfast, and he looked at me curiously.

"I've never known you to cook like this, kiddo," he said.

"I guess I've learnt a few things from living on my own." I shrugged.

"I guess you have. So, what time are you planning on leaving? Will you stay for a while before driving back?"

I nodded. "Yes, for a while. I'd like to have a wander around Almanbury to see what's changed, you know."

"Not a lot has changed, Layla."

"Well, this place has."

He tipped his head. "Fair enough. Just promise that you'll save some time for your old dad before you go," he mumbled. "It would be nice to spend some time together before you disappear again."

"Sure, Dad." I smiled. "But, just so you know, I'm never going to disappear again. I'll call lots, and even come down to visit every couple of weeks if you like."

He speared a piece of bacon. "We would like that very much."

I nodded. "So how is breakfast?"

"Surprisingly good."

I breathed a laugh. "So, did you decide on, tea or coffee?"

My dad stopped chewing and pressed his lips together. "How about one of those coffees of yours? Only without the sugar."

"Coming up."

The kettle clicked off, and I flittered around, making a hot beverage for us both, and then served myself up a plate of food. We sat in silence for a long while, just enjoying each other's company. When my dad had finished his last bite of toast, he sat back with a groan.

"Well, that was really great, kiddo, thanks."

"You're welcome." I grinned. "I'm glad you liked it."

He smiled an eye-creasing smile. "You know, I really missed you. Please don't ever disappear again."

I swallowed, feeling my eyebrows pinching together. "I promise I won't. I missed you too, you and Mum. More than you know."

**

I waited until Mum was up and had eaten her share of breakfast before I headed off for my tour of the neighbourhood. I didn't know what I was hoping to find. I didn't know whether it would be worse to see that everything had changed, or seeing that everything was exactly as I remembered. I started small, heading in the direction of the cemetery where I'd already been before circling back around towards the Almanbury forum and my old high school.

High school.

It was here that held the most memories for me. It was a place where I'd spent most of my time, and the place where I'd first laid eyes on Christian. He'd moved to Almanbury the year we both turned fourteen, and we started dating almost immediately. From the moment that I met him, I knew there was something special about him. It was as if our hearts were drawn towards each other, like magnets. From then, until four years ago, it was Christian and Layla, Layla and Christian.

Being back on the familiar grounds of my high school was as haunting as being at the cemetery. My memories floated around like ghosts.

"Layla?"

Funny, that voice sounded real.

"Layla Thomas," the voice repeated.

I tensed because it *was* real, and turned to find myself before two guys with folded arms.

"Wayne, Stuart, hey," I sighed. "Um, how are you?"

Stuart was supposed to be Christian's best man, and Wayne was a groomsman. I was probably on the top of their hit lists.

They exchanged a glance.

"Is it actually you?" Wayne mumbled. "Well, better late than never."

"I'm just visiting," I replied. "I'm heading back home later today."

"Home," Stuart groaned, shaking his head.

"So, where exactly is home now?" Wayne asked.

"Or are you still keeping that a secret?" Stuart snapped.

I exhaled. "South Coast is home now."

They exchanged another wary glance.

"I know that Christian is there. I've already seen him," I sighed.

Wayne bit his lip. I had always been good friends with Wayne.

"So, we missed you at the reunion last year, amongst other things," he said. "What's the deal, Layla? Why'd you bail?"

I shook my head. "It's a long story."

"I'll say," Stuart scoffed. "Like four years long. What the hell are you even doing back here? Did you think it would be safe to finally see your parents again because Christian's not here?"

"No, that's not—"

"Whatever," Stuart groaned, running his hands through his light brown hair.

He turned to walk away, and I looked at Wayne who seemed to be a little more forgiving.

I frowned. "Wayne, I—"

"You know, you didn't just leave Christian and your folks when you left, Layla," he replied evenly. "You left friends too – friends that were worried about you. A call is all it would have taken just to let us know what was going on."

"I'm sorry," I whispered. "I don't know what else to say. I've made a lot of mistakes, and I'm just trying to do what little I can to make things right again."

Wayne shook his head. "It's going to take more than an apology, you know, especially for Christian. That was his life that you walked away from too. It's been a long road to recovery for him."

"I know." I nodded. "And I heard about Nancy. It must've been awful for him."

"You don't even know the half of it."

I looked down.

"Anyway, I'd better go and find Stu," he sighed. "It was, um, good to see you, I guess. Have a safe drive back, um, home."

"Thanks," I murmured. "It was good to see you too."

He nodded and turned, running his hands through his scruffy orange hair.

I watched as he continued across the oval, and took a deep breath. I had considered that our friends would have been disappointed and angry with me, but seeing those emotions in action was something I wasn't prepared for. Not thinking about it didn't negate the fact that I had singlehandedly disappointed everyone that had ever mattered to me with one spontaneous act. My reasoning behind it didn't matter now. All that mattered was that it happened. Wayne was right. It would take more than an apology for everyone, not just for Christian. But I owed Christian way more. I just didn't know where to begin.

I circled back towards home and passed the park where I had made the promise of forever to Christian that, apparently, didn't translate. By the time I got back to my house, I felt a sense of homelessness that I couldn't explain. I didn't tell my parents about it because it wasn't their burden to bear, it was mine. I couldn't even comprehend it myself, so I knew that it was up to me to deal with alone.

I stayed for lunch in Almanbury, and then started my drive back to South Coast. The daylight was beneficial in keeping me alert since I hadn't slept too well the night before. Regardless, the trip back up felt longer than the ride down.

When I got home, Madeline wasn't there. I tried not to think about where she was or who she was with. Instead, I wrote her a note telling her I was home, and then had a shower and went to bed. The trip to my hometown had been emotionally exhausting. It figured that I'd felt so lethargic all the way back, but now I was curled up under my blankets, the shadows returned. I felt wide awake again as memory lane reopened, and I knew it meant that I was in for another sleepless night.

Chapter Five
Back to the Present

In the morning when my clock ticked over to seven thirty, my hand stopped the alarm before it had the chance to chime. I sat up slowly, my head spinning from sleep deprivation, and I twisted my body around to stand. As much as I'd tried to get some decent rest last night, the enormity of my dilemma had kept me awake. Four years of hiding meant a lot of bridges that needed to be repaired. My mind ran over and over the long list of loved ones that I needed to make amends with, and I was overwhelmed. I felt as though there weren't enough hours in the day to sleep.

I pushed my beige curtains open and frowned at the morning sun – another day, another week. It was Monday again, which meant the start of a new issue of *Flash,* and the beginning of another mountain of planning. Any other week, I would have welcomed the challenge. But, today, I honestly didn't know how anything more could be crammed into my already full and struggling mind. It didn't matter if I was ready for it or not. Time waited for no one, not even those who made stupid decisions and refused to face up to them.

Game face, Layla.

I dragged my feet over to my door and opened it. Maddie was right outside.

"Good morning, sleepy!" She beamed.

I groaned at her enthusiasm. "Morning, Maddie."

I could smell coffee so headed straight towards the kitchen to get a cup. The upside of Maddie already being up meant that it was already freshly brewed. I took a mouthful of black coffee and choked on the hot bitterness that caught in my throat.

"When did you get home yesterday? It must've been early because I wasn't late," she said.

"Um, I think it was about six thirty." I shrugged tiredly. "Where were you anyway?"

As soon as I asked the question and saw her face light up, I wished that I could retract it.

"Well," she sighed. "Christian and I went to the Sunday session at Crescent. It was so amazing."

"Christian."

I swallowed the wrong way and started to cough the liquid up my windpipe. The tears that had only temporarily been absent from my eyes came pouring out again. I put the mug down.

"Are you all right, Layla?" Maddie asked, jumping off the couch she sat on.

I nodded mid-choke and brushed my wet cheek, and then took another mouthful of coffee to try to recover.

Maddie waited as I continued to struggle to clear my throat. It was a decent minute before I got a grip of myself.

"Are you good now?" She frowned.

I cleared my throat one final time and nodded. I chose not to dwell on how *good* I was, but at least I wasn't trying to breathe in coffee and flood my lungs now.

"So, yeah, it was really nice," she continued. "Christian is a great guy."

I nodded, too afraid to speak. I also tried not to think about *how* great he was and how much better of a person he was than me, or how much better Maddie was for him than me.

No. Stop, Layla. Not everything is about you.

"So, how was Almanbury?" she asked. "Did you enjoy seeing everyone again?"

I opened my mouth, but it was a few seconds before any words came out.

"It was… okay. Kind of weird, actually," I said. "It's been a long time since I've seen everyone, so they were a bit annoyed that I hadn't kept in touch."

Understatement of the century, Layla.

Maddie gave a half smile. "At least you're making an effort now, right?"

"Maybe." I shrugged. "Some thought it was too little, too late, but I'm glad I went. It was long overdue."

"Good." She nodded.

I exhaled in relief as I saw resolve colour her expression. The topic of my trip to Almanbury was dropped.

"So, did you end up getting shoes for the ball?" I asked, for good measure.

Maddie wrinkled her nose. "Kind of."

"What does that mean?"

"Well, I found a couple of pairs, but I couldn't choose. Do you mind if we go after work sometime this week so you can help me pick?"

I felt my forehead crease. "You're asking me for fashion advice? Wow, you must really be desperate."

She rolled her eyes. "You're pretty fashionable. I mean, you are the chief photographer of a fashion and lifestyle magazine."

I forced a laugh, and it sounded forced. "I suppose. Speaking of which, we should get organised for work."

Maddie smiled. "We've got plenty of time. I just need to get dressed."

"Well, I think I need a shower and a pile of makeup to look half-way decent."

"You do look kind of haggard," Maddie agreed. "What's the deal with the *night of the living dead* look?"

I frowned at her honestly. "I haven't been able to sleep for the last couple of days."

"I guessed that much. How come?"

"Who knows?" I yawned, and it made my lie sound more convincing. "But I'm certainly not looking forward to the onslaught of planning this week, that's for sure."

"I can't wait." Maddie bounced. Her energy honestly made me feel even more exhausted.

I picked up my coffee and headed into the bathroom to paint some colour onto my sallow cheeks.

Game face, Layla.

**

Maddie and I arrived at work to find Ebony sitting in our office. I froze with stress, hoping that something hadn't gone wrong with the last issue. I hadn't given it any thought since Friday morning – since seeing Christian again.

Ebony smiled. "Relax. You don't need to look so scared. You haven't done anything wrong."

I exhaled, glancing at my watch. I wasn't late either, so that didn't explain her presence.

"So, to what do we owe the morning welcome?" I asked.

"Actually, I wanted to ask you for a favour," she said as she stood up and bit her lip.

I shrugged. "Sure, what is it?"

I glanced at Maddie who looked as confused as I did.

"You're coming to the ball this Friday night, right?" Ebony asked.

"Yes."

"Well, Layla, I was hoping, I mean, you can say no, but—"

"Ebony."

"Well, you are our best photographer, so I was hoping that you might bring your camera with you and take some snaps of people?" she said. "I'd be happy to pay for the ticket for you and your partner."

I blinked. Partner? I didn't know that I'd need one of those.

"Oh, um…" I sighed.

Ebony smiled a little apologetically. "You'd really be doing me the biggest favour."

"No, I mean, yes, of course." I nodded. "But I only need the one ticket."

"Nonsense, a pretty girl like you? Invite someone."

I pressed my lips together.

"Well, thank you for agreeing to it, Layla," she said with an exhale. "I suppose I'll see you and Maddie in ten minutes for the ideas workshop."

I nodded, and Maddie waved. Ebony smiled before leaving.

"Sweet," Maddie squeaked. "You get two free passes to the ball just for taking a few photos."

I huffed. "Two. Do you want one?"

"No, Ebony said that you've got to bring someone," she replied. "Besides, I've already invited Christian."

"What? You what?"

"Is that bad? Because he already said yes."

I willed my head to shake. "No, I mean, I… you've only known him a few days, and you invited him to a work ball? That's a little fast, isn't it?"

"It's not a marriage proposal, Layla." She smiled. "So, who are you going to invite?"

"I, um…"

I tried to think of all the guys I knew but, other than the ones I worked with, there really weren't any I could think of. I hadn't dated anyone since Christian. I never could. In fact, the only guy I'd really been alone with for any length of time was Jeffrey from the jewellery store. But, I'd known him as long as Maddie had known Christian, less in fact since at least Maddie had the weekend… I could hardly finish the thought because it still felt wrong to think of Christian with anyone else – wrong but selfish. He owed me nothing because I'd forced him into living without me.

"Layla!" Maddie gasped.

I jumped. "What?"

"Have you been holding out on me?"

My head shook, but my shoulder lifted against my will. "Maybe, I don't know. I might know someone."

"What! Who?"

"Just some guy I met when I was lost at the shops on Friday afternoon."

Her mouth hung open. "Lay-la. Tell me everything."

"It's nothing, really. I hardly know him," I sighed. "Besides, we've got the workshop in a few minutes, and I need to grab a coffee on the way."

"I'm not letting you off that easily."

"Have you ever?" I groaned. "Come on, let's go."

"Okay, um, actually, I'll meet you there. I want to make a stop in fashion on the way," she answered with a giggle.

"I'll see you in five then," I replied, heading towards the door.

My pleasant façade slipped the second I didn't have an audience.

I walked quickly to the kitchen without making eye contact with anyone and made myself a coffee before heading to the ideas workshop in the boardroom. I wasn't the first one there, but I wasn't the last. Maddie arrived about a minute after me, and sat down opposite. I opened my file to a new page, even if I wouldn't be writing much down. I never did.

The ideas workshop was more for the feature writers and editors who had their finger on the pulse of what was up-and-coming. Maddie, as the fashion editor, was also crucial in planning the fashion trends spread. The meeting was a bit moot for photographers since the type of photos that I shot never dictated the story. I suppose it was just handy to know what photo shoots I'd need to brainstorm before I needed to liaise with individual columnists. Despite their flair for words, most were struck with illiteracy when it came to describing what they needed. This never helped when we were all working towards a deadline for publication.

Each issue had a threading theme, which most ideas in the magazine revolved around. Ebony usually came up with the subject, but she was always open to ideas.

Ebony was the last to arrive and, as soon as she was in the room, the meeting began.

"Welcome, everyone, to another edition." She smiled. "As you know, in the last issue of *Flash*, we focused on all things Spring. Now, since there seems to be a lot of high profile weddings lately, I thought that the next edition could be a bridal special."

I absently reached for my coffee, but my mind slipped into auto-pilot. Was this a joke? Was my past actually coming back to haunt me? Did karma have a sense of humour?

My hand missed the handle of my mug, and I knocked it over, sending a wave of beige liquid over the conference table.

"Crap, I'm so sorry," I gasped as the writers groaned and gathered their papers.

Maddie looked at me curiously and slid her books to the side.

Ebony cleared her throat. "Layla, is everything okay?"

"Yes, I'm so sorry. I'm such a klutz."

"It's fine," she replied.

She passed some napkins down the table, and I began to mop up the spill. It was easier to zone out and ignore the wedding talk when I focused on cleaning.

When I was finished, I sat back and frowned at my empty mug, fleetingly considering slipping out to make another one. Surely no one would notice that I was gone.

"What do you think, Layla?" Ebony asked.

I looked up. "I'm sorry, about what?"

"Is it possible to get in touch with different designers to get a spread of the latest fashion gowns?"

"Um, isn't that more Maddie's area of expertise?"

Maddie shrugged. "Yeah, I can see what I can do."

"Actually," one of the writers interrupted. "I don't know if you've heard of it, but there's this relatively new store in the city called *Montage*, and they liaise quite closely with the designers. They're sort of a warehouse for all the surplus stock from the factories."

Maddie nodded enthusiastically. "I know it. Layla and I were there last Friday. We can go in and check it out."

"Why do I need to be there, Mads?" I asked.

"Well, I'll need your opinion on the palette and such to see what will work with the shoot," she answered.

I frowned. Choosing clothes to match the shoot wasn't usually something I had a say in. Again, it was more Maddie's call for the garment selection, and I just worked the shoot around them.

I glanced up at Maddie, concluding that this was definitely penance for my past sins, and then looked at Ebony.

"Sounds fine." I nodded.

"Wonderful." Ebony grinned before turning back to her notes.

I could see that she had already planned out a mock-up of all the pages and story ideas. She really was amazing. I don't know where she found the time to do it all. I just took photos, and twenty-four hours each day didn't feel like long enough. I zoned back out, staring at my coffee-stained page as more ideas for stories were thrown around the table.

I really needed a coffee.

"Layla, Maddie, since we're all finished here why don't you two go to check *Montage* out," Ebony said. "Then, Layla, if you could start thinking about nice settings and such for bridal shoots, I'll touch base with you towards the end of the day to see what you've come up with."

"Great." I nodded.

I picked up my empty mug and damp notes.

Maddie jumped out of her seat with excitement. "Montage!"

I tried to smile, but it didn't quite come off. This was certainly not how I planned on spending my week. Sure, I expected it to be chaotic and stressful with a new edition's worth of planning to do, but not to spend it talking about weddings with my ex-fiancé and his new girlfriend.

Nope.

I tried to remind myself that it was my fault it was going to be so awkward. It was lucky that I'd decided to stop running –

so maybe this edition was the perfect thing to ensure that I did just that.

"A wedding issue, oh, this is going to be fabulous!" Maddie grinned, clapping as we returned to the office. "We're going to have so much fun."

"Mm." I nodded, dropping my file onto my cluttered desk.

Maddie frowned at my lack of enthusiasm. "Aren't you excited? We get to plan a wedding, haven't you always wanted to do that?"

"Not so much," I answered, sounding slightly strangled. I felt like someone had stabbed me in the heart, but Maddie didn't seem to notice.

"I can't believe how un-girly you are," she sighed. "I think it's going to be a blast. Do you think we'll get to try on some of the dresses?"

I grabbed my bag and camera and looked up. "We should go. I... we have a lot to get done."

"Fine," Maddie mumbled. "I can't believe we get an awesome assignment like this, and I'm stuck with the Grinch of weddings."

"You asked for me to tag along, Mads."

"Yeah because you have a great eye for colours and stuff, Layla. I need your creative opinion."

I nodded. "Okay."

"We're a team, you and me," she said, and her blue eyes turned pouty.

"I know we are, Madeline. So let's just do this, okay?"

She smiled. "I'll drive, and you can tell me about the guy from the other day on the way."

I sighed loudly, following her towards the door. How on earth was I going to avoid this one?

When we arrived, Maddie and I wove our way through the unusually busy shopping mall to find *Montage*. I'd managed to stall on the Jeffrey subject on the drive here by calling the modelling agency, and then asking Maddie what she had in mind for the spread. It was a good distraction until she realised what I was doing.

"So, what's this guy's name?" Maddie asked. "The guy you met the other day, I mean."

I sighed. "I figured."

"So?"

"So, after we find designs today, I need to scout for locations," I said. "Then tomorrow we need to meet with potential models, and then Wednesday and Thursday I want to start shooting just in case we need to do any reshoots."

Maddie rolled her eyes. "Lay-la, you know that's not what I meant."

"Yeah," I exhaled. "His name is Jeffrey."

"Jeffrey?"

"Yes?" a voice replied.

Maddie and I both jumped, and I turned to find him behind us.

"Are you talking about me?" He smirked.

"Are you stalking me?" I frowned.

He chuckled and pointed to the side. My head turned to see *Reflective Jewellers*.

"I'm heading to work," he replied. "What's your excuse?"

"I… I was just telling Maddie about the strange guy I met who was pretending to work in a jewellery store." I shrugged. "And presto, here you are."

He laughed again. "You must be Maddie."

Maddie smiled. "Hi, Jeffrey was it?"

"Yeah, it's nice to meet you." He nodded. "So, there really is a Maddie. I thought Layla was just making you up."

"How have you heard about me, and yet I'm only just hearing about you now?" She frowned.

"Ouch," he sighed. "You'd better ask her that. Anyway, I need to get to work."

"You know, since you work at a jewellery store, you might be able to help us."

"No, Maddie," I murmured.

As if involving Christian wouldn't be awkward enough.

"Why not?" she asked. "We'll need to get it from somewhere."

Jeffrey blinked. "Um, get what?"

I rolled my eyes. "We're doing a spread for *Flash*. I guess it's a wedding special. Maddie meant loaning the jewellery for the shoot."

"Oh." Jeffrey smiled. "Sounds like a good business opportunity. I'll check with my folks. I'm sure they'd be willing to help out."

I shook my head. "No, Jeffrey, it's fine, we were just—"

"Layla," Maddie sighed. "Give him your number."

"What?"

Jeffrey grinned. "I like this one."

Maddie laughed. "Well, he'll need to call you after he checks if he can help us."

"Oh, right." I nodded. "Well, wouldn't it make more sense for you to give him your number? I mean, you're the fashion editor."

Maddie shrugged. "I lost my phone yesterday."

"No, you didn't. I—"

"Layla, just give him your flipping number."

243

I exhaled and reached into my bag for my business card. "It's best to reach me on my mobile. I always have that with me."

"Okay, thanks." Jeffrey nodded. "I'll be in touch."

"Great," I sighed. "Come on, Maddie, we need to see about those designs."

Maddie smiled. "It was nice to meet you, Jeffrey."

Jeffrey waved. "You too. See you, Layla."

I waved back and gripped Maddie's wrist, tugging her sharply after me.

"Real smooth," I hissed.

"What?" She shrugged. "You know that Ebony will ask us about the jewellery, too."

"Right, because *that's* what I meant," I groaned, stopping short in front of *Montage*.

Maddie took a few steps and then frowned.

"Well, are you coming in or not?" she asked. "You dragged me all the way here."

I forced my legs forward. I wasn't quite sure just what I was going to say to Christian after my weekend in Almanbury. I knew that I needed to say a lot but, with Maddie here, I knew it probably wasn't the best time. Regardless, with all the flurry of this morning, I hadn't managed to prepare any brilliant or profound speech for the occasion.

I followed Madeline as she made a beeline to the desk where she had obviously spotted Christian on her way to the wall of designer gowns. She didn't look back to check I was following her, but maybe she didn't care if I was. With Christian here, I was obsolete, the third wheel.

Maddie reached the desk before me and cleared her throat. Christian looked up and raised an eyebrow.

"Hey, Maddie, I didn't expect to see… Layla," he sighed. "What brings you two here?"

"We need to see all of your designer wedding gowns please." Maddie smiled.

I felt my brow crease with stress as Christian looked to me because he looked a little pale. I wondered if I did too. I couldn't even find my voice to explain what Madeline meant.

"We're doing a bridal edition for the next issue of *Flash*," she said with a laugh. "Relax, it's not for us."

He nodded, not seeing the joke in it. I squeezed my eyes shut, willing myself to disappear.

"—Layla?" Maddie asked. I hadn't even heard a question.

My eyes opened slowly. "Sorry?"

"Are you okay? You look a little flushed."

I shook my head. "Fine. What was the question?"

"What did Ebony say we needed?" she asked. "I know that I'm the fashion editor, but I didn't bring my notes. Do you remember?"

I looked down and blinked. "Um, the numbers of designers so we can get in touch with them, maybe loan some stock now if they have any here that we can borrow—"

"I'll check with the manager," Christian said.

He stepped down from the landing and hurried off towards the back of the store. When he was gone, Maddie turned to me.

"What is with you?" she whispered. "Now you look like you're going to faint."

"It's probably just the lack of sleep. I'll be fine."

Maddie nodded but didn't look entirely convinced.

"Maddie," Christian called.

We both looked up, and he gestured for us to go over. Maddie gripped my arm.

"Are you okay? You can wait in the food court if you like," she offered.

"No, I'm fine."

We headed over, and Maddie released me to talk to the manager who was an older woman with white-blonde hair who was impeccably dressed.

Christian stepped back and folded his arms as he looked over at me. I was a little surprised when he walked over.

"So, what's up with you? Not thrilled about wedding planning?" he murmured.

I shook my head. "Once was enough. And let's face it, I wasn't exactly Jennifer Lopez."

Christian huffed. "From memory, you did an all right job. In the planning, I mean."

"So I, um, I went to Almanbury on the weekend to see my parents."

"Maddie mentioned. It's about time."

I nodded. "I'm so sorry about Nancy. I wish I could have been there."

He looked up, and his eyes were wild with unmasked pain. "You weren't. You missed a lot of things."

My heart sank to my feet and then felt like it had been stepped on.

"Christian—"

"Don't," he breathed.

I let my head fall and heard footsteps as Maddie danced towards us. I glanced up and saw her smile fade.

"What's going on?" she asked.

"Nothing," Christian said, and I almost believed him. "So, what did she say?"

"She said we can grab a few gowns and run them through on a receipt of loan," she explained. "So, I guess we should start looking."

Christian nodded. "I'll leave you to it. Let me know when you're done, and I can sort it out for you."

"Thanks." Maddie beamed. "Unless you want to give us a hand... maybe a male opinion?"

Christian looked at me and then mashed his lips together. "I need to get back to work. Besides, Layla is an expert on weddings, so you'll be fine."

I groaned internally at the comment as Christian walked away.

Maddie looked at me in shock. "Expert? You? What does that mean?"

I shrugged weakly. "I, um, helped a friend of ours who got engaged right out of high school."

"Oh, how very small town."

"Yeah." I frowned. "Well, let's get this over and done with."

"Don't sound too enthusiastic."

"Sorry, there are just a million other things I need to do today."

She nodded. "But, Layla, we get to shop for *free* designer wedding gowns."

I mashed my lips together, unable to reach her level of excitement. Maybe if it was anything else – a debutante ball edition, or literally *anything* else then I might have been more convincing. But planning a wedding issue was like walking wide-eyed down memory lane, especially right after seeing Christian again after all this time. It just felt like another cruel reminder of the mistakes I'd made and the life I had walked away from.

Maddie snapped into action, heading straight to the Ambrosia White collection. She picked up the white dress that she'd made me try on the other day and handed it to me.

"One," she said. "You can help select, or you can carry the merchandise."

"I can carry." I nodded.

She smiled and spun in the opposite direction towards the corner where there were more dresses. I followed slowly.

"So, do you think that any white dress could be a wedding dress?" she asked.

"I think that *any* dress could be a wedding dress," I answered flatly. "Why does it need to be white?"

Maddie turned around, and her brows pulled together at my tone. "Wow, you really are anti-weddings aren't you? Why on earth would anyone ask you to help with their wedding?"

I smiled weakly. "No, I'm really not anti… I just… I'm just stressing about this issue. It sounds like a big one, and I don't want to mess it up."

"Oh my gosh, are you kidding?" she gushed, dumping three more dresses in my arms. "You'll be great. You're the best person for the job."

I groaned. "Right. *The Grinch of weddings.*"

Maddie grinned and turned back to the racks. A few minutes passed, and she turned back towards me.

"You know, I think you're right," she said.

"You think I'm going to mess this up?" I frowned.

Maddie laughed. "No, silly. I meant about the whole white-dress thing. Who says it needs to be white? I think we should shake things up a bit and go for, like, gold or silver, or—"

"Black?" I offered.

Maddie rolled her eyes as my phone began to ring. I dumped the dresses into her arms and pulled it out.

"Ugh," she groaned. "I hope that's not Ebony because we're nowhere near—"

"Private number," I mumbled. "Hello, it's Layla."

"*Hey, it's Jeffrey,*" the voice down the receiver said.

"Jeffrey, what's up?"

"*I just spoke to my folks, and they'd love to help out with the magazine thing,*" he replied. "*Do you want to swing by later on and see what we've got?*"

"Can we make it tomorrow? I'm actually pushed pretty hard for time today," I said, walking up a random aisle.

"*Sure, that should be fine. Morning would be better though. Does that suit you?*"

"That's fine. I'll come by first thing. Say, nine o'clock?"

"*Cool, I'll see you then.*"

"Great, thanks."

He hung up, and I slid my phone back into my work trousers. Maddie's head popped out from the end of the aisle.

"Jewellery-Jeffrey?"

"Yeah, he—" My voice cut off as Christian's head appeared beside her. "Um, he said that his parents are happy to contribute, so to go and see what they have."

"Oh, great." Maddie smiled. "Are we going there after here then?"

I shook my head. "No, tomorrow morning at nine. I need to check out locations after this."

"Right."

"Is that okay with you?" I asked hesitantly. "You don't have meetings then, do you?"

"No, but I don't think he was inviting *me* Layla, the guy is clearly hot for you. Don't tell me that you don't see the way he looks at you. It's like he's just seen the sun after years of clouds."

249

"Don't be stupid, Maddie, it's not… no," I answered.

My cheeks felt warm, and I noticed that Christian made it a point to find the back wall interesting. The way she spoke reminded me of something that he would say, like the way he used to describe love between two characters in one of his stories.

"Why not?" she sighed. "It's not like you've been out with anyone in the *entire* time I've known you, maybe—"

"Madeline," I snapped. "Enough."

Christian looked back at me, and his brow was creased with curiosity that he swiftly evened out.

I bit my lip. "Mads, we need to finish up here, are you done?"

Maddie shrugged. "Almost, except for the boys."

"Boys? What does that mean?"

"Suits," she answered and then drew in a staggered breath. "Oh, how am I going to get the right size if I don't know who the model is? It's not like I can clear out all of the stock here."

"But we're not interviewing models until tomorrow. We don't have time to come back to sort out the men's clothing—"

"Hey, relax." Maddie smiled. She looked as if an idea had struck her like lightning. "After all, we have a man right here."

She turned to Christian who raised one eyebrow.

"What?" he asked flatly. "No. Whatever you're thinking, just no."

"Honestly, you are as bad as Layla is," she sighed. "Is it an Almanbury thing?"

Christian looked at me, and I saw amusement in his blue eyes that I hadn't seen since we were younger.

"Come on, Christian," Maddie pleaded. "You're a guy. Please help us."

Christian was still shaking his head. "I really can't. I'm just finishing up here. I have uni in an hour."

"This won't take long. Please, it would really help Layla and me out."

Christian glanced in my direction again, and I mashed my lips together.

"I don't know," he sighed.

"Maddie, leave him alone," I replied. "Besides, it doesn't matter how well the thing fits him, it needs to fit the model."

"You're right." She nodded. "So, Christian, how would you like to earn a few bucks?"

"No," he said quickly. "I don't like being photographed."

I felt my eyebrows drop because he never used to have any concerns about it in the past. In fact, he had been my subject for years. But then, I suppose we'd both changed since then.

"Why not? You're a good-looking guy." Maddie shrugged. "It's not that hard, is it, Layla?"

"Maddie, no," I replied. I wanted to expand, but I couldn't. I didn't want to offend him or encourage him. The wedding issue was hard enough without seeing him as the groom to another girl.

I glanced up at Christian who looked as though he was considering it for a moment.

"No, I really can't," he answered finally. "Between uni and work, I don't have a lot of free time."

Maddie pouted. "Okay, fine. But we're still on for Friday night, right?"

Christian's gaze flickered to me and then blinked back to Maddie. "Of course. If I say that I'll be somewhere, I'll be there."

I frowned at my feet and ignored the dig.

"Anyway, I've really got to go," Christian said. "If you need help with the suits, talk to Troy over there. I'm sure he'd be happy to help."

I scoffed and then covered it up with a cough. Troy, Mr Underwear from the other day, the guy that Christian had to drag me away from decking.

Maddie glanced at me and then looked back at Christian. "Have fun at uni. I'll talk to you later maybe?"

I found myself strangely pleased that Maddie seemed uncertain about the prospect, and then kicked myself internally because it wasn't a rational response.

"Sure, I'll talk to you later." He nodded. "Bye, Layla."

I raised my hand to wave, a little taken aback that he was directly addressing me now.

"Bye, Christian," I sighed.

It was harder to say than I thought it would be. But then, I'd never said the words before.

Chapter Six
Unsuccessful Distractions

We took longer than I'd hoped to get the clothes for the photo shoot. The manager of *Montage* ended up assisting us in the selection of the latest couture for both men and women, and we left with three dresses—two white and a gold—and three different black and dark grey suits. They were all packed in two large boxes that barely fit into Maddie's silver Mercedes.

After *Montage*, we set out to look at places for the bridal shoot, which was planned as the main fashion spread for the issue. I already had some places in mind. One was a hotel owned by James Butler, Madeline's father, which was also the venue for our work ball on Friday evening. It was a difficult subject to broach with Maddie since she didn't have the best relationship with her dad. She never liked to talk about it, so I never asked about it. Since I've known her, she's called her dad about as much as I've called my parents.

"Hey, so I was maybe thinking that, since it's getting all dolled up for our ball, maybe we could use the *Eclipse* grand ballroom for part of the shoot," I murmured. "Do you think they would mind?"

Maddie shrugged indifferently. "We can ask. It should be okay, but I guess it'll be up to the manager."

I nodded. "And I was thinking about maybe doing some sets down at South Beach. What do you think?"

"Sounds perfect." Maddie smiled. "Are you still aiming to shoot Wednesday and Thursday?"

"Yeah, I thought we could start at the beach and work our way in."

"Okay. Do you want to swing by South Beach now then? Maybe get some angles and scout an exact location?"

I laughed lightly. "You knew that I was going to ask that next."

"I know you too well." She grinned.

"Right," I said. I bit my lip and felt the guilt creep up my legs.

"So, are you going digital or standard do you think?" she asked, pulling my attention back to business.

I thought for a moment, deciding which of the single-lens reflex cameras I'd use.

"Definitely digital for outside since I like being able to preview the image as close to the moment of exposure," I replied, forgetting not to be so technical. Maddie raised her eyebrows, and I smiled. "Sorry, I'll probably just stick to digital, I think. I prefer it to standard."

She chuckled. "Sounds good."

When we pulled into the street side parking along the fringe of South Beach, Maddie exhaled, unclipped her seatbelt, and pushed the car door open. I followed her lead, and climbed out of the expensive car as the cold breeze whipped my auburn hair around my face. I tried to peel it off my lip-gloss, but it was pointless since the wind just blew it back.

"So, what do you think?" Maddie asked, folding her arms across her chest. "What catches your eye, shutterbug?"

I stepped back, letting my gaze pan the incredible scene. South Beach was one of the most pristine beaches that I'd ever set eyes on, and had glorious golden sand that stretched for miles against the crystal blue ocean. But, I had to admit, as beautiful as the beaches in South Coast were, they didn't hold a candle to some of those in Almanbury.

I turned towards a grassed patch outside the surf-club that backed onto the ocean. The contrast between the green, blue, and gold was breathtaking.

"Maybe over there," I said.

I didn't wait for an answer. I was already walking towards it, slinging my camera around in front of my eye to take in the view through the viewfinder. I scanned until I found a good angle and adjusted the lens before taking my first shot.

I was pretty familiar with the landscape of South Beach. It had been my first subject when I'd moved here, though it had changed a little since then. There were a few more square metres added to the surf club, and a couple more statues erected. In my humble opinion, it wasn't as untouched as beaches should be, but that didn't mean it wasn't an aesthetically pleasing sight.

I walked around for a while longer, checking different spots, and taking a few more shots. I had taken about five when Maddie finally caught up to me.

"Here?" Maddie asked, sounding confused.

I pulled the camera back from my face to look at her.

"Don't you like it? I think if we have the bride and groom standing there, her train flowing down here…" I gestured curling my hand around in an arch. "I'd be able to pick up on all the colours. It would look lovely if we maybe have some subtle blues in the bouquet." I took a deep breath and let it out. "Maybe some daisies too."

Maddie nodded and then frowned. "Flowers, right. I suppose we'll need to get some of those as well."

I laughed. "For someone who is so excited about planning a fake wedding, you certainly haven't considered all the aspects of actually planning one."

"Well, *I'm* sorry if *I* haven't done it before," she groaned.

I shifted uncomfortably. "Well, anyway, we'll need flowers and a couple of rings for the models, so it at least looks authentic."

"Right, rings." She nodded, pulling out a small spiral notebook to jot down my suggestions. "Anything else, oh wise wedding sage?"

I huffed. "It's common knowledge, Maddie. But, no, not unless you want the whole bridal party in the shot too."

She pressed her lips together. "I'll have to check with Ebony first."

I nodded. "Well, I'm good here. At least I know what I'm working with and I can run it by Ebony. I can assess the rest tomorrow pending the weather is okay."

"Okay, let's get back to the office so we can look at our goodies."

"Plus, Ebony would probably like to know how we got on."

She exhaled theatrically. "And I need to call a guy about a bouquet."

**

"Oh, wow," Ebony gushed. "You guys did *great*. These are fantastic."

"Thanks." Maddie beamed. "And Layla was thinking about doing the shoot at South Beach and also maybe in the ballroom at *Eclipse* since it'll be set up for our ball."

Ebony looked up. "Sounds perfect. Have you spoken to the hotel manager yet?"

"No, but, well, I thought maybe I could just give my dad a call." Maddie shrugged.

"That's right. He owns it, doesn't he?"

She nodded. "But Layla also reminded me that we'll probably need a bouquet and some rings too."

"But, in regards to jewellery, Maddie and I are meeting with a jewellery store tomorrow morning who are willing to loan us some," I added.

"Oh, Jeffrey." She chuckled. "I forgot about him."

Ebony's brow lifted. "Jeffrey?"

"He works for his family's jewellery store," Maddie replied. "He's totally hot for Layla."

Ebony smiled. "I see."

"Anyway, we're meeting him tomorrow, as well as the modelling agency," I continued, guiding the conversation back to subject.

"Perfect." Ebony nodded. "It sounds like you're all on track. I'll let you two run the show."

Maddie and I exchanged a glance. I didn't know what my expression was, but hers looked like it was a little more excited than mine.

I looked back at Ebony.

"What about the other features?" I asked. "I could take close-ups of bouquets, wedding bands, and champagne glasses or something in case you want to use them."

"That would be cool." Ebony nodded. "Maybe we could talk to a bakery and get them to make us a cake, too."

"Cake," Maddie gasped, flicking open her notebook.

"Actually, that would be good to have for the *Eclipse* shoot," I murmured.

"Oh, speaking of which," Maddie said, looking up. "Is it okay to have just the bride and groom, or did you want the whole wedding party?"

"Whatever you think," Ebony replied. "I'm giving you total creative power."

"I think just the bride and groom," I answered. "We can do a lot with just the two of them. Maybe even add a few black and white or sepia shots too, so it'll give it a timeless feel."

"Great." Ebony smiled. "So, tomorrow is finalising arrangements, and then Wednesday and Thursday you're shooting?"

"Yes," Maddie and I said in unison.

"Wow, I love that you're so organised."

"We need to be to use *Eclipse*." I shrugged. "So, hopefully Friday will be an office day sorting the shots. That will give us time for reshoots if necessary."

"Perfect. That sounds amazing." Ebony grinned. "I'll leave it in your capable hands and check back in with you later in the week."

Maddie smiled. "In the meantime, we'll organise a cake and a bouquet."

"Planning a wedding is stressful, isn't it? Gosh, I remember trying to plan mine. Rob was great though. He came along to almost everything with me."

I smiled sadly, remembering when Christian and I were planning ours. I thought I knew what I was doing, but Nancy and my mother ended up nearly doing the whole thing. Sure, we selected the specifics—the designs, the colours, the location, the music—but they pulled it all together for us.

I frowned at the thought that I never got to see the end product. I'd always imagined it to be like a dream that was constructed around both Christian and me.

"Are you all right, Layla?" Ebony asked. "Are you feeling a little sentimental?"

I blinked out of my nostalgic reverie.

"Layla doesn't like weddings," Maddie answered for me. "She's been a sad-sack all day."

"I never said that I didn't like weddings. I just…" I paused and considered how to explain it without giving too much away, but came up empty. "Okay, maybe I just don't really like weddings."

Maddie laughed, but Ebony raised her eyebrows.

"What's not to like?" she asked, and I could tell that she didn't buy my explanation.

I shrugged and smiled. "Bad experience?"

Both girls laughed, and Ebony headed towards the door, while Maddie proceeded to arrange the gowns and suits into sets.

"Well, I hope this experience is better for you then, Layla," Ebony said. "Good luck to both of you."

Maddie looked up and flashed a bright smile that made her eyes twinkle.

I mashed my lips together. I could only hope that this experience was better. At least this time I'd make it to the wedding reception.

**

By the end of the day, we had managed to organise a local bakery to donate a cake for the shoot. Maddie had also convinced a florist to arrange two bouquets for us free of charge, one of pale blue roses and Madonna lilies, and of white and gold frangipanis. Most independent businesses were co-operative with donations if it meant that they appeared in an acclaimed magazine. In fact, before we left for the day, Maddie got a call from another local store that had caught word of our spread from the manager of *Montage*, and offered to loan us some of her uniquely designed shoes for the shoot. We planned to go to check them out after meeting with potential models the next day since there was more of a need to be exact for shoe sizes.

By the time Maddie and I got home, I felt physically and emotionally drained. The day had felt longer than usual, and although I tried to distract myself from Christian with my work, it wasn't a welcome distraction since it bore too much of a resemblance to my nightmares.

Ever since I left Almanbury, I felt as though I'd been pierced with an arrow in the heart. But, instead of pulling it out so the wound could heal, it had been snapped off, so the spearhead was still beneath the skin. Every movement pulsed with pain, every breath, every twitch. I had no one to blame but myself, but that didn't make it any easier. It was wearing me down until I would be unable to function – and it was worsened by my lack of sleep. I just prayed that my exhaustion meant that I could get some decent rest tonight.

I stuck to a light dinner and turned in to bed early. But the second I switched off the light and rested my head on the soft, ivory pillow, I was wide awake. I gave up after a couple of hours of staring at the ceiling and reached for my laptop, which was beside my bed. I waited for it to glimmer to life, then typed in my password, *laylaturner*. Another reminder, and waited for my settings to be generated.

I knew that what I was about to do was dangerous for my sanity, but I couldn't seem to stop myself. My fingers grazed over the mouse pad as I went into my documents and to the zip file that I hadn't opened in years.

In my haste to leave Almanbury, I would have forgotten to bring my laptop and digital camera had they not been left in the boot of my car. I was thankful that I had brought them when I began studying, I just didn't remember that the memory card of my camera still had a handful of photos of Christian and I that I hadn't copied across to my drive yet. At the time, I didn't have the strength to delete them because I was afraid that I wasn't going to see Christian again and his face would fade in my memory. So, instead, I copied them to my laptop and zipped them up, careful not to tempt or torture myself with them. Well, until now.

The file popped up, showing a list of seven photos. Only seven photos were left of our time together. We'd been apart now for almost as long as we were together. It felt like we were together for longer, and it had been lifetimes since we had been that way. I hadn't allowed myself to look at the images before now. Even while copying them, I knew that the second I saw his face, my resolve would waver, and it would take a lot of self-control not to get in the car and go back. But then I remembered what made me leave, and it was a little easier to resist the urge.

I moved the cursor over the first listed photo and took a deep breath. If Christian was going to keep me up at night, I might as well remember some of the good times I had with him. Even if I knew that it would torment me more. Love had the power to do that – to change you, uplift you, or even ruin you if you let it… if you walked away from it.

I double-clicked, and the first picture popped up, stretching across my screen like a digital slap in the face. I flinched with pain at the happy image of Christian and me. The framing was lopsided, the result of Christian flipping the camera on us as he clicked. His arm was tight around me, holding me against him as his lips pressed to the hollow beneath my ear. My eyes were squeezed shut, but I was smiling so big that it looked as bright as the morning sun. My hair was short, falling just an inch below my ear, and I recognised the sundress I was wearing as the one I had worn when he had proposed. The photo was from that day.

I hit the right arrow key to scroll to the next photo, and my brow creased. It was one of Christian lying with his hands behind his head with a small smirk on his face as he glanced up at the lens, his sparkling eyes squinting into the sun. I remembered when it was taken. I was sitting across his abdomen, as suggested by the angle.

It amused me a little to see him so comfortable in front of the camera. I suppose he would've been used to it though. I'd always brought my camera along with me when we were together. It was habit, mixed with the fear of forgetting. I wanted to capture every emotion so I could relive them. Maybe it hurt less when you knew that you still had whatever was in the photo. Goodbye wasn't hard – the memories and flashbacks were.

I swallowed and clicked to the next one, smiling at the photo of him struggling against my hand as it attempted to push his still-buttoned-at-the-time black shirt up without any luck. I could almost hear his protests ringing in my ears.

The next photograph was an image of my left hand stretched out to show the perfect gold diamond ring that he'd just put on my finger. Sometimes I wished that I'd kept it, but I had left it with the note for my parents, hoping that they would return it to Christian. I guess keeping it didn't seem right to me since I wasn't sure if or when I'd be back, and I thought that, if I took it with me, it would be harder for him move on.

I flicked to the next photo, and it that had obviously been set up. I could see the blurry rim of the picnic basket that the camera had been sitting on, but the focus was on Christian and me as we locked lips. My left hand was resting on the side of his stubbled face, and I could almost feel his lips over mine at the memory.

I hit the across button quickly, and the next photo was another one that Christian had taken of us. I was curled into his side clutching the small bunch of daisies that he'd given me. My hand rested on his chest as his lips pressed to my forehead.

I exhaled as I pressed the right arrow to the last photo, and felt tears pinch in my eyes. The last one was more artistic. It reminded me of the kind of picture seen on the front of a romance novel. I sighed when I realised that was exactly what things were like for Christian and me before it all went wrong. Before I made it go wrong.

The photo was another setup shot of the two of us. I was sitting back against his chest with my face turned towards his, and our lips lingered only a breath apart. My hand was curled around to rest on the back of his neck as he wrapped his around to rest on the back of mine. It was as if we were both guiding the other into the embrace. His eyes were closed, but mine watched him. I always felt as though closing my eyes when he was near was a waste, like keeping the cap over the lens in a photo shoot. I wanted to take in everything, remember everything. Now those memories were keeping me up at night. Irony was as cruel as karma.

I sucked in a staggered breath and reached for a tissue to mop up the tears that were rolling onto my keyboard, but the movement sent my laptop tumbling backwards onto the floorboards with a loud crash. The noise sobered me, and I blotted my moist eyes just in time for Maddie to fling my door open.

"Layla!" she gasped, making me jump again.

She switched my light on, and I flinched, squeezing my eyes closed.

"Maddie, kill the light," I groaned, reaching out to touch my lamp on.

I waited to hear a click before opening my eyes again.

"What the heck are you doing? It's quarter to twelve," she sighed as she folded her arms across her pink nighty.

"I was just looking through some pictures on my laptop to, uh, get inspired for tomorrow."

"Pictures? Pictures of what?"

"Um, South Beach. I don't know. I wanted to see if I'd taken a better shot when I was last there."

Her eyebrows pulled together. "Okay. So, why is your laptop on the floor?"

I sighed. "It fell off the bed."

"How? And why are you crying?"

I wiped my eyes on my shirtsleeve. "I'm not. I, um, sneezed."

She nodded slowly and stepped towards my computer to pick it up. I remembered what picture was left on the screen and felt my heartbeat in my ears.

"No!" I near shouted.

Maddie already had the machine in her hands. "What?"

"I... I..." I stuttered. She turned it over, and I noticed that the screen was black, so relaxed a little. "I was worried you might get electrocuted. You know how laptops can be faulty."

Maddie raised her eyebrows as if to question my sanity. She rested the computer on top of a pile of clothes on one of the kitchen chairs that was just inside my door.

I bit down hard on my lip to silence myself.

"Maybe you should get some sleep," she said. "Clearly you need it."

I breathed a laugh. "Right. So, what are you doing up anyway?"

"I was brushing my teeth. I've been reading something that Christian recommended."

I frowned. "Oh. Well, goodnight."

"Goodnight. I'll see you in the morning."

I nodded and slipped down under my covers then reached to tap my light off. I heard my door click closed and waited until I heard Maddie close hers before sitting back up and tapping on my lamp to check if my laptop was okay. I was terrified that I'd lost the photos, afraid that the last remaining evidence of good memories with Christian were now gone forever.

I pressed the on button again and waited, but nothing happened. I pushed it harder, but there was still nothing. I could feel a whimper building up in the back of my throat, and felt the last ounce of hope disappear with each frantic press of the small round button. I let my hands fall hopelessly onto my blankets and then looked down at the floor, noticing the power cord. It had fallen out when the machine had tumbled to the floor.

I sniffled and closed my eyes to compose myself. Once upon a time, my laptop could last on the battery. But now, being several years old, it relied on being plugged into a power socket to function. I rested my hand on the computer to keep it in place and leant over to grab the plug. My breathing stopped as I pressed the power button again, only this time, it hummed back to life. I rested my head back on my bed head, waiting for the system to start.

To my relief, I hadn't lost the photos. My memories were still intact. I bit my lip and re-zipped the file, and then shut the system down properly before sliding it safely under my bedside table.

I tapped off my lamp and waited for sleep to come. I wasn't even surprised when it didn't. So, instead, I thought about what Mitch had said and wondered if the promise I'd made him was a realistic one for me to keep. Maybe Christian and I would never be how we were before, but I needed to believe that we would be better than we had been in the last few days. But then could we ever be just friends after everything we'd been through? Could we watch on and support each other as we both found other people to love?

A resounding 'no' echoed in my head. Mostly because I couldn't imagine loving anyone else the way that I loved him. Plus, moving into friendship with him meant that he would need to hear me out and forgive me for what I did – or at least get past it.

I couldn't even get past it.

I couldn't get past him.

What had I done?

How could I have acted so impulsively and thrown away everything I'd ever wanted? What did I really expect to happen when I left him and our life behind? Did I really think that if I did see him again that everything would be bygones? Maybe I hoped as much, but maybe it was more than that. Maybe I had just hoped that, even though I wanted more for him, he wanted me enough to try to find me.

Somewhere between my hypothetical torments, my mind drifted off into another world. It was a world where the hypothetical didn't matter because everything was as it should be. In this world, the Christian and Layla now were the same Christian and Layla as the people in the photographs.

They were together.

They were happy.

They were in love.

Chapter Seven
Between a Rock and a Hard Place

"Layla!" Maddie's voice rang, piercing through my subconscious.

I sat up, a little disorientated, and looked around. Surely I hadn't been asleep. Surely it wasn't time to be awake already.

"Layla, why are you not up? We have to meet Jeffrey in half an hour," she said from my doorway.

I grabbed my pulsing head and pulled back my covers, standing shakily on my feet.

"Why did you let me sleep in then?" I groaned.

"I thought you were awake."

"Oh, God. Give me two minutes to throw something on."

Maddie looked at me warily. "We'll need to get you coffee on the way."

She stepped out, closing the door behind her, and I reached for the closest shirt I could find. I pulled it on and found a pair of black slacks and, on my way out the door, I stepped into my only pair of comfortable heels. I stumbled as I reached for the handle though, and smacked my head on the corner of some shelves. I shrieked and twisted the door open, lifting my hand to my head as it pulsed like a tribal drumbeat. Maddie was standing in the doorway with her arms folded.

"What is going on, Layla?" she muttered. "You're a hot mess."

I groaned, and removed my hand. There was a bloodstain on my palm. "I hit my head. Can you get me a Band-Aid?"

Maddie frowned and went to get the first aid kit from under the kitchen sink. She returned with a dampened tissue and lifted it to my head. It was lucky that she was a little taller than me.

"It's okay," I whispered. "I'll do it in the car. We're already going to be late."

Maddie pressed her lips together. "Maybe you should stay. I don't know if—"

"I'm fine, really." I nodded. It was a bad idea because the motion made my head spin. "Come on, Jeffrey's expecting us."

**

Maddie didn't speak much on the way to the South Coast City shopping centre, but I did notice a few side glances in my direction when she thought I wasn't looking. I dabbed the dried blood from my forehead as best I could and then carefully put the Mickey Mouse plaster in place. I was a little impressed that I'd managed to avoid spotting my white shirt, but then realised I had gotten a few drops on my left collar.

As we drove, I tried my best to make myself presentable. I ran my fingers through my hair and twisted it over my shoulder to hide the blood drops. At least it was still straight from the day before, so it was relatively manageable.

"There is eyeliner and mascara in the glove box," Maddie said, watching as I dabbed my fingers under my puffy eyes.

"Thanks," I murmured, and then clicked open the compartment.

Maddie glanced back to the road as the light turned green, and the car moved off slowly. By the time we got to the shopping complex, I looked much better. Luckily, Maddie also had a tub of lip-gloss and a foundation stick in the glove box, so I was able to hide the dark circles under my eyes too. If it weren't for the Disney Band-Aid plastered on the slight rise of my forehead, I would have passed as normal – or as close to what passed as normal this past week.

"Are you sure you're all right to do this?" Maddie asked.

I looked over at her and saw that she was looking at me with pity.

"I'm fine. I'm better than fine." I shrugged, and then glanced at my watch. "Let's go. We're already five minutes late."

Maddie sighed, opening the driver's side door and watched as I heaved myself up, clutching the doorframe for support. I noticed her looking and recovered myself. I even managed to force a smile.

It took us probably five minutes to get to *Reflective Jewellers* and, when we walked in, Jeffrey was already with a customer. He looked up and held up his index finger when he saw us. Another female sales assistant saw the transaction and took over from him, allowing him to come over.

"Hey, you made it." He grinned, glancing between Maddie and me. He looked back at me and mashed his lips together. "Uh-oh, what happened to you?"

I felt my cheeks flush and raised a hand to my wound. "I tripped."

"Mickey to the rescue, huh?"

I breathed a weak laugh.

"Okay, feel free to have a browse at our selection," he said. "I can help with anything you'd like to look at."

"Great." Maddie smiled. "Is there anything you can recommend?"

"You said a wedding theme, right?" he asked. "So, you'll need earrings, necklaces, perhaps a bracelet, and definitely some wedding bands."

Maddie tipped her head. "That sounds about right."

Jeffrey nodded contemplatively. "You have the dresses. What are they like? Simple, traditional, contemporary, intricate…?"

Maddie looked to me for support.

I blinked twice. "Does it make a difference?"

Jeffrey smiled. "If you want something that will go with the gowns. Did you have anything particular in mind?"

Maddie and I exchanged another glance, and he laughed.

"Like gold or silver," he said. "Pearls, diamonds, rubies, sapphires…?"

"I'm not sure. Layla's the wedding expert," Maddie answered.

I rolled my eyes. "I wouldn't go that far. I'm more the artistic director."

"So, what are you thinking then, Layla?" Jeffrey asked.

"Well, we have two white dresses coupled with a pale blue bouquet. So, maybe white gold and, like, blue stone or something could go with that." I shrugged. "Then we have a gold gown, so I'd say maybe yellow gold with a yellow topaz stone or something could work nicely with that. But, I don't really know. You're the jeweller, so you tell us."

Jeffrey tipped his head back, brushing his fingers under his chin in thought.

"At least now we're getting somewhere in regards to colour themes," he said. "So, I suppose… what bouquet are you having with the gold dress?"

"Frangipanis."

He nodded. "I think maybe if you added some diamond or crystal in the setting it would look nicer. It will tie the tones together a little better."

"Whatever you think."

"Okay." He smiled. "Follow me. I think I have something that could work."

He paced behind the counter and made his way around to the back of the store where there was a small display. He pulled out a bunch of keys attached to a plastic spring clip on his belt and unlocked the cabinet. Then, he removed a stand and placed it on the glass counter.

"So, this is diamond and citrine gemstone," he explained, gesturing towards the stunning gem-studded necklace coupled with matching earrings. "As you can see, the stones are set in yellow gold and alternate around the entire necklace. The earrings are similar but, yeah, they drop down in the same pattern."

"Wow," Maddie gushed. "They're exquisite."

Jeffrey smiled at her enthusiasm and then looked at me. "What do you think, Layla?"

I shrugged. "They're pretty perfect. Do you have a bracelet that would go with that?"

Jeffrey tipped his head contemplatively. "Well, with this, you could put a studded diamond bracelet set in yellow gold. For the ring, I would do the same thing with maybe a princess cut diamond. You could use one in a white gold setting."

"Okay, sounds great." I nodded. "Can we see them?"

Jeffrey laughed. "All business."

He turned and disappeared to get them. Maddie sighed and turned to me.

"You could be a little nicer about it," she whispered. "He's doing us an incredibly huge favour here."

I felt my forehead crease and winced. "Am I not being nice?"

"A little more enthusiasm wouldn't go astray."

"Well, I think you're enthusiastic enough for the both of us." I smiled, nudging her lightly in the arm.

Maddie tried to hide a smile but failed.

Jeffrey returned with the pieces of jewellery, and both Maddie and I agreed that they were perfect as a set for the golden dress. Since they were locked in, we needed to look for a couple more sets in for the more traditional white wedding gowns. Maddie skipped off to look at the selection of bridal jewellery not far away, and as I went to go after her, Jeffrey stopped me.

"Layla," he called. I turned and saw him leaning against the counter. "How are things? I mean, apart from the sore head."

I smiled humourlessly. "That is really just the icing on the cake."

"Bad week?"

"Bad decade."

He laughed. "You're a little too young to be so jaded. What are you, like, twenty-two, twenty-three?"

"Turning twenty-three next month." I shrugged. "Age is just a number."

"Fair enough."

I glanced over at Maddie who frowned at me, so I cleared my throat.

"So, how have you been?" I asked. "You're not working in the museum this week?"

Jeffrey's nose wrinkled. "No, my parents need me here. They take priority over the museum."

"That's very loyal of you."

He smiled. "That's just how I was raised. Family first."

I looked down, not knowing what to say in reply.

"Listen, Layla, I was thinking—"

"Look, Christian—" I stopped and shook my head. "Sorry, Jeffrey, I… sorry. I'd better go help Maddie with, um… stuff."

I went over to Madeline and exhaled, still kicking myself internally at the slip.

"See anything that you think will work?" I asked, trying to make my tone sound light.

Maddie looked up at me. "What are you doing? Why aren't you talking to Jeffrey? Or, I don't know, making out with him?"

"Maddie, please don't try to set me up with—"

"Jeffrey." She beamed.

I mashed my lips into a tight line.

Maddie glanced at me before looking back to him. "I think some white pearls would be nice and sort of classic, then maybe an aquamarine stone in white gold as an alternative. Hey, what are you doing tonight?"

Jeffrey went from nodding about her selection to raising his eyebrows. "Tonight?"

"Tonight." Maddie smiled. "This guy I'm sort of seeing is coming over for dinner so, rather than make Layla a third wheel, I was wondering if you wanted to join us?"

Jeffrey glanced at me warily as I glared at Maddie. "Well, I mean, if Layla—"

"Great," she said with a nod. "That's settled then."

Jeffrey moistened his lips. "Um, okay. What time?"

"Seven. I'll give you our address before we go."

"Sure. So, um, if you get the pearls and aquamarine in white gold, then you'll need a white gold ring too. Plus, a couple of bands for the guy as well."

"Oh, right." Maddie nodded. "The only thing is, we don't know the models' finger sizes. But I don't think we'll have time to come back before the shoot to size them properly."

Jeffrey frowned in thought. "Well, I could bring a few different sizes out to the shoot? Where are you doing it?"

"South Beach and then *Eclipse*," Maddie answered. "You'll have to bring a bunch out, Jeffrey."

"I'll tell you what," he said, walking around behind the counter to bring out a collection of what looked like key rings. "Take this. It's all the ring sizes available. When you cast the models, just get them to try on what fits best, and call it into me. If I know the style you like, I can bring them down for you."

"Great." Maddie smiled. "So, do you want to put through the rest now?"

"Sure, I'll make out a receipt and just staple the one for the rings on later."

"Perfect, Jeffrey, perfect," she said. "Um, Layla, we need to meet the modelling agency in an hour, and I want to go back to the office beforehand. We should probably start to make tracks."

I nodded, unable to speak, so didn't bother trying. Maddie frowned at me and then glanced at Jeffrey.

"Do you mind if we take care of this now?" she asked. "I'm sorry to smash and grab, but…"

"No, that's fine." He smiled. "Just give me five minutes, and you'll be on your way."

**

The jewellery ended up totalling quite a few thousand dollars, so Maddie and I thought it was best to leave it with

275

Jeffrey until tomorrow since he was bringing the rings out to the shoot anyway. From there, we headed back to *Flash* so Maddie could pick up the dresses and suits to compare colourings with the models. It was difficult to get them all to try on the pieces we wanted, especially when they were on loan, and wear and tear was a concern.

As we made our way to meet the agency, I picked absently at my fingers.

"What's eating you, Layla?" Maddie asked. "You're making me nervous."

I looked up. "When were you going to tell me about dinner?"

"I thought I did. Maybe I forgot."

"What if I had plans of my own tonight?" I asked.

Her eyebrow lifted. "Do you?"

"No."

"Well, now you do."

"Madeline Alice Butler," I groaned. "Please stop trying to set me up with Jeffrey when I specifically asked you not to."

"That doesn't sound a thing like something I would do."

"Actually, it sounds exactly like something you would do," I mumbled. "Exactly like something you *did* do."

She giggled. "What? He's cute, and he's totally into you. Plus, it's about time you had a date."

"That doesn't mean I need your help."

Maddie pulled into the car park and looked at me incredulously.

"Why?" she huffed. "Because you've done so well on your own in the past three and a half years?"

I exhaled. "If I wanted a date, I could probably get one, but I don't. Why is that so hard for you to understand?"

"Because, Layla, I know you get lonely sometimes, and yet you never do anything about it. I'm just trying to help you."

I didn't know that she'd noticed. The thought made me frown.

"Look, Jeffrey seems like a nice guy, so just give it a chance." She shrugged. "It's not as if you have to *marry* the guy."

I felt the blood drain from my face and nodded mechanically.

Maddie cleared her throat. "Anyway, let's go to get ourselves a couple of models."

I tried to smile. "Right."

**

The agency offered us a choice from four girls and four guys, but only three of the guys were there when we arrived. So, we decided to start with the girls. We got each of the girls to pose for test shots, and then did the same for the boys. We then paired them up to take some couples shots and, it was only when we were about to brief them that the fourth guy arrived. I nearly choked when I looked up to see Troy from *Montage* swagger in.

"Sorry I'm late," he sighed. "I came straight from work."

I looked at Maddie whose eyes widened as she glanced at his Calvin Klein suit. He stepped forward and handed Maddie his audition sheet.

"That's fine," Maddie breathed, blinked, and then shook her head. "Um, if you want to pair up with, um, yeah, we'll do individual shots after."

I straightened from my camera and tripod. "Wait a minute, no, you're late."

"I know, sorry." He nodded. "I promise I won't make a habit of it."

I folded my arms. "Well, we're working on a tight schedule here, and you're nearly an hour late."

"Come on," he groaned. "I said I'm sorry."

"Right, well, *sorry* doesn't sell magazines and, like I said, we're on a tight schedule."

Troy lifted an eyebrow. "Well, do you know what *does* sell magazines? Good looking models. And, hey, you can't deny that I look great in a suit."

Maddie giggled, and I turned to glare at her. She sobered quickly, and turned her snigger into a cough.

Troy smirked at her, and he flicked his styled short brown hair out of his chocolate brown eyes.

I exhaled slowly, trying to control the rage that threatened to surface. Maddie cleared her throat and glanced at his audition sheet.

"Um, Troy?" she said nervously. "Um, how about for now we just take the couples shots, and then we can discuss this afterwards."

He lifted his hands. "Whatever you'd prefer."

Maddie glanced at me.

I took a deep breath, and the other models that were still waiting mostly in pairs looked about as impatient as I felt.

"Okay, I'll give all of you a couple of minutes to get acquainted with each other and then you'll have three frames to show me what you've got. As you know, it's for a bridal shoot, so we're looking for more, um, romantic stances."

"We'll call you in couple by couple," Maddie added.

The four pairs filed out, and Maddie wandered over to me.

"I totally hope that Troy guy can strike a pose because he is insanely cute," she whispered.

"He's a creep," I mumbled.

"How do you know?"

"I had the unfortunate fate of encountering him in *Montage* the other day."

"When?" she frowned.

I cursed internally since she didn't know that I'd gone back after she left. I had only told her that I had things to do.

"I, um," I started, trying to think on my feet. "Well, when I got lost, I went back to ask for directions and he was there. Needless to say, he wasn't very helpful."

She shrugged. "Well, this isn't a personality contest."

I sighed. "I know, and if he is the best we've got, then I guess we'll just have to hope that he's on time."

**

Troy ended up being the best, much to my acute disappointment. I shouldn't have been surprised, really, since that's just the way my week was panning out. On the plus side, he fit most of the suits and offered to exchange the ones that didn't in time for the shoot. The girl that I favoured to be his magazine-bride was a redheaded beauty who I later found out was Holly Forrester, Maddie's cousin. She and Maddie weren't that close and barely spoke as friends, but even Maddie had to agree that she was the best person for the job.

After we'd sized them for the rings and shoes, and made sure the couture fit, we then arranged to meet the two of them at South Beach tomorrow for the first day of shooting. From there, we went to the shoemaker who would be donating the footwear to select appropriate matches. Maddie and I picked out a closed-in white satin pair and a golden strappy pair to go with the dresses, and two pairs of gents' shoes for the different suits. Then we finally headed back to the office.

I made a call to Jeffrey regarding the wedding bands, and Maddie finally called her father about using the *Eclipse* ballroom for our Thursday shoot. I wasn't aware that she hadn't called him yet but, luckily, it wasn't a problem. He even offered to cater for us and, although Maddie was hesitant in accepting his offer, he insisted. I hated to think of what we would have done if he'd declined, but I couldn't afford to dwell on the negative. Enough were going around without fabricating more.

Things seemed to be on schedule for tomorrow so, at around five thirty, Maddie and I ventured home to start on dinner for Christian and Jeffrey. I tried to help as much as I could but, after ten minutes, Maddie kicked me out of the kitchen and told me to get a shower. By the time I was out and decent, Maddie had put whatever she'd prepared into the oven and laid out some dip, crackers, and cheese on our coffee table. I was a little impressed.

"So, what's for dinner?" I asked, yawning as I made my way to the couch.

"Apricot chicken and vegetables," she answered, and then glanced up from setting the table. "Tell me you're not wearing *that*."

I frowned at my T-shirt and jeans. "What's wrong with it?"

Maddie sighed and disappeared into her room. She resurfaced a second later and threw something blue at me. I unravelled it to find it was a strappy dress.

"I'm not wearing this," I muttered. "It's too dressy for dinner."

"It's dinner with *male* company," Maddie sighed. "It's a size too big for you, but put it on. You're not going to impress anyone by dressing like a boy."

"These are not boy clothes, and I'm not *trying* to impress anyone."

"Layla, please, would you just put on the dress," she said in an exhale. "I don't have time to argue with you. They'll be here in less than half an hour and I need to get a shower."

I groaned and headed to change. "Fine, but go and get a shower now. I don't want to have to entertain them on my own."

"That would be entertaining."

I pulled the dress over my head and kicked off my jeans. I was still struggling with the zip when I stumbled back out.

"You look great." She smiled. "But maybe fix your hair and ditch the Mickey Mouse Band-Aid."

I raised my hand to tear the plaster off my forehead. "Anything else?"

She frowned in thought, and I rolled my eyes.

"Just get a shower," I sighed.

She giggled and headed towards the bathroom.

I pulled out the elastic that was holding my hair back and went to pour myself a glass of water. I had only just brought the glass to my lips when a knock sounded at the front door. Ice shot through my veins as I tipped the water out, rested the glass back upside down on the sink, and then went to answer it.

I stopped and ran my fingers quickly through my hair before taking a deep breath and turning the handle.

"Christian," I exhaled. "Come in."

"Layla." He nodded. "Thanks."

"Maddie's in the shower."

"Okay. You look, um, are you going out somewhere?"

I blinked, hanging onto the doorknob for support. "Um, no, didn't Maddie tell you? I'm staying... here."

"Oh," he breathed. "On your own?"

"Well, actually—"

"Layla," Jeffrey's voice rang.

I jumped and tried to arrange my face into a smile. "Jeffrey, hey."

"Wow, you look *amazing*, Layla," he sighed, and then looked up at Christian. "Oh, this must be Maddie's boyfriend."

I winced at the word. "Um, Jeffrey, this is Ch-Christian."

"*Christian*," Jeffery repeated slowly. "It's good to meet you."

"Likewise," Christian answered taking Jeffrey's hand to shake.

I was a little annoyed that he didn't seem more jealous, but then realised that he had no reason to be. We weren't together any more. I'd made sure of that.

"I brought some after-dinner chocolate things," Jeffrey said as he held them up.

"I brought alcohol," Christian added.

I nodded. "Oh, great, alcohol. I'll get some glasses."

Christian smirked.

"What about Maddie? Shouldn't we wait for her?" Jeffrey asked.

I froze mid-step and turned. "Maybe? I don't host a whole lot, but I don't think she'll mind."

Christian chuckled. "Well, as a hostess, it's polite to offer the guests a drink."

I nodded. "Great. I'll get glasses. You, um, sit."

The boys sat on the couch, and Jeffrey put the box of chocolates on the corner of the coffee table. I went into the kitchen for wine glasses and prayed that Maddie's shower was quick.

"So, Christian, how long have you known the girls for?" Jeffrey asked.

The glasses slipped between my fingers and smashed into a million fragments on the floor at my feet. I jumped instinctively, and felt my bare feet crunch on the glass. Of course I wasn't wearing shoes. It was a walking-on-broken-glass kind of week. A second later, I felt myself being lifted and then lowered on the edge of the kitchen table.

Christian stepped away from me, frowning. "What are you playing at, Layla?"

I blinked back tears. "You seriously think that I did that deliberately?"

Christian's eyebrows softened.

"What happened?" Maddie asked. I looked up and saw her rushing out towards us. She looked down at my feet and sighed. "What is with you today? First the head, now this. You're never this clumsy, Layla."

I just shrugged and felt someone rub my shoulder. It was Jeffrey.

"You should go and put some shoes on, Maddie," Christian said as he took a step towards her. "Um, Jeffrey and I can clean up this mess."

"Okay." Maddie nodded. She tiptoed over and wrapped her arms around him. "By the way, hello, you."

He breathed a laugh, loosely wrapping his arms around her. "Hi."

The aching in my feet took my mind off my hurting heart.

"Is the pain bad?" Jeffrey asked.

I looked up. "What?"

"Your feet."

I nodded. "It all hurts."

"Maddie do you have tweezers or something?" Jeffrey asked. "I think we should get the glass out."

"Of course, I'll go and get them." She smiled. "Such a gentleman."

"Mads, where do you keep your dustpan?" Christian asked.

"The bottom of the pantry," she called back.

I glowered, *Mads*. Great, nickname of a nickname basis.

Maddie disappeared to get shoes and tweezers while Christian swept up the glass. Maddie then mopped up the blood while Jeffrey removed the slithers of glass in my feet. It was all a little ironic that, once again, I had made a mess of things and left other people to clean it up.

Generally speaking, my feet weren't cut up too bad, but there was a rather large slice to my left heel that caused the most pain. The rest of the cuts were rather superficial, so Jeffrey dabbed some disinfectant on the wound and plastered it up with more Mickey Mouse Band-Aids. I made a mental note to buy some adult plasters if my clumsiness was likely to continue. Apparently, Maddie thought the same.

"If this keeps up, we're going to run out of those soon," Maddie sighed.

I ignored her jibe. "Maddie, can you grab my socks for me?"

"Sure, but I really need to check on dinner first. I don't want it to be ruined."

I wondered if that was her way of implying that the food was the only thing about tonight that I hadn't ruined.

"I'll get them if you like," Christian said.

"You're an angel." Maddie smiled.

It was probably a bad idea, but I'd disappointed Maddie enough tonight. Plus, it wasn't as if Christian had never been in my personal space before. I just hoped that I hadn't left anything incriminating around.

"Um, my room is to the right of the bathroom," I said. "My socks are in the second drawer beside my bed."

Christian nodded and turned to make his way towards the small hallway. It felt like he had been in there for minutes when he finally resurfaced with a pair of fluffy purple socks and handed them to me. Jeffrey took them and carefully slid them over my feet.

"Dinner's probably got about twenty minutes," Maddie announced.

I slid off the corner of the table and cautiously pressed my feet onto the floor. It stung a little, but I ignored the pain. It was concerning how second nature that was becoming.

"Are you right? Do you need a hand?" Jeffrey asked.

"No, I'm right," I breathed. "Where's that alcohol?"

Maddie smiled and handed me a glass. I took a big gulp.

"So, what is for dinner anyway?" Christian asked. "It smells great."

"Apricot chicken with some vegetables," Maddie replied. "I hope you guys like it."

Jeffrey's lips pressed together.

"What?" I smirked.

He shrugged. "I'm sort of vegetarian. I probably should have mentioned that, huh?"

I couldn't help but laughed. Christian also looked a little amused but tried to hide it.

"But you're Italian," I said.

"This is a disaster." Maddie pouted.

"No, it's not," I replied. "Hey, Jeffrey, do you like macaroni and cheese?"

"Layla, you are not serving him—"

"Well, are you going to force-feed him meat?"

"It's fine, really. I'll just eat the vegetables," Jeffrey said. He was starting to look a little uncomfortable.

"Nonsense," I sighed.

I limped towards my room to grab the T-shirt I had been wearing earlier, so I didn't mark the dress. When I returned, I saw Christian's lips twitch as I pulled my hair back and fastened it with the elastic around my wrist.

"Jeffrey, sit," I said. "It'll take me twenty minutes, and it's honestly no trouble. Plus, my mac and cheese is what people write songs about. It's amazing."

Christian's gaze dropped to his feet, but I could still see the smile that he was trying to hide.

Maddie was suddenly behind me as I stretched to boil the kettle and grab an onion. She went to get the pasta from the cupboard and the cheese from the fridge.

"Christian, can you grate the cheese?" I said. I didn't even realise that I'd asked until the words were out. They sounded too familiar as they hung in the air.

Christian stepped forward, but Maddie lifted her hand towards him.

"No, you sit too," she groaned. "Layla, you can't put him to work. He's a guest."

He shrugged. "I don't mind."

Jeffrey stood. "Then what can I do, Layla?"

"Um, when the water is boiled, can you put the pasta on to cook? You can be in charge of that," I answered.

"We are like the worst hostesses ever," Maddie mumbled.

With the four of us working together, we got the macaroni cheese ready to bake in record time, and it was ready about ten minutes after the chicken came out of the oven. We didn't talk much during dinner. Maddie did, mostly quizzing Jeffrey because I wasn't. It was a little awkward, but it wasn't the worst dinner I'd ever had.

When we were finishing up, Jeffrey looked over at Christian again.

"Hey, you never mentioned how you knew the girls," he said.

Christian didn't even flinch.

"I met Maddie last week when she came into my work," he replied. "I went to high school with Layla."

"No kidding?" Jeffrey smiled. "So, you've known each other for a while then?"

I looked up when Christian didn't reply and realised that Jeffrey was directing the question at me.

"I suppose so." I shrugged. "So, Jeffrey, you must be the only vegetarian Italian in South Coast."

Jeffrey laughed, but I saw Christian frown from the corner of my eye.

"There certainly aren't a lot of us. Apparently, it's not bad enough that I spell my name with a 'J'. The letter 'J' isn't even in the Italian alphabet. So, basically, I'm the lousiest Italian ever." Jeffrey chuckled. "But I am sorry I didn't mention the vegetarian thing. I didn't even think to."

"Please don't apologise," Maddie replied. "I hope it was all okay. I should have asked you today what you liked."

"It was great, actually. I'll have to get the recipe for that mac and cheese, Layla."

Christian looked at me. I took another sip of wine.

"I don't use a recipe," I answered. "I've been making it so long that I wouldn't even know what amounts to write down."

Christian leant over towards Maddie.

"Why don't you go and sit down in the lounge. I'll take care of the dishes," he whispered.

I cleared my throat. "I'll give you a hand, Christian. Jeffrey, you can and keep Maddie company. Ask her about the models we got for the shoot."

Jeffrey's mouth closed, and I guessed that he was about to offer to help with the dishes.

"Okay, if you're sure." He shrugged. "In my house, the cook never does the cleaning."

I smiled. "Go and relax. We won't be long."

Christian stood up, shaking his head infinitesimally as he cleared away the plates and then backed towards the kitchen. I stacked the remainder of the dishes and followed him in. Maddie and Jeffrey went into the lounge room.

Christian was leaning over the sink when I placed the plates beside the ones that he'd brought in. As I hobbled up next to him, he turned his crystal blue eyes on me. After four years, they still had the power to make my heart melt, even when they looked as annoyed as they did now.

"What are you playing at, Layla?" he whispered.

I huffed. "Me? What about you, Christian?"

"And what is that supposed to mean?"

His eyes were blue flames, and I had to look away to regain control over my brain function.

"I mean that there are a thousand other girls in South Coast that you can date," I muttered. "Why does it have to be my best friend?"

"Why does it even matter to you, Layla?" he snapped. "You asked that jeweller guy to dinner, and you don't see me getting all crazy about it."

I recoiled in the sting of his words.

"Maddie invited Jeffrey, not me," I said. "And that wasn't the question."

He turned on the hot water tap and squirted detergent into the sink. "Whatever. The point is that you lost the right to complain about who I date the day you walked out on me. I never wanted to date anyone else ever again. You were the one who didn't love me enough to stay."

"I—" My throat suddenly felt thick, as though his words had been shoved down to block my airways. "I love you. I mean, Christian, I loved you. How could you even think—?"

"I don't…" he shook his head and cut off the water. "I don't want to have this discussion with you. Not now, or here, or…"

"Christian," I whispered as he backed away and left the room. I frowned at the water in the sink and then jumped when Jeffrey suddenly appeared beside me. My hand rested over my beating heart.

"Gosh," I sighed. "How long have you been standing there?"

He shook his head. "Not long. So, you and Christian used to date, huh? Were you and he high school sweethearts or something?"

I closed my eyes and exhaled. "Something like that."

"Does Maddie know?"

"No. And I'd really like to keep it that way."

"She won't hear it from me," he replied. "So, were you two serious?"

I cleared my throat. "We were engaged."

Jeffrey laughed and shook his head. "Wow, okay."

"But I messed everything up, and now he can hardly stand being in the same room as me."

Jeffrey began cleaning the plate on the top of the pile.

"What did you do?" he asked. "If you don't mind me asking."

I blew out a breath. "Four years ago, I left town the day of our rehearsal dinner without telling him or anyone why. Up until last week, I hadn't seen him or spoken to him since."

"Ouch."

"I know. It was cruel, but I… I had my reasons. They seem stupid now."

He waited but, thankfully, didn't ask me what they were.

"Do you still love him?" he asked instead.

I didn't know which question I would have preferred, but I couldn't lie.

"Yes, I never stopped," I whispered.

Jeffrey handed me the clean plate, and I rinsed it before drying it.

"Well, it must be hard for you to see him with Maddie," he said. "So if you need a shoulder, or hey, even someone to make Christian jealous, I'd be more than happy to help."

"Thanks, I'll keep that in mind." I laughed, but it sounded a little flat. "Actually, there's a work ball thing I have on Friday night if you're interested. It should be sufficiently painful, but I have to go to take photos. Do you want to be my plus one?"

He smiled. "Let me guess, Maddie is bringing Christian?"

"Look, I understand if you don't—"

"Sure, it sounds like fun."

"Oh, I promise it won't be," I sighed. "But it might be a little more bearable with you there."

"Good. I'm definitely in then," he replied. "And, hey, if you change your mind about the whole dating thing…"

I rolled my eyes. "You'll be the first to know."

Jeffrey passed me another plate, and I rinsed and dried it. We continued in comfortable silence until footsteps sounded behind us.

"What's going on in here?" Maddie asked.

I sighed. "I know what it looks like but, honestly, we're just washing the dishes."

Jeffrey chuckled. "Actually, Layla just asked me to that ball of yours on Friday night. It's going to be awesome."

Jeffrey's enthusiasm was almost infectious.

"Oh, yay, I'm so excited," she squeaked.

I glanced over my shoulder and saw that Christian was hovering behind her and my almost-smile cracked. I turned back to rinsing and drying.

"Layla, make sure you tell catering that Jeffrey is vegetarian, or you'll have to whip up another mac and cheese," Maddie said with a giggle.

"That I wouldn't mind." Jeffrey smiled, giving me a playful nudge. "Food of the gods, right there."

I smiled tightly, stealing another glance at Christian who seemed to maintain an even expression. It confused me a little that everyone in Almanbury seemed to think that Christian was still pining for me when I could hardly even get him to speak to me. Maybe they had the story wrong, or maybe he'd just gotten over it. I mean, it had been four years, and it wasn't as if I expected him to stay single forever. I just didn't expect to have a front row seat to him moving on. But maybe Maddie wasn't the first girl he'd been with since I left. It hurt to think that she wasn't, but I had no right to be annoyed about it. Regardless of my reasoning, it was my choice to leave. All I'd ever wanted was for him to find happiness in his life and, if I never planned to return to Almanbury, it wasn't right for me to expect him to wait for me.

I sighed out loud, and Maddie laughed.

"Are we boring you, Layla?" she asked.

I blinked. "Sorry?"

"You're not even listening to us, are you?"

"Sorry, no. I was just… drowning in my thoughts," I mumbled. "Were you talking to me?"

She rolled her eyes. "Jeffrey and I were just talking about that movie we saw last week. It was so funny."

I tried to smile. "Yeah, it was pretty funny."

"Are you okay?" she asked for what felt like the millionth time in the last few days.

I lifted my hand to my head. "I, um, you know, my head and feet kind of ache, so I might go lie down for a while. I'm sorry to be rude, but I want to be on point tomorrow. I can't afford to mess up the shoot."

"That's true." Maddie nodded. "You should go to bed. The guys and I can take care of the rest of the cleaning."

Christian and Jeffrey exchanged a look, and for some reason, I felt like crying. I didn't know where it came from, but I hoped it was only from exhaustion.

"Thanks," I whispered. "Sorry and thanks. I'll just see you in the morning."

Maddie tapped her index finger on my nose. "Just make sure you actually wake up tomorrow."

I laughed weakly. It sounded forced. "Okay. Goodnight. Goodnight, guys, thanks for coming."

"Night, Layla." Jeffrey smiled. "See you in the morning."

He put one arm around me in a half-hug, and I weakly patted his back.

I stepped back, and Maddie waved. Christian was staring at his feet and didn't even look up.

By the time I got into bed, I ached everywhere. The physical pain was unbearable, the mental throbbing was intolerable, but it was the emotional agony… that was absolutely insufferable.

Chapter Eight
Murphy's Law

I woke up from my light slumber a few minutes before my early alarm chimed. It was probably a fragment of a millisecond before my feet and head started to pulse again, reminding me that I was still alive. As I lay there, I wondered if they were as red and as swollen as they felt. But, then again, they didn't balloon up the room, so I took that as a 'no'.

I got up slowly, pulling off my bed socks and examined the damage. My left heel looked unsightly, but I couldn't dwell on it because the sound of rain distracted me. Surely it couldn't be raining. It was the middle of spring in South Coast. It didn't even rain in winter here.

I crawled to the end of my bed and pushed back the curtains as beads of water ran down the outside glass. I groaned internally. Doing a bridal photo shoot at the beach would not be a possibility, even if it did stop anytime soon. If the dresses got sullied, it would breach the lease agreement.

I flopped back on my pillow as my alarm went off. I silenced it before it made the second ring.

"Layla, it's raining!" Maddie yelled from her room. "What are we going to do?"

"I don't know," I called back. "Maybe we could put up a marquee or something?"

"Where are we going to find one of those?" Her voice sounded closer and I waited a moment to reply as my door burst open.

"We'll figure it out," I sighed.

She frowned. "How are you feeling today? Better?"

"Somewhat. I think I'll survive."

"Good. I'm going to get a shower. Breakfast in ten minutes?"

"Okay, I'll toast some crumpets."

She grinned and turned, pulling my door closed as she left. I swung my legs over the side of my bed, feeling a sting as the blood ran down to my wounded heel. As I shifted my weight off the bed and onto my feet, I reached for the support of my bedside table and my fingers knocked a pile of crap onto the floor in front of me.

I frowned at it all. There was a book that I'd started but hadn't read much of lately, a pocket torch, my alarm clock, and something gold. What was that? I lowered carefully and picked up the coiled chain, letting it hang loosely to examine it.

I felt my heart squeeze. It was my necklace – the goldstone pendant wrapped in the woven yellow-gold cage. It was the first piece of jewellery that Christian had bought me. He'd given it to me on our first anniversary and said that the stone reminded him of the gold twinkle in my eyes. I hadn't seen this since… when? Years, not since… since I'd left Almanbury four years ago. But how was it here?

I frowned. I remembered taking it off the morning of the rehearsal dinner to shower, but I had forgotten to put it back on. Other than that, I never usually took it off. I was so mad that I'd left it behind. So, how was it here? Why was it here?

My heart whipped into a sprint. Christian. Christian had been in my room last night to get my socks. Had he planted it here for me knowing how much it meant to me? Or was I officially paranoid and going insane?

I opened the clasp, fixing the necklace around my neck and then straightened. Another shot of pain ran through me.

I reached for nearby track pants and pulled them on, limping with my laptop into the kitchen. I plugged it in and pressed the power button, organising the crumpets to toast, and then made some coffee while I waited for it to start. By the time Maddie had finished her shower, I had coffee made, the crumpets dripping with honey, and was searching for a place on the internet that hired out marquees.

"Casual Wednesday?" Maddie smiled. She looked stunning in a pale pink shirt, and a pair of light grey slacks coupled with a matching vest.

"Hey, I've made breakfast and think I've found something that can help us," I murmured. "Can you pass me the phone?"

"What 'cha got?" she asked, sliding me the hands-free. She picked up the crumpet and took a bite, clasping the coffee mug in her other hand.

"I think I found a marquee."

"Don't forget you'll have to clear it with the South Beach Surf Club first," she said, gulping a mouthful of coffee.

I pressed the hang up button. "Crap, you're right."

I opened another search tab and looked up the number of the Surf Club.

Maddie frowned. "What's that necklace? I've never seen it before."

She reached towards it, and I flinched.

"Relax, I'm not going to strangle you with it." She laughed.

I exhaled. "Sorry."

"It's nice. What stone is that?"

"Goldstone."

"Mm." She nodded. "The colour sort of matches your eyes."

I grimaced, dialling the number of the Surf Club. Maddie took another bite of her crumpet as I waited for the phone to pick up.

"*Good morning, South Beach Surf Club, this is Lila.*"

"Lila, hello, my name is Layla Thomas. I'm a photographer for *Flash Magazine*," I replied, playing with my necklace. "I spoke to someone yesterday regarding a photo shoot that my colleague and I are doing on the grounds there today."

"*Yes,*" she answered. "*What can I do for you, Miss Thomas?*"

"Look, as luck would have it, the weather is not looking so great for an outside shoot today, so we were wondering if it was possible for us to maybe get someone to come in and put up a marquee so we can still go ahead with it? We would postpone it, but we're on a deadline, and I understand that you already have a function booked there for tomorrow."

"*That's right,*" Lila replied. "*But, actually, you wouldn't need to get someone to come out for the marquee. We have some stored up out the back so I can arrange maintenance to put a couple up for you. How many will you need?*"

My eyebrows lifted. "Oh, um, well, maybe two... one for the actual shoot and one for the crew and extras."

"*Okay, sure. You're due here at about eight thirty, aren't you?*"

I glanced at my watch and noticed it was just going on seven fifteen. "Yes, that's right."

"*Great, I'll let them know to make sure it's done before you arrive,*" Lila replied.

"Thank you, that's wonderful," I sighed. "See you then."

"*You're welcome, Miss Thomas, bye now.*"

I hung up and exhaled. "Well, the Surf Club already have them, so they're going to put them up for us."

Maddie beamed. "Seriously?"

I nodded. "It seems a little too easy though."

"Ever the sceptic. Why can't you just accept the fact that sometimes things just work out?"

I gave her a wry smile. Maybe it was just because I knew better. I reached for my mug and took a long sip of coffee, enjoying the calm before the inevitable storm.

**

After breakfast and a shower, I tried on every pair of shoes that I owned to find the pair that hurt the least. I was sure that, by the end of the day, it wouldn't matter which pair I chose anyway. But surprisingly, the heels were the best since they pushed the weight onto the balls of my feet.

Maddie frowned at me when I walked out.

"Layla, you look as if you're dressed for a funeral, not a wedding shoot," she sighed.

I straightened my black shirt and black pinstriped slacks.

"Well, I can't wear jeans, and I don't have anything else that's clean," I replied. I slung my camera bag over my shoulder and reached for my tripod. "Can you grab that reflector for me? We'll need it today."

"We're going to be late. It's lucky that we brought the clothes and shoes with us, or it would be heaps worse," Maddie said. "When is Jeffrey meeting us?"

"Nine. You called hair and makeup and told them to meet us then too, right?"

"Yes. I think."

I frowned. "You *think*?"

"I'll call to remind them on the way. Can you drive?"

"Maybe not with my feet all cut up."

"Right, you call. I'll drive," she said.

When we arrived at South Beach, everything was set up just as Lila had promised. We checked in with her first and then headed down to where we were holding the shoot. I got Maddie to drive her car down to park as close to the marquee as possible for easy access. Then we started to unpack.

Holly arrived a little before nine and slipped into the Surf Club change rooms to put on the first dress – the white Ambrosia White gown that Christian had found me wearing in *Montage*. The makeup artist arrived not long after, and the beautification process began. Jeffrey was a little late with the jewellery, but it didn't matter. Holly wasn't ready to start until after nine thirty, which was when Troy decided to rock up. Troy needed a bit of touching up before we started, and that set us back further. We didn't get started on the first round of proofs until nearly ten thirty. It was then that it also started to rain.

The shots were good but not great, and the connection between Holly and Troy that we were relying on seemed to flicker and fade as time progressed. The pressure began to get to me, and it was evident to everyone at the shoot. After about an hour, Maddie suggested that I take a short break, so I headed to her car for a bit of quiet. I rubbed my eyes, trying to centre myself. After a moment, a shadow moved over me, and I looked up to see Jeffrey. He crouched down at my side, and I noticed that it had stopped raining for the first time since we started.

"What's up, Andy Warhol?" he asked. He patted my knee in what I thought was supposed to be a comforting gesture.

"Andy Warhol was more of a painter and filmmaker," I replied.

Jeffrey laughed. "Oh. Are you all right? You look a little… glum."

I shook my head. "This is disastrous. We never should have picked Troy, he's a complete tool. He's supposed to look like he's in love with Holly, not himself."

Jeffrey chuckled. "It's not that bad."

I looked up at him and flicked on my camera, then turned the viewfinder around to show him a shot. Troy's chest was pushed out like a pigeon, his body slightly in front of Holly's as he dominated the frame. If I was shooting promotion pictures for suits, it might have been acceptable, but I wasn't, so it was ridiculous.

Jeffrey cleared his throat. "Oh, well, it didn't look as bad when you took a step back to see the whole picture."

"People don't see the whole picture. They only see what I capture," I said. "I don't know what to do. The only shots I can really use are the ones of just Holly."

"Well, weddings are all about the bride anyway."

I nodded and drew in a breath. I was midway through exhaling when a squeal sounded. Both Jeffrey and I looked up at the same time that Holly paced into view, her long scarlet curls bouncing as she ran over to us with Troy right behind her. The glorious pearly gown she wore was gathered in her hands.

"Layla, Maddie!" she shrieked. "Troy spilt coffee on my dress."

"For the love of all that is holy," I groaned, climbing out of the car. Jeffrey straightened and helped me to stand.

"It was an accident," Troy called. "She nudged me, and it just splashed."

Maddie's head puckered in stress. Jeffrey looked at me as if waiting for me to snap and burn the place down. Instead, I took another slow breath.

"Jeffrey, would you do me a favour?" I asked.

He nodded. "Sure, anything."

"I was hoping you would say that."

He blinked curiously.

"Troy," I called. "Pack your things and get off my shoot. You're fired."

Maddie's eyes peeled into full moons as Troy's mouth dropped.

"What?" he grumbled. "You cannot be ser—"

"Do I look like I'm kidding? Now go before I get someone to throw you out."

"What about my pay?"

"You'll get paid if you leave now," I replied. "However, you did ruin one of our dresses, so I'll have to deduct that from your cheque."

"What?" he squeaked. "You can't do that!"

"Well, it was on loan, and I can't return it soiled."

Everyone around us remained silent while Maddie, Holly, and Jeffrey looked at me as if I had completely lost my mind.

Troy huffed. "You still need a groom."

"He's right, Layla," Maddie whispered, trying to be subtle.

Troy lifted his eyebrow as an arrogant smirk stretched across his face. I wanted to smack it off.

"Jeffrey can do it, he's about Troy's size," I answered.

Jeffrey cleared his throat. "Um, Layla?"

"Him?" Troy chuckled, pulling the silver ring off his finger. "Whatever, it's your career."

He walked over and handed the ring to Jeffrey, then headed towards the car park. Wary eyes slowly returned to me, and I pressed my lips together.

"Jeffrey?" Maddie breathed. "Please tell me that you will help us."

Jeffrey bit his lip. "I can cover today but not tomorrow."

"That's fine." I nodded. "Thank you."

"Layla, that's half a shoot," Maddie hissed.

"It's better than nothing."

Jeffrey smiled tightly, and Maddie snapped into gear, walking over to him with a garment bag.

"Please go and change then," she said then turned to Holly. "Now, about that coffee stain. Layla, any ideas?"

I rubbed my head and looked up as a droplet of water broke its way through the cover above me and fell onto my cheek.

"The dress is ruined," Holly sighed. "Maybe we should just get another one?"

"We won't be able to give it back," Maddie sighed.

I bit my lip. "Well, since it's already ruined…"

"Why? What are you thinking?"

"Holly? How are you with water?" I asked as another drip fell and splashed on my cheek.

Holly's perfect eyebrows lifted. "I'm fine with water. Why?"

I smiled and turned back to the car. I knew that Maddie kept plastic bags in there because she was a clean freak. I pulled one out to wrap around my camera.

"Okay, I don't think I'm going to like this," Maddie said. She was nearly hyperventilating. "Layla, I'm just reminding you that the dress is an Ambrosia White original, handmade —"

"And covered in coffee," I finished. "It's going to get a little wet, Mads. Are you okay with that, Holly?"

Holly grinned. "Just tell me where to stand."

Maddie's head was shaking. "Layla, are you—?"

"Maddie, hand me the bouquet," I said, pointing to the cluster of roses and lilies.

I paced over the threshold of the marquee and into the rain. It was cold but refreshing, like sticking your face into the freezer section in a supermarket and inhaling. Maddie handed me the flowers, and I passed them to Holly who had followed me into the falling water.

"So, stand facing with your back to me and maybe hold the bouquet in one hand. Okay now glance over your shoulder towards the camera," I said.

Holly did as I asked, blinking through the water as it trickled down her face. She was a natural, not too over-the-top like some of the other girls had been. She was pretty, and she relied on that to work for her. She didn't apologise for being attractive.

"Part your lips a little, but don't pout," I murmured, lifting the camera to my face. "Good."

I pressed the button down, capturing her smouldering beauty in several shots. Jeffrey returned from changing and cleared his throat.

"Where do you need me?" he asked, fixing his pale blue tie.

I glanced up and mashed my lips together. "How do *you* feel about water, Jeffrey?"

He sighed. "The things I do for you."

I smiled, and he walked into the rain, over to where Holly was standing. I saw him smile at her and say something that looked like 'hello', but I couldn't hear him over the pitter-patter around me.

"Rest your hand on her lower back, Jeffrey," I said motioning towards Holly. "And I need you to look at her as if… as if she was the most beautiful woman you've ever seen. Like your heart beats only for her."

"Poetic." Maddie smiled. "Who knew that you were a romantic, Layla?"

I glanced at her and then turned back to Holly and Jeffrey who were now dripping wet but still managed to look great. Water droplets ran through the lengths of her ruby-red hair.

"Okay, Holly, if you could wrap your arms around his neck," I directed.

Holly blushed and moved towards him, Jeffrey rested his hands on her waist. They looked at each other, squinting through the rain and then smiled. The look of adoration on their faces was evident, and it was what I had been looking for all day. Holly closed her eyes, letting the raindrops caress the plains of her face, and Jeffrey dipped his head to lightly brush her cheek. It was a simple gesture, but perfect. Actually, the sweetness of it made me a little sad. I remembered when Christian and I had been like that, the personification of love, devotion, and affection. It was a long time ago now.

"I don't suppose you guys can give us a kiss, could you?" Maddie called from the marquee. I was glad that she had been the one to ask because I couldn't seem to get the words out. My throat felt thick with emotion.

Holly ran her hands through Jeffrey's hair, guiding his lips to hers. They met lightly but sparked like electricity. Her body bowed against his as the bouquet dropped to her side. My finger kept clicking, despite my urge to cry. It was a little pathetic, even for me. Outward displays of affection never used to pinch a nerve in my heart. But I guess knowing that I'd had that with someone and thrown it away made it harder to bear.

I cleared my throat. "Okay, perfect. Um, maybe if you two could hold hands and just have a stroll around a bit. Holly, just try to keep the bouquet over the stain."

"This is adorable," Maddie gushed. "Jeffrey is so cute!"

I smiled, lowering my camera. "He certainly saved the day."

Maddie nodded fervently. "But what are we going to do for tomorrow? Can we even have a different groom?"

I mashed my lips together. "I don't know what we're going to do, Maddie. Let's just get through today first."

I lifted the camera back to my eye. One day at a time was all I could handle. Luckily, it was also all that was on offer.

**

After a few more scenic shots in the rain, Holly and Jeffrey dried off and changed into the next lot of outfits. Holly looked amazing in the golden dress, and Jeffrey looked very handsome in the Armani suit. It was really a stroke of luck that it fit him so well. I hoped that meant that my luck was changing.

It took the team a while to dry Holly's hair and do retouches to her makeup. But, by the time she was ready and holding the frangipani bouquet, the sun was out, and the sky was blue. The blades of grass still glistened, but it only added to the image. We just had to be careful not to ruin another gown, so took extra precaution to lay out the blankets that the Surf Club lent us.

We managed to get some brilliant photos of the two of them, and after a collection of shots in the golden gown, Holly made her final change into the last white dress. We got a little bolder then, moving down into the sand for some snaps with the afternoon sun dipping down into the ocean. I loved living on the west coast. It was weird to think that not everyone in the world had the opportunity to see the sunset over the beaches. South Coast was amazing for that. Almanbury, being a little more south, didn't quite get as scenic views of the sunset, even if I preferred the beaches down there.

The sun was kissing the horizon as we packed up for the day. I had taken a few memory cards worth of photos, and I was completely thrilled with how many of them were useable for the magazine. Holly and Jeffery could easily pass as young lovers.

I leant against the car, waiting as Maddie rattled on to Holly about tomorrow's shoot. I took the opportunity to go over some of the images.

"How was my first stint as a model? Did I pull it off?" Jeffrey asked.

I exhaled into a smile, and it felt like the first real one to cross my face in days.

"You were amazing," I replied. "I don't know how to thank you. You saved the entire shoot."

"You don't need to thank me. Seeing you smile is thanks enough."

I opened my mouth and then closed it again, shaking my head. "Jeffrey, I—"

"Okay, I'm sorry." He grinned. "I didn't mean—"

"It's fine," I breathed. "Any girl would be lucky to hear those words from you. I'm just not—"

"You're not any girl."

I sighed and looked around the car park. Jeffrey did the same.

"Well, I'd better go," he said. "My folks are probably wondering what happened to me."

"Did they expect you to help out at the shop today?"

"No, but I told them I'd be back before closing," he answered, glancing at his watch. "Which is in three minutes. I don't think that I'll make it."

"Well, thank you for everything," I replied. "You really came through for us."

"Anytime." He smiled. "Well, except for tomorrow, I guess. Sorry I can't be there. I hope it all works out."

"Right, we still have to figure that out." I frowned. "We might need another bride if we get another groom."

"Sorry. I wish I could help but—"

"No, don't be. You've already done so much. I mean, loaning the jewellery then stepping up, I really—"

"Layla, it's okay." He chuckled. "It was kind of fun. But if you tell anyone I said that, I'll deny it."

I nodded. "Speaking about the jewellery, I can get it back to you probably Friday depending on whether we need to do any reshoots or more shots for fillers. I hope to finish it all tomorrow though."

"No hurry." He shrugged. "But Friday is your work ball, right?"

"Right, the ball," I exhaled.

"Do you want me to meet you there? Where is it?"

I shook my head. "I'll have the ticket, so we should probably go together. Um, it starts at six forty-five. So, maybe come to our place around quarter past six, then we can go from there."

"Sure," he replied. "What colour is your dress?"

"Why?"

He raised a brow. "I don't want to clash."

I smiled tightly. "Gold lace."

"Okay. I'll see you Friday. Good luck tomorrow."

"Thanks. We'll need it."

Jeffrey winked, sliding his hands into his pockets. I watched as he strolled towards his black Subaru, and then snapped back into action.

It was another little while before Maddie and I were finally heading homeward, and the sun had been completely swallowed by the grey-blue horizon.

"For the record, I think you did the right thing in firing Troy since Jeffrey was completely perfect," Maddie said as we pulled up home. "But you do realise that we're completely screwed for tomorrow, right?"

"I know," I sighed. "If we replace Jeffrey, we'll have to replace Holly, too. It'll look odd if we're talking about everlasting love, and the groom is different."

Maddie pursed her lips. "But I wanted it to look like the wedding and then the reception. Plus, those two were so cute. We don't have time—"

"I know, Maddie. I screwed up. I'm sorry."

"I didn't say that. I'm not blaming you, Layla."

I rubbed my eyes and rested my head on the dashboard. "Why is nothing easy any more?"

"What are you talking about?" she sighed. "We'll figure it out."

I looked at her and frowned. "How is it supposed to look like a wedding and reception anyway? They're wearing three different outfits."

Maddie burst into laughter. "I never thought of it like that."

I pushed open my car door and hit something as a groan sounded.

I looked up. "Christian. Sorry, I didn't see you there."

He held the door open for me, and half smiled. His cheek dented with a dimple.

"No problems, Layla," he replied. "How did the shoot go today?"

I blinked. "Um, good."

"Good after some early drama," Maddie added.

I jumped and looked over at her because I'd forgotten she was here.

"Drama?" Christian asked. He looked amused but unsurprised. I didn't know whether to be offended.

Maddie rolled her eyes. "Layla fired Troy, so Jeffrey had to fill in, but now he's unavailable tomorrow for the second half of the shoot. So, we may have to recast both him and Holly. Crap, I guess you're going to make me tell her."

Christian looked at me. "You fired Troy?"

"Yeah, he's a tool." I shrugged. "It was quite painful to take photos of him."

Christian smirked. "Jeffrey to the rescue. Lucky he was up for it."

"Oh, he was so adorable and *so* convincing," Maddie gushed. "He'd never done a shoot before, and he was great. I think you'd be a natural too, Christian."

"What?" both Christian and I answered in unison.

"Think about it, Layla, he's perfect." She smiled. "He's gorgeous, he would look *great* in a suit… I just think he would make the perfect groom."

Christian scoffed, and I had to bite my tongue so I wouldn't add more of the traits that made him perfect.

"Regardless, we still don't have a… girl," I mumbled, refusing to say the word *bride*.

Christian noticed my discomfort and cleared his throat. "I don't see why you don't just do the shoot with the girl you have. Just don't use a guy. It could be like a runaway bride – or groom, as the case may be."

I frowned at him because he wasn't playing fair.

Maddie didn't notice the building tension.

"Like Cinderella," she mused. "Layla, that could work you know – better than having a different girl in the same dresses. You could do a bunch of those arty shots that you're so fond of."

I shook my head. "I don't know, Maddie, I—"

I choked on the words I was about to say when Christian lifted his hand to scratch his neck because on his right ring finger was the wedding band that we'd picked out. I hadn't

308

noticed it before. How long had he been wearing it? What was he trying to do to me? Get a reaction? Check. Make me feel guilty? Successful. Mess with my head? Enough.

Christian noticed my face and slowly dropped his hand.

"Just think about it, Layla, it could totally work," Maddie finished. She headed towards the front door, still completely oblivious to the discomfort oozing out of all my pores. She started to unlock the doors.

Christian folded his arms as his eyes dropped to my throat.

"Nice necklace," he whispered. "It matches your eyes."

I took a calming breath. "Nice ring."

"Are you two coming in or what?" Maddie called from inside.

We both glanced towards the door.

"I need to grab my equipment. I don't want to leave it in the car," I replied.

"Oh, I forgot about that," Maddie said. "I need to come and get the dresses and stuff."

Christian tipped his head but kept his eyes on me. "I got it, Mads."

My eyes narrowed, and his eyebrow lifted in response.

"You think *I'm* playing games," I hissed. "Well, what about you, Christian? Do you really like Maddie, or is this just a way to get to me?"

"I'm not even going to dignify that with an answer," he muttered as he walked around to the back of the car.

I exhaled. "Right, dodge the question."

"Don't lecture me about dodging things, Layla. You've been dodging everything and everyone for the last four years."

I opened the back door to pull out my camera and tripod.

"I made a mistake, and I'm *trying* to make it up now," I grumbled. "So stop—"

I gasped as Christian's hands took hold of my upper arms and spun me into him. My back gently pressed against the cold metal of the car, and his sudden closeness made my heart stutter over several vital beats.

"Stop, Layla," he said quietly. "You need to stop. Stop trying to make me feel guilty for moving on. You left, so what did you expect me to do?"

"I'm not trying to make you feel guilty. I know I gave up my right to have any kind of a say in what you do in your life, but if all of this is about punishing me, then there's a better way to go about it without involving Maddie. She deserves better."

Christian's face crumpled, and his grip on my arms loosened until his hands dropped back to his sides. He took a step back.

"Layla Louise Thomas," he sighed. "And here I thought you knew me better than that."

I swallowed, feeling as though my heart had risen to my throat. I did know him better than that. A part of me just wished that he didn't want to move on because I had never been able to. I was ashamed of it because it was selfish, but it was there. It was a big part of me.

Christian paced back to get the boxes of clothes from the boot of the car.

I frowned down at my hands. "Did you know that last Friday, the day that I bumped into you in *Montage*, was—"

"Five years since the day I proposed?" he finished, glancing over the hood to look at me. "Of course I remember. I didn't think you did though."

I smiled humourlessly. "How could I forget?"

"There are a lot of things that you seem to have forgotten."

"Layla!" Maddie called.

I jumped and turned in the direction of the house.

"Maddie," I breathed.

She beamed an adoring smile. "Your daddy is on the phone."

"He is?"

She waved the handset around next to her head. I turned to grab the rest of my equipment and struggled with it as I headed towards her.

"Tell Henry I said hi," Christian said.

I glanced back and nodded once before dropping my things inside the door. I reached for the phone from Maddie's outstretched hand.

"Dad?" I sighed.

"*Hey, kiddo,*" he replied. "*Was that Christian I heard?*"

I looked up. "Uh, yeah, he says hello. So how are you? How's Mum?"

"*Good, she's cooking dinner,*" he answered. "*Are you and he hanging out again?*"

"Um, not really," I whispered, continuing into my room and closing my door. "He's hanging out with my roommate."

"*You live with a guy?*"

I paused. "No."

"*I'm sorry, kiddo. That's got to be hard. But, hang in there; he never could stay angry at you for long.*"

"I've messed up pretty big this time though, Dad."

"*Regardless, we're always harder on those we love, but it's only because we love them. Hang in there, Layla.*"

I didn't want to say out loud that Christian didn't love me any more because it didn't feel right to even think, even if I knew it was true. He had always loved me more than I deserved, but even this was expecting too much after everything I'd put him through.

"*So, how's work going?*" Dad asked. "*Have you been busy?*"

"Super busy, actually," I sighed. "I've been run off my feet since I got back. The magazine is doing a wedding issue, so I'm stuck photographing all things bridal."

"*The punches just keep rolling.*"

I laughed. "I guess some would call it karma. So, how are you and Mum going?"

"*Oh, we're fine,*" he answered. "*She keeps fussing over me though. You know how she gets.*"

"Does she have a reason to fuss?"

"*Nuh, I've just got a bit of a sore back and neck, but I'm fine. Not that she listens to me. The woman carries on like a pork chop sometimes.*"

I smiled and then heard my mum shout something like "I heard that, Henry," in the background.

My dad just chuckled. "*So, do you think you'll come and visit again soon?*"

I drew in a breath. "I'd love to, but I'm not sure when. It might be in a couple of weeks before things calm down at work."

"*Oh,*" he sighed. "*Well, weeks are better than years, I suppose.*"

"I promise that I'll come as soon as I can, Dad."

"*Sure, kiddo. I just miss you.*"

"I miss you too," I said. "I love you, Dad. I hate that I let years go by and not tell you that more often. I promise that I'll be back soon, even if it's just for a night again."

"*Sounds good, kiddo,*" he replied, and it sounded like he was smiling. "*I love you too.*"

Chapter Nine
Love is Hopeless

I hung up from my Dad after about an hour of talking to him, then Mum, then him again. Despite everything that seemed to be going wrong in my life at the moment, I was glad that at least things were back on track with them. Before I'd left, I was really close with my parents, and I honestly didn't know how I'd kept myself away from them for as long as I did. All my reasoning for keeping my distance seemed ridiculous now. I wanted like crazy to make it up to them, but I knew that it would be difficult to get down to Almanbury in the middle of a shoot.

When I returned to the living area, Maddie had reheated the chicken and macaroni for her and Christian. The two were camped on the couch with their plates on their laps. I was jealous of the ease that they seemed to have with each other, but it reminded me of the way siblings were with each other. Or maybe I was just trying to fool myself into thinking there was nothing romantic between them. A long time ago, Christian had pledged to me that he'd never love anyone else and, even if I'd released him from that promise, I held onto the idea.

"Hey, how are your folks?" Maddie asked.

I rested the phone on the bench.

"Good, they're fine." I nodded.

"Your dad sounds really nice. Hey, there's a plate in the microwave for you if you're hungry."

"Thanks."

I walked over and put one minute on the clock then pressed start. I leant against the kitchen counter as I waited for it to heat, and my arms folded across my chest.

Maddie glanced at Christian and then back to me.

"Um, Layla," she said cautiously. "What's going on with you?"

I frowned. "What do you mean?"

She scratched her brow and placed her plate on the table. "You've been acting weirdly this past week. Plus, since when do your parents call?"

"Since now, I guess."

"You mean since you actually gave them your number," Christian clarified.

I shot him a dark look as the microwave sounded. My food was still cold when I stuck my finger in it to test the temperature, and I contemplated eating it despite the cold patches. I scooped a spoonful into my mouth, and it was disgustingly cold, so I stirred it and put my plate back in. It seemed that I would just have to deal with the third degree from my best friend and ex-fiancé for another minute.

"And *what* is going on between the two of you?" Maddie asked. "Am I missing something?"

I ignored the blush I felt tickle my cheeks. "What do you mean?"

"Quit playing dumb, Layla, it doesn't suit you," she sighed. "Did you two have a falling out or something? You've had this strange vibe-thing going on ever since we met. And why does Christian know so many things about you that I didn't know?"

I took a deep breath. "Well, it's kind of complicated."

"Layla and I were family friends back in Almanbury, that's all." Christian shrugged. It was the most casual-sounding

314

almost-truth I'd ever heard. "When she left so abruptly, I saw what it did to her parents, and I guess I've been holding it against her."

"Oh." Maddie nodded. "I guess that explains all the hushed arguments."

I bit my lip. Here I thought we had hidden them so well. Madeline clearly saw more than she let on.

"Is there anything else?" she asked. "I mean, there's nothing else to it, is there?"

I glanced at Christian and then jumped as the microwave chimed.

"That's all," Christian said for me. I could see in his eyes that he disapproved of keeping our history from her, but I also saw that he had no intention of divulging it.

"So, about tomorrow," Maddie said. Her tone was normal again, and it instantly lightened the mood. "Are we sticking with just Holly or finding a new couple?"

I rubbed my forehead, trying to smooth the creases that I was sure were permanently etched into it.

"Let's stick with Holly," I said. "I think we can make it work."

I turned back to the microwave for my food.

"Great." She smiled. "That'll save tension at the next Butler-Forrester family occasion. Not that we've had one in, like, years."

I waited for Christian to make some kind of remark about how I hadn't had a family occasion in years either, but he didn't. So, I just nodded to myself, grabbed a fork, and headed into my room to eat.

"Layla, you can stay out here with us," Maddie called.

I half turned and forced a smile that felt wrong.

315

"I'm just not real keen on being the third wheel," I answered as lightly as I could manage. It didn't really transfer, and my words seemed to hit the ground with the force of concrete.

Maddie didn't seem to notice. She just rolled her eyes. "Well, I guess I'll just see you in the morning then."

I nodded, letting my eyes fall on Christian and then back to her. "I'll see you in the morning."

**

The sanctity of my room began to feel like a prison. I wished that I had my camera and memory cards from today with me, so I at least had something to do while I was hiding and trying *not* to think of Christian and Maddie who were together on the couch. I got restless and decided to free myself from the self-inflicted banishment to wash my plate and grab my camera.

The reasoning I gave to myself was because I needed to copy the photos across to my external hard drive to free up my memory cards for tomorrow. But I knew that, way in the back of rationality, I secretly wanted to spy on Maddie and Christian. It was all very childish, but I was relieved to find that I didn't interrupt anything. The two were still sitting on the couch watching something I didn't recognise. I tried not to notice that Christian's arm ran along the back of the couch because Maddie was hugging a pillow to her chest. Clearly it wasn't a move on his part, or maybe she just wasn't responding to it.

After I left the kitchen, I crept past them to the door where I'd left my camera.

"Hey, you all right?" Maddie asked.

I sighed. "If I had a dollar for every time someone has asked me that in the past few days…"

"We're just worried."

"I know, but you don't need to be," I replied. I pulled the camera bag over my shoulder and straightened. "I'm fine."

"Well, if for some reason you're not, you can talk to me," she said.

I looked at her and noticed that Christian was glancing at me from the corner of his eye. It hurt to know that once upon a time it would have been him trying to cheer me up. Now it seemed like he couldn't care less. I suppose I deserved it. I'd brought it on myself.

"I know, Maddie. Thanks." I nodded belatedly.

"You know, you're a bit damaged, Layla." She smiled. "And I mean that in the nicest possible way."

I blinked, and Christian grimaced as he scratched his jaw.

"Well, goodnight," I sighed. "Don't stay up too late, Maddie. We've still got a big day tomorrow."

She rolled her eyes. "Yes, Mum."

I frowned and headed back to my room without another word.

It took me a while to upload all of the photos from my camera. I tried to force myself to look through them when they were done, but the reminder of love was a painful rub of salt in my wounds. So, I just backed them up on my drive and computer then turned off my light and prayed for sleep to come quickly.

It didn't.

As much as I willed it, my brain couldn't let me forget that the love of my life was in the next room, on a couch canoodling with my best friend. I tried not to listen out. I tried, but I failed. Regardless, I couldn't hear anything. I wasn't sure whether that was a good thing or a bad thing, but I did know that it was an incredibly unhealthy thing.

By the time dawn broke, I was relieved that I didn't need to keep up the sleeping façade any more, but I was exceptionally exhausted. I held a flame of hope that I would at least be able to sleep tonight so I didn't have dark circles under my eyes for the ball. My skin seemed to be permanently tinted with dark circles so, needless to say, it was a pretty small flame.

After a shower, I tried in vain to make myself look human before starting on breakfast. By seven thirty, I was not only dressed and ready, but I had also cleaned the entire house. Maddie still wasn't anywhere to be seen. I found it odd that she hadn't come out of her room yet, but I was too frightened to go in to wake her in case I found something or someone in her room that shouldn't be there. So, I waited until the latest possible second, and then stood at the end of the hallway to call down to her.

"Madeline Alice Butler, I hope you're up."

A silence followed that concerned me, so I took a few steps down towards her room.

"Uh, Maddie?"

There was a tired groan. "What, Layla?"

"It's seven thirty. We need to go soon," I replied. "Are you almost ready?"

I heard her yawn. "Oh, crap, I slept through my alarm."

There were a few bumps and another yawn, and then her door opened. I couldn't help but try to look past her, and was relieved to see that her bed was empty.

"Um, big night?" I asked, handing her a coffee.

"More like late night," she yawned big. "Christian didn't leave until nearly two."

I struggled to understand her, and after a moment of processing, I nodded while also regretting the pleasantries. "Well, Mads, I did tell you—"

"I know, I know, you told me so," she grumbled. "I should shower."

I nodded. "Make it quick. We're meeting your dad at half past eight."

"Oh, *wonderful,*" she groaned. "That's exactly how I like to start my days."

"Sorry."

"It's not your fault that my dad's a jerk."

I frowned. "I'm sure he's not that bad."

She shrugged. "You'll see soon enough that James Butler is not the great guy the business magazines make him out to be. He's a total sleazebag."

"He's still your dad."

"Only by blood. He was never around when I was growing up."

I bit my lip. "Well, you get a shower. I'll start loading the car."

She blinked so slowly I thought her eyes were going to stay closed.

"Thanks, Layla. I really need to try to wake up."

I smiled. "Maybe I should drive."

"Deal." She yawned. "I'll be ready in ten… make that twenty minutes."

I chuckled lightly. "I'll even give you twenty-five."

"Twenty is plenty."

**

We ended up leaving about forty minutes later, when my watch had ticked over to ten past eight. With traffic, it took us close to half an hour to get to the *Eclipse* hotel and, when we arrived, Mr Butler was waiting by the bar. The waitress he was talking to looked like she was trying to flirt with him, but he didn't seem to mind. Maddie scoffed and rolled her eyes. Her hand reached up to ruffle the back of her short blonde hair.

"*Dad*," she groaned loudly.

It took him a beat to realise it was him being called and then he turned slowly. The waitress turned scarlet.

"Madeline." He smiled as he pushed off the bar and swaggered over to us.

Maddie glanced at me with lifted brows, and then looked back to her father. "Hey."

"And this must be Layla Thomas." He lifted a hand towards me, and I took it.

"It's nice to meet you, Mr Butler."

"Oh, please, call me James."

Maddie gave a forced smile. "Okay, we're already behind. I'm going to go and set up."

She turned on her heel and started towards the ballroom.

I exhaled. "Thanks for letting us use the hotel for the shoot, Mr Butler."

"Layla, it's James," he said. "And it is such a tragedy."

"What is?"

"That a beauty such as yourself is behind the camera instead of in front of it."

I mashed my lips together. "I'd better go and help Maddie."

"Layla?" he said.

I half turned but didn't respond. It was sad to think that Maddie had been right about her father. No child should ever have to feel ashamed of their parent's behaviour, especially

320

when they were being inappropriate towards someone their own age.

"How is Madeline doing?" he asked. "She doesn't talk to me much. Actually, other than asking for the favour, I haven't really heard from her in the last few years."

Who would have thought that Maddie and I were more alike than I realised? I suppose the only difference was that my parents hadn't done anything wrong to have me ignore them. I was a bad daughter. James Butler was just a bad parent.

"She's great." I nodded. "She's exceptionally talented and one of the best friends I've ever had. You should be very proud of how she's turned out."

He smiled and instantly looked aged. "Thank you for saying."

"I'm only speaking the truth."

I turned to make my way up the grand double staircase to the ballroom. I found Maddie spinning around on the dance floor like a toddler in a tutu.

"Isn't it pretty, Layla?" She grinned.

I nodded. "I think it'll be great."

She slowed to a stop and exhaled. "Did James hit on you?"

"No." I didn't even flinch. "He was actually asking about you. I think he misses you."

"I'm sure he does."

I folded my arms. "You should try to talk to him more. He might surprise you."

She laughed darkly. "He always surprises me, but in the wrong way. Did I ever tell you why my brothers don't speak to him any more?"

"You never really went into detail."

She pulled her lips into a line. "He tried to seduce their girlfriends. He succeeded with Jake's girlfriend, Scarlett. But

Dean's girlfriend Tash didn't buy it. She was seventeen at the time, and Dean didn't want to believe it at first. I believe it. He's just a sleazy businessman. I don't want anything to do with someone like that."

I frowned. "Wow, that's... I'm so sorry, Maddie. I didn't know."

"It's okay. I don't like to tell people because he's still my dad, you know? But, just so you know, I have my reasons for freezing him out."

I nodded as footsteps sounded behind me. Maddie and I both turned to see Holly walk in.

"Hey, girlies." She beamed. "Mads, I just saw Uncle James. He asked us all out to lunch."

Maddie smiled, and it looked almost genuine. "I don't think we'll have time, Hols."

Holly twisted her ravishing red hair around her finger. "Speaking of which, we should get started. Did you find a replacement for Jeffrey?"

Maddie and I exchanged a look, and Holly's forehead creased.

"What?" she said.

"We've actually decided to go a different way with today's shoot," I explained. "We're not going to have a groom. It's going to be the bride's perspective. Just the bride's perspective."

"Like a bride who's been left by the groom at the reception kind of perspective?" Holly said flatly.

"Like an artistic contemplative perspective."

Maddie smiled. "Look at it this way, Hols, you won't have to compete for the spotlight."

Holly straightened, and her smile was blinding. "Well then, let's do this."

Two people filed in behind Holly with the cake we'd ordered, and Maddie guided them over to a stunning round jarrah table to set it down. A heartbeat later, the hair and makeup artists appeared, and the preparations could begin. I ushered them over to a corner to set up their station and, while they got to work on Holly, Maddie went to get the dresses. I began scoping the room.

The *Eclipse* grand ballroom was pretty extravagant. It was probably about a football oval in length, and even had its own private bar. The stage it held was big enough for a circus act, and it had an upper gallery that stretched around the entire room. I couldn't imagine that there were enough people in South Coast to fill the space – there definitely weren't enough people in Almanbury. South Coast may be small compared to some cities, but Almanbury was smaller. I looked towards the far left wall, which was almost completely made up of glass windows and doors that led out to a vast grassed area complete with a large concrete fountain. The right wall accommodated the enormous wooden door that marked the entrance from the hotel. Most of the room was filled with round tables, and each had a place setting for eight. There was a space in the middle of each for a table decoration. But given they were missing, I assumed they would be decorated with flowers, and they were waiting until tomorrow to place them. They had decorated the ballroom in trimmings of gold and brown. It looked like a snapshot of something right out of the 1940s. The chandeliers were blinding and the tapestry, intricate. I hadn't given it enough credit when I'd first entered – it was truly breathtaking. The decorators had done a commendable job.

"What are you thinking?" Maddie asked.

My hand brushed my chin. "I think we should use the back left corner. That way, we can still have a bit of the dance floor and use some of the golden hues streaming through the window."

"Typical that we're inside today and it decides to be sunny, right?"

"Maybe not for too long. We should get started soon."

She nodded and glanced over at Holly. "It looks like they're almost… well, nearly halfway done. Can I get you a coffee?"

I smiled. "I would love one."

She pulled her phone from her pocket, and I frowned.

"Madeline, what are you doing?"

She shrugged. "Calling Christian. He can drop some off on his way to uni."

"But they serve coffee downstairs."

She made a face. "Have you tasted the coffee here? It's horrible."

"You know, I don't really need a coffee."

"Too late. Text already sent."

I shook my head. "Maddie, you shouldn't treat Christian like a waiter."

"Relax," she sighed. "He was coming anyway. He won't mind."

I scratched my neck. "Why don't you go and organise the first dress for Holly. We'll only have to shoot with two of them today since the third was ruined yesterday."

"Which do you want to start with?"

"Maybe the gold one while there's sun," I answered. "The white one will look better in black and white if we need to go that way—oh shoot."

"What's wrong?"

"I forgot to do close-ups of the rings yesterday when Jeffrey was here," I groaned. "I need a male's hand."

Maddie shrugged. "Christian's on his way. He can do it."

"No, it's fine. I'll just do it back at the office. I'm sure one of the columnists can do it."

"But you said you'd take the rings back tomorrow," Maddie reminded me. "And I'm sure Christian won't mind."

Christian might not mind, but how did I feel about it? Did it even matter?

I gathered my camera equipment and began setting it up. I was fastening the legs of the tripod when Christian arrived with a tray of cups.

"Hello, you." Maddie beamed. "Thanks for the coffee."

"I think I owed you after keeping you up so late," Christian replied. "I am sorry about that."

"I'm not. It was fun."

A sharp pain shot through my chest. If I weren't almost twenty-three and healthy, I would have sworn it was an onset sign of a heart attack.

Christian glanced down and extended a cup towards me. "Coffee, one sugar, extra foam."

It took me a moment to remember how to move my arms but, when I did, I quickly reached out and clutched it.

"Thanks... you. I mean, thank you, Ch-Christian."

His eyebrows lifted.

"Hey, before you go, can you help us with something?" Maddie asked him. Her hand slid onto his shoulder, and I worked not to make a face.

"Um, is it going to take long?" He frowned.

"Maddie, let him go," I sighed. "We'll sort it."

"Come on, Layla, it's hand-held," she groaned. "It will take no time at all. We just need one of those tables, the bouquets and a couple of hands with wedding bands on."

Christian's eyebrows rose. "You want to photograph my hand? With a ring on?"

"We forgot to do it yesterday with Jeffrey. I promise it won't take a second," Maddie replied.

I frowned. "Maybe a second."

Christian exhaled. "Where do you need me?"

Maddie passed Christian the small gold ring. I adjusted my camera to the right settings.

Christian slid it on his finger then handed it back. "It's too big."

Maddie dropped the bouquet on one of the tables.

"Big?" She frowned. "Are you sure?"

Christian smiled. "Pretty sure."

I focused intently on my camera because I couldn't deny that I was a little relieved that...

"Hey, you can wear your ring," Maddie said. "Just change fingers."

Christian glanced at the ring on his right hand. The ring, our ring. The one that would have been on his left hand – it should have been there. I should have put it there four years ago.

I couldn't stop myself from watching as he removed his wedding band from one ring finger and replaced it on the other.

He cleared his throat. "What now?"

Maddie walked over to get a suit jacket. She then called Holly and handed the blazer to Christian, and he shrugged it on. I guessed she was being thorough since we would still see the sleeve in a close-up.

"Holly!" Maddie called again.

Her head popped out from behind the mirror.

"What? I'm not done yet, Mads," she answered. Her eyes panned to Christian, and despite her makeup, her cheeks flushed. "Oh, hi. Did you guys change your mind about a groom?"

"This is Christian," Maddie replied. "He won't be a groom, but we need to take some shots of the rings."

He won't be a groom.

Christian glanced at me. "So, how do you want to do this, Layla?"

I blinked. "Um, if you want to just rest your left hands kind of overlapping by the bouquet, but so we can see the rings, that would be, um, good."

Maddie gave Holly the gold ring. She slipped it on then placed hers over Christian's waiting hand.

I lifted the camera to my eye and then lowered it again. The placing looked a little awkward.

"Holly, can you try to relax your hand a little?" I said. "Make it look soft and as if his hand is like an extension of yours. Like you want to hold it... like you could hold his hand for the rest of your life."

Maddie's eyebrow lifted, and Christian's eyes burnt through me.

Holly bit her lip. "I don't think I know what you mean. Can you show me?"

I opened my mouth and then put my camera down. Holly withdrew her hand and went to remove the ring.

"No, you keep the ring on, uh," I sighed.

My hand shook as I extended it to place on Christian's. My skin prickled against his, and he tightened his grip. I fell in love with him all over again at the touch. My thumb tucked under his palm. I was too afraid to meet his eyes.

"Oh, I see," Holly said. "Your hands sort of fit together, sort of like a glove."

I removed my hand and picked back up my camera. I tried to be as quick as possible in taking the snaps, but I was also mindful that we needed them to be useable. After a moment, I stepped back.

"Thanks, guys, that's great."

"Are you sure you got it?" Christian asked. He began shrugging out of the jacket.

I nodded. "It, I, um, yes."

He glanced at his watch. "I've got to go. I'll be late for my first class."

"Thank you for the coffee and for your help." Maddie beamed.

Christian leant into her for a weak hug. "Good luck. I'll talk to you later."

Maddie giggled and nodded. Christian turned around and headed towards the door. When he was out of sight, Holly nudged Maddie.

"Nice work, cousin, he is totally hot!" she gushed. "Weird that he didn't kiss you goodbye though."

Maddie blushed. "We haven't exactly done that yet."

That was news to me. My head snapped up from adjusting my camera.

"You haven't kissed him yet?" I asked.

She shook her head. "He just came out of a serious relationship, so we're taking things really slowly."

My optimism instantly melted away at the words. Christian was in another relationship? When? Who with? Did I know her? How serious had it been? My heart felt like it had stopped beating. My eyes began to water. My throat started to close on itself. My hand pressed against my chest.

Pull it together, Layla.

"Will you excuse me for a moment?" I choked. I didn't wait for an answer, I just scrambled towards the door.

I made it to the bathroom before the tears began to fall, and all the sleepless nights hit me like a tsunami. I pulled a handful of toilet paper off the roll and mashed it against my face to silence the sobs. When that didn't work, I bit down hard on my lip. I tasted blood.

"Layla? Are you okay?" Maddie asked.

I exhaled and made sure that I had control of my voice before answering. "Yes, just give me a minute."

"Okay, as long as you're all right."

She waited a moment before her footsteps faded, and the door banged to a close. I unlocked my cubicle and dowsed my face in water, then instantly regretted it. My cleverly covered dark circles reappeared as the foundation wept off my skin.

I blotted away the moisture with a paper towel and took a deep breath.

I had no right to be upset that Christian had moved on. After all, he was sort of seeing Maddie now, and that had bothered me when I thought she was the only one. But someone else? Someone serious? I suppose I should be happy that he could continue with his life without me but, truthfully, I was gutted. Our forever had certainly not lasted anywhere near close, but it was naïve of me to think that everything stayed the same after I left. Life wasn't a photograph. The world kept spinning, and life goes on.

It was then, looking at my sallow face in the mirror, that I realised that inside I still held on to hope that maybe things could be the same as they were between Christian and me again. But, we would never be those two people ever again. Once you lose someone, even if they do come back, they're never the same person. Four years have passed, but it might as well be four lifetimes. Maybe it was time that I moved on with my life too.

I straightened myself and strode back to the ballroom, ready to throw myself into the only thing I could control in my life right now.

Holly was dressed when I returned, and Maddie was adding the finishing touches of jewellery to her golden goddess look. I walked straight to my camera and took it down to the tripod I'd set up before Christian had arrived. Maddie and Holly looked at me and exchanged a glance that questioned my sanity. I ignored it and cleared my throat.

"All right, let's get started," I sighed. "Holly, can I get you to face the window? Maddie, can you fix the train so it flows around towards me please?"

The two girls snapped into action. I focused the lens.

"Okay, Holly, just lower your head slightly and relax your shoulders… great."

I took a few shots and stepped back, pressing my index finger to my lips.

"Holly, can you sit?" I asked. "On the floor where you are, I mean."

"Sit? Um, sure." She shrugged, lowering to the floor.

Her dress mushroomed and then flattened. She rested her bouquet in her lap.

I took the camera off the stand and walked towards her, twisting a spiral of hair over her shoulder.

"Just turn towards me and lower your eyes." I raised the camera. "Great, now think of something sad."

She frowned. "Sad?"

"I know it sounds strange, but just work with me."

She bit her lip and looked down. The corners of her lips turned down, and a small crease appeared between her eyebrows. The pucker at her lips softened as her full lips separated slightly. Her brown eyes glistened, and her gaze drifted sideways. I clicked the shot on a high shutter, capturing each and every muscle movement as the brimming tears spilled down her rosy cheek. After I'd captured the shot, I rested my camera on the floor and pulled a tissue out of my pocket.

"Beautiful," I murmured. "But don't ruin your makeup."

She looked up and smiled crookedly. "It's waterproof."

"Well, that's lucky. What do you say we make this shoot a little more upbeat?"

Holly nodded.

Maddie helped her cousin stand, and I could see the questions prickling on her face. I didn't stand still long enough to give them the opportunity to surface.

The rest of the shoot went well and, although we were one groom down, Holly managed to carry the wistful gazes, and Cinderella glances all on her own.

I gave everyone a short break for lunch but worked through myself to make sure I'd gotten enough shots of the inanimate objects like the set, the cake, shoes, bouquets, and the incredible chandeliers and gold trims of the ballroom. Maddie disapproved of me not eating so tried to force-feed me some lasagne that James had sent up from the restaurant. It was too hot, so I told her I'd eat the rest later. Later never came.

**

After lunch, Holly changed into the white dress, and the process started again. I got some shots of her with the cake and even one of her taking the groom off the top of it to leave the bride alone. Maddie thought it was a great idea so the writers could weave in a '*weddings are all about the bride*' story. For me, it was easier to capture a moment when I considered that all endings were not necessarily happy. Sometimes they were just endings, just a fade to nothingness. Some endings kept you breathing but fundamentally changed. They were endings, but somehow life kept going, torturing you, and reminding you of the loss. It wasn't the endings that were hard, but the recollection of what once was.

I knew that I'd become jaded in the five years since Christian had proposed to me. The girl from five years ago would never have thought ill of happy couples because she was *in* a happy couple. I knew that I had no right to wallow. I knew that I was selfish.

We worked through until around four thirty and, at the end of the shoot, Holly went to change, and the rest of the crew went home. Maddie and I started packing up the clothes and camera equipment.

"Do you want the cake?" Maddie asked.

"What am I going to do with a three-tiered wedding cake?" I replied as I zipped up my camera bag.

"Eat it?" she offered, picking up my plate of untouched lasagne.

"Oops, I totally forgot about that."

"You haven't eaten a thing all day."

"Not true," I answered. "I had toast for breakfast and a bite of the lasagne."

She laughed. "Oh, well, *excuse* me."

I smiled tightly, and Maddie folded her arms.

"What?" I asked.

She shook her head. "You don't smile any more. Not really."

"I've been busy—"

"Too busy to smile?" She laughed. "More like you haven't had anything to smile about. What's going on, Layla?"

"Like I said, I'm just busy. I have a million things on my mind right now."

She sighed. "I'm not going to push it because I can see that you don't want to talk about it. But just for the record, I don't believe that being busy is the reason for all the pouting lately."

I lowered my eyes. "Thanks, and for the record, we should probably just return the cake to the patisserie. Maybe they can on-gift it."

Maddie nodded as Holly returned.

"Hey, Mads, are you busy tonight?" she asked.

Maddie glanced at me then frowned. "Uh, I don't think so. Why?"

"Because you're going to have dinner with Uncle James," Holly said as she reached out and pulled him inside the doorway.

Maddie shuffled uncomfortably. "I can't. I need to take Layla home."

"She can join us," James offered.

"No, she can't. She was just saying that she needs to go into work to upload the photos from today."

I forced a smile. "Right, though you really don't need to come with me if you—"

"Great, it's settled." Holly clapped. "See, Uncle James? I told you I could get her to stay."

Maddie glared at me. "But, Layla, *how* will you get home?"

"I can drop her." Holly shrugged.

"Aren't you staying with us?"

Holly beamed a breathtaking smile. "Sorry, I can't, cousin. I have a date. Are you ready to go, Layla?"

"Ready here." I nodded. "Maddie, are you right to take the clothes and cake, or do you want me to?"

"I'll take them," she answered, giving me a meaningful look. "Don't leave me here, Layla."

"You'll be fine," I whispered. "Text me if you need an exit excuse."

"Can I text you now?"

"Give him a chance. I'll see you at home."

She frowned but nodded.

I gathered my things and hobbled over towards Holly by the door. My feet still bothered me, but the pain kept me awake, so I used it during the day. Now I just wished that it would go away.

"Was that your idea?" I asked.

Holly took the tripod off me to carry. "She's got to forgive him eventually. Madeline used to think that her dad was the bee's knees until she found out about his indiscretions. The boys tried to keep it from her, but they didn't want to lie to her."

"You mean her brothers? Jake and Dean?"

Holly nodded. "When Maddie was born, and my Aunty Alice died, Uncle James made it a point to never stay home for long. Maddie reminded him too much of her. So, Jacob and Dean raised Madeline, and she never really got to know her father. It's not her fault at all, but I don't think it's his either."

"Sounds tough," I sighed.

"Well, growing up rich isn't as glamorous as people seem to think. Most of the time it means you're poor in other areas of your life. It's a balancer. It all evens out in the end."

I followed Holly to her red BMW. On the dashboard was an ID badge of employment for South Coast Memorial Hospital that said she was a receptionist there. Holly noticed me looking and laughed.

"My parents didn't want me to turn out spoilt," she said. "Right before handing me keys to my new car. Go figure."

I smiled. "Did you ever think about studying?"

"Not really, I mean, I thought about doing a makeup course and working freelance between modelling jobs, but I don't know. At the moment, the hospital gets me out of the house, and I get some pocket money out of it."

"Oh, to work for fun."

Holly started the car and laughed. "Like getting paid for your hobby? You're a photographer, Layla. You work for fun every day."

It didn't feel much like it lately, but she was right. "True."

She shook her head and smiled as she shifted into reverse. "So Maddie mentioned that you knew Christian in high school," she said. "Small world, huh?"

I flinched at his name. "Really small considering we went to school in Almanbury."

"No kidding. I wouldn't have picked you for a country girl. How long have you lived in the city for?"

"Four years."

"Nice. Which do you prefer?" she asked.

"They both have their pros and cons," I replied. "So, you have a date tonight?"

"Mm, with Peter, he's a nurse who used to work with me." She grinned. "Actually, his brother was in my sister's class at school."

"Small world."

"Small South Coast."

"Your sister's name is Anna, right?"

She nodded. "Right, Anna. She's a year older than me. She works at Ambrosia White."

"Maddie mentioned." I smiled. "So, you said that Peter's brother was in Anna's year at school. Is he older or younger than his brother?"

"Older. Like five years older. But he's been asking me out for ages."

"Age is just a number."

"True."

**

When I got home, I wasn't entirely sure that I was going to stay there. Being alone unconstructively didn't sound too appealing. So, I wrote Madeline a note, grabbed my hard drive, and headed into the office to upload the photos from the last two days to begin sorting them.

By the time I got to *Flash*, it was about quarter to six, and the last of the columnists were leaving. Ebony was just finishing her last meeting for the day, and she frowned at her watch when she saw me.

"Layla, what are you doing here?" she asked. "Surely you're done for the day. Weren't you shooting at *Eclipse*?"

"Yes, but Maddie's out, so I thought I'd come in for a bit," I replied. "That's okay, right?"

"It's okay with me but, seriously, you should relax and have a warm bath or something. You work longer hours than me."

"Yes, but I don't have anyone to go home to."

"You're still young." She smiled. "You'll have all that and more."

I couldn't return her smile because I didn't feel the same hope about my future that she did.

"Don't stay too late, okay?" she said. "You still need your rest."

"Okay, I'm just going to check through the photos while it's fresh in my mind. Plus, I need to clear my memory card for the ball tomorrow night."

"Thank you again for that," she answered as she began backing away. "I don't want you in tomorrow before ten if you're working late, deal?"

"Sure." I nodded. "Goodnight, Ebony."

"Night, Layla."

I continued to my office and hooked up my camera and hard drive. While I waited for all the photos to upload, I went to get a giant coffee. I hadn't had one since this morning, and my body was crying out for the caffeine hit. I ended up downing two before I headed back to my desk with the third. The photos were all on the system when I returned, so I began moving the good ones that could be used for the publication across to the *Flash* photo editor. Here, everyone at the magazine could be access them to look through.

The photos had all turned out well and, from the looks of things, reshoots would be minimal if at all. I didn't want to delete any, even if a couple were slightly overexposed or out of focus. If I'd learnt anything from the past, it was that it was harder to go back and fix things if you tried to erase them.

It took a long time to sort through the hundreds that I had taken, but I didn't care. It was a worthy distraction, and far more productive than staring at my ceiling for another night.

I wasn't sure what time it was, but I was well into the shots from *Eclipse* when everything started to move in slow motion. With every passing second, I began to slouch closer to the keyboard, and every blink made my eyes harder to open. I contemplated driving home but knew I was too tired to operate any kind of heavy machinery. So, instead, I pushed my keyboard back and folded my arms in front of me to rest my head on. Maybe if I had a short nap, then I'd be better equipped and alert to drive. Besides, it would probably only be a couple of minutes. It wasn't as if I had been sleeping longer than that for the last few nights. Regardless, I welcomed it.

I welcomed the darkness.

Chapter Ten
Total Eclipse

"Layla Thomas, tell me that you haven't been here all night," Maddie's voice rang as I felt her fingers jab me in the ribs.

My arms retracted towards the tickle, and I groaned. They felt so stiff. Had I been here all night? Was it morning already? My dead arms collapsed to my side.

"That depends." I yawned. "What time is it?"

"It's eight o'clock on Friday morning."

"Then, yes, I have been here all night." I glanced at my phone and saw that I had four missed calls. "Did you call me?"

She nodded. "I saw your note last night, but I thought you would have been back by this morning. I was worried about you."

"Sorry. How did dinner with your dad go?"

Maddie rolled her eyes. "Fine. He won't be winning father of the year anytime soon, but at least he's trying."

I tried to give a weak smile but wasn't sure if I pulled it off.

"Good morning, girls," Ebony said as she appeared at the door.

Maddie turned towards her while I shook off the pins and needles that burnt their way down my arms.

"Tell me that I'm mistaken, and you are not wearing the same clothes that I saw you in last night, Layla," Ebony said. "Did you go home at all?"

I looked down and frowned. "How do you remember what I was wearing yesterday?"

"I like that shirt." She shrugged. "But seriously."

"No, I fell asleep," I replied. I looked at my computer and woke it from standby. It glowed to life, and I raised my eyebrows. "Wow, I got a lot done."

Maddie laughed. "You are a complete worry."

"A worry that needs sleep," Ebony added. "Go home, Layla. I'm officially giving you the rest of the day off."

"The whole day? Even tonight? Do you not want me to take photos at the ball?" I asked.

Ebony smiled. "Let me rephrase. I'm barring you from the office until Monday. Go home and sleep, or get your hair and nails done, whatever, just get out of the building. There are a handful of other photographers here that can cover for you today."

"You're banishing me? Can I at least finish organising the photos? There are only, like, two dozen left."

Ebony eyed me suspiciously. "How long will that take?"

"Ten minutes maximum. You can even get Maddie to stay to make sure I leave after it's done."

Ebony turned to her. "You'll escort her out?"

Maddie raised her hand. "You have my word."

I felt like a five-year-old.

"I'll work fast," I sighed.

"I'll get coffee." Maddie smiled. "You look like you need coffee."

Ebony followed Maddie out, and I moved my numb hand back to sift through the remaining photos. By the time Maddie got back with my coffee, I was on my last row of six.

"There you go, girlie," she sighed. "And Ebony said that you have four and a half minutes to go."

I continued to flick through the photos with one hand while the other reached for the mug.

"Wait, move that last one to the photo editor," Maddie said.

I turned to look at her. "Which one?"

"That last one where Holly's looking out at the rain. It's pretty."

I scratched my head, and double clicked on it. "This one?"

She nodded.

"But there's a reflexion in the window," I said. I pointed tiredly at the screen.

"Oh, even half-asleep you're on the ball."

I left the photo and smiled weakly, scrolling through the remaining two. I moved one into the editor and left the other on the drive.

"So, you're done?" Maddie asked.

I stretched back and yawned. Both of my elbows cracked, and I moved my hand slowly towards the mug. I felt the muscles in my arm seize as I tried to pick it up, and it slipped through my fingers and sent a wave of hot coffee over my lap.

I gasped and pushed back in my chair. The boiling droplets ran off my slacks.

Maddie exhaled. "I'm not making you another one."

"I'll get one at home. Aren't you supposed to escort me from the building or something?"

"You can't drive, Layla, you're a wreck."

"You're going to make me walk?" I asked. The idea didn't exactly appeal to me.

She drew in a breath and then blew it out. "I'll drive you in your car and then catch a cab back."

"No, Maddie you—"

"Layla, you're my best friend. I'm not letting you drive when you're four degrees away from being a complete zombie."

I nodded and flicked my hair from my eyes, then picked up my phone and camera.

"Let's go, then," I sighed.

Maddie took hold of my elbow and towed me all the way out to my yellow Beetle. She took the keys from me and opened the door to the passenger side, ushering me in.

We didn't talk all the way back to our place. Maddie didn't even complain about how rusty and old my car was. Maybe she was trying to let me rest. Regardless, I couldn't fall asleep with her sudden stops and erratic driving. But I still appreciated the gesture.

When I got home, I had a shower and went straight to bed. Maddie made sure that I was tucked in before calling a taxi to take her back to work.

I dozed for what felt like hours but, when it seemed like I couldn't sleep any more, I saw that it had only been forty minutes. I looked around my room at the piles of clothes that needed washing and cut my losses. If I couldn't sleep, I may as well be productive. After I'd put a load in the washing machine, I gave my room a once over, made myself a ham and cheese sandwich, and then retired to the couch for some lousy daytime television. When my washing was done, I changed it to the dryer and set to painting my toenails gold to match my ball dress. After I'd finished that, I started reading a backlog of newspapers that I hadn't had the time for in the last few weeks.

Most of the news was outdated by now, so I gave up and turned back on the television and tried to rest some more. It felt like I had merely closed my eyes when the front door opened and Maddie stepped in.

"Hey, sleepy." She smiled.

I sat up and yawned. "What time is it?"

"A little after three. Ebony let me go early so I can get ready for tonight. Whoever thought it was a good idea to have a ball on a Friday night was obviously a male."

I huffed. "Right."

Her eyes caught sight of my toes, and she folded her arms. "Look at you, Layla, you even sprung for some polish on those sad feet."

"My feet aren't sad."

"They're all cut up."

"They're healing. They're almost healed," I mumbled. There were still a few cuts on the top of them, but underneath they were still a miserable sight.

"P.S. I'm doing your hair tonight," she said. I opened my mouth to object, and she lifted a finger. "No complaints. You're going to look great whether you like it or not."

I pushed myself off the chair. "That's all well and good, Madeline, but I just remembered that I need to return the jewellery from the shoot to Jeffrey."

"Today? Now?" She blinked. "I don't think he'll mind if we return it tomorrow. Or even, like, Monday."

"No, it's worth too much to hold on to."

"Fine," she sighed. "Let's go."

"I'll go, you stay. You need to have a shower and all that. I just need to throw everything on."

"You make me nervous when you say things like *throw everything on*."

I grinned. "I'll see you soon. I won't be long."

"Okay, you win."

I grabbed my car keys and the small box of jewellery still at the door from yesterday and headed out. I took my time driving, cautious of my slow reflexes. The last thing I needed was to have an accident because, even if I wasn't really looking forward to the ball, I was not suicidal.

I couldn't see Jeffrey at the shop when I got to *Reflective Jewellers*, so I walked up to an older woman with similar features to him who stood behind the counter.

"Excuse me," I said. "Is Jeffrey in today?"

She looked up from her small, black-framed glasses.

"He was, darling, but he just left," she replied with thick Italian pronunciation. "Can I help you?"

"Yes, I actually came to return some things."

She pursed her lips. "I am sorry, but we do not accept refunds, darling."

"Oh, no, I'm sorry," I sighed. "My name is Layla Thomas. I'm the chief photographer for *Flash Magazine*—"

"Ah, *si, si.*" She nodded. "You had them on loan for a photography shoot, of course."

"That's right. I wanted to make sure that we returned them as soon as possible. We really appreciate your generosity in lending them to us."

She grinned widely, reached under the counter to pull out a receipt, and began checking through the items. I let my eyes wander while I waited.

"You are a pretty girl," she said. She didn't look up from the listing, so I wasn't sure if she was speaking to me. After a moment, she looked up and smiled. "Yes, you, Layla Thomas. My Jeffrey likes you. It is you that he's going to the ball with tonight, *si?*"

"That's right," I breathed. "He's a really great guy. You did well with him."

"Thank you, it is nice of you to say." She smiled. "Well, Layla, it looks like it's all here."

"Great." I nodded. "Do I need to sign anything?"

"No, darling, that's all."

"Okay, thank you." I smiled. "We'll be sure to credit you in the magazine."

She nodded, and her brown eyes twinkled. "It was a pleasure to meet you, Layla."

"You too."

I turned towards the door and walked as quickly as I could manage back through the shopping centre. I was mindful of the time, and that Maddie would probably still insist on doing my hair even if I was late. I may as well not delay us both. Resistance was futile.

When I got back to the car, I struggled to pull out my keys out of the pocket of my jeans.

"You should really get some new ones," a voice said.

I jumped, and the keys tipped out of my pocket and onto the floor. I lifted a hand to rest over my beating heart.

"Christian, you scared me," I sighed, and then shook my head. "Um, new what?"

"Jeans," he said, pushing off the hood of my Volkswagen. "I didn't mean to scare you."

"Uh, why do I need new jeans? They still fit."

"Because you've had those for years," he replied, raising an eyebrow. He glanced down and pointed at a small rip in the right leg. "You caught them on my dad's ute when we were sixteen."

I breathed a laugh. "I remember. I was so mad. They were brand new."

His eyes met mine. "So, maybe it's about time you threw them away and got some new ones."

"What if I don't want to?"

He leant over to pick up my keys then handed them to me and took a step back.

"Sometimes we're forced to do things that we don't really want to," he said. "I guess I'll see you later for the ball."

I watched him go and then turned back to my car and started for home.

**

Maddie had showered, done her makeup, and was making the finishing touches on her hair by the time I got back. Even if her hair was short, she never failed to surprise me with her creativity. She had twisted the front of it and clipped it all down with little silver clasps. It looked amazing.

I stopped at the bathroom door and leant on the frame.

"Ta-dah." She smiled. "All settled?"

I nodded. "All settled."

"Great. Now, go and take a seat at the kitchen table. I'll be right out."

I opened my mouth and then sighed. "Just promise me nothing too extravagant."

"You have my word. Do you want me to get you a book or something? Or put the television on?"

"How long is this going to take?"

"As long as it takes," she replied.

She surfaced with the rollers and plugged them in. My stomach twisted. The last time my hair had been curled, it was the day of my wedding rehearsal.

"Uh, Maddie." I frowned. "Why don't you just straighten it?"

"It's always straight. I think it will look nice curly."

I sighed and reached for some catalogues that were on the table.

Maddie was very quick with the rollers and, once she was finished, turned her attention to my makeup. I didn't bother trying to object because I knew that any complaint would fall on deaf ears.

When she had finished, she carefully removed the rollers and pinned up some wayward curls before covering me with hairspray. Then she stepped back and appraised her handiwork.

"See, nothing extravagant." She smiled. "It's perfect."

"Am I done?"

"Yes, now get dressed. It's quarter to six, and the boys will be here in half an hour."

"Oh, right."

I'd forgotten that we were going out with people after this. I suppose I was trying to tackle one torment at a time.

Her eyes narrowed. "Don't mess up the hair or smudge the makeup."

"Maddie, I don't think gale-force winds will mess up my hair," I sighed. "Plus, my dress is a halter neck with a zip, so I can step into it."

She nodded once and spun towards her room. I stood up and headed to mine.

I dressed carefully, making sure that I didn't catch my gown on anything, then pulled out my comfortable black heels. I didn't really want to risk wearing any other shoes since the cut under my heel was still pulsing. Like other pains in my life though, I'd just learnt to live through it. I was putting in my gold stud earrings when I heard a knock at the front door. Maddie's door opened, and then there was a *clip-clop* of high heels, then I heard the front door squeak open.

"Hey," Maddie said. "Come on in."

I froze to listen to whose voice would reply. Was it Christian or Jeffrey?

"Sorry I'm a little early," the gruff voice answered. Jeffrey. "I figured I'm better early than late."

"I completely approve of that philosophy," she replied. "Layla should be ready. Layla!"

I exhaled. "Give me a minute."

I made sure my earrings were fastened properly, and then sat down on my bed. I could hear Maddie and Jeffrey laughing in the next room and sighed.

Tonight was going to be tough. I knew that much. I was just relieved that I had work as a distraction. I looked down and flattened the gold lace overlay on top of the silky golden material of my dress, and then tucked an auburn spiral of hair behind my ear.

Game face, Layla.

"Layla Louise Thomas!" Maddie yelled.

"I'm coming, Madeline Alice Butler," I groaned.

I waited a moment before pushing myself to my feet. I walked carefully to pick up my camera, and then took a deep breath, plastering a smile on my face as I pulled the door open.

"Hey, Jeffrey," I sighed.

There was a short silence, and Maddie and Jeffrey just stared at me. I noticed that Jeffrey was wearing a gold tie.

"What?" I shrugged. "What did I do?"

Jeffrey cleared his throat. "Nothing, you just look unbelievable."

I blushed, looking down at my camera. "Oh, um, thanks."

Maddie grinned. "You do scrub up rather well."

"You too, Miss Madeline."

Her deep pink dress looked as if it had been designed for her. It had a sweetheart neckline with thin straps and a ruffled silk overlay that cut off unevenly below her hips. The length of the gown reached the floor.

348

"Oh, before I forget," Jeffrey said, patting his black suit pockets. He reached into his blazer. "This is for you, Layla."

He extended a maroon coloured box towards me, and my forehead creased. The last time I'd received jewellery was under very different circumstances, from a very different person, and for a very particular reason.

"What is it?" I asked.

"Open it."

I took the small *Reflective Jewellers* box from his hands and tried to ignore Madeline's squeaks of excitement. My hands were shaking a little as I pushed the lid open. Inside the box was a beautiful gold bracelet with some kind of oval stone attached to it.

"Wow, Jeffrey, I can't accept this," I gasped.

"Sure you can." He smiled. "I'm giving it to you."

"What's the stone?" Maddie asked, now jumping up and down in excitement. Shiny things always make her act like a kid at Christmas.

"It's smoky quartz," he explained, taking the bracelet out and fastening it to my wrist. "It's supposed to have healing qualities. Plus, I thought it would go with your dress. I was right."

"Jeffrey, it's too much."

"Stop, Layla. I wanted to. It's not too much, it's just enough."

I looked down at the bonded gold swirls encircling the incredible dark brown gemstone and frowned. "Thank you."

I felt his fingers under my chin then he tipped my face up. "You don't like it, do you?"

"No, I do. I really do," I answered, forcing a smile. "I just… it's too much."

He chuckled. "It's not, really. I have connections."

I laughed. "Right."

"Hello?" Christian called from the door.

I looked at Maddie, who still had a dumb smile on her face, and cleared my throat. She snapped back to reality and hurried towards the door. She took quick, little steps.

"Hey, Christian." She beamed. "Come on in."

"Thanks. You look great, Mads," he answered. He stepped over the threshold, and casual stuck his hands in the pockets of the charcoal-grey trousers he wore.

She grinned. "You look pretty great yourself there, sparky."

He smiled then looked up at Jeffrey and me.

"Hey, guys." He nodded. He slipped his arm around Maddie, and I had to work to keep my expression even.

Jeffrey fell into step beside me, moving his arm around to rest his hand on my hip.

"Hey, Christian," Jeffrey replied.

I glanced up at him, and he gave me a wink. I wasn't sure if I agreed with what he was doing, but I didn't do anything to stop it. Maybe it was because I was still trying to convince myself to move on. Maybe it was just because I liked feeling wanted by someone, even if it was the wrong someone.

I pulled my lips into a line, but Maddie had a giant grin on her face. I stepped forward to break the feeling of petty competition between the four of us and headed into the kitchen.

"Does anyone want a drink?" I asked.

I took a glass from the sink and filled it with water.

"Layla," Maddie gasped. "Tell me you're not wearing those shoes."

I swallowed the mouthful and looked down at my feet. "Do you want me to lie?"

350

"You wear those shoes to work. You can't wear them to a ball."

I glanced at the boys and then back to her. "Why not?"

"Because there are unwritten rules in fashion and you're breaking one," she groaned. She headed to her room, and I made a face. I knew what was coming.

Jeffrey and Christian laughed.

I rolled my eyes and lifted my hand to run it through my hair as Maddie returned.

"No! Don't touch the hair," she shrieked. I dropped my hand back to my side as she held some gold-cord shoes towards me. "Put these on."

"Maddie, they look horribly uncomfortable," I said.

"Fashion is not about comfort."

I stepped out of my black shoes and into the gold ones. As I pulled the strap over my heel, I sucked air through my teeth. Maddie took a step back to appraise me.

"Much better." She nodded.

"For whom?" I groaned. "They hurt my heel."

"Layla, please."

Jeffrey glanced at his watch. "Should we go?"

Maddie looked up and blushed lightly. It was as if she had forgotten we had company.

"Yes." She smiled. "Christian, you said you'd drive, right?"

I frowned. "I thought we were catching a taxi?"

Christian shrugged. "I don't mind driving."

"Me neither," Jeffrey added. "I don't drink."

"You don't drink?" Maddie smirked. "Are you sure you're Italian?"

"Pretty sure."

"We'll need to go in two cars then," Christian replied. "I only have a two-seater."

My brow furrowed. Christian used to drive an old Holden sedan. He loved that car. Why would he get rid of it?

Jeffrey nudged my arm gently. "That's no problem, I don't mind taking Layla."

I looked up at him and smiled tightly. "Great, let's go."

I poked my phone in my camera bag and followed Maddie and Christian to the door. It turned out that Christian was now driving his dad's utility. It was the half-cab truck that, once upon a time, I had torn my jeans on.

Jeffrey took my hand and led me towards his black Subaru. He opened the door and helped me in, and I narrowly missed bashing my head for the second time this week.

**

When Jeffrey and I arrived at *Eclipse*, I got straight to work photographing people as they sipped on cocktails outside the grand ballroom. I welcomed the distraction because it made me feel more like a fly on the wall rather than someone actually attending.

Jeffrey followed me around like my shadow and even saved me from tripping over my shoes a couple of times. I appreciated him being here but, after a while, his presence felt more like a hindrance than anything else. He made me stand out. He struck up conversations with my subjects. He took the spontaneity out of the shots. I was relieved when we were invited to sit down to begin the introductions and entrées. I had to take a couple more photos, and then I was able to sit too. I was ravenous by the time the food came out, but there was a mix-up in the kitchen which saw both Jeffery and I receiving vegetarian meals. Apparently, catering misunderstood my email.

"So, what kind of music do you like?" Jeffrey asked as we finished the main course. "I need to know what to request to the DJ for us to slow-dance to later on."

I opened my mouth to reply but was interrupted by Maddie.

"Layla doesn't like music," she said.

Jeffrey frowned. "Why don't you like music?"

I rolled my eyes. "I don't *not* like music."

"Layla, in all the time I've known you, I've never heard you listen to music," Maddie sighed.

"I just don't listen to it that often, I guess."

"Why?" Christian asked. He looked equally as confused as the other two.

I lifted my head. "Too many memories."

"So, listen to the new stuff." Maddie giggled.

I glanced over at her and forced a smile. "I'd better do another round."

I made my way around to all the tables and took photos of everyone just before the final speeches started and we were left to our own accord. Ebony thanked everyone for their contributions over the past five years, and then introduced a slideshow of *Flash*'s achievements. I waited for the lights to come back on to continue my shots since there wasn't much to see in the dull glow of the PowerPoint presentation.

"Nice bracelet," Christian whispered in my ear.

His breath made me shiver, and I looked up at him and then glanced back to the screen.

"Jeffrey gave it to me," I said.

"That was nice of him."

I frowned. "I didn't ask for it."

"Okay." He shrugged. "The details don't matter much to me."

"Is that why you came over? To admire my jewellery?"

Christian smiled to himself and looked down. "I was just on my way to the bathroom."

"Did you get lost?"

"Apparently."

He huffed, and then walked towards the exit. As he left, the lights came back on, and Ebony took her place back at the podium.

"Okay, guys and girls." She smiled. "It's nine twenty-five, and dessert will be served in about five minutes. Please feel free to fill the dance floor, and I hope you all enjoy the rest of your evening."

I looked over at our table and sighed, readying my façade as I put the lens cap back on my camera. I took another breath and started over.

"Layla," Ebony called.

I felt a strange sense of relief at the delay to return.

"Hey, Ebony, great speech," I replied.

"Thank you, Layla, and thanks so much for taking photos tonight. I hope it didn't disrupt your evening too much."

"Not at all, I can safely say that it was a welcome distraction," I answered honestly.

Her delicate eyebrows pulled together, forcing a pucker to develop between them. "Distraction from what?"

I glanced back at our table as Christian settled. "Life, I guess."

"Life can't be that bad." She smiled. "I see that you're here with the model from the South Beach shoot. I must say, I'm a little impressed. He's cute."

"No." I laughed. "I mean, yes, he is. But it's not like that. We're not dating, we're just friends."

Ebony nodded. "Okay, whatever you say. I hope that you can enjoy the rest of your night."

"Thanks, you too."

Ebony gave a small wave and headed towards her table where her husband Rob was sitting. He smiled up at her as she returned.

I exhaled and continued back to my table.

"Hey, you're back." Jeffrey smiled. "Tell me that you don't need to take any more photos tonight."

I opened my mouth, but it took me a moment to speak. "Maybe, I'm not sure."

"I think you've shot enough," Maddie said. "Ebony will be pleased with what you've done. Take a break and dance. You've been working since you arrived."

I fit my camera back into its bag and pulled out my phone. It didn't have any missed calls or messages but left it on top.

"I'll be right back," Christian said as he stood.

We all watched as he made his way over to the DJ and whispered something to him. The DJ nodded, and Christian turned on his heel and made his way back over. He sat down noiselessly with a look on his face that I didn't entirely trust. A beat later, a familiar song filled the arena, and I felt my body stiffen.

Surely not. Surely Christian hadn't just requested Eric Clapton's *Layla*.

Music pumped from the speakers, and the live acoustic version of the classic song bellowed. The strings of the guitar curled their way around the notes.

"Hey, Layla, it's your song." Maddie giggled.

I forced a smile and let my gaze wander to Christian as the lyrics started. The words of the song felt like accusations as his eyes found mine.

Running, hiding, foolish pride...
No.

This wasn't fair. He wasn't playing fair.

I shuffled uncomfortably in my seat, trying in vain to look away from his taunting face.

Jeffery's hand rose to my back. "Are you all right?"

I looked up and nodded silently. My eyes glanced back at Christian as the second verse started. I thought I could see his lips moving to the lyrics, but at least his eyes were no longer probing.

Falling in love, turning worlds upside down.

Enough, Christian.

I rubbed my forehead and pushed my chair out, unable to handle it any more.

"Layla?" Maddie and Jeffrey both said in unison.

"I just need some air," I replied. "Please, stay. I'm fine, really."

I paced as quickly as I could towards the exit without seeming suspicious and pushed open the large wooden doors. The cool foyer air was like a splash of cold water on my clammy skin. I sucked in a deep breath and exhaled. It felt good to finally have some oxygen filling my lungs. I felt like I hadn't breathed properly in days.

A second later, I heard the door open behind me and turned to see Christian looking at me with a mixture of curiosity and complacency. I exhaled in a whimper and crouched down by the wall.

"What? What now? Come to finish the job?" I breathed. "I get that I hurt you, and I'm really sorry that I did, more than you'll ever know, but enough of the torture."

Christian folded his arms. "Torture? Guilty conscience?"

I wiped my watery eyes with the back of my hand, leaving a black smudge trail on my skin. "If you care so much about the fact that I left then why won't you let me explain myself to you?"

"What you say isn't going to make a difference, Layla," he replied. "It's been four years."

"So what does that mean? That you're over it? If that's what you're saying then just please *be over it*. Let it go, Christian. I can't take it any more."

Christian sighed and knelt beside me. "I didn't request the song, Layla."

I looked up through tears and rolled my eyes, the motion sent another wave of water down my cheek. "I'm not stupid. We all saw you talking to the DJ."

He brushed away a salty tear from my chin before it dripped onto my dress.

"I didn't request it," he repeated as the Eric Clapton song strummed to an end.

I frowned and looked up at him, trying to read his eyes to see if there was any truth in them. They were clear blue, like the sea. He raised his eyebrows earnestly.

I sniffled. "Well, what did you request then?"

He tipped his head to the side as another song started and then looked back to me.

"*Here Comes the Sun* by The Beatles," he said, and his fingers swept another tear off my chin.

I frowned because we'd both loved this song. It was one that never got old no matter how much we listened to it. It was one of the three songs in the running for our first dance at our wedding.

"Why?" I asked, and my voice was thick from crying. "Why request this one? It's just as bad."

He shrugged and stood up, offering me his hand. "I like the song. I've always liked the song. You know that."

357

I wiped my cheek and put my hand in his and he pulled me up.

"I know that you like it," I whispered. "I do too, but—"

"Memories."

I exhaled, and he cleared his throat. He pulled his hand away and looked back towards the door. We stood in silence for a couple of minutes, but it wasn't uncomfortable. It was actually the most comfortable I'd felt in a long time.

"We should get back," he said. "Our dates will be wondering where we are."

"Christian," I sighed. He turned to face me again, and I mashed my lips together. "I'm really sorry."

"For what?"

"A lot of things." I shrugged. "But mostly for the way—"

"It's okay, Layla."

"It's really not okay, Christian. I think about that day all—"

"Layla, I said that it's okay," he murmured. "Please. I'll just see you inside, okay?"

I took a deep breath and let it out. "Okay."

He turned back and reached for the brass handle. An Ed Sheeran song began to play, and I wanted to cry even harder.

"No, wait. Do you know what, Christian? It's not okay," I said. "It's not okay. What I did to you was *not* okay."

Christian closed his eyes and turned back around.

"Layla, please don't do this," he sighed. "I'm begging you. Please don't do this now. For me, just don't."

I shook my head. "But we need to talk about it. I need to explain what happened. I owe you that much."

"It's in the past."

"But it's not. If it was then it wouldn't be so hard being around each other now. If it was, it wouldn't hurt like hell that we're not the ones going home together at the end of the night," I replied. "If it was, Christian, it wouldn't be so damned painful to look at you and see every mistake that I've ever made in your eyes."

"Layla—"

"I loved you, Christian, so much, I loved you," I whispered, and my eyes grew glassy again. "It wasn't that I didn't love you. It wasn't that at all. Not a day goes by that I didn't think about you and what our life would have been like if we—"

"Layla, please—"

"But I got scared. Four years ago, I got really scared of the future, and I didn't trust myself not to ruin everything for you. So, I left. I left so you wouldn't be held back by me. I thought that I was setting you free. I thought... I thought wrong and for that, I am eternally sorry. I'm so sorry."

I bit my lip to stop myself from sobbing hysterically because it wasn't about me right now. Regardless, another tear spilled down my cheek.

Christian looked to the side, and his blue eyes were brimming. His expression was tormented, and I thought for a moment that he might not answer. I wasn't sure whether I wanted him to or not.

"I wish you'd just said something," he murmured. "But you didn't say anything. For four years, I waited for you to come home. I waited, even after you disappeared and left me to face our families and friends alone. You could have called, you... you didn't even leave *me* a note, Layla." His voice cracked. "Even if it might have hurt worse, at least I would have known, but there was nothing."

The thought that I had left him, not only to deal with the heartbreak, but also with all our guests had always haunted me.

"I'm sorry. I'm so sorry," I whispered. "I wasn't thinking rationally that day."

"And what about the next day?" he asked. "The next week? The next month, or year? Don't you think that I at least deserved an explanation then? It's been *four years*, Layla. It's too much, too late now."

"I tried... I tried calling," I breathed. I looked up at him as another cascade of tears poured down my cheeks. I only started to sob harder when I saw the unguarded pain on his face. "But, I knew that you wouldn't be able to forgive me for what I did. I was so ashamed because I knew that didn't deserve your forgiveness."

Christian brushed his cheek, and I only noticed then that it was wet.

"How could you think that?" he groaned. "Layla, I loved you more than anything, more than life itself. Whatever you were feeling you should have told me. I might not have understood, but I wouldn't have pressured you into anything. *How* could you think that leaving was your only option?"

"I... I..."

I didn't have an answer, so I just hid my face and sobbed into my palms. I was aware that I was crying hysterically, but I couldn't even stop myself to breathe. So, when I felt Christian take me in his arms and pull him against his chest, I stopped breathing all together with shock. It took me a second, but then I started up again, tucking myself into him and clutching his blazer to hold myself against him. His hand stroked my hair, and if I weren't so frenzied, I would have otherwise savoured the gesture.

"Don't cry," he sighed. "Tears won't fix anything now."

"You shouldn't be the one comforting me," I sniffled. "It's not right."

His hold tightened. "Well, we never were a conventional couple."

"Sure we were."

Christian exhaled, and I felt his grip weaken. "Layla—"

"Layla!" Maddie's voice exclaimed.

Christian and I both stepped back at the same time as she burst through the doors. Maddie's brows pinched together for a split second before she snapped back into action.

"Um, your phone is ringing," she said, handing me my camera bag.

I pulled my phone out and noticed that it was an out of area number. I hastily wiped my face, and turned away from my audience as Jeffrey appeared behind Maddie. I lifted the phone to my ear.

"Hello, it's Layla," I sighed, covering my other ear.

"*Layla, it's Mum,*" her frantic voice said. "*I don't want you to panic, but your father's in the hospital.*"

I felt the blood drain for my face and looked up at Christian.

"What? Why? What's happened? Is it bad? Is he going to be okay?"

Christian's brow creased.

"*I don't know yet. They're running tests,*" Mum replied. Her voice broke, and I felt tears begin to form in my eyes again. "*They think he might have had a heart attack.*"

Watery drops spilled over my eyes.

"I'm coming home, Mum. Just hold tight and I'll be there soon."

"*Honestly, Layla, you don't have to—*"

"I want to," I interrupted. "Just try to stay strong, okay? I'll be there in a few hours."

"*Please be careful driving at this time of the night, honey.*"

"I will, Mum. I love you."

"*I love you, Layla.*"

I turned back to three pairs of questioning eyes, and Christian was the first to speak. He also looked by far and away the most worried.

"What is it?" he asked.

"My dad is in hospital. I have to go." I tucked my phone under my arm and struggled with the zip on my camera bag. Christian took the bag off me and sealed it in one movement.

"You're driving to Almanbury tonight?" he asked. "I don't think that's a good idea."

"It's my dad, Christian," I sighed. "I don't care."

Maddie looked at Jeffrey and then glanced back at us.

"He's right though. Maybe you should wait until the morning to go, Layla," she offered calmly.

I was already shaking my head. "No, it might be too late by then."

Christian nodded, and was already pulling his keys from his pocket. "I'll drive you then."

I blinked. "What?"

"What?" Maddie echoed.

Christian shrugged. "It's Henry. I love him too."

I nodded and glancing to Maddie who now looked as if she was trying to solve a difficult math problem.

"Maddie, can you take my camera home and just leave it on my desk for when I get back?" I asked, handing it to her.

"Oh, um, okay." She nodded.

I smiled tightly, and then remembered that Jeffrey was standing in the background with folded arms.

"Jeffrey," I sighed. "I'm sorry. I—"

Jeffery raised his hand. "Go. I understand."

I nodded. "Can you make sure that Maddie gets home okay?"

"Absolutely."

Christian rested his hand on my lower back. "Come on, let's go home."

Home. Almanbury. With Christian. People will talk.

Chapter Eleven
Too Many Memories

I was convinced that the radio was against me. We were two and a half hours into the drive to Almanbury, and the songs that had been playing seemed to be the best of betrayal and heartache. I may be paranoid but, as Eric Clapton's *Change the World* strummed to an end, I sighed.

Christian glanced over at me. "I can't go any faster. I'm already doing ten over the speed limit."

I shook my head. "It's not that."

"Then what?"

The familiar introduction to *Layla* filled the car, and I groaned. "Seriously, is it Eric Clapton's birthday or something? What is with all this depressing music on the radio?"

Christian's lips twitched. "It's a USB drive."

"Oh, of course it is," I sighed.

He pressed the FM button to change to the radio, and the sound of the rising antennae echoed from the outside. As it lifted, a song that I recognised to be *It Must Have Been Love* by Roxette crackled through the speakers.

Christian huffed, and I reached out to press for another channel. Missy Higgins' *Where I Stood* filled the car and Christian's smile faded. I pushed the *off* button, and silence replaced the disturbing lyrics that lingered between us.

"Maybe you should try to get some sleep," Christian said.

I shook my head. "I'm not tired."

"If you say so."

I rested my head against the door and saw him glance in my direction. The silence stretched on and became almost deafening. I sat up to turn the radio back on, and was relieved that it was advertisements.

"I thought you decided that you didn't like music," Christian replied.

I took a deep breath. "Anything is better than this painful silence."

I froze as the music started, and a remake of John Waite's *Missing You* filled the vehicle. I couldn't think of how to move to make it stop, and I could feel Christian's eyes flicker to me as he waited for me to do something. It was the lyrics, those truthful yet horrifying lyrics caught me short. I don't know why it took me so long to understand how hard it must've been for Christian not knowing what went wrong between us but, in that second, it hit me like lightning.

I felt the car slow.

"Layla?" Christian said.

I was aware that I must look ridiculous with my hand frozen over the power button, but it was as if I didn't have control over my limbs any more.

"Layla," Christian repeated. There was worry in his voice.

The car swerved into the emergency lane and stopped. His hand pushed mine aside to turn the radio off.

"Layla," he said again. His hand rose to my cheek to turn my face towards his, and he brushed away a tear that I didn't even feel fall.

I swallowed. "I…"

"Shh, it's okay," he soothed.

I shook my head. "You must hate me so much."

He frowned. "That's the worst part. Even after everything, I could never hate you."

My frown deepened, and I let out a sob. "Stop being so nice to me. I don't deserve it."

"I didn't think that was nice."

I continued to cry.

"Layla, look at me," he said. His words were redundant since his hands tipped my face towards his. "You need to calm down."

I bit my lower lip, looking into his eyes and tried to regulate my breathing. Without thinking, I leant forward to catch my lips on his. It was the first time in four years that I'd kissed anyone, but my lips seemed to remember the taste of his. Only a few seconds had passed when Christian moved his hand from my cheek to my shoulder to pushed me back from him.

"I can't," he whispered. "I'm sorry."

I exhaled. "No, it was my fault. I'm the one who's sorry."

"It's not... I'm just..."

I shook my head. "We should just keep driving. We're still a couple of hours away, and it's only getting later."

He nodded rigidly and started the car again. We drove in absolute silence for nearly twenty minutes. I was too scared to speak just in case I started to get emotional again. This time, it was Christian who broke the silence.

"So, you didn't like the main course tonight, huh?" he said.

I looked at him curiously. "Um, sure I did."

"No, you didn't."

"What makes you say that?"

He shook his head. "Not even you can change that much. You used to say that it wasn't a meal unless there was a slab of meat on your plate. Polenta and a side salad is not even a course."

I looked over at him and sighed. "Fine, I hated it. It was horrible."

Christian chuckled. "I knew it."

"How did you know?"

He slowed to give way at a roundabout to the only other car on the road. He took the opportunity to look over at me, and his crystal eyes glittered in the street lamps.

"You make this sound when you don't like the taste of something," he said.

I blinked. "Sound?"

"Yeah, like..." He mashed his lips together. "*Mm.*"

"What? Really?"

He nodded, laughing lightly and accelerated to continue on his way.

I shook my head. "How do you know that?"

"We spent a lot of time together, Layla. Plus, I know that you didn't like my mum's hambone soup, but you still used to eat it. You did the same thing with that."

I made a face. "She used to make hambone soup every time I came over. I didn't have the heart to tell her that I hated it."

He laughed reminiscently. "She always liked you."

"Your dad didn't though. I didn't think it was actually possible but, going by the way he acted towards me, I'm pretty sure he hates me even more now."

His brow furrowed. "When did you see him?"

"Um, I bumped into him at the cemetery last weekend. He told me to stay away from you."

"Oh."

"I think he was worried. He said that it took you a while to recover after... and, well, seeing me would undo all that."

Christian pulled his lips tight to one side. A dimple appeared on his cheek. "He shouldn't have said that to you."

I looked down, not bold enough to ask what he meant – that Mitch shouldn't have told me to stay away from him or that Christian had taken a while to heal from my leaving.

"So, are we going to talk about the kiss?" I asked, trying to change the subject. It was only after the words were out that I realised it probably wasn't ideal by way of subject changes.

Christian's expression tightened. "I'd actually rather not if it's all the same to you."

"I'm sorry. I shouldn't have done it. I was just—"

"Layla," he sighed, and his eyebrows lifted.

"Sorry," I breathed. "I keep messing up."

He shook his head. "Why don't you get some sleep? We're still a couple of hours away yet."

I considered objecting but then thought of the alternatives – listening to disheartening music or sitting in uncomfortable silence. So, I shuffled down in my seat and rested my head against my seatbelt. My eyes closed lightly, and I focused on Christian's even breathing beside me as my awareness drifted off.

**

It seemed like I had only just closed my eyes when I felt Christian's hand shaking my shoulder to wake me.

"Layla, we're home," he whispered.

I gasped, opening my eyes. "We are? Already?"

He smiled, but it was small. "Yes."

He unclipped his seatbelt and walked around to help me out of the car. I stumbled into his arms, and he held me up.

"Why don't you take off those ridiculous shoes?" he said.

I smiled, kicking them off as I took in a deep breath of the cool Almanbury air. Christian picked them up and threw them into the back cab of the car before taking my hand.

"Come on," he murmured, leading me towards the hospital's main entrance, which also doubled as the emergency department. It was one of the drawbacks of a regional hospital. There were fewer funds, so everything was jammed together. Not like the hospitals in South Coast.

I felt suddenly wide awake as I burst through the hospital doors, like a hurricane of nervous energy. I rushed up to the clerk behind the desk, and she looked as if she'd been awake for weeks on end.

"Hi, my dad is here, Henry Thomas," I said. "He would've come in a few hours ago."

She tapped something on her computer and pursed her lips.

"He's actually in our Coronary Care Unit which is accessible through our Intensive Care Unit," she replied. "So if you just go through the corridor—"

"Thank you, I know where ICU is," Christian replied.

I began hyperventilating, and his hand curled around mine as he tugged me in the direction the girl had pointed. I was in autopilot, and he pulled me into his side, helping to guide me through the corridor, past the lifts to a glass door. He shoved it open and pulled me inside. We struggled a bit since the width of the doorframe wasn't wide enough for the two of us at the same time, but Christian didn't let me go.

My mum looked up from a seat in the small waiting room as we entered. The dress was constricting to walk in, but I finally found my feet again and hurried over to her.

"Mum," I sighed. "How is he?"

"Layla," she cried. "Ch-Christian? You two didn't have to come all this way at this time of the night."

"It's fine, Pattie. There's nowhere else we'd be," he replied.

My mother brushed my cheek and then stepped into Christian's arms. Her eyes were wide, and I wasn't sure whether it was because she was surprised to see us together or because of something that had happened with my father.

"Look at you," Mum breathed. "You both look lovely. Were the two of you out somewhere together?"

I shook my head trying to remember that far back. "Um, it was a work ball. Mum, how's Dad? Is he okay?"

She pulled away from Christian and pressed her lips together.

"The doctor and nurses are in with him now so I thought I'd give them some space, but he seems better than he was. They think now it wasn't a full heart attack, it was most likely some kind of arrhythmia," she explained. "They still want to keep him in for observation tonight and probably tomorrow too. I've asked to board with him here because I didn't want to be too far away, or on my own in that house."

"I'm here now. I'll look after the house," I said, rubbing her back. "You stay here though. Can I get you anything?"

"No, honey, I'm fine," she whispered. "Just a little tired."

"Go and get some rest. I'll sit with dad for a bit when the doctor is done."

"But—"

"Christian's with me. I'll be fine."

Mum pouted at Christian before looking back to me. She patted her pockets and pulled out something silver, then folded it into my palm. It was a key.

"Honestly, Layla. Promise me that you'll go home and sleep. Don't stay here all night in the uncomfortable hospital chairs," she said. "Christian, make sure she goes home."

Christian nodded. "I promise. Leave it with me, Pattie."

My mother smiled weakly and glanced back at me. "Layla, honey, have you been looking after yourself? All the makeup in the world can't cover those dark circles under your eyes."

I grimaced. "I... sort of. I've been trying."

"And the cuts and bruises?" she pressed, gesturing towards my head and feet.

I sighed. "It's been a tough week."

Mum yawned, gave us another hug, and then headed out the door. I guessed she was going to her room, but I didn't know where borders to ICU and CCU patients stayed. I didn't think they slept in the unit.

Christian watched her go and then looked back to me as I fell into one of the waiting chairs.

"I might go to find a vending machine. Are you hungry?" he asked.

I shook my head. I might have been, but I couldn't think about food right now, never mind eating it.

Five minutes later, Christian returned holding two foam mugs.

"I got you coffee," he murmured. "It's from a machine, but I think it'll do the job."

"Thank you, Christian."

He nodded. "Any word yet?"

I shook my head. "Not yet."

"I'm sure you'll hear something soon."

I took a sip of the coffee. It wasn't that hot, but it was at least drinkable.

"Thanks for being here," I said. "Seriously, Christian, I don't know what I would've done if I was alone."

He looked down. "You would have been fine, like always."

I frowned into the foam cup.

371

"Besides, I don't have to tell you that your dad has always been like a father to me," he added. "I would have driven down myself just to make sure he was okay."

I looked at him and wondered if it was possible to continue falling in love with the same person on deeper levels every single day.

"Excuse me, are you here for Henry Thomas?" a nurse asked.

I looked at her and stood. "Yes, I'm his daughter. Can I see him?"

"He's exhausted, but—"

"I'll be quick, I promise," I said. "Where is he?"

She waited a moment before lowering her head slightly. "It's room four."

I nodded and blew down the white passage, counting the doors until I realised there were numbers on them. I stopped at four and took a deep breath, then pushed it open.

"Dad?" I murmured. "Daddy?"

"Layla?" he mumbled. "Hey, kiddo, what are you doing here? Isn't it your ball tonight?"

I took a seat by his bed and clutched his hand. "Yes. If you wanted me to visit, you could've just asked. You didn't need to fake a heart attack."

My dad chuckled weakly. "I'll keep that in mind next time."

He brushed his thumb over my hand, and we both sat in silence for a while. I rested my chin on the mattress and let my eyes close. Dad's hand rested on my head, and I looked up.

"I hate to say it, kid, but you look almost as bad as me," he sighed.

I frowned. "It's been a tough week."

"You've been through the wars a bit lately."

I nodded. "Dad?"

"Layla?"

"Please don't do that to me again," I sighed. "You really scared me. I thought that I was going to lose you."

"You won't lose me, princess," he whispered. "I'm not going anywhere."

"Me neither."

"Good, kiddo. I like having you around."

I smiled. "Dad?"

"Yes, Layla?"

"I love you."

I grinned. "I love you too, kid."

Chapter Twelve
Feels Like Home

I woke up the next morning in my old bed and couldn't for the life of me remember how I got there. My arms and legs felt like I had lead weights in them, so it took me a little while to get up. When I was finally standing, I unfastened the stud holding the halter in my dress and unzipped it. I hadn't emptied all of my drawers in my quick getaway four years ago, so I found a pair of jeans and a long-sleeved top and headed out to the kitchen.

Christian was asleep on the couch, draped over it like a throw rug. He was almost two feet too long for it but looked as comfortable as if it was two feet longer. His face was angelic, peaceful, and beautiful. He looked exactly the way that I remembered him in my mind.

I crept past him towards the kitchen and flicked on the kettle, setting out two mugs. When the water had boiled, I had filled the cups just in time for Christian's eyes to flutter open. It was like seeing a patch of blue skies amongst the clouds.

"Hey," he exhaled. His voice was thick with sleep, but it was my favourite sound in the world.

I smiled weakly. "Hey, I made you coffee."

He stretched out and then pushed himself off the chair, dragging his feet towards me. I tried and failed not to notice how his tanned chest expanded and constricted beneath his mostly unbuttoned shirt.

I nudged a mug towards him. "It's white, no sugar. I hope you still take it that way."

I was a little disappointed that I was now uncertain of how he took his coffee. He must have detected the edge in my voice so looked up. His lips arched over the rim of the bone-china mug.

"Yes, I still like it this way," he replied.

I looked down at my coffee and raised it to take a sip.

"So I feel kind of silly for asking," I said, running my finger around the lip of the mug. "But how did I get home last night? The last thing I remember is going in to see my dad."

Christian nodded. "Yeah, you fell asleep by his bed, and the nurses came out to get me. I carried you back to the car and drove us back here. I told your mum that I'd make sure you got home, and I'm a man of my word."

I frowned at the jibe. "Apparently."

"Sorry, that wasn't fair."

"Maybe, but I think I've revoked all my rights there."

He shook his head. "Well, you had your reasons. Mind you, not very good ones, but reasons nonetheless."

I looked back at my coffee and took another mouthful. Christian chuckled to himself, but it sounded flat.

"Do you know the worst thing?" he asked.

I shook my head. "No."

"Do you remember the last thing you said to me that day?"

"No. Why? Was it bad?"

He smiled. "No, not *bad*."

I bit my lip. "Well, what did I say?"

He ran his hands through his overgrown hair. "You kissed me, and then you traced your finger around the outline of my lips, looked me in the eyes and said…"

I swallowed, and he looked down at me. I felt as though I was about to go into cardiac arrest myself.

"What, Christian?" I asked. "What did I say?"

He took a deep breath and blew it out. "You said, *Christian, I think you need a haircut.*"

He chuckled again, and I exhaled.

"You still do," I said.

He mashed his lips together. "I did get it cut after I left here that day. It was the last day you were here. I haven't had it cut since."

I wasn't sure how to answer, so it took me a moment before I spoke again.

"Christian," I sighed. He looked up over his coffee, and I bit my lower lip. "I think you need a haircut."

He laughed easily, and the sound made my heart want to sing. "I think you're right."

We exchanged a glance that, for the first time in a long time, didn't hold any ill feelings, sorrow, or bitterness.

"I might call the hospital to see how my dad is," I said. "Maybe you should call yours and let him know that you're in town."

"Good idea." He nodded. "He'll probably be disappointed that I didn't call last night to tell him."

"If he gets annoyed at you for one night, tell him to talk to my parents about having a neglectful child."

His eyebrow lifted. "He doesn't need another reason to dislike you. He'd probably think that you were rubbing off on me."

"No wonder he told me to stay away from you."

We smiled at each other, and I couldn't help but feel surprised that we were even joking about this. I never thought that he'd ever talk to me again, never mind laugh with me. It was more than I'd ever hoped for, but less than I wanted in my heart. I wished that we could be the Christian and Layla from five years ago, but I knew that would never happen. If this was all I got then I would take it and be glad.

I dialled the number for Almanbury Public Hospital and waited for the receptionist to answer. It was a little after nine o'clock, so I mustn't have been asleep for very long here. We had arrived at the hospital just before two.

I spoke to a nurse in the CCU who told me that my dad was resting but doing a lot better judging by the monitoring they'd done. She went into a whole lot of technical talk that I didn't understand, but Mum came on the phone after and translated it into English. I told her that I'd go in to see them both later and then hung up.

Christian was still on the phone to his dad when I went to get a shower, and when I returned, I found him sitting on the edge of the couch twisting the phone between his hands. He looked up when I appeared.

"Everything okay?" I asked.

He nodded. "You?"

"Yes, Dad's doing better. I told Mum I'd go in later."

"Good."

"So, what are your movements today?"

He smiled. "I was going to head over to my place to see my dad, and maybe change my clothes. I was just waiting for you."

"Oh, sure," I sighed. "Well, you didn't have to wait for me, I can catch a bus. You do what you need to."

"I waited because I was going to ask if you wanted to come with me," he said. "We can go to the hospital together from there. Or I can come back and get you after I'm done at mine."

"You want to come with me to the hospital?"

"Yes, is that okay?"

"Of course." I shrugged. "I just thought maybe you might want to catch up with everyone while you're back."

377

He blinked. "Layla, I came back to make sure that Henry is okay. I want to make sure he's okay and that your mum is going to be all right too."

I smiled. "You really are something, Christian Turner."

"So, do you want to come with me?" he asked.

"You mean, to your house?"

"Yes."

I frowned. "With your dad?"

"Uh, yes."

"With Mitch?"

"Yes, Layla."

"The same guy who told me to stay away from you," I clarified. "As in, you're asking if I want to go *with* you to *his* house. Like, with *you*."

His eyebrows rose. "Look, if you're too chicken—"

"I'm not chicken. I'm fine." I shrugged. "As long as you're fine."

"I'm fine."

"Fine. Well, let's go then."

"Fine." He smirked, and then stood and headed towards the door.

I followed obediently, more confident than how I felt. I may have wanted to be fine with seeing Mitch again, but I was scared of seeing him with Christian. I was afraid because everything he'd said to me the last time I saw him was entirely reasonable. He was a parent looking out for his child. He wanted to protect his son from anyone who threatened harm. Any parent would have done the same. I know I would have if it were me.

The entire way to the Turner house, as in the whole four-minute drive, my foot tapped restlessly against the dashboard. Christian kept glancing at it with an amused smile on his face, and I would have been more annoyed by it if I wasn't so nervous. Or maybe I wouldn't be. It was difficult to be annoyed at Christian when I owed him four years and countless apologies for what I'd done. It was also hard not to feel elated to be back hanging out with him in a place that held so many good memories for us.

We pulled into his driveway at the same time that the front door opened. Mitch stepped out and had his arms wide to welcome his only son home. Christian headed over and into his embrace, and the two mumbled something and patted each other's backs. It was only when they parted that Mitch noticed me standing there by the truck. His expression changed from delight to displeasure.

"What is she doing here?" he grumbled.

Christian glanced over at me. "Layla and I are just on our way to see Henry."

"Together?"

"We drove from South Coast together, so, yes, Dad."

Mitch frowned.

"Look, we're not going to stay for long, so if you have a problem with Layla being here then can you just put it on ice for a while?" Christian said. "I'm just here to grab a change of clothes."

Mitch's face crumpled. "You're not staying for morning tea or anything?"

"*We* can stay if you want *us* to."

Mitch looked from his son to me, and then gave a firm nod. "I'll put the kettle on."

Christian smiled and waved me over. I trotted over and raised my eyebrows at him.

"You didn't tell him that I was coming with you?" I whispered. "Are you crazy?"

"I didn't know at the time." He shrugged. "But see, he's fine. Everything's fine."

"Fine," I sighed. "This is going to be insanely awkward, Christian. Who has tea with their former fiancé and his dad?"

He smirked wryly. "You, apparently. By the way, the *former* part isn't my fault. Now, look alive."

I groaned and followed him through the door, down the passage, and into the Turner family room. The last time I was here was the night before the planned rehearsal dinner. I had helped Nancy cook a banquet for Mitch and Christian. Being here now and knowing that she was gone made me want to cry, but I kept myself in check. I knew that Mitch had a very limited tolerance for me, and tears would only make things worse.

Christian headed straight down the hallway to where his old room was, while Mitch peeled away to the kitchen to prepare the morning tea. I stood uncomfortably in between the two places because as much as I didn't want to be alone with Mitch, I didn't want to invade Christian's privacy either. Luckily, the discomfort didn't last long, and Christian resurfaced a couple of minutes later pulling a T-shirt over his head. My heart raced when I recognised it as one of the ones I'd bought him years ago.

"So, when did you get here?" Mitch asked.

I didn't bother answering since I knew it wasn't me that he was talking to. He would have otherwise spoken sooner and filled the awkward silence that lingered between us when Christian was absent.

"We started from South Coast late last night," Christian answered as he tucked a corner of his shirt into the side of his jeans. It was one of my favourite quirks of his. "We were at a function when Pattie called Layla, so we literally just jumped in the car and drove right down here."

"How is Henry?"

"He's doing better, it was a heart scare," I said.

Mitch glanced at me then nodded. "Give him my best."

"We will."

Mitch huffed. "*We*. You were together last night then. In South Coast."

I shuffled uncomfortably, and Christian turned around to look at me.

"Technically," he replied. "I was there with a friend of Layla's, and she was with some jeweller-model guy."

I rolled my eyes. "He's not a model, he's a historian."

Christian shrugged. "I don't care."

"So, you *haven't* been spending time together?" Mitch pressed.

Christian looked at me, and then turned back to his father.

"Does it really matter, Dad?" he replied. "So what if we have?"

"Nothing," Mitch sighed. "It's just interesting, that's all."

Christian straightened, and I knew that he was about to get defensive, so I sat down at the table.

"What is interesting?" Christian asked. On cue.

"Well, just that after everything she did to you, son, I find it interesting that you seem to have so willingly forgiven her."

I swallowed. I had fooled myself into thinking that he *had* forgiven me, but he had never said it in so many words. It was more of a *don't ask, don't tell* with us. As long as we were getting along, I didn't need for him to spell it out.

Apparently, Mitch did though.

"Look, Dad, what happened between Layla and me was between *me and Layla*," Christian said, and his tone was like dried concrete. "So, if I choose to forgive her then that is my decision, not anyone else's."

If.

"Yes, son, but—"

"I know that you're worried, but please just leave this to us. We're both grown-ups now."

I bit my lip and risked a glance up at the two of them. There was a tense silence for a moment, and then Mitch continued making the hot beverages.

"You're a better man than me, son," Mitch mumbled.

Christian shook his head. "You would have done the same thing for Mum."

My forehead creased with emotion, and I lowered my eyes.

Mitch cleared his throat. "Tea or coffee?"

"I'll have a coffee, Dad."

"And for you, Layla?" Mitch continued.

I wiped my eyes and looked up. "Coffee for me too please, Mr Turner."

He nodded. "Do you still take it one sugar? I don't know if I've got cream though, just milk."

"Milk is fine. One sugar and, yes, milk is fine."

I was surprised that he had remembered my coffee preference. After four years, he'd remembered. Christian's father remembered a lot.

"Why don't you take a seat with Layla, son? I won't be long."

Christian looked over and sat beside me. I ran my hands through my crusty, tangled hair and wished that I'd washed the knots out of it this morning in my shower.

Christian leant towards me. "Is everything okay?"

I nodded but didn't want to risk speaking. I didn't trust my voice.

Mitch joined us with the three coffees and a packet of cream biscuits. I admired his hospitality when I knew that he would have preferred that when I'd packed up, I'd stayed away.

Nevertheless, the conversation was pleasant through our impromptu morning tea. Admittedly, I didn't do much talking. Instead, I let Mitch and Christian catch up since he seemed eager to hear about how his son was settling back into university this semester – and so was I. Christian said that he was enjoying it, but keeping on top of the readings was a bit challenging with work and other commitments. I wanted Mitch to ask him what other commitments he had, but he didn't. I was scared that he thought spending time with Maddie was some kind of *commitment* since he'd been doing a lot of that lately.

When we'd all finished our coffees, and the conversation had dried up some, Christian pushed out his chair.

"Dad, we're going to head off in a second," he said. "But before we go, Layla, I have something for you."

"For *me*?" I asked. I didn't really like the sound of that.

He brushed the biscuit crumbs off his jeans and moved his arm around me, walking me in the direction of his room. I stopped at his door.

"You can come in," he said as he walked straight over to a set of drawers. "It's nothing that you haven't seen before."

I looked inside, half expecting to find a box of my things in there, but there was nothing like that in sight, in fact, everything was as orderly as I remembered. Christian was always very clean.

I stepped in as he threw a piece of yellow fabric at me, and my hands caught it reflexively. I unravelled it to find that it was my yellow dress, the one I'd worn the day he'd proposed. That was probably the last time I'd worn it too. I'd looked for it a few times since then but couldn't find it. I guess I knew why.

"I'm pretty sure that's yours." He smiled. "It's not my size."

I breathed a laugh. "Why do you have this?"

"I think you left it here when you stayed over," he replied. "I didn't steal it, I promise."

I smiled. "No, I... I thought I'd lost this."

His forehead creased. "When did you look for it?"

I pressed my lips together. "In recent times, last weekend when I was home but couldn't sleep. I had a dream about *that day* just before I saw you last Friday. It just made me think... made me wonder if I still had this dress."

"It always was my favourite on you." He nodded then frowned. "*That day*? Do you mean—?"

"The day that you proposed to me," I replied as I lifted my hand to play with my necklace.

He bit his lip. "I like that necklace on you too."

"I could have sworn that I didn't have it with me in South Coast but, funny thing, one night it just appeared on my bedside table."

"That is funny."

I nodded. "Did you leave it there?"

"Was it childish to leave it rather than to give it to you directly?"

I smiled and shook my head. "Thanks for returning it, and for my dress."

"You're welcome."

"So, is there anything else of mine lying around here?" I sighed, looking around his room. It looked the way it always had — very neat, except for the corner where his desk sat. In that corner, there were books piled everywhere, pens overflowing their holders, and post-its stuck to different objects containing what I could only guess were old story ideas.

I wandered over and picked one off his desk lamp.

"*Girl and boy at park, early spring, boy pops question,*" I read aloud.

Christian shuffled his feet. "It's a work in progress."

"Does it have a happy ending?"

He shrugged. "Jury's still out."

"Are you writing something about us? About our story?"

"Not exactly about us, but I've drawn from experience," he said "I wrote it as a short story, but I've started to develop it into a novel."

"So, why the post-it?"

He walked over and took it from me, then scrunched it up and dropped it in the waste bin beside his desk.

"That's an old note. I've already written these ideas out. I'm about halfway through the novel."

I nodded. "The novel that's not quite about us?"

"Well, it's about love. Loss."

I looked down. "Experience."

"It's hard to write about things you don't know," he answered.

I sighed. "So, you said it was a short story?"

"Yes, it's actually what got me the scholarship," he replied. "My mum encouraged me to write when you left because she was worried that I wasn't coping. When I finished it, she sent it into SCU. I had no idea that she'd done it, but I got an acceptance letter one day before she died. I deferred it for a while because I knew that I couldn't leave my dad but, eventually, he sent me on my way. It's what she would have wanted."

I went to sit on the edge of his bed. "I'm sorry. It must've been tough for you."

He shrugged. "It was, but I survived."

"I'm sorry that you had to go through it alone."

"But I wasn't alone," he replied, and his head tipped. "I had Pattie and Henry, Wayne, Stuart. I just didn't have you."

I covered my eyes as tears brimmed.

Christian sighed, and I felt him kneel in front of me, then peel back my hand. He brushed the moisture away from my cheek.

"You need to stop all this crying, Layla," he said quietly. "You're going to dehydrate yourself."

I breathed a humourless laugh. "I don't care. I probably deserve it."

He rested an elbow on either one of my knees and tipped my chin up towards him.

"Layla, you need to forgive yourself," he whispered. "You can't change what happened by dwelling on the past."

I shook my head. "Sometimes I really wish that I could. Most times, I wish that I could. I'd do things so differently."

His fingers brushed my cheek and then moved to stroke the ends of my hair. My eyes found his, and I drowned in them. Time, distance, bad decisions, everything seemed to melt away. Christian had always had such a calming influence on me. I'd always been convinced that it was because of his kind soul, but maybe it was more than that. It scared me how much more than that it seemed to be.

His hand fell to rest on mine in my lap, and only a beat had passed when a ringing filled the room.

Christian pressed his lips together and stood as I scrambled to pull my phone from my pocket. I hit answer without stopping to check the caller ID.

"Hello?" I breathed. My voice sounded odd, even to me.

"*Layla, is that you?*" Maddie asked.

"Madeline, yes, it's me."

She exhaled. "*You sounded not like you. Anyway, I was just calling to make sure that you and Christian arrived safely. I thought it was too late to call last night and you'd be at the hospital anyway. How's your dad doing?*"

"Um, he's doing better," I answered. "We're just going back to see him now."

"*Oh, good, I'm glad to hear. The way you left, well, Jeffrey and I were worried.*"

Jeffrey.

"Well, hopefully, he'll make a full recovery," I sighed. "I'm going to stay at least another night to be sure, so I should be back tomorrow evening sometime."

"*Oh, sure,*" she said, and her voice was a little higher than normal. "*Well, call me if you need to.*"

"Thanks, Maddie," I breathed. "I'll see you when I get back."

"*See you, Layla. Say hi to Christian for me.*"

"Will do. Bye, Maddie."

I glanced up at Christian as he brushed his slightly stubbled cheek and I ended the call.

"Maddie says hi," I said.

Christian nodded. "*Don't Dream it's Over* is your ringtone?"

I looked down at the mechanism and brushed my thumb over the screen.

Don't Dream it's Over by Crowded House. It was also one of the songs that made the cut for our wedding song. Actually, I think it was the one we'd finally decided on.

It had been playing one time when our car broke down on one of our random adventures down the coast. We were seventeen, it was summer and, after being on the road for two hours, we'd run out of petrol. I hadn't been so good at reading the fuel meter back then. The song had been playing just before the car stopped, and it had resided with the both of us while we waited for help. As well as being one of my favourite songs of all time, it always reminded me of the way things were between Christian and me.

Christian lifted an eyebrow because he was still waiting for an answer.

"I, um, I thought it was on silent," I answered finally.

He looked down. "We should get to the hospital."

Christian walked from his room, and I followed to say goodbye to Mitch. We headed back to his car in silence while I cradled the dress in my arms. Christian had a scent of aftershave and fabric softener, mixed with a kind of musky scent that all guys seemed to have. The yellow fabric held onto the fragrance, making a flood of memories come back to me. As if the dress alone didn't do that.

Christian reached over to switch on the radio, and I snapped out of my reverie. I pulled out my phone again and turned it to silent. Christian glanced at me as he turned the music down.

"Can I ask you something personal?" he asked.

I huffed at the question. "Of course."

He hesitated, and it suddenly made me nervous. A few beats of music passed when he swallowed and moistened his lips.

"Maddie once said that you hadn't been out with anyone in all the time that she's known you," he said. "I know it's not my business, and I have no right to ask, but—"

"There's been no one else," I murmured. "How could there be?"

"No one until Jeffrey, you mean?"

I shook my head. "Not even him. That was more Maddie pushing it. I told Jeffrey that I wasn't ready for anything."

"Wasn't ready?"

"I guess I've always felt like being with anyone else would mean being unfaithful to you. My heart didn't come with me when I left."

Christian's brow creased, but I couldn't see his expression properly because his eyes were forward, fixed on the road.

I shook my head. "It probably sounds silly—"

"No, it doesn't."

"But you've been with other girls since I left," I whispered.

Christian pulled into the hospital car park and cut the engine. "What gives you that impression?"

I looked up and was surprised to see that his expression was a little angry.

"Maddie told Holly and me that you two were taking things slow because you had just come out of a serious relationship," I said. "So I thought that—"

"We were pretty serious, weren't we?" he asked.

I blinked. "Y-yes, but that, we, Christian, four years—"

"Well, as it turns out, you're not so easy to get over."

I sat back in confusion.

"Are you okay?" he asked.

I looked at him. "Are you telling me that after four years of being single, the girl that you decide to move on with just happens to be my best friend?"

"We were more just hanging out." Christian shrugged. "As you know."

"But I'm sure that other girls would have been interested in *hanging out* with you," I replied. "Other girls that weren't my best friend."

389

"Layla, the other girls in Almanbury knew better, and when I moved to South Coast—"

"Why did you really go out with Maddie, Christian?" I asked. "Was it just because she was my best friend?"

He exhaled. "I'll admit that, with her, there was the small incentive of finding out about you. Not *torment* you, like you thought, but just seeing how you were doing."

I raised my eyebrows. "You could have just asked, you know."

"Right," he mumbled. "Because it's so easy to go up to the girl who left me at the altar and ask what she's been up to."

"I didn't leave you at the altar."

"You might as well have."

I shook my head. "So, instead of just talking to me, you recruited a nice and unknowing girl to act as your spy?"

"It wasn't like that, I just... I wasn't leading her on or anything. We weren't doing anything that I wouldn't do with any of my other friends."

I rolled my eyes. "Well, that makes it okay then."

"Why are you getting mad about this?" he asked. "You were doing the same thing with that Jeffrey guy."

"Christian, Jeffrey knows about us," I replied. "I told him that we used to be engaged. I told him that I was still in love with you, so nothing was going to happen between him and me. He knew that when I said nothing was going to happen, that meant *nothing* was going to happen. Maddie still holds onto hope that one day something might happen between you two. Unless she's right?"

"So, why did he give you that bracelet then?" he asked. "That's not something that a guy gives a girl who he considers just a friend."

"I don't know why he gave it to me. He just gave it to me." I shrugged. "I didn't ask for it, and I tried to give it back, but he said that it went with my dress and that the stone promoted healing."

"Whatever," he sighed. "But I seriously don't know why you're getting angry about me not telling Maddie about us. You were the one who was trying to be all covert about our history."

I opened my mouth to rebuke him then closed it again because he was right. I sank down into my seat.

"God, we are a completely messed up pair," I mumbled.

He breathed a humourless laugh. "Nothing much has changed, has it?"

I looked over and frowned. "Some things have changed."

He nodded. "Well, we should go in. I don't want your mum to worry. We're later than we said we'd be."

"Okay."

Christian exhaled and pushed his door open. He was already around beside me by the time I'd climbed out the car myself. Neither of us moved for a moment, and then he held out his hand towards me. I didn't need to think about reaching out to take it. Our fingers laced together, a perfect fit as always, and we both walked in unison towards the hospital.

Chapter Thirteen
Seeing is Disbelieving

Christian squeezed my hand then released it when we arrived at the entrance to the CCU. I looked down and saw him slide them in the pockets of his jeans then rubbed my hands together, feeling the absence of his warmth. My eyes lifted to his, and he smiled as his right eye closed in a wink.

"Can I help you?" a nurse asked flatly.

"We're here to see Henry Thomas," Christian replied.

"I'm sorry. He's not taking visitors."

"But I'm his daughter," I said. "He's expecting me."

She frowned at me, then at Christian. "Well, only immediate family can go in."

"Well, this is my husband so he is family," I answered. The way it just rolled off my tongue scared me a little. It sounded too casual, too familiar, too close.

I felt Christian's arm slip around my waist, drawing me against him, and the nurse exhaled.

"Fine, follow me, please," she said.

She turned to walk down the clinical hallway, and Christian and I exchanged an incredulous glance as we followed her down to room four. She stopped by the door and folded her arms.

"Try not to stress him out," she mumbled.

I fleetingly considered making a joke about burning the house down or something but thought better of it. She apparently did not have a sense of humour, and it wasn't worth being turned away for. Christian's hand moved up to my shoulder, and it, too, felt too natural for comfort.

"Don't be too long. He needs his rest," she added, then turned on her heel and muttered something to herself.

I sighed and pushed open the door. Mum and Dad looked up with aghast looks on their faces that quickly turned into beaming smiles. Christian's hand dropped from my shoulder.

"Hey, Mum, Dad, you're looking better," I said.

"Pattie, Henry, how are you today?" Christian asked.

My mum and dad exchanged another look, and I walked to sit by the bed as my eyebrows lifted. Mum blinked out of her trance-like state.

"Did we miss something?" she murmured.

I looked back at Christian as he leant against the wall.

"Uh, no." I shrugged. "The nurse just wasn't going to let him in. I think she takes her job a bit too seriously."

Mum's and Dad's eyebrows lifted simultaneously. It was a little funny, actually.

"So, Dad, how is everything today?" I asked.

He groaned. "I'm great, fit as a fiddle. But they're paranoid and want to keep me in another night to be sure."

"Henry, they are not paranoid. Your heart was beating irregularly again this morning. They're only doing their job," Mum sighed.

"This morning?" I frowned. "You didn't mention anything when I called."

"It happened after you hung up," Mum said. At the same, time Dad replied, "It was nothing."

I glanced back at Christian who looked a little amused by the three of us.

"Well, if it's okay with you, Christian, we'll stay another night, and we can head back tomorrow afternoon," I

393

murmured, still locking eyes with him. "I'd stay longer, but I don't want you to fall behind with your studies, plus I'm under a deadline too."

Christian shrugged. "It's fine with me. I'll stay as long as you want."

I smiled then turned back to my parents. They were looking at me strangely again.

"What?" I sighed. "What is that look?"

Mum shook her head. "Nothing, honey. It's just nice to see you two together again."

"Calm down, Mum, we're just…" I stopped and bit my lip. What were we exactly?

"So, Pattie, are you staying here tonight as well?" Christian asked, walking over to the foot of my dad's bed.

"I don't know yet, darl. Probably," she answered. "If they let me."

"So, what do you kids have planned for the rest of the day?" Dad mumbled.

"I was thinking about stocking up the food supplies," I replied. "But then I remembered that I left South Coast without my wallet, so there goes that idea."

Mum reached down the side of her seat and pulled out her purse. "You need money?"

I shook my head. "No, mum, don't worry about it."

"Nonsense, honey, take my card. You remember the pin don't you?"

"Mum, I'm not taking your card."

She flapped it in my direction. "Why not? Honestly, Layla. You said you wanted to buy supplies for the house. I live there more than you, so let me pay for them."

I looked at my dad, who raised his eyebrows, and then rolled my eyes and plucked it from her. "Fine."

"You, my dear, are the hardest person to give money to," Mum exhaled. "I don't know how on earth they pay you at work."

"With peanut M&M's."

Both Dad and Christian laughed, but it took my mum a moment to comprehend that I was joking. Then she just rolled her eyes and said the two words that I probably heard the most from her in my foremost years.

"Honestly, Layla."

**

Christian and I only stayed for a little while longer, talking to my parents about nothing of consequence. When the first pause came in our conversation, Mum sighed.

"So, are you kids going to stay or head off? I'd hate to upset the nurses, and there's probably not much you can do here," she said. "You probably want to go and enjoy your day."

"We don't mind staying," I answered, turning to check that Christian felt the same. He had moved to sit on a chair beside my mother, which was opposite to me. He looked just as comfortable here amongst my family as any of us. But then, he had always been family to me.

"Absolutely, who cares about the nurses?" Christian smiled.

"Kids, if I could leave here, I would," Dad said flatly. "Go and have fun. Enjoy the day for all of us."

"Are you sure?" I asked. I rested my hand on his, and he gripped it firmly.

"Surely sure," he replied fervently. "You go. Just don't go too far."

I breathed a laugh and glanced at Christian. "Are you right to go?"

"I'll do whatever you want." He shrugged. "We could get those provisions for the house that you were talking about."

"Okay, sounds good."

I stood up, and Christian followed suit.

"So, you're going?" Mum asked. She sounded a little too excited.

"Yes, why?" I frowned. "Are you going to start singing?"

"No." She laughed. "Have fun."

"I'll call to check in later."

"Okay, honey," she sighed. "Love you both. Be careful."

"We will, Pattie, I promise." Christian smiled. "Take care, Henry."

"See you, Christian," Dad replied. "Bye, kiddo."

I stepped forward to kiss my dad on the cheek. "Bye, Dad. Love you. I'll talk to you later."

He smiled a crinkly-eyed grin.

Christian and I backed out of the small room and headed straight to his car. He strode ahead to open the passenger's side door for me then jogged around to the driver's side.

"Thanks," I said.

He started the engine.

"For letting you in the car?" He smiled. "No problem."

My lips twitched. "I meant thanks for driving me to Almanbury. Thanks for being here. Thanks for always being so nice to my parents. Thanks for defending me to your dad before. I really don't know if I deserve any of it – any of your kindness, but I am truly grateful for it."

Christian mashed his lips together. "I didn't do any of that for you, Layla. I drove you here, and I'm nice to your parents because, as I said, they are like parents to me too."

I deflated a little but nodded. "And when you defended me to your father?"

He took a breath and smiled. "That was more for me than you. Sometimes my dad forgets that I'm not five, and I don't need protecting."

"Parents are like that. They always want the best for their kids," I murmured a little absently.

Christian pulled into the car park of the only forum in town. "But sometimes parents don't know what's best for their kids."

"Maybe." I nodded. "But if it was me, and my son was in that position, I wouldn't trust me either."

He cut the engine and looked me in the eye. "Is there a reason that I shouldn't trust you?"

"No," I answered. "I would never lie to you, Christian."

It was true. That's why I had to leave.

"Well, I believe you," he said.

I looked down and wondered if now was the right time to tell him about the phone call that had made me leave Almanbury so suddenly that day. I wondered if there would ever be a right time.

"Christian, I—"

"Please don't, Layla," he sighed. "Don't go on about what great a guy I am."

I looked down and couldn't help but smile at his humility. "Okay."

"So I know that we need groceries, but I think first we should get lunch, or breakfast, or whatever we're up to first. I guess biscuits don't really count as a meal."

"Okay."

He nodded. "Okay."

He pushed open his door, and I waited a moment before following. I needed to tell him eventually, I knew that I did. Or did I? Was it just my conscience that I was trying to clear, or was it essential for Christian to know why I left? If he didn't want to know, then wasn't that enough? But then, would we ever be the same as we were? Could we be that way again? We were hardly the same people as we were four years ago. Maybe it was too much to hope that we could be that couple again.

I was getting ahead of myself. We were only just on speaking terms. Plus, Christian would need more than an apology and my word to trust me again. Wouldn't he? It had always been all or nothing with us, and we'd always given it our all until I walked away, and then there was nothing. So that just stood to question whether this Christian and Layla were still those two people that gave it their all when they were together. The idea started to seem not so impossible to me any more.

"Where do you want to eat?" Christian asked, sliding his hands into his pockets.

I shrugged. "You choose."

Wordlessly, we both gravitated towards a coffee shop, which used to be a popular hangout for us when we were in school. It felt bizarre to be back after so long had passed, especially with Christian. But, in another way, it was almost as if no time had passed at all. The only bad thing about the forum was that it was always buzzing with people, and since it was the weekend, and the only forum in the small town, if we sat there long enough, everyone that we'd ever knew would probably pass by.

Everyone knew everyone in Almanbury, and everyone knew what I did. Four years meant nothing. It might as well have been yesterday. If it were, I probably would have gotten less judgemental glares, but maybe I was just being paranoid.

We ordered some hot drinks and pre-made rolls and took a seat in a booth that was tucked into a corner. I felt safer in there, like maybe the rest of the world didn't count – like it was only Christian and me.

"Are you okay?" he asked. "Is it weird being back?"

I shrugged. "A little. I mean, I was here last weekend."

Christian laughed and leant forward. "Why are you whispering?"

"I'm scared of seeing someone we know."

"We know everyone." He smiled. "It's Almanbury."

"Right."

"Are you embarrassed to be seen with me?" he asked. He lifted an eyebrow, and I melted a little.

"I'm actually worried about what they'll think of you being seen with me," I whispered. "It's a small town. News travels fast."

"You're telling me."

I shook my head. "If your dad gave you lip for hanging out with me, what will everyone else say?"

I sat back as the waitress came over with our order. She didn't look that much younger than Christian and me, so I wondered if she went to Almanbury Senior High with us.

My suspicions were silently confirmed when her glare turned on me and then she glanced almost sympathetically at Christian. It looked as if she recognised us from somewhere at least.

She peeled away and headed back to the counter.

Christian sighed and shook his head. "Layla, I don't care what people think. You shouldn't either. We don't even live here anymore."

"Yes, but these people used to be our friends."

"These people." He laughed. "Layla, you never used to care what people said. If you did then you never would have gotten engaged to me at eighteen."

I frowned at him. He made it sound so casual now, as if we were talking about the colour of the sky, or whether the local football team had won their last game.

"It's different now though," I said. "I wasn't ashamed of my actions back then."

Christian picked up his roll without answering and took a bite. I looked down at mine and poked it before taking a sip of coffee.

"You should eat something." He nodded. "And for someone who doesn't sleep very well, maybe you should consider changing back to tea."

"I don't think it's the coffee," I sighed. "And I'm not especially hungry."

He opened his mouth to say something but then closed it again. His brow creased.

"Look alive, Layla," he whispered. "We've got company."

I turned in the direction his eyes were and felt my stomach lurch. This was bound to be suitably unpleasant.

"Hey, guys." Christian smiled. "What's going on?"

"Hey, buddy, I didn't know you were back in town," Wayne replied. Stuart and Abbie, my would-be maid of honour, we with him. I hadn't kept in touch with Abbie either, not a letter or a call. She wasn't at the top of my contact list despite her standing in my wedding party, she was actually the least of my concerns after I left. Needless to say, there was probably a voodoo doll somewhere with my name on it that she stuck pins in.

"Dude, what are you doing?" Stuart asked Christian. His tone laced with horror, but I couldn't see if his expression matched it since his back was turned on me.

"I'm having lunch with Layla. Do you want to join us?" Christian answered.

I gave a startled laugh, and Abbie's head snapped towards me. Her fierce brown eyes made me recoil.

"No, I don't want to join you," Stuart muttered. "Turner, what are you doing here with her? I never took you for a masochist."

I rubbed my forehead. Sure, it was unpleasant, but what did I really expect? I expected it to be worse, though I still willed myself to disappear. Christian sat up.

"Don't talk about Layla like that," he said, saying what I least expected him to. "She was your friend too, remember?"

"What? That far back?" Stuart huffed.

"I remember," Abbie said. "I also remember when she left without as much as a word and then didn't call or write or even tell me that she was alive. I remember hearing that she was here last weekend and didn't *bother* paying me the courtesy of a visit even then."

I exhaled. "I would have come to see you, but last week was really just about making up ground with—"

"Right, well, you have made where I fall on that list crystal clear."

"Abbie," I sighed.

She rolled her eyes, so I gave up.

"Look, Christian, we're just worried about you, man," Wayne said, ignoring the dialogue between Abbie and me. "You may not remember what things were like when she left, but we certainly do. It's not worth it."

"I was there." Christian frowned. "Of course I remember."

I stared into my coffee cup. Apparently, people were going to continue talking about me as though I wasn't here. I guess they got a little too used to my absence.

"Did she tell you why she left then?" Stuart asked. "Care to share?"

Christian shook his head. "I'm not talking about this here."

"How could you forgive her, Turner?"

"It's none of your business."

Stuart groaned. "Well, it was my business when she up and left you heartbroken, and Wayne and I had to pick up the pieces."

Christian exhaled slowly. "Stu, seriously. She doesn't have to explain herself to—"

"I got scared, okay?" I burst out.

Four sets of eyes turned on me. Then one set disappeared as Christian looked down.

I shook my head. "I wanted more for him than to be tied down to me forever."

"And you didn't think of that in the twelve months you were engaged to him for?" Stuart quipped. "Or even to tell him on the day or, I don't know, in any of the days over the last four years?"

Christian looked at me and I bit my lip. A phone call wouldn't have fixed anything. After all, a phone call had been the thing to ruin it all in the first place.

"I…" My throat closed. "I guess it didn't hit me until it was too late."

"Well, then," Stuart mumbled. "I'm sold."

"Don't," Christian breathed.

"You know, I do remember when we were friends, Layla," Stuart continued. "I remember everything from when we met in pre-school to when you and Christian met in ninth grade. I thought I knew you then, but I was wrong. The girl I knew wouldn't have done something like this. That girl didn't have a cold heart like this one does."

"Stop," Christian near shouted. His hand slammed on the table, causing our coffees to spill. "Just. Stop. What happened between Layla and me is between Layla and me. She can't change what happened, and she knows that she messed up. Open your eyes and see that she is trying to make up for it now."

I felt my cheeks flush as bystanders turned to stare. I'd never seen Christian so outspoken in public. Normally, he wasn't one to make a scene.

He took a steadying breath. "I know you're all hurting too and that you're concerned about me, but paying out on her does not help me try to move past everything. So just stop."

Abbie scoffed. "Whatever."

She turned on her heel and walked away from our table. Christian drew in a breath, not even flinching.

Stuart glanced over his shoulder at Abbie's departing figure then walked after her. Wayne took a side step, so he was standing evenly between us.

"I hear what you're saying, Christian, and I know you're sorry, Layla," he said. "But, honestly, you had to know that it wasn't going to be easy coming back."

I nodded. "I know that I've got a lot of making up to do."

Wayne sighed. "Well, I guess sorry is a good start. So, how long are you guys here for?"

"Until tomorrow night at this stage," Christian answered, visually calmer now. "We only came down to make sure that Layla's dad is okay."

"Is Henry not okay?"

"He's in the hospital for his heart." I frowned. "He's stable and hopefully getting released tomorrow."

Wayne nodded. "Send him my thoughts. He's a good guy, your dad."

"He is," I agreed. "And I will, thanks, Wayne."

Wayne smiled weakly then glanced over his shoulder in the direction that Abbie and Stuart had gone.

"Well, I'd better go and find Stu and Abs," he said. "Stuart probably isn't the best person to calm Abbie down."

Christian's eyes rolled. "Right. Catch you later then."

Wayne extended a fist towards Christian who knocked his against it. He then turned to me and opened his hand for me to shake.

"It's good to have you back, Layla," he said. "Don't be a stranger."

I took his hand and squeezed it. "I won't. I promise."

"Christian and Layla." Wayne smirked. "See you, guys."

He turned and walked away. When he was out of earshot, I glanced at Christian.

"I'm really sorry about that," I sighed.

"Why are you sorry?" he asked. "It was Stuart and Abbie who were out of line."

"It was only because they were reacting to what I did that you had to defend me."

He shook his head. "I didn't have to, Layla."

"But you did, Christian," I replied. "I'm just saying that I'm sorry I've caused tension between you and your friends."

"Well, they're your friends too. They just needed reminding."

"Well, I don't know if that worked since they still hate me. For good reason," I exhaled. "God, I'm a complete idiot."

"They don't *all* hate you. Wayne still likes you." He shrugged. "And you're not a *complete* idiot, just a little one."

I huffed. "Thanks. Add some salt."

He chuckled and rested his hands on mine. "I'm kidding. Sort of."

"You think you're helping, but you're not."

404

He smiled and withdrew his hand to pick back up his roll. He took a bite then noticed the spilt coffee so moved to mop it up.

"Layla, eat your food," he said. "We've got to get groceries yet and then think about what we're going to make for dinner."

I froze midway through trying to figure out how to best attack my giant salad roll.

"Dinner?" I sighed. "How can you be thinking about dinner when we haven't even finished lunch yet?"

He waited to finish his mouthful before replying. "Because we need to know what to buy."

I frowned at the food. "I don't know if I'll be able to eat dinner if I eat this."

"Yeah, you've gotten a little thin."

I opened my mouth to argue and then saw the amused smile on his face.

"You're not funny," I mumbled.

"That's because I'm serious." He laughed. "Layla, I don't think you're as good at looking after yourself as you think."

"Well, I'm still alive, aren't I?"

"If you don't count the fact that you look as if you haven't slept in months, and have cuts on your head and feet. Plus, I'd be willing to wage a bet that you don't do a lot of cooking... unless you count the times when your vegetarian boyfriend comes over."

"He's not—" I started and then sighed when Christian laughed again.

"You're so easy to rile." He grinned.

I shook my head incredulously.

"But, seriously, I'll cook tonight," he said. "Like a steak inside a turkey, stuffed with chicken, with a side of bacon."

"Sounds great." I laughed. "But maybe just pick one protein."

"It sounds like the vegetarian Italian is having an impact on you already."

"Hell no. Give me a steak over a cabbage any day of the week."

Christian chuckled. "That's my girl."

**

When Christian finished his roll, and I'd eaten as much of mine as I could, we headed to the grocery store to get supplies. Christian and I hated lingering while food shopping, so we weren't long in the supermarket.

Once we were done, we headed back to my house. My parents' house. It was good to be home.

"I think I need to wash the can of hairspray out of my hair," I said when we got back. I hadn't washed my hair since Maddie had curled and sprayed it for the ball. It all seemed to clump together like strands of hay.

"Okay, well, while you do that, I might go and grab some more clothes," he replied. "That is if you want me to stay here again with you tonight."

"I do. I mean, sure. That would be nice. Only if you don't mind."

He smiled. "I don't mind."

I looked down and tried to stop myself from blushing, but the burning on my cheeks told me that I was unsuccessful.

"So, I'll see you when I get back," Christian sighed. "Do you want to lock me out?"

I walked him to the door.

"Why don't you just take a key in case you get back before I'm out of the shower?"

"I don't think that will happen unless you're planning on taking a long shower."

My forehead creased. "Are you going to be a long time?"

He shrugged. "You know how my dad can be."

"Right." I smiled. "Well, be careful. I'll see you soon."

"Okay." He nodded. "Enjoy the shower."

I took a step back and pressed my lips together. He'd taken maybe four steps when he stopped and turned, then walked back towards me.

"Why don't I take that key, just in case?" he said.

I pulled one out the back of the door and handed it to him. My eyes never left his face, and his didn't leave mine.

"I'll try not to be too long," he murmured. "If I'm not back in four years then you can start to worry."

I exhaled. "You're still not funny."

"Sure I am." He chuckled.

He winked and walked back towards his car then slipped in behind the wheel. I waited until he had pulled away before closing the door.

It occurred to me as I was heading down the hallway to the bathroom that one thing had never changed between us despite the time that had passed. Christian didn't turn his back on me, and I had never really closed the door on him.

I took my time in the shower. Longer than I ever really took in the shower, but there was no reason for me to rush. Christian had taken a key, and there was no one else in the house. So, at a leisurely pace, I gently smoothed the tangles from my hair and let the warm water loosen the knots in my muscles. I couldn't remember the last time that I wasn't in a hurry to be somewhere. I knew that, come tomorrow, things would go back to chaos but, for now, time was mine.

After my shower, I tiptoed to my room to find something to wear. There wasn't much left in my drawers by way of jeans. I'd cleared most of those out when I left. I didn't have a lot of tops left either since my clothing item of choice had always been dresses.

I dried my hair and found some clean underwear, again in short supply, and then headed out to the kitchen to find the yellow dress that Christian had returned. It had been five years since I'd worn it, so I knew it probably wouldn't fit.

I pulled it over my head, expecting a struggle, but it fell over me perfectly, even loosely over my hips. Maybe Christian was right when he'd said that I hadn't been eating properly. I suppose I had been a little strapped for cash when I left, then lately, I'd been a little preoccupied with work. At least I ate breakfast. Well, most days.

I glanced at the clock and saw that Christian had been gone for almost forty-five minutes, which meant that I'd spent an unreasonable amount of time in the shower. I made my way back to the bathroom for my old brush and began combing through my hair. I hadn't had it cut in the four years since I'd left either. I could probably do with a trim myself.

I heard the front door close and paused.

"Layla?" Christian called. "Are you still here?"

"Still not funny," I shouted.

I put the brush down and headed out to find him.

Both Christian and I froze as we saw each other. All of his shoulder-length hair had been cut into the short style crop that it used to have.

"You, um, you got a haircut," I sighed. "It looks great."

"And the dress still fits," he noted. "That's a little scary."

"I know. I was surprised too."

We fell silent, but the look between us spoke volumes. The years of gap felt like they were closing again. For a second, I could almost fool myself into thinking that we were still the same people we had been – the same Christian and Layla that were happy and in love.

Then Christian's gaze dropped, and his soulful eyes released me from my sweeping nostalgia.

"So, uh, you managed to get the knots out of your hair?" he asked.

"Yes," I replied. "It took a lot of conditioner."

He chuckled, reaching up to brush his hand through hair that was no longer there. Instead, he ran it down his neck and then let it fall back to his side.

My fingers found the bottom hem of my dress, and I looked down at it. Things might appear to be the same, but everything had changed. I *was* only fooling myself. As much as I wanted it to be the same, as much as I wanted Christian to take me into his arms and kiss me like he used to, and as sorry as I was, that wasn't going to change what I did. It wasn't going to change the Christian and Layla we are now into the Christian and Layla we once were.

I cleared my throat. "I might go and change. I probably look ridiculous."

Christian looked up, and his forehead was creased. His eyebrows slowly lifted as he let his gaze brush over me. I hesitated for a moment before turning towards the hallway.

"Layla," he said.

I stopped and dropped my eyes to the floor. From the corner of them, I saw him step towards me, and I'd barely lifted my head when his hands were guiding my face towards his. His lips were on mine before I knew what was happening, and they moulded together the way light wraps around a vortex, perfectly harmonised in movement as if we were two halves of the one whole, meeting like opposite charges of magnets.

His hand dropped to my waist as the other rested on the back of my head. His fingers wove through the damp tresses as he drew me towards him. My hands lifted to his shoulders, clutching him to bring him closer towards me. I moved my arms around his neck, lacing my fingers through his freshly cut hair. I could feel his heartbeat as it hammered fiercely against mine. They beat together in quick thuds as if they were synchronised with only flesh and fabric separating them.

But, as much as it felt right, something felt wrong. I needed to tell him. I needed to be honest about the phone call. It was something that was more of a barrier between us than our clothes were – and they were quickly not becoming a non-issue.

Christian's hands ran up my thighs, lifting me up around his waist. He walked me towards the kitchen counter and sat me down. My breath hitched in my throat.

"Christian," I panted. "I need… there's something I need to tell you."

His lips traced a line down my jaw to my neck. "Can it wait?"

His mouth was hot against my left shoulder as his fingers peeled off the strap of my dress. Could what wait? What was I saying? I exhaled as the sensation tingled all the way to my toes. I caught the bottom of his T-shirt and dragged it over his head, my hands re-familiarising themselves with the muscles of his chest, his shoulders, his back. His lips pressed to my neck once more, and then he lifted his eyes to mine.

"Layla," he breathed.

He ran his fingertips through the damp hair framing my face, and I brushed my hand down his cheek and neck to settle on his chest. I could feel his beating heart thumping under my palm, and it was a wonder that it didn't burst through his ribcage.

"I—" he started, but his words were cut off by the sound of keys in the front door. He looked at me, and I saw my confusion reflected in his eyes before I gasped.

"It's Mum," I whispered.

Christian stepped back and scooped up his T-shirt, swiftly pulling it over his head.

"Layla? Christian?" Mum's voice echoed down the hallway. "I hope I didn't startle you. I had to use the spare key since I gave you mine."

I wiped my mouth and slid off the counter, flattening my yellow dress.

"H-hey, Mum," I sighed. "How's Dad?"

"No change except he's grumbling more now," she replied as she stepped into the doorway leading to the kitchen and sitting area. Her head tipped curiously as she appraised me.

"Honestly, Layla, don't you think it's a little chilly for a summer dress?" she asked.

"Yeah, I know." I smiled. "I just wanted to see if it still fit."

Christian glanced up at me as he paced around the counter into the kitchen. My cheeks felt like they were on fire.

Mum looked between us. "Didn't you lose that dress, Layla?"

I shrugged. "I guess it showed up."

She nodded slowly. "Christian, you got a haircut. It looks lovely."

"Thanks, Pattie." He smiled. "I thought it was time."

Mum laughed. "Gosh, you two look just like you did when you were eighteen."

I hoped that she was just referring to clothes and haircuts rather than the look of being sprung that we both wore.

"So, what's up?" I asked. "Are you home for dinner or just checking in?"

"Actually, I came to pick some things up for your father," she said. "Although the doctors are probably releasing him tomorrow, he's restless. I came to get his book and a change of clothes for him."

"Oh, okay. Well, we are probably going to start on dinner just after I get changed."

"Lovely, what are you having?"

I couldn't remember so turned to Christian. He leant back against the sink and folded his arms.

"Uh, steak, I think," he answered. "It was steak, wasn't it, Layla?"

I nodded. "Sure, steak."

"I hope there are some vegetables with that steak," Mum said.

Christian chuckled. It sounded so natural that it warmed me. "Of course, Pattie. Would you like to join us?"

"No thanks, sweetie. I'd better get back to Henry, I think." She smiled. "I'm just going to gather some things, and maybe get a quick shower, and then head back to the hospital. Don't let me interrupt whatever you were doing."

I swallowed the wrong way and started to choke, and it took me a moment to pull myself together. Mum's forehead pinched as she watched, and Christian nudged a glass of water towards me. I took it and gulped it, then nearly started coughing again.

"Thanks... and sorry," I gasped. "I'm just going to get changed."

I backed away quickly to escape the curious glances that Christian and my mum were exchanging. Christian had begun to gather the appliances for cooking.

"Why is Layla acting so strange?" I heard Mum ask.

I bobbed around to see Christian shrug and then smirk as he saw me looking.

I changed into the pair of jeans I'd been wearing during the day and rummaged through until I found a plain black T-shirt to wear with them. On my way back to the kitchen, I pulled on the bottom of the shirt to tie a knot in the left corner. Christian looked up and shook his head at me. My mum wasn't anywhere in sight.

"Are you still doing that to your T-shirts?" he asked. "You know it stretches them out of shape."

I shrugged. "It makes them fit better."

"Whatever you say."

I looked down and saw that Christian was busily marinading the steak.

"Is there anything I can help with?" I asked.

"You can chop the onions if you like?"

"Do you want to make me cry?"

Christian stopped and smiled. "Well, it's either that or peel the potatoes, and I know you hate it when your hands smell like potato juice."

I pressed my lips together. "Okay, I'll do the onions."

Christian grinned widely. "I thought you might."

Chapter Fourteen
Unravelling the Truth

It took my mum an extraordinary amount of time to shower and get her things together. By the time she was ready to leave, Christian and I were already sitting down to dinner with our steak and vegetables.

"I'm almost gone. I'm just grabbing some snacks for your father." Mum said with a smile as she rummaged through the freshly stocked cupboards. "That dinner smells delicious."

Christian looked up at me and grinned triumphantly.

"We make a pretty good team." I nodded.

"Mm, you certainly do," Mum answered. "Always have."

I cleared my throat.

"You know, Mum, by the time you get back to the hospital, you'll have to come right back home with Dad," I said.

She groaned. "I know, I know. I'm going. Thanks for doing the shopping, Layla. I know how much you hate grocery shopping."

"No problem," I replied. "By the way, your card is on top of the fridge."

She closed the cupboard with the arm that wasn't holding the food and looked at me curiously. "Honestly, Layla. How on earth am I supposed to see it up there?"

"That's why I'm telling you."

Christian chuckled. "I told her to leave it on the counter, but she was adamant."

"Yes, I know how she gets," Mum mumbled. "Stubborn as a mule."

"Hi, I'm right here," I said, raising my hand.

Mum smiled. "And I'm heading off. Have a good night, you two."

"Bye, Pattie." Christian waved. "Tell Henry we said hi."

"Will do."

"Bye, Mum," I added.

She waved and headed down the hallway. I heard the door lock and looked back at Christian, and his blue eyes were already on me. My heart gave a squeeze, and I drew in a breath to try to slow it.

"You did a great job with dinner," I said. "It was really delicious."

"We," he corrected. "You helped too. Maybe not with your blood and sweat, but with your tears."

I breathed a laugh. "I haven't hurt myself in a while. I'm a little surprised I didn't accidentally chop a finger off."

"I'm glad you didn't. I don't like seeing you hurt. Plus, I've already cleaned your blood up off the floor once this week."

"Right." I nodded.

I looked down and pushed out my chair, taking our empty plates into the kitchen. I put them in the dishwasher since we'd been cleaning as we cooked, and there weren't any others left to wash.

I took a deep breath and made my way back to where Christian was standing by the table.

"So, about before," I sighed. It was better not to delay the inevitable awkward conversation.

Christian nodded slowly. "Yes, before."

"That was…" I stopped and searched for the word.

"Weird?" he offered.

"I was going to say '*nice*' but okay."

"I mean, it was nice but still a bit weird."

I felt my cheeks blush and rubbed them. "Weird how?"

"Weird because it felt just the same," he said. "Like as if no time had passed at all."

"I know what you mean."

He smiled weakly and looked down. There was a beat of silence between us, and then he exhaled. "Listen, Layla, there is something I've been meaning to ask you."

I folded my arms. I knew that I couldn't hide from this forever. "Okay, what is it?"

"What you said at the ball last night, did you mean it?" he asked quietly.

I blinked. "Um, remind me what I said."

"That not a day goes by when you don't think about me and the life that we would have had if you had stayed."

Had I said that?

"Yes." I nodded. I walked over to sit on the couch before my knees gave way. "Yes, I meant it."

Christian came over to sit beside me. "What did you think about?"

I frowned and shook my head. "Christian, I don't—"

"Please."

I took a deep breath. My hands were shaking, so I laced them together.

"I think, by now we would have a little place of our own." I shrugged. "It's a white cottage-style house with little window gardens with lots of daisies and a blue front door. It would have probably been in Almanbury, or close by, since we both suffer from chronic homesickness."

Christian sighed. "Not so much any more, I guess."

I shook my head. "No, even more so now."

He looked up at me and nodded. "What about kids? Did we have any of those?"

As the words came out his mouth, tears flooded my eyes. I took a staggered breath. There was no hiding from the truth now. My head fell.

"Yes," I whispered. "A little boy, just like you. He's three and a half."

Christian was silent, so I looked up. I could see the confusion on his face that slowly began to soften into comprehension.

"Three and a half," he said, and then head shook. "That would mean… were you pregnant?"

My lips turned down into a pout.

"Is that why you left?" he asked. "Is that what you meant by not wanting to hold me back?"

My head fell into my hands, and the sobs shook my shoulders.

"Layla," Christian murmured. "Layla, look at me."

He tugged on my wrist, and I looked up at him. His blue eyes had turned glassy.

"You were pregnant," he said. It wasn't a question, it was confirming a suspicion.

"I panicked," I sighed.

Christian ran his hands through his hair and stood up. He began to pace, and his head was shaking. He looked angry, but as though the anger was fuelled by the disappointment and sadness that reddened his features.

"Tell me what happened," he said. "Tell me everything. I want to know when you found out, why you thought that *leaving* was the best decision and, since you don't have a toddler on your hip, what the hell happened after you left."

417

I wanted to cry harder, but it wasn't my time to grieve now, it was his. He had every right to know and every right to be as angry, disappointed, and sad as he looked. So, I took a breath to compose myself and wiped my cheek.

"I got a call a couple of hours before the rehearsal dinner. It was the doctor," I explained. "He was concerned that I'd be drinking that night, so he called to let me know the results of the tests that he'd run earlier in the week. I had been feeling—"

"You were sick. I remember." He nodded. "Then what?"

I shrugged. "After he told me, it hit me that we were nineteen, and we were going to be married and have a kid. We weren't equipped to raise a child, and you had your whole life ahead of you. If I'd have stayed—"

"What?" he shouted. He stopped pacing, and the anger outweighed the other emotions on his face. "What would have happened, Layla? Tell me."

"You wouldn't be studying, Christian, you would have been stuck."

"I would have taken care of you and the baby," he exclaimed. "I would have figured something out. We both would have figured it out *together* like we promised we would when I proposed. We were stronger than that – than for you to doubt that. You had *no right* to make that decision for me, Layla. *No right*."

Christian smacked his hand into the wall, and I bit my lip. I knew he'd be upset, but seeing him like this made my heart physically hurt. It was what I had been trying to avoid – it was what had made me hang up all those times I'd tried to call.

"I'm sorry," I mumbled. "I just thought you deserved so much more."

"Than a wife and kids?" he asked. His voice cracked. "That was my dream, our dream. Maybe we thought we'd be older, but we always talked about having a family, Layla. How could you take that away from me?"

My heart sank to my toes. He was right. I had taken it all away from him. I'd always thought about it from the other side, from him reacting badly about the baby since we were so ill-equipped to raise a child. But he was right – we had talked about it. We'd both wanted it, and we'd both wanted it with each other.

Christian walked over to stand in front of me and folded his arms.

"Did you change your mind about us?" he asked. "Were you scared about having a baby because you didn't want that with me any more?"

"No," I sighed. "No, I loved you. I wanted everything with you. I just freaked out when it all started to happen so soon. Sure, we'd talked about kids, Christian, but we talked about having them when we were at least out of our teens. I knew that you wanted so much to study and get a good grounding before we started a family. I thought, I mean, I was obviously wrong, but I thought you'd be disappointed that I let it happen."

"You *let* it happen? Layla, I know that you didn't fail human biology. I don't need to tell you that it takes—"

"I know, but it was my fault that we were careless. I'd missed my appointment for the injection, and I knew the odds."

He frowned. "It... you only missed it by a week or so, didn't you?"

"It was enough."

He exhaled. "Then what? You got the call so you left and went to South Coast. Did you keep it?"

419

His voice shook again, and I glanced up to see a teardrop trickle down his cheek. He ignored it, but I couldn't ignore the ones that fell from my eyes. I rubbed them with my palm.

"I… at first I didn't know what to do. I didn't think that I could go through with it," I said. My throat felt dry, but thick. I had to pause to swallow. "I considered coming home so many times, but I couldn't bring myself to face everyone."

Christian shuffled, and his frown deepened.

I swallowed again. "About seven weeks in, I got rushed to hospital after collapsing one day. I heard the baby's heartbeat for the first time, and it was then that I decided I would find a way to go through with it."

Christian's jaw hardened. "So, you did? Then where is he?"

I shook my head and a whimper escaped me. "I miscarried a week later."

Christian's head fell back, and the moisture in his reddened eyes fell down the sides of his face.

A moment later, he dropped to his knees in front of me, folding his arms over my legs to cry into my lap. I leant forward to hold him, and we stayed like that for a long time.

**

"I wish you'd have called me," he whispered. "I should have been there. You shouldn't have gone through it alone."

We were sitting on the couch facing each other. Our knees overlapped like Jenga pieces, and our hands were a tangled pile on top of them.

"I wanted to call. I tried to," I breathed. "But I felt like such a failure. After everything I'd put you through and the way I'd left, I thought it would be better for you if I just stayed away. Maybe it would be easier for you if I were gone. Maybe you could move on or hate me easier if you didn't know why. But then, I couldn't handle the idea of you hating me, and I couldn't rationalise telling you that I'd left and hurt you for nothing. I was ashamed of myself for leaving and even more so that I thought it was the right thing to do."

Christian shook his head. "I hate that you didn't trust me enough to let me help you."

I was already shaking my head. "I did trust you. I just wanted more for you."

"More than what, Layla?" he asked. "Nothing else in my life meant anything without you. God, you had to have known that I would have given up everything for you."

"I just didn't want you to have to."

"So you played the martyr and gave up everything for me instead? How is that fair?"

I blinked. "I didn't give up everything."

"You didn't?" Christian asked, and his eyebrow lifted. "What else did you have but your family, your home, your friends, your future... me?"

"I... I didn't think of it like that."

"Honestly, Layla," he sighed.

I looked down at our hands, and he removed his to rub his face. He always did that when we were about to have a conversation that he didn't want to have.

I bit my lip. "What? What is it?"

"What am I supposed to do now?" he asked.

"What do you mean?"

"Well, after four years of trying to understand why you could have left. This is a far cry from thinking that you didn't love me enough or—"

"How could you ever think that?" I sighed. "Christian, you are my whole world. You always have been."

"And you were mine. But you left, so what was I supposed to think?"

"I know," I murmured. "I know. I messed up, and I know that you probably hate me and can't ever forgive me, but please—"

"Layla, I forgave you a long time ago."

I blinked. "But how? Why? But you didn't even know the whole story before."

"And now that I do, I standby that forgiveness," he said. "You made a mistake, and I can't hold it against you forever."

"So, now that you know, you can forgive me, but you also hate me, right?" I mumbled. "I understand. I would hate me too."

"Layla, have you not been listening to anything I've been saying since we were fourteen?" he asked. "I could never hate you. For some reason that I can't comprehend, I love you in a way that doesn't disappear, even if you do."

"Are you saying…?"

"I love you, Layla. I always have. I know that I always will."

My lower lip jutted into a frown. "No, you don't. You can't. I don't deserve it."

"Layla, stop," he whispered, taking my hands in his again. "You don't get to decide this for me."

I looked up at him sadly.

"Sorry, wrong words," he sighed. "I just meant that, from the moment I saw you in the ninth grade, I fell in love with you, and your yellow sundress. From that day, not even I could control what I felt for you."

"But—"

"And over the last four years, every second has felt like a dream, like I haven't really lived it without you. I need you,

Layla, now more than I ever have. You frustrate the hell out of me sometimes but, damn it, I still love you."

I let out a sob. "But how can you after everything I've put you through? I've made so many mistakes."

His hand brushed my cheek. "That only makes me love you more. You made them all for me."

I shook my head. "Christian Turner, I love you, but you are far too good for me."

"No, Layla Louise Thomas, I'm just right for you."

He leant towards me, resting his open lips on mine and let them close. The kiss was salty from my tears but, for some reason, it only made the embrace sweeter. He moved his legs from their tangle with mine and backed me against the cushions of the couch. My knees hooked over his to bind him closer against me.

"I'm sorry, I'm so sorry," I breathed against his mouth.

"Stop apologising," he panted.

"I just—"

He exhaled. "I know."

My hands ran up his body, and he sighed against me.

"Christian, I never want to leave you again," I said.

His eyes glowed like blue fairy lights. "You'd better not."

"I never will."

His hands moved up my abdomen, over the knot in my T-shirt, and then he groaned against my lips.

"Makes it fit better," he mumbled.

I breathed a laugh and pulled out the coiled fabric. He pushed my shirt up my body, and his mouth was hot as his tongue brushed over the skin on my abdomen. My hands ran through his hair.

"Christian, are you sure—?"

"I've waited long enough."

I tipped his chin upwards, and he returned his lips to mine. I felt alive for the first time in over four years. Every cell in my body was on fire, every breath burnt like I was breathing in flames, but it was exhilarating.

My T-shirt left my body, and a shot of adrenaline ran through me. No one had ever touched me the way that Christian had. Time may have passed, but it seemed to mean nothing to the way our bodies moulded together.

"Not here," I panted. "What if—"

"Your room?" he gasped.

I nodded and before I could contemplate using my legs, he had swept me up in his arms. Like muscle memory, he carried me to my room with his lips still pressed to mine.

He smiled a familiar eye-crinkling smile as he dropped me onto my mattress. Back to where it had all began.

**

Awareness sank back to me, and it was heavier than my body felt. I tried to move my arms and legs, but it was almost as if they didn't belong to me any more. I didn't mind if they didn't work. I didn't need them. All I needed was Christian.

I drew in a deep breath, but it caught in my throat on the exhale. What if everything that had happened was just my overactive imagination? I had dreamt about Christian so many times over the years, so what if everything, the conversation, the caressing, what if…

"Not a dream," he whispered.

His fingertip ran from my hairline to my chin, and I opened my eyes and found his eyes looking at me. They glowed in the morning sunlight that peeked through the rim of my curtains.

I smiled and felt a spot of moisture leak from my eye. It ran down the side of my nose and fell onto the pillow.

"Christian," I sighed.

"I hope those are happy tears. My ego can't handle any more of the other kind."

"I'm happy, I promise," I said. "I'm bursting with happiness."

He propped himself on his elbows and ran his fingers under my eyes to dry them. "You're so beautiful."

My thumb brushed over his lips. "I like waking up to you. I'm glad it wasn't a dream."

"Some dream."

He rested his head on my chest and moved his arm around my body.

"So, what happens now?" I asked. I hated the question and its uncertainty. But, even I couldn't deny that the thought of us only being a passing thing was even worse.

"I don't know," he replied. "We could get breakfast?"

I shuffled around to sit up and pulled the sheet with me. "I meant with us. I'm not really keen on losing you again anytime soon."

He smirked. "Well, I'm not the one who has a history of running."

"I told you that I'm not leaving you again. Besides, you know all my hiding spots now."

He tucked a piece of my hair behind my ear. "Good."

"So, what do you think?" I asked. "What do we do now?"

"We stay together. Simple as that."

"But is it as simple as that? What about our parents and friends? What will they think?"

He mashed his lips together. "To be honest, it doesn't matter what they think. It's never bothered us before. Plus, we're not teenagers any more. We're better equipped to make this work now."

"But we have to go back to South Coast today," I sighed. "And then everything will change again."

He shrugged. "It doesn't have to."

"And what about Maddie? We have to tell her about us."

"So we will."

"She's going to hate me. She likes you, you know."

Christian smiled. "She has good taste."

I glared at him. "You're still not funny. She's my best friend."

"I know, Layla, and, to be fair, you probably should have been honest with her sooner," he said. "I know you think you're protecting people by lying to them, but it's really not helpful."

I frowned. "Noted. But, to also be fair, you probably shouldn't have started dating her in the first place. That wasn't helpful either."

"Noted." He nodded. "Clearly we are both terrible people, and we deserve each other."

I laughed. "I sure hope so."

"So, are we done with having the talk now? I'm thinking pancakes for breakfast."

I bit my lip. "Actually, just one more thing. Call it a favour, I guess, and I know I don't even have a right to ask, but—"

"Layla, I know things are different between us than the last time, but you've got to quit with the self-deprecating stuff. Bringing it up won't help us move past it," he said.

"Okay, but—"

"What's the favour?"

I moistened my lips. "I need you to keep what I told you about the baby between us. You're the first person I've told, and I wanted you to know because you had a right to know. I just don't think it's anyone else's business."

Christian stood up and pulled on his jeans. "You don't even want to tell your parents?"

"Especially not them."

"Why not?"

"Because they'll hate me," I replied. "I mean, I got pregnant before I was married and then, to make matters worse, I didn't tell them, ran away, and barely kept in touch for four years. They'll think less of me than they already did."

"You told me, and I don't think less of you," he answered. "Actually, it kind of makes me understand a little better. I don't agree with how you dealt with it, but I get why you reacted so unlike you."

He rested his hands on the bed and leant towards me. His forehead settled on mine and I closed my eyes.

"I'm just scared that it'll make them mad," I whispered. "And they won't look at me the same way."

"They forgave you for leaving," he murmured. "You owe them an explanation as to why."

I exhaled.

"What about my father? Can I tell him?" he asked.

My eyes shot open in horror. "No! Christian, he hates me enough."

Christian lowered to his knees beside the bed. "Well, I actually think he'd be a little nicer to you if he knew what you went through. You only ever had my best interest at heart. All the reasons why you left were all the reasons why he didn't want us to get married to begin with."

I frowned. "He didn't?"

"You knew that."

"I suspected that, but I didn't know he actually hated me *before* I trampled his only son's heart."

Christian's lips pressed together. "Well, he came around."

"And then I went and messed it up again."

"Layla."

I shook my head. "Sorry."

He sighed, and I moved towards the edge of the bed. He sat back on his heels and watched in amusement as I pulled the bed sheet with me.

"I know you think that telling our parents is a good idea, but I really don't," I said. "They won't see it the way you do. If anything, the fact that I was pregnant was even more reason to stay and marry you. I stole that future from them too."

He nodded and moved his hands up my legs. It was distracting.

"I understand what you're saying," he answered. "And if you are absolutely adamant that you don't want them to know then I won't say anything."

I nodded.

"But, Layla," he sighed. "For what it's worth, I think you need to tell them. If we've learnt anything from all of this, it's that keeping secrets doesn't work. It doesn't allow those who love you the chance to love you enough. They might be upset about it all, but they will heal. We all will. We just need to bleed first."

His hands settled under my thighs, and I moved my hands around to hold them.

"I'm just scared," I whispered. "I know that I made some bad decisions. They know I did too. But I'm just ashamed to tell them how bad they really were."

He lifted to kneel, and pressed his forehead against mine again.

428

"But this time you don't have to go through it alone," he said. "I'll be there with you. I'm not going anywhere."

I nodded as best I could. "Okay then, we can tell them."

"We," he whispered. "You're doing the right thing."

"Finally."

"It was bound to happen sooner or later."

I smiled and dipped down to reach his lips. I didn't have to reach far because he stood, catching his mouth on mine and forcing me back against the mattress. His hand rose to my cheek and then made a burning path all the way down to my waist.

I gasped, trying to get adequate air into my chest. My heart was beating so fast that it felt like all the oxygen in the world wouldn't suffice. Christian gave a throaty chuckle and dropped his lips to my neck.

"You're too cute," he murmured, and then straightened.

It took me a moment to get my breathing under control before I could be suitably mad at him for putting things on ice so suddenly.

"What was that?" I panted. "Why did you stop?"

He smiled. "I heard the front door. Your parents must be home, and I figured they will eventually come looking for us. This wouldn't exactly be an ideal way to tell them that we're back together."

My anger melted away. "We are?"

"I hope so. I mean, we can take things slow. There's a first time for everything."

I leapt into his arms, and he cleared his throat.

"Layla, love, you should probably put some clothes on," he said.

I laughed. "There really is a first time for everything. I never thought I'd hear you say those words to me."

His blue eyes smiled from the dimple in his cheek. "I'll get started on breakfast and keep your folks occupied."

"Okay. I might grab a quick shower."

He nodded and leant down to kiss me. I didn't want to let him go.

"See you soon," he whispered.

"Yes, you will," I replied. "Thank you, Christian."

"Always, Layla."

He grinned and turned to leave but then stopped to spin around and kiss me one more time. Then he picked up his T-shirt and continued out the door. I pressed my lips together because they still tingled from his kiss.

I collected the nearest change of clothes and pulled on my dressing gown, then made my way to the bathroom for the quickest shower I could manage.

My stomach was in knots as I dressed in the brown cotton dress that I'd grabbed. Regardless, the day looked bright outside with not a cloud in sight. I hoped it was some kind of sign that things were finally looking up.

**

When I walked out to the kitchen and lounge area, the first thing that I saw was a plate of pancakes on the counter. Behind them, Christian and my mum stood arranging hot beverages for the two people sitting at the table. *Two?*

Dad and... Mitch.

Christian looked up first, and his blue gaze made my heart beat faster and slower at the same time. He smiled, and I smiled back. Then my dad turned around, and Mum looked up. Mitch barely glimpsed over his shoulder.

"Hey, kiddo," Dad said.

"Hey, Daddy." I leant in and kissed his cheek.

"Look who stopped by for breakfast."

"I see. Good morning, Mr Turner."

"Hello, Layla." Mitch nodded.

"Morning, honey." Mum smiled. "How did you sleep?"

I felt my cheeks warm. How, indeed. "Very well, thank you."

I walked towards the counter, and Christian smirked. "Have a seat, Layla. We won't be long."

I nodded and went to sit at the table.

"How are you feeling, Dad?" I asked.

"Tip top, kid," he answered. "I don't know what those quacks were so worried about."

"Your heart, Henry," Mum groaned.

She walked around and set two mugs in front of my dad and Mitch. Christian was suddenly beside me, resting a cup beside my joined hands. Mum reached for her mug and the plate of pancakes. I took a sip from mine and then started coughing. It wasn't what I expected.

"Tea? Really, Christian? Tea?" I choked.

He chuckled. "I think you drink too much coffee. It's not healthy."

"I completely agree," Mum said.

I took another sip and groaned. "It's going to take a little getting used to."

"So, what did you kids end up getting up to last night?" Dad asked.

I choked on my mouthful, and Christian rubbed my back. It was almost theatrical.

"We turned in early," Christian answered. "We were pretty tired."

431

Mitch's brows pulled together, and I felt Christian reach under the table to hold my hand.

"Layla, your mother said that you made dinner," Dad said, and I admired his dedication to keeping the conversation going.

"I, well, Christian did most of it. I just chopped the onions, really," I answered. I took another sip of tea and shivered as I swallowed the mouthful.

"Is everything okay, Layla?" Mum asked. "You're acting rather strange this morning."

My eyebrows lifted. "Stranger than normal?"

"She's fine, Pattie," Christian sighed as he gave my hand a gentle squeeze.

I pushed my mug of tea forward and reached for Christian's coffee. I took a gulp, but it was equally as distasteful.

I made a face. "Ugh, how can you drink that with no sugar?"

"Are you right there?" Christian laughed.

"You're the one who gave me tea. What is tea anyway? There is no point to it."

"For goodness sake, Layla. I'll make you a coffee if you really want it."

He pushed out his chair and went to stand. I tugged on his hand to pull him back.

"No, stay," I said.

The moment the words were out, I realised that it probably wasn't the smartest thing to say or do. Simultaneously, three throats cleared.

Christian glanced at our parents before sitting back in his seat. He lifted our still-adjoined hands up to rest on the table.

"Layla, Christian, would you like to tell us what is going on?" Mum asked calmly.

I turned to face them and cowered under the scrutiny. I glanced over at Christian for help and saw that he was failing to hide his smile.

"Pattie, Henry, Dad," he said. "There's something we need tell you. It's about why Layla really left."

I opened my mouth to protest, but Christian shot me a look.

"Layla, if we're going to do this, they need to know the full story," he reminded me.

I knew that he was right, but I didn't think that right now was the most ideal time for this conversation. But then, there would probably never be a perfect time to disappoint my parents again.

"Do what?" Mitch snapped.

"What full story?" Dad asked.

"Are you two back together?" Mum gushed.

Christian and I exchanged another look.

"Yes, we are," I murmured.

"You are not serious," Mitch muttered.

Mum's eyebrows lifted. "When did this happen?"

"Last night, Pattie," Christian sighed. "And, Dad, before you start, just let us explain."

Mitch shook his head. "It is one thing to forgive, Christian, but it's quite another to forget."

"Mitch, let them talk," Dad said. "Go on, kids. Tell us what you need to."

I gave my dad a small smile as Mitch folded his arms. My dad sank back in his seat – clearly ready to defend my honour. There was a short silence, and Christian looked at me. He gripped my hand with both of his.

"Well, last night, Layla and I got talking about what happened," he said. "During our discussion, she told me

433

something about why she left. It was because something happened that compelled her to leave. She made a mistake and perhaps a misjudgement in the way she went about dealing with it, but she thought that, by leaving here and leaving me, it would mean more opportunities for my future."

"Christian, honey, I don't understand what you're trying to say," Mum answered.

"Layla, why don't you just tell us what you told Christian?" Dad replied. "Help us to understand too."

Christian gave my hand a gentle squeeze, and I took a deep breath. This wasn't exactly how I expected this conversation to go. It certainly wasn't something that I wanted to discuss over tea and pancakes.

"Just before the party… I, well…" I shook my head. "Mum and Dad, last weekend I told you that I left because I was scared and I wanted more for Christian than what he would get by being married to me. But I didn't tell you everything about what he was getting."

"Oh, for Pete's sake," Mitch grumbled. "Will the two of you stop talking in riddles and just spit it out."

"I, well, I…"

"Layla," Mum sighed. "What are you trying to tell us?"

I looked at her in desperation. "Mum, do you remember leading up to the wedding when I was sick? Do you remember that?"

She blinked. "Yes, honey, it was a stomach bug."

I shook my head. "No, it wasn't a bug. It was morning sickness."

My dad who was midway through taking another forkful of pancake dropped his fork. The metallic noise echoed louder than it otherwise might have as silence fell over us all.

I looked down. It was cowardly, but I was too afraid to see their expressions.

After a moment of deafening silence, I peeked up to make sure that they were still in the room.

"Morning sickness?" Mitch repeated. His hand was half over his mouth.

"Layla, honey," Mum whispered. Her voice sounded unsteady, and I saw that it was because there were tears in her eyes. "Were you pregnant?"

I opened my mouth to answer, but before I could answer, my dad pushed out his chair and headed towards the front door. It was an odd reaction, considering the subject matter, but understandable nonetheless. I had disappointed him.

I looked at Christian in panic, and he lifted my hand to his lips and kissed it. "I'll go to see if he's all right."

I nodded, but then he released my hand, and I wished that he'd come back. I dropped my head into my hands and then heard Mum clear her throat. I'd almost forgotten that she and Mitch were still there.

"Layla," she murmured. "What happened to the baby?"

I frowned. "I miscarried about eight weeks in."

Mum shook her head, and her forehead creased with emotion. "Honey, why didn't you come home? You shouldn't have gone through that all alone."

"I couldn't come home. I was too ashamed."

"Honestly, Layla," she sighed. "Why didn't you say something in the first place? Why did you leave to begin with? For Christian? Did you think that he wouldn't support you?"

"Of course he would have," Mitch grumbled. "We all would have."

"I just panicked." I shrugged. "I didn't want you all to hate me, and I didn't want to be Christian's only accomplishment."

"Christian would have been fine with that. He would have done the right thing by you. He loved you, Layla. You had to know that," Mitch answered.

"I know that he did," I said, blinking back tears. "I see that now."

Mitch sighed. "Look, I am sorry for your loss, Layla, and I can understand why you might have acted the way that you did but, honestly, it doesn't change anything."

"Mitch," Mum breathed. "Please."

Mitch Turner put his napkin on the table and pushed out his seat. "No, Pattie. She still left my son broken-hearted and without a single word. He might be a good enough man to forgive her and forget, but it's going to take more than a few words to show me that she's worthy of him again."

"Again?" I said. "Mr Turner, you've never approved of me."

"And it seems that my instincts were correct."

"Mitchell Turner, do not speak about my daughter like that," Mum replied. "She is a good girl who got scared and made a bad call."

"I am only looking out for my boy, Patricia. Christian was a wreck because of your girl, and if the situation were reversed, you would have reacted in the same way, and I wouldn't blame you in the least."

I hated that he was right in everything he said. He wasn't too hard on me. He was just as I would have been as a concerned parent, I would think. But to speak to my mother that way?

Mitch took a step towards the door, and my awareness suddenly snapped into gear. I sprang to my feet.

"Mitch—Mr Turner," I called. "Wait."

I saw my mother reach for me from the corner of my eye but ignored it.

"I get it, okay, I know how much I hurt Christian, and I know that it was unacceptable," I said. "It hurts me how much I hurt him, but I want you to know that everything I have ever done was for him."

He scoffed, and I lifted a hand.

"Please just listen to me," I sighed. "I understand that I didn't go about things the right way, and my logic may have been a little fuzzy, but I love your son, and there isn't anything in the entire world that you can say that will change that." I stopped and took a breath. "I know you don't like me very much, and I can appreciate that. Maybe you're right. Maybe I'm not worthy of being with Christian. Maybe I never was. But I will spend every day for the rest of our lives proving to him, to you, and everyone else in this sleepy little town that he didn't make a mistake in giving me a second chance."

Mitch frowned, and I looked at my feet.

"Mr Turner, I have and will always love your son with every fibre of my being," I added. "There will never be anyone that will ever love him as much as I do. But if one day for some reason he stops loving me then I'll let him go, but just know that even then, I will never stop loving him."

I heard footsteps and looked up. Christian's arms encircled me, drawing me into him as his lips sank to mine, and I melted into his kiss. It was a moment before someone cleared their throat, and we slowly parted. Christian rested his forehead against mine.

"I love you too," he whispered. "Always."

"So, what happens now?" Mum asked. "Are you going to give marriage another shot then?"

I looked over at her. "We have some making up to do, so we're just going to take things slow for now."

Mitch huffed, but Christian ignored him.

"We haven't really discussed any of that yet," he added. "We're together, and that's all that matters."

I glanced at him and smiled. From the corner of my eye, I caught a shadow and turned to see my father standing in the doorway.

"Dad," I exhaled. I stepped towards him, but he turned his head away from me. "Dad, I'm sorry. I—"

"Were you trying to give me a heart attack?" he asked. "Or just break it?"

"Dad, I—"

"How could you do it, Layla?" he growled. "You go and get yourself pregnant and then, to make matters worse, you just up and leave? Were you ever going to tell us?"

"No." I shrugged. "I didn't want to tell you because I didn't want you to look at me the way you are right now. I knew that you'd be ashamed of me. I knew that you'd raised me better than that."

Dad shook his head. "But you were still just a kid, Layla. What was going through your head?"

"Nothing, Dad, I was scared. I just wanted to disappear. I knew that if I stayed, it would turn everyone's life upside down, not just mine and Christian's. It might have been wrong, but I did what I thought was best at the time."

"But *you* were just a *kid*," he repeated. "Did you think that you'd be able to raise the baby on your own?"

I looked down. "To be honest, I wasn't sure if I was going to keep it. Then I lost it anyway."

"You're right. We did raise you better than that."

"Henry," Mum sighed.

"Pattie, I just don't understand any of it," Dad muttered. "I don't understand how it could even happen when we taught her to be responsible."

438

"We didn't plan it, Dad, obviously," I replied. "We were being responsible, but I don't know what happened when—"

"Layla, please. You're my little girl. I don't want to even think about that."

"I don't know what else to say, Dad," I sighed. "I'm sorry. I messed up. I'm going to do better, and I'm going to make you proud of me again."

Dad frowned but reached one arm around me in a half hug. I didn't know what it meant, but I hoped it marked the beginning of our healing. I wasn't sure how much more I could bleed for my parents before my heart stopped. But words were just words. I needed to follow them through this time.

Mitch cleared his throat. "I'm going to go. I have some things to do. Son, do you think that you'll visit before you and, uh, Layla head back to the big smoke?"

"Sure, Dad, we can do that." He nodded. "Um, thanks for dropping by this morning."

Mitch lowered his eyes and then reached out to ruffle Christian's hair.

"I like the haircut too, son," he said. "It suits you much better than that overgrown mop you were sporting."

"Thanks, um, Dad," Christian answered. He mashed his lips together to hide his smile.

Mitch looked to my mother. "Pattie, thanks for having me. I hope I didn't overstay my welcome."

"Don't mention it, Mitch." She smiled. "It was an unexpectedly emotional morning, but it was lovely having everyone together again."

Mitch pulled his lips into a tight line. It was his way of discretely disagreeing. He turned towards my father. "Henry, glad to see you on your feet again."

"Mitch." Dad nodded.

He extended his hand towards Christian's father, and their hands met with a force that was not unfriendly, but more like they had a mutual understanding. Maybe it was their years of their differing opinions of me had caused kind of a rift. Regardless, it was well known to all that both men loved Christian as a son, so that they had always agreed on. It bothered me a little that Mitch Turner resented me so much, but the resentment was more for Christian's sake than mine. Maybe it would take time for him to see that I wasn't going to leave again. Maybe it would take more than that. Whatever it took, I would do it. Even if he never started to like me, maybe we could at least come to a mutual understanding over our love for Christian just like he and my dad had.

Mitch released my father's hand then glanced at me. "Bye, Layla."

"Goodbye, Mr Turner."

He turned away and started towards the door. As he left, I wondered if anything he'd heard today had made a difference. Maybe it hadn't. Maybe it had. I knew that telling anyone would be difficult. I knew that, to varying degrees, our parents were disappointed in me, but I also knew that Christian and I would face the toughest audience outside of Almanbury. After all, the entire town and everyone in it had seen us together. They'd grown up with us, and they knew what we were like. They knew us best when we were Christian and Layla.

In South Coast, it was different. The people there only knew us as Christian Turner and Layla Thomas, individuals who came from the same town, the same high school. Whatever. Maddie knew us as individuals, but she didn't know that we'd lied about our history when she'd asked us point blank about our association. Christian was right about telling lies – they had a habit of catching up to you. It was selfish, and I could only hope that it didn't cost me more than I'd already lost. Maddie had been a good friend, and she deserved better.

I should have been better.

**

Christian and I finished breakfast with my parents and then gave them some space. They didn't say much to me, and I didn't push it. I'd had four years to get my head around what happened, whereas they'd had forty minutes. It would take time – more time than what I'd already cost us all through my spontaneous act. I couldn't blame anyone but myself, but I was trying not to do that any more. Failing, but trying nonetheless.

Christian and I spent the afternoon together walking around town. It reminded me of the walk I had done the weekend before but, this time, it was easier because I wasn't alone. Places that held memories of the two of us sang as we passed. The ghosts in my memory seemed to ascend into a better place.

In the mid-afternoon, we went back to my parents' house to gather our few belongings ready to drive back to South Coast.

"Thanks for coming, honey," Mum said. She captured me in a hug at the front door. "I know you're both so busy, but it means a lot that you came."

"Don't even mention it," I whispered. "I'm glad that we could be here."

She nodded. "Layla, I don't know what happened to make you feel like you couldn't come to us before, but I want you to be able to come to us if you ever need to. Now, I know that you've been out on your own for a while, but you'll always be our baby girl. Our only baby girl."

I hugged her again. "I know, Mum."

"You grew up too fast, Layla," she sighed. "Parents always say that about their kids, but you were different."

"I know, Mum. I'm sorry."

"I don't want you to be sorry. I just want you to let us be there for you. Let us be a part of your life even if you can do it by yourself."

"I'll always need you, Mum." I looked up at Dad. "Both of you. I meant it when I said that I'll be around more. I'll call more. I promise that you'll be sick of me."

"Honestly, Layla," she replied. The phrase was as endearing as her 'I love you'. "We could never get sick of having you around."

Christian hugged my mum then turned towards my dad. When he stepped away from the embrace, he gave me a wink and headed towards his car.

I looked over at my dad. "I'll talk to you soon, Dad. I'm sorry for everything, but I'm glad you're okay."

"When I was in the hospital, Layla, your mother called you to tell you that I was there," he replied. "Not because you knew any of that medical mumbo-jumbo, but because sometimes being there for someone you love is all that you can do, and that is enough."

I nodded slowly.

"Kid, I don't ever want to hear about you going through something like you did on your own again," he continued. "I don't care how badly you messed up or disappointed you think we'll be; I want to know about it so I can be there for you. Layla, all that we care about is *you*. Honestly, the hardest thing about dealing with all that has happened is knowing that you were alone through it all. As a parent, that's a whole other level of helplessness."

"I'm sorry."

He sighed. "I know."

"I'm going to tell you everything from now on."

Dad glanced over at Christian then looked back to me. "Maybe not *everything*, just the highlight reel," he said. "You're still my daughter, so some details are best kept under blanket forts."

I smiled at the memory. It seemed like another lifetime ago. I guess it was.

"I love you, Dad."

"I love you too, kiddo."

I stepped forward and wrapped my arms tightly around him. I heard him squeak under my grip but didn't loosen it. He didn't either.

"Tell Christian to drive home safely," he said.

"We're not going home," I murmured. "Almanbury will always be home."

He nodded. "Yes, it will."

**

We made a stop at Mitch's place on the way out of Almanbury, but I didn't leave the car. I figured it was best that Mitch and Christian say a proper goodbye without me causing another argument or tension between the two of them. It was the least I could do.

Half an hour later, we were back on the road and bound for South Coast. It felt strange to leave together the way we were, but I knew that it wouldn't be for long. Something told me it was the first of many road trips between our hometown and our new address.

Christian held my hand as he drove, resting them interlocked on the gearstick between us just like he used to.

The radio was on, but this time the crooning songs that played didn't bother me. An Ed Sheeran song started to play.

"Your dad gave me the talk," Christian said.

I looked over at him, watching as the afternoon breeze tousled his hair. I was suddenly jealous of it.

"Wait, the what? The talk?" I replied belatedly. "What do you…?"

Christian lifted his eyebrows, and then I understood.

"He's a few years late for that, isn't he?" I mumbled. "What did he say?"

Christian smirked. "He said that I should have taken the lead on responsibility and waited until we were married before I seduced you."

I laughed. "You seduced me? That's not exactly how I remember it."

"Well, I needed no convincing." He chuckled. "From memory, it was quite a mutual need."

I bit my lip, and he glanced over at me. I felt like I was seeing the memory of it all reflected in his eyes. If he wasn't driving, I was sure that we would probably have made an attempt to relive the experience.

"To be fair, we were together for four years before we got engaged." I shrugged. "And, initially, we did wait for a little while before we did anything."

"Two years, yes, I remember quite vividly."

"It was worth the wait though, wasn't it?"

Christian smiled. "Absolutely."

"When did my dad talk to you?" I asked. "I was with you for most of the day."

"It was when I went after him. I guess he decided to direct the anger at me since I was there. It got a little awkward, but he calmed down pretty quickly."

444

"I'm sorry that he got mad at you because of me."

"He wasn't mad at me. He was just frustrated, I think. I understand that."

I nodded. "Your dad was mad at me though."

"It sounded like you had him under control."

"How much did you hear of my little outburst?"

Christian frowned. "I came back as you were telling him that you might not be worthy of me."

"Oh. So, it was mid-outburst then."

"Did he really say that to you?" he asked. "That you weren't worthy of me?"

I exhaled. "He said something about it taking more than a few words to prove that I was."

"I'm sorry he said that to you."

"Well, he's right anyway. Words are futile."

"No, they're not," he answered. "Words are power. People have this misconception that they're weaker than actions, but they have the power to leave scars deeper than any flesh wound."

"But it was my actions that hurt you, not my words," I said. "I didn't leave you any words, and that was the problem."

Christian shook his head. "You're wrong. I mean, okay, it was confusing not knowing where you were or why you left, but not having words in black and white saying that you didn't want to be with me, that kept me going. It didn't keep me sane, but it kept me going. Somewhere in the back of my mind, I convinced myself that if you wanted to leave, and if you didn't love me, you would have said so. You would have let me off the hook and just said it in plain words."

"But I could never say it."

"I know." He nodded. "Just like I could never move on without hearing it."

I looked down. The reminder about moving on made me think of Maddie. She would probably be waiting for us when we got back, and we needed to tell her sooner rather than later. Today had been the day for ripping off painful Band-Aids and letting scars bleed.

"We need to figure out what to say to Maddie," I murmured. "She's been through so much and been let down by so many people in her life, I just hate that I'm another one of them."

"Do you want me to talk to her?" he asked.

I shook my head. "I think I need to be the one to tell her. I'm her best friend and the one who chose to keep it from her in the first place."

"If you're sure. You don't have to tell her alone though. I can be there."

"Okay." I nodded. "I would like that."

He squeezed my hand. "Together then."

I smiled weakly. "Together."

Chapter Fifteen
The Butterfly Effect

It was a little after eight thirty in the evening when we pulled up my street. A part of me wanted to find Maddie asleep, but then I realised that I didn't have a key. Christian helped me carry in my ball dress, and I grabbed Maddie's gold shoes then went to knock on the door. My fist had barely landed twice on the wood when I heard a small scuffle, and the door flew open.

"Hey, you're home." Maddie smiled. Her arms were around me before I knew what was happening. "I'm glad you got back before I went to bed because I wanted to talk to you."

"Hi, Madeline. What's up?"

"Layla, you're wearing a dress." She frowned. "What happened down there in A-berry?"

"Almanbury."

"Same thing." Maddie shrugged. She looked at Christian and smiled. "Hey, you."

Christian nodded. "Hello."

I stepped in and dropped the shoes just inside the door. Christian followed me and laid the dress over the couch. Maddie spun to look at us.

"So, how's your dad?" she asked.

"He's, um, fine. He's doing much better," I replied.

"Is everything okay? Did something else happen? You look like you're about to sit a math test that you haven't studied for."

I scratched my neck. "I actually wanted to talk to you too."

"Okay, you go first," she said.

"Why don't you come and sit down?"

"I'll stand thanks. What's up?"

I drew in a breath and lowered to sit on the corner of the couch. "I need to tell you something that I should have told you a long time ago. I didn't tell you before because I didn't want to have to answer a bunch of questions that I'd been avoiding since I left Almanbury."

She breathed a laugh. "Sounds serious. What's it about?"

"It's about Christian and me."

"You... *and* Christian?"

"Yes," I sighed. "We, um, well, we—"

"We were more than just family friends," Christian said. "We actually dated for most of high school."

She folded her arms. "So, you *were* a couple. But when I asked you, Layla, you said—"

"I know I did. I lied, and I shouldn't have," I answered.

She frowned. "Why did you lie about that?"

"Because we didn't just date in high school, the year we turned eighteen, Christian proposed to me... and I said yes."

Her eyes popped. "Are you telling me that you were married? How very country town."

"We weren't married. We were engaged," Christian replied.

I glanced at Maddie and watched as her head tipped contemplatively.

"The wedding that you planned right out of high school," she said. "That was yours?"

"Yes." I nodded.

"So, you were engaged, but you *didn't* get married," Maddie clarified. "Well, that explains the weird tension and bickering between you two. But, Christian, you said it was because Layla left abruptly, and it affected her parents. Is that a lie or the truth?"

448

"That was true," Christian answered.

He glanced at me, and I looked at Maddie.

"On the afternoon of our rehearsal dinner, I packed a bag and left Almanbury for South Coast," I explained. "I didn't go back or make contact with anyone there until last weekend."

Maddie frowned. "How many years ago was that? Four?"

I nodded. "Four."

"Layla, we've been friends for three and a half years, and we've been living together for three. Why didn't this ever come up even before Christian came into the picture?"

"It's just not easy for me to talk about."

"But it was you who left." She shrugged. "Why did you leave? Why not just call off the wedding?"

I exhaled. "I still loved Christian. I just wanted more for him. I didn't want to hold him back."

"So, why did you say yes to his proposal then?"

"Because marriage was one thing, but it got a little more complicated," I answered. I looked up at Christian, and he gave a small nod of encouragement. "I found out I was pregnant."

Maddie raised her eyebrows. "Oh. Well, that changes things. But, hey, you weren't pregnant when we met."

"No, I lost the baby in the first trimester."

Christian's hand found my shoulder, and I leant into him.

"When did you tell Christian about it?" Maddie asked.

"Last night."

"He didn't know all this time?"

I shook my head. "Last Friday was the first time I'd seen him since."

"In the white dress?" She frowned. "That's awkward."

I nodded. "I'm just really sorry that I didn't tell you sooner. And I'm sorry I wasn't honest with you when you asked me."

"Okay," she sighed. "I guess I can understand why you wouldn't want to talk about it. But, Layla, if you had told me, I would never have pursued Christian."

"I could have said no," Christian replied.

"Why didn't you say no?" Maddie asked. "Do you still love her?"

"Yes. I still love her."

"Are you back together?"

Christian and I exchanged a look.

"Yes," I answered. "And Maddie, I—"

My words cut off as my eyes caught sight of a gold tie in the corner of the lounge area. Maddie took my distraction as an opportunity.

"It's okay," she said as she started to fidget. "Nothing happened between Christian and me anyway. And, for real, if I wanted to be with a guy and not make out with him, I'd call my brothers."

I blinked up at her. "What?"

She laughed. "Nothing, I'm happy for you, I guess. I mean, it's weird but… Hey, does that mean you're not into Jeffrey?"

Jeffrey. Gold tie.

"Maddie, I was never into Jeffrey," I said slowly. "Speaking of Jeffrey, did he get you home okay after the ball?"

Maddie flushed as pink as her dress had been. "Um, fine. Yes, he, um, great."

"What was it that you wanted to talk to me about?" I asked.

"Oh, um, it… it's not important tonight," she stuttered. "You're probably tired. It can wait."

I stood up from the couch and walked over to the gold piece of silk. I picked it up and looked at her.

"What, um, what's that?" She blinked.

"You don't recognise it?" I asked.

"Should I?"

I shrugged. "Jeffrey was wearing one identical to this one on Friday night."

"Was he?"

"Madeline Alice Butler."

She rolled her eyes. "Okay, fine. It's his tie. I was going to tell you, but your news of your prior engagement sort of trumped mine."

"News?" Christian asked. "You and the jeweller, Mads? Looks like you got dumped, Layla."

I threw the tie at him, and he leant away from it.

"Okay, yes, we sort of hooked up... like all weekend." Maddie giggled. "Which I actually felt guiltier about half an hour ago."

My eyebrows lifted. "All weekend? Maddie, what if I *was* interested in Jeffrey?"

"Oh please, Layla," she sighed. "I saw your face on Friday night when he was following you around. Besides, when your mum called, it was obvious that I was interrupting something between you and Christian. Then you guys run off together on a road trip in the middle of the night. Oh, oh, and don't even get me started on the fact that you were acting like a complete robot whenever Christian and I were together – and Christian wouldn't stop asking about you whenever we were alone..."

Christian and I exchanged a look.

"Honestly, Layla, give me *some* credit," Maddie scoffed.

Honestly, Layla.

If only I had been honest from the beginning then I wouldn't have had to spend so much time apologising in the last couple of weeks. Even with best intentions, trying to protect people by omitting truths clearly wasn't the answer. I

451

had disappointed a lot of people. I was just lucky that the people who meant a lot to me had overlooked my faults.

"Layla," Maddie said.

I blinked over at her as Christian moved to my side.

"Yes, Madeline?" I smiled.

"Everything is going to be okay. You know that, right?"

"I hope so."

Maddie looked between us and stifled a yawn. "Well then, I'm *exhausted*. I'll leave you lovebirds to it."

"You don't have to—"

"Sure I do." She smiled. "Just promise me one thing. When you two try to get married again, promise me that I can be a bridesmaid."

"If he ever agrees to marry me again, you'll be the maid of honour," I replied.

Maddie did a five-second victory dance.

"Night, Laystian," she said. "Christyla? I'll work on your shipper name later."

Christian and I laughed, and Maddie skipped off to her room.

"By the way, if… when we get engaged next time, we're eloping," Christian whispered as he drew me into his arms.

"Deal." I nodded.

His lips dropped to mine, and I could feel the love in his kiss. I wondered if things might have been different if I'd gotten everything I'd wanted when I was eighteen or nineteen. I know that I would have appreciated what I had, but I wasn't sure if I could have appreciated it as much as I do now after everything that had passed. That's not to say that I wouldn't have willingly taken back all the hurt and heartache I'd caused to everyone. But, now I would make sure that none of the pain they had felt was felt in vain.

I loved Christian. I had always loved Christian. I would always love Christian. I would spend the rest of my life showing him just how much I loved him and how much I needed him in my life. I had survived without him, but I didn't want to live without him. For the four years we were apart, I had lived as an echo, a shadow of myself. Christian illuminated me. He lit up the dark corners of my soul. Without him, I was an underexposed photo, out of focus, a negative image. With him, I was so much more.

"Layla," he whispered. "Maddie is right. Everything is going to be okay."

"It is," I answered. "It is now."

"Hey, I know that you blame yourself for a lot of things, but not everything is your fault."

"Maybe, maybe not," I murmured. "But a lot of things are."

He brushed my cheeks with his fingertips. "You should have more trust in people. You can't save them from everything, and you can't shield them from things because you think you know what's best for them."

"You're right. I can't fix everything. I need people, and I need you. I don't want to do this life thing alone any more."

"You've never been alone. I've been there," he whispered. "But like the stars in the daytime, you just couldn't see me."

"I'm so in love," I whispered. "God, Christian, I love you."

He chuckled. "You do?"

"Yes, is that okay?"

"More than okay." He nodded, and his forehead rested against mine. "Do you think we're crazy?"

"Probably, but does it matter?"

He smirked. "Not to me."

He took me in his arms and kissed me again, and I felt it from my head right down to my toes.

Yes, everything was going to be okay. It would be more than okay. It was our version of perfect.

Epilogue
Ever After

"You're not honestly going to make me say it, are you?" I groaned.

Christian smiled down at me from his lazed position underneath me on the picnic rug. His blue eyes twinkled with amusement in the rays of the spring afternoon.

"If you're really doing what I think you are, Layla, then you are going to do it right," he said.

I rolled my eyes and leant over him, letting my lips lower towards his. "Christian David Turner."

"Come on, you can do better than that."

I laughed. "I'm asking you to marry me."

"Yes, I got that much." He grinned. "So go on then."

I sat back and bit my lip. "Will you marry me?"

"Why?"

"Because I love you… and my life is meaningless if I don't have you to share it with," I replied. "Because, Christian Turner, I don't want to spend a single day without you. Every day from now until eternity, I want to wake up beside you so I can remind you over and over just how much I love you."

"Which is how much?" he asked.

"Too much," I sighed.

I leant down to press my lips to his, and his hand lifted to my cheek and then laced through my hair. When we parted, he let out a breath.

"Well. That was a little better."

"So, are you going to give me an answer?" I whispered. "Or do you need me to go on?"

He chuckled lightly and guided my lips back to his. The warmth of his breath sent a shiver down my spine. It set all the nerve endings in my body on fire.

"Yes," he murmured between kisses. "Of course the answer is yes."

I pulled back to look at him, running my fingertips over his lips.

"I'm not going to let anything tear us apart ever again," I whispered. "The three of us, this is just the beginning."

He smiled up at me, his sky-blue eyes sparkling as his hands moved over my swollen abdomen where the new life grew inside me. A life that was half-him, half-me, and would link us together forever.

It was a long time coming, but at last, we could have it all, everything that we'd always wanted with each other since we were fourteen years old.

I couldn't help but smile as my hands moved under his open white shirt and onto his golden skin. I could feel his heart in his chest beating with such vitality that it shook his body with each thud.

Our lips met again with a passion that seemed too big for two people to endure. But we did, we encompassed it as if we had been made for the sole purpose of loving each other.

On this day we pledged forever to each other again, only this time, forever wasn't just a dream. It was my reality, our reality, for as long as we both shall live.